MICE IN THE WALLS

MICE IN THE WALLS

WALLS

Coming of Age in a Shooting Revolution

~ Butch Denny ~

ISBN: 0692109633
ISBN 13: 978-0692109632
Library of Congress Control Number: 2015918422
Bent Sun Productions, Lockhart, TX

PREFACE

Over the years, arthritis and other discomforts have claimed me. My gripes outnumber pleasures, but it was not always so. Every day over fifty is a day of pain.

It seems especially so in Wyoming, where I was born and raised. Though it can sometimes be harsh, I remember such pleasures there, but now I split my time between properties in Montana and warmer Texas, where I spend the winter fishing alone on the Gulf Coast. I don't catch much, but my knuckles and back seem to work better there, and I enjoy hummingbirds in the oleanders outside my window of an evening. I walk sort of bent-over now; it's embarrassing and distresses me. Though I'm an attractive and available widower, the snowbird ladies never glance my direction. To heck with them.

About twenty years ago, I was driving through Wyoming. First, my *alma mater* in Laramie, and then an obligatory stop at the Virginian Hotel in Medicine Bow. I usually have dinner at the hotel and enjoy a whiskey in the historic Shiloh Saloon before continuing on to spend the night in Casper.

That year, however, as I partook of a glass of temporary cheer, I saw a couple come in and sit near the door. The man faced the icy glass of the inner doorway of the mudroom; the woman had her back to the painted wall, facing the other tables. The wind outside was fiercely cold; the outer door rattled in the hurricane-strength winds and made a lot of noise. I was hoping I could get my truck started; my battery was not so good. The couple ordered Coors draft, in pre-frosted mugs. I thought I knew the young man.

"You're Danny, Dunn MacCreary's oldest boy, aren't you?" I asked, approaching the table.

He moved his right hand to the front of a black field jacket, then relaxed. I found out later he had a Browning Hi-Power nine mil in a holster hidden just an inch away from his hand. "Sit down, Mr. Denny," he said graciously. "I haven't seen you in ten years or more. How have you been?"

I did sit down, my back to the door, the last time I ever did it. We passed pleasantries. I inquired about his family. His father, my long-time friend, had passed away earlier that month. I hadn't heard, and I was sad. It was natural I inquire after him, the son no one talked about.

"I'm alright," he said. "My days of adventure are over."

The woman looked up from her beer and wagged her head skeptically. She had been a looker in her day, but now she was a brittle blonde in a cold bar in southern Wyoming. I didn't know she had a gold-plated Walther .380 automatic fitted with an (illegal) suppressor under her jacket, right side, with a quote engraved in Arabic-script on the pearl grips. I saw the gun later, one of the few times she granted me anything. If I remember the translation of the inscription, it was something like, "What does it matter if I were once beautiful, I will only grow old and die." I didn't have an appreciation for such fatalism then, so I blundered into unknown territory. I asked for more. I asked for the whole story. I had been a journalist. I have always looked for a good story.

It was 4:15 p.m. The wind outside was brutal. The door rattled in its frame. I don't know why I looked at my watch. The bar closed much later. The owner served us a last drink and went to bed after showing us how to lock the door on our ways out. It was snowing and windy that night. It was Wyoming in October. And it was 4:45 in the morning when Danny finished.

Yeah, we sat there (with several breaks...) for twelve hours.

As he went silent and looked down at the table sadly, the woman—who had been mostly quiet during the telling—reached over and affectionately took his left hand in both of hers. I was overcome. I hadn't paid attention to his deformity up to that point.

It brought home to me that there are three kinds of scars one can get in this world. Some are from cuts and surgeries; some are from blunt-force traumas like bullets and blows; some are from events. Across the table from me, Danny MacCreary had all three.

دیوار در ها موش

"Listeners, listen!
Of a time and a place,
So very far away,
Only remembered by me
And the many dead...."

Al Kuhula
Ali Mustafa Mazhar
Marrakech, Morocco, abt 1260 A.D.

دارای دیوارها

Based on a true story

– 1 –

THE COURIER

"He could come in, unload a suitcase with a million dollars in cash on the table, spread it out to dazzle us, leave, and no one could recall his face. He was the best privately employed international courier that ever was."
—*Mustafa Ibrahim "Yolli" Gholli, Ventura, California, 1994*

As Sophia Scagnelli hurried home from a greengrocer's, she spotted an unfamiliar man standing in the narrow street leading to her tenement apartment. The moment she sighted him, her heart raced fearfully, but she averted her eyes, praying he wouldn't notice as she passed. She knew *his* type well. Though the foreigner tried to blend in with the Italians around him, there was something about the way he watched passersby that told her all she needed to know. She recognized him for what he was: a killer of hopes and dreams.

Neatly dressed in a blue sport jacket, white slacks, a cream silk shirt with an open neck, and expensive shoes, the stranger had his left arm in a sling. His hand looked freshly bandaged. Glancing through an English-language newspaper held awkwardly in his right hand, the man noticed every*thing* and every*one* around him. She knew his type well. Like her ex-husband, he referred to himself as "rough trade," but what such men traded for money was not a bargain for the recipient.

She darted across an alley and scurried down the crowded street. Her mother was probably angry. Every evening the older woman had dinner waiting at eight o'clock, but today the bus had been delayed, and Sophia was late. Tired from a long day at work, the young woman knew she would have to endure her mother's complaints until bedtime. What were they having for dinner tonight? Rewarmed *zuppa di coze* again, she smiled wryly, and by this time the mussels had been boiled so often in the broth they would have lost all flavor. Too bad. At least her mother made fresh pasta everyday. Tonight they would have buttered *pasta bolognese*, as they did every Friday night. Sophia had bought a bottle of wine and a loaf of bread to dip in the soup; it would be a good dinner if her mother weren't in a bad mood.

On an impulse, Sophia hesitated at the end of the street to look at her reflection in a shop window. After the long ride on the bus, she looked disheveled. Her clothes were as wrinkled as if she'd slept in them. Just thirty years old, she was nearly worn out from working long hours as a machine operator in a Roman textile mill. Her income barely paid their bills. Her hair graying prematurely, she didn't have the energy to dream about the future; she thought only of the past.

Squinting to see her reflection better, she noticed new lines at the corners of her eyes. They had once been so bright men would remark on them from across the street, but now, no one noticed her, not even the teenagers at the bus stop. She had studied to be a fashion artist, but art school had become too expensive. Her best designs adorned the walls of the tiny apartment she shared with her mother.

Brushing her hair aside with a hand, Sophia glanced furtively over her shoulder. The stranger had moved a bit in her direction, but as she watched out of the corner of her eye, he paused at a window fifty meters away. After a moment's scrutiny of the merchandise displayed there, he tucked the newspaper under his bad arm and entered the shop. Thank God, she realized. He wasn't following her after all.

Slipping into the blistered door of her tenement, she ran up the worn green stairs. On the fourth landing, she stopped to dig in her purse for a key, but at the sound of her at the door, her mother snatched it open.

"*Il 'omo—*" her mother warned, joining her in the fetid hallway.

"*Si,*" Sophia said wearily. Her mother had seen the stranger too. In fact he had been at the entrance door below and at the foot of the stairs earlier in the afternoon, but then he had walked away.

Shaking her head mournfully, the old woman happened to glance over her daughter's shoulder. "Sophia!" she cautioned, pointing an arthritic finger down the stairs. The dangerous man was coming up to the third landing!

"Sophia Scagnelli?" he inquired, hesitating just out of reach, three steps below the landing.

"*Si,*" the young woman answered warily, pushing her mother back into the apartment. Somewhere, a child began to cry, and the sound of its wailing echoed eerily up and down the stairwell in the squalid tenement.

The stranger motioned inside, and the two women backed away from the door to let him in. The living room was small, the furniture old and heavy. Boldly taking a seat in the middle of a day bed, the stranger motioned for Sophia to sit in a stuffed chair opposite him. Hovering near the kitchenette, her mother watched every move the man made; Sophia noticed she was hiding a butcher knife behind her back. Glancing to her right, Sophia spotted a pair of scissors on the sill, near the greasy window.

The stranger had seen a hard life. His forehead was creased with a scar; he had deep scars on either side of his jaw, and his one good hand, the right, had prominent, thin scars running up under his sleeve.

Crossing, then uncrossing her legs, Sophia decided the stranger's left hand looked crippled under the white bandages. Glancing at the scissors again, she hoped she and her mother might be able to overwhelm him if he gave them a chance—

But the moment she looked back at him, she realized he already knew. He was good. He had learned his trade well. The scissors were too far away to be of use. She should have recognized he was this smart. Here it was a cloudy day, yet he wore sunglasses to hide his intentions. He was probably carrying a gun under his jacket. Accepting it was useless to resist, Sophia sighed and waved for him to do his worst.

With his right hand, the foreigner unbuttoned his sport jacket and took out two manila envelopes—one very thick, the other quite thin. Pulling a large knife from his pants pocket, he flicked it open in a practiced way. It made no sound at all, a knife carefully honed for use in the dark. He awkwardly held the thicker envelope at the edge of the table with his bandaged left hand and slit it open.

It was money! Lots of money. There were American hundred-dollar bills, English pounds, and Swiss francs. She guessed the envelope held fifty thousand dollars—a veritable fortune to her and her mother.

The stranger separated the cash into currencies, placed a slim gold ring and two gold Pahlavi coins on top, and then held the envelope open to show it was empty. When Sophia nodded, he crumpled the envelope and put it aside. This man—a professional courier—had delivered such things so often it had become a ritual for him. Opening the next envelope as ceremoniously as the first, he withdrew a handwritten letter, showed her there were no enclosures, then reinserted the letter at an angle and laid it on top of the money.

"Grazie," she whispered, inwardly cursing herself for never learning any English.

"Khahesh mikonam," the man replied in Farsi, revealing he had come from her ex-husband, Masud Pooinak.

She wondered if the man could speak the language well.

"Farsi miduneed?" she asked. *"Americae hasteed?"*

"Balle," he nodded. "Yes, I'm an American," he answered her second question in English.

Sophia had avoided reading the news lately; she knew things were bad now. Children were fighting on the front now; they were dying by the tens of thousands...and were not even buried because they were children. Their bloody little carcasses littered every battlefield in eastern Iraq. For God's sake! Children! And they were calling them "martyrs? What about her son? How recently, she wondered, had this man left the fighting? Was her son okay? Had her son been forced to fight on the front too? What about her ex-husband...?

"Koja mireed?" she asked in Farsi, wishing there were more time. Her throat was thick with conflicting emotions. There was so much she needed to know, but could she even ask this man? Could she trust him? Would he know the answers or was he just an employee?

"Beh manzel miram," he answered tiredly. "I'm finally going home," and he rose from the sofa. Reaching into his coat pocket for a photograph, he gave it to her and said, *"Khodahafez,"* in Farsi and *"Addio,"* in Italian.

From the door, she watched him walk down the stairs and into the street, and then he was gone forever before she looked at the photo. In the picture, her ex-husband and this mysterious courier were sitting on a car's fender, grinning and holding guns. She noticed the stranger's left hand was normal in the picture, so it must have been taken some time ago. Behind her, her mother was griping about dinner. Putting the photo in her pocket, Sophia stood in the doorway and began to sob. She hadn't learned the stranger's name, but she now knew he was one of Masud's associates.

– 2 –

THE CONTRACT

"Money, travel, and adventure! What more ever you could want?"
—Major Mahmud Ahmadi, Iranian Liaison Officer, Defense
Language Institute, Lackland Air Force Base,
San Antonio, Texas, September 1975

Unemployment. The situation faced him like a sentence of death. Two years out of the University of Wyoming, with a bachelor's degree in history but no experience at anything professional, Danny MacCreary faced unemployment with dread.

He had beat Denver's empty streets, gone to soul-less Dallas, tried hippie Austin, and wound up in San Antonio, broke. Twenty-four years old, he accepted a temporary position at the Defense Language Institute. He had been surprised in his interview to learn such a training center existed. This unique school offered American English to foreign military allies. Danny was hired as a fulltime (temporary) "GS-1712-07, Training Instructor, (Language)." He wore a tie to work the next day.

There might be a future for new instructors, something called conversion to career status, which sounded like a stable job, so Danny worked hard to be the best instructor DLI ever hired. Plowing through textbooks at night, intensively studying English grammar, pronunciation, idioms, listening attentively to advice from other instructors about something called the "audio-lingual" approach to teaching a language, and after a year he was fairly proficient in ESL, or English as a Second Language. There was a whole science—indeed a lifestyle devoted to teaching foreigners.

"Which is correct," a Turkish student asked him one day. "On the corner, in the corner, at the corner, by the corner, or near the corner?"

"A good question!" Danny said confidently. "The simplest answer would be they're different kinds of corners and different places in relation to a corner."

"Which different kinds of corners? I must know in case it's on a test," the student persisted.

"A corner of a block is where two streets intersect, or a corner is where two walls meet. In other words, you're *on* the corner of a block, but you're enclosed *in* the protection of two walls," Danny answered with a smile. Yes, he had become proficient at explaining the concepts of American English to a speaker of another language, but it wasn't good enough for the Defense Language Institute, which announced in August 1975 that all temporary positions would end in September.

"It just galls my butt," Barbie Hansen, another temporary instructor, complained shortly after she got the notice. "I just had to sign with the Iranians. It's my only chance at a good job."

Danny was intrigued. A job? "Where did you find out about this?"

"At the Iranian Liaison Office," she answered. "They have sixty positions posted for overseas."

"How much do they pay? What kind of job is it? Do they provide housing?" Danny asked.

"I don't know the details," she replied evasively.

"Thanks for the tip," he said, and soon afterward, he made his way to the Iranian Liaison Office, the point of contact for thousands of students studying in the United States.

"May I help you?" an Iranian Air Force captain greeted him.

"I'm looking for the Iranian Liaison Officer," Danny answered. "I hear there is work for experienced language instructors in Iran."

"Yes, there is," the officer laughed amiably. "Come, I introduce you to Colonel Ahmadi."

The colonel's office was full of low-ranking enlisted students in tight, white navy uniforms, but at a harsh word from the colonel, imposingly dressed in dark air force blues, the men got up and sullenly left the room. The colonel strode around his desk, brushed aside some candy wrappers a sailor had left on his most important papers, then smiled hopefully at the young American standing before him. Behind the desk, an ornate portrait of the Shah hung over a bold, plastic sign proclaiming:

His Imperial Majesty
The Shah
Shahanshah Aryamehr
Mohammed Reza Pahlavi

Looking powerful, aristocratic, and determined, the king reminded Danny of an eagle with his hard, pitiless eyes glowering over a beaked nose. The Shah wore about twenty military medals, a red sash, a Sam Browne belt and golden epaulets. There was something sinister, yet pathetic, about the way the king presented himself in his official portrait.

On the other wall hung a slightly smaller picture, equally well-framed, but oddly tilted to one side, titled:

The Empress
Shahbanou
Farah Diba Pahlavi

Dressed in an ermine robe with a splendid crown on her head and enormous pearl earrings dangling from delicate ears, the empress was the perfect image of beauty, sophistication, and intelligence. Though she had the dreamy expression of an artist, she had as commanding a presence as her husband.

Scattered around the walls of the room were framed newspaper clippings of the Shah and Shahbanou skiing in San Moritz, receiving diplomats, and collecting honorary degrees from American and French universities. That was the total of what Danny knew about the Shah, too. In fact, he had always confused the Iranian aristocracy with the rulers of Monaco, Princess Grace and Prince Ranier. Perhaps it was the elegance, the ethereal beauty, the fast cars and luxurious villas, all shrouded in the romance only wealth could purchase.

"You want to go to Iran?" the colonel inquired after giving him time to survey the pictures.

"I'm looking into it," Danny answered cautiously. There was no sense in telling the Iranian too much.

"Is good contract. One hundred and five t'ousand rials a month, plus living allowance." Like many Iranians, the colonel had a hard time pronouncing double consonants and added a breath before words beginning with an "s" sound. Also inconsistent with sounds like "th" and "w/v," everything the colonel said was broken with extra syllables. For an Iranian, an American expression like "salted French fries" sounded like, "eh-sal-ah-ted f-ah-rench-a f-ah-ries," ten syllables, not four.

"The school exactly like here," the colonel said. "Same buildings, same books, same tests, many the same teachers. Everyone happy. Housing? Good housing. We can provide quarters on base, or you live off base in private apartment of your choice. Swimming pool, private car— whatever you want! Eit'er way, housing similar to America. Persian carpets every the room, because you buy some souvenirs, I'm sure. Persian carpets more cheaper in my country.

"We pay plane fare to Iran, give you buses to and back from work if you live off-base, and free medical care. Thirty days vacation every the year, paid ticket home at end of contract, round trip if you wish to sign for another tour. What you say?"

"Sounds good," Danny answered, though he knew enough to haggle. "I was hoping for more money. How much is 105,000 rials anyway?"

"Exchange rate is seventy-two rial to a dollar," the colonel smiled.

A bit over fourteen hundred dollars a month, Danny figured quickly—more money than he had ever earned in any job. "To put it into exchange terms, I was hoping to make a hundred sixty thousand rials."

"Oh? You married?"

"No, I was hoping to send money home," Danny lied. Accidentally glancing at the Shah's picture over the colonel's desk, he looked away quickly when his eyes met the hard black eyes of the king.

"A hundred sixty thousand is too much. I have flexibility with salaries. Let me see what I can do," the colonel smiled ingratiatingly. "Special, you know? You don't tell nobody. I try to get you … hundred thirty thousand, okay?"

"Yeah." For the first time since he'd learned he would be laid off, Danny felt a rush of excitement. Maybe this was his big chance, the one people said came only once in a lifetime—he had to grab it!

"Okay!" the colonel exclaimed, hugging himself in congratulation. "Ali?" he shouted to the captain waiting in the outer room, *"Sizdah hezar toman."* Turning back to Danny, he said, "Get a passport. Send it to the consulate in Houston for a work visa. I must have a statement from your doctor certifying you for employment, plus a notarized copy of your will, in case of accident, *enshallah*. I will arrange your plane tickets. Someone will meet you at the airport in Teheran and take care of you. Nothing simpler."

In minutes, the captain ran in with a freshly completed contract, twenty pages thick, ten in English, ten in Farsi. "Read this after signing it," the captain instructed Danny. "Don't worry. The Farsi is esame-esame as English. I translated it myself."

It would have been bewildering for a person with normal emotions, but Danny was too excited to care. It was a job with a good salary. Thanking the officers for their time, he hurried away to find an Iranian student to translate the Farsi.

"Sizdah hezar toman! Thirteen thousand tomans!" a sailor gasped.

Taking Danny by the arm, he whispered, "One hundred-thirty thousand rials is thirteen thousand tomans. Ten rials are one toman, you see. Good contract! You no tell nobody about this. Nobody."

Danny was satisfied. He went home that night, made appointments with a doctor, dentist, and an optometrist and then signed the papers.

"You're headed to Iran?" a friend asked him the next day. "I hear Barbie Hansen's going too."

"I probably won't even see her," Danny responded. "I think Iran's a big country—"

"You think it is?" his friend asked in surprise. "Don't you know?"

"Not yet," Danny admitted. "I need to go to the library to find out. I've never been able to tell Iran from Iraq."

"Hell! They're completely different," the man said as he hurried away.

–3–

THE WRONG ELEMENT
OF SOCIETY

"You talked to whom? I cannot believe you'd talk to her!"
—Barbie Hansen

As luck would have it, Danny MacCreary and Barbie Hansen were booked on the same flights from San Antonio to London. Since they had a two-day layover there, they visited as many tourist traps as they could. On their last night in England, they visited a neighborhood pub down the street from their hotel.

The place, however, ended up being not as quaint as they expected, for it was filled with stale cigarette smoke; most of the taciturn customers were drinking alone; and though there was a crowd around the bar, they weren't friendly. Seating Barbie at a table along the wall, Danny sauntered up to the bar to order a *pina colada* for her and a whiskey sour for himself.

"A what, mate?" the bartender asked. Nearby customers eavesdropped so obviously they paused with mugs of beer halfway to their mouths.

"A *pina colada* and a whiskey sour," Danny repeated. If the bartender weren't hard of hearing, he certainly wasn't paying attention. Behind the bar were huge bottles of whiskey and gin hanging upside down along one wall, but there were only a few glasses on a counter nearby, one mirror, and just half a dozen taps for beer. Used to the wild saloons and legendary honkytonks of Wyoming, his home state, with mounted deer heads and guns adorning the walls, where total strangers might offer you a bar stool or bust you in the mouth at some perceived slight, where bartenders and cocktail waitresses could run twenty table tabs in their heads simultaneously, he felt disappointed with this, his first pub. The place had little of what he expected in the way of atmosphere, but even so, it seemed to be filled with interesting people. The strangest thing was, though, few of the people indulged in conversations. Most looked like hard-core alcoholics in no mood to talk or socialize. They were concentrating on their drinks.

"Whiskey I know," the bartender said, scratching his balding head. "D'ya mean a whiskey neat?"

"No, a whiskey sour," Danny said. It was his favorite drink, but he didn't know how it was made. "I think it's whiskey and lemon juice."

"Oh, I can make one of those," the bartender said. "In England, though, most people prefer their whiskey neat."

"Okay, I'll try it neat. I've never had one before," Danny agreed. "And a *pina colada* for my friend."

"Oh," the bartender said, shaking his head. "I s'pose that's another of those sour drinks?"

"No, it's rum, coconut milk, and—I don't know what else," Danny admitted, for he was better versed in the drinking than the making. He wasn't impressed with this bartender's skill.

"How about a white wine for the lady, then?"

"That's fine, I guess," Danny said, making a mental note to skip pubs after this. Next time he visited London, he would go where bartenders worked American-style, like wizards able to create thousands of complex drinks from memory.

"What's this fucking shit?" Barbie complained the instant he returned to the table. "I didn't order white wine."

"The bartender didn't know how to make a *pina colada*."

"You should have told him," she snapped. "Here, you drink this god-damn piss-water. I'll go order my own drink."

Handing her a pound note, Danny sat back against the wainscoted wall and took a sip of his whiskey neat—and coughed. His eyes watered and his throat burned. It was pure scotch, but it tasted like rubbing alcohol. The Scotch was the worst thing he'd ever swallowed. "Wow," he gasped, "So that's what they mean by neat." Jim Beam, Wild Turkey, Jack Daniels, or Old Yellowstone could put this English scotch to shame....

He coughed again and took another sip. It didn't burn so badly going down the second time, and when he looked up, he spotted a beautiful redhead at the bar laughing at him over the top of her own glass. Dressed in a tight red dress, the woman was six feet tall, and she sported at least forty-inch, triple D knockers. She had wide hips, stiletto heels, long legs that stretched all the way to the floor, and a wicked smile promising a long evening ahead. Furtively glancing at the bar where Barbie was deep in argument with the bartender and half a dozen scruffy men, Danny sauntered over to the red-head with Barbie's white wine in one hand and his whiskey in the other.

"American?" she asked, taking his right hand in hers and dumping the whiskey into her own empty glass.

"Yeah, how did you know?" Danny asked stupidly. She was a little forward about the whiskey, but he liked white wine, and he certainly liked the look of her. He had never seen high heels so ... high ... before! In those shoes, she stood at least four inches taller than he did. He noticed she had a firm, tight ass and was *lush* everywhere in between. She was the most desirable woman he'd ever seen.

"Got a light?" she asked, looking him in the eye as she pulled a Gitane cigarette from her purse.

Although she spoke with an accent Danny had never heard before, he understood the seductive language of her lips as the cigarette dangled expectantly at her mouth. Lips that could suck the label off a beer bottle, he imagined, embarrassed at the nasty thought. He stuttered, "No, I ... ah ... don't... ah—"

"Don't smoke?" she asked, surprised. "I don't know anyone what doesn't smoke." Poking the man next to her at the bar, she motioned toward her cigarette, and he grudgingly lit it with an expensive Dunhill lighter, using the opportunity to give Danny a look.

"Don't smoke," she repeated, testing the sound of it. "Nothing wrong with you, is there?" she said, draping her left hand on his shoulder and mussing with his long auburn hair.

"No," he smiled. "I don't smoke." He liked her touching him. It sent shivers down his spine.

"M'name's Maggie," she said, raising her glass in toast, her bountiful boobs stretching her dress to its limit. Her cleavage was so deep he could have buried his head in the front of her dress, and she had a full, red-lipped mouth he wanted to lick dry. Her fingers were tipped with curved, red nails— the kind a tiger would be proud of—and he imagined what she could do.

"Danny MacCreary," he introduced, taking a breath to calm himself. She was the most attractive woman he had ever talked to, and he was pleased she was so interested in him.

"MacCreary!" she exclaimed, pulling him closer. "Me maiden name's McClanahan. Married name's Tompkins."

"Oh, you're married?" he asked, disappointment showing on his young face. Why couldn't he pick women better? He had come from a town in Wyoming so small its high school graduating class had less than a hundred students, but couldn't he at least pretend he was sophisticated?

"Don't worry, love. Me husband's a bastard. Fucked off w'some whore from Lancashire two years gone. Been on me own since." Boldly taking his arm, she squeezed him belly to the bar and asked, "Order us drinks?"

Surprised her glass was dry, Danny realized she drank whiskey like it was water, but he motioned to the bartender and turned back to the luscious woman beside him. When he did, she blew a cloud of cigarette smoke straight into his face, all the while looking at him with lovely blue eyes that were somehow cold, disinterested, and deep as crystals.

"Excuse me," Danny spluttered, his eyes watering. Her rudeness was surprising, but what could he say to such a beautiful woman without offending her?

"For what? You getting randy, love?" she laughed, oblivious to his discomfort. Blowing smoke into his eyes again, she cuddled closer and rubbed so much thigh and butt against him he was warm from knee to shoulder.

Danny didn't like cigarette smoke, especially at such close range. His father had lung cancer…. "Randy, what's that?"

"Oh c'mon, love. You know the drill! Let's not play games." Stubbing her cigarette in a chipped saucer on the bar, she surreptitiously reached down to cup his testicles in her left hand.

"Whoa? What?" He had never had anyone do that to him—let alone in public—but he was reluctant to pull away. Her long fingers felt wonderful.

"Twen'y, and cheap at that," she whispered, leaning closer to show him more cleavage. He could almost see her navel down the front of her dress. "Worth it, even if I say so m'self."

Danny had never met a prostitute before, never even *seen* one except in movies, and here was Maggie, so blatant about it, yet no one within earshot paid her the slightest attention. "Oh," he gulped. "I've never—I mean—I've never done it with a—I'm not interested in a—I don't have the money to—"

What rotten luck! First desirable woman he meets overseas, and she ends up being a hooker. He cursed his innocence.

"That's the way me evening's been so far," she sighed. "Never mind, love, but stay awhile. Buy me another whiskey?" She took her hand back, but even so, she gave him a thrill by rubbing her thigh against the rising front of his trousers.

Again he was surprised her drink was gone, but he anted up and then told her he was on his way to Iran. "Iran!" she laughed. "I've fucked a few of them, I'm sorry to say. They pay well, just like the Arabs, but Arabs they're not. They think they're God's great gift to womankind, they do. It's too bad, for the men tend to be nice looking. Big hairy chests, nice asses, tight pants, gold necklaces, but they think for twenty pounds they own you the night, and they want to bugger up your ass and down your throat for free.

"Did you ever hear the limerick what someone wrote about the Iranians?" she asked.

"No," he said, shaking his head.

She raised her nose theatrically and recited:

"A marvelous race was the Persians.
They had such won'erful diversions.
They did it all day,
In the very straight way,
And saved up the nights for perversions."

"Funny!" Danny laughed. He maneuvered himself closer and managed to look down the front of her dress again.

"I think it's true," she swore, putting her arm through his as she leaned closer to whisper some of the notorious Persian perversions in his ear.

At that moment, however, Barbie Hansen reappeared from around the corner of the bar. "Danny, what the fuck are you doing?" she asked incredulously, her face contorted in horror when she spotted the prostitute.

"Oh, hi, Barbie," he said. "Let me introduce you to—"

"I think it's time to go," Barbie replied haughtily. "We have a very early flight to catch tomorrow."

"C'mon, love," the prostitute tempted him. "Tell 'er to bugger off. Buy me a drink, and we can go somewhere else."

Danny was filled with desire, but he knew he had to go. Regretfully, he pried himself loose from the beautiful woman, bought her another drink, and wished her a good evening. "Maybe we'll meet again sometime," he waved.

"I'm 'ere every evening," she said tiredly, already smiling at a man across the room.

Minutes later, after an angry walk back to their hotel, Barbie turned on Danny in the hallway and hissed, "There are the desirable people in this world, and there are the undesirables. I'm convinced you're destined to attract the wrong element of society once we get to Iran!" Her hand shaking as she unlocked her room, she yelled, "I want you to stay the hell away from me once we get there."

-4-

MEHRABOD

"You know you are not welcome in my country."
                                                            —*A taxi driver*

It wasn't a pleasant name for an airport like Heathrow or Dallas Love Field, nor was it as romantic as Schiphol or as businesslike as O'Hare. It was just Mehrabod, and it sat on the edge of Teheran like a toad on a log, a brooding, sinister promise of things to come.

Looking out the plane's window as they approached the airport, Danny caught a glimpse of a flat-roofed adobe-brown city under a gray cloud of air pollution, then the plane banked once, landed bumpily, and taxied to a stop three hundred yards from any building. Minutes later, a reticulated bus picked up the disembarking passengers.

"We're here," Danny announced as cheerily as he could, loading his and Barbie's suitcases onto the bus. There wasn't a baggage handler in sight, and a hundred people, young and old alike, struggled to get everything aboard. Though it was nearly November 1975 it must have been ninety degrees on the tarmac. He broke into a sweat. He had never gotten used to the heat in Texas, and Iran was supposed to be much worse. The distant mountains had snow on them, but they were brown and treeless otherwise.

"I can't believe we're expected to ride to the terminal in a goddamn bus," Barbie complained. "Are we expected to carry our luggage inside? You would think in a modern international airport—"

"It looks more like a military base than an airport," Danny observed, noting the rows of F-4 Phantom fighter planes and military transports on the other side of the runway.

"Two weeks ago," an experienced passenger whispered as they got on the bus, "the international terminal collapsed under a light load of snow. The domestic terminal is being used to receive international flights now."

"Why are you whispering?" Danny asked.

"Don't criticize anything in Iran," the man said. "They remember every word. Everyone hears you here. Everyone is listening to you."

At first, the terminal appeared large, airy, and up to date, but the baggage carousels weren't working, and half the lights were burned out or stolen. The tile floor was immaculately clean, but everything else was layered in dust. Only two photos broke the monotony of the walls: the obligatory portraits of the Shah and Shahbanou. Farah's picture, Danny noticed, was tilted in exactly the same way it had been, seven thousand miles away, in the liaison office in Texas. Was it a coincidence?

There was no one to meet them. Their fellow passengers cleared customs and departed, and the two hapless Americans were left standing alone with twenty policemen in blue uniforms, a bored customs agent, a mysterious loiterer in a black suit, and a derelict in a sports jacket who was sweeping the floor in a sideways motion with a witch's broom ten feet long.

"I think we should collect our luggage and get out of here," Danny suggested. "What do you say we—"

"Absolutely not!" Barbie snapped. "We're supposed to meet someone from the Imperial Iranian Air Force, and we are not leaving this airport until he gets here. We have a contract with the government!"

Shrugging indulgently, Danny dragged their suitcases to a round bench in the middle of the floor and then walked over to a bar to get something to drink.

"Do you have—?" Danny tried.

"*Farsi miduneed?*"

"Excuse me? I need something to drink—"

"*FARSI MIDUNEED?*" the bartender shouted, subscribing to the theory if foreigners don't understand, shout.

"Ah, no. No Farsi whatsoever," Danny admitted.

"*Miduneed?*"

"Do you speak English?" Danny asked, feeling silly.

"*Nemidunam,*" the man answered.

Stymied, Danny tried again. "Do you have something to drink?"

"*Chai?*" the man asked, raising his eyebrows.

"*Chai,*" Danny agreed.

"*Dota?*"

He looked for some sign in the man's eyes but there was only scorn. "*Dota*," he agreed.

The man instantly produced two little glasses. Placing them on a saucer with six sugar cubes, he whirled around and filled the glasses half with hot water from a samovar and half with concentrated tea from a teapot simmering on top. "*Doh toman*," he demanded.

Luckily, Danny had changed money in London, so he handed the man a bill. Rummaging in a cardboard box for change, the Iranian gave him an assortment of silver coins and small bills. Danny smelled a rat immediately.

"Excuse me," he asked a nearby policeman. "Do you speak English— um, I mean, English *miduneed?*"

"Yes, I understand English terminology."

"Can you tell me how much this is?" Danny asked, holding out the money.

"No," the policeman said, walking away.

Puzzled, Danny turned to another policeman and asked,

"English *miduneed?*"

"Yes."

"Can you tell me how much this is?"

"Yes," the policeman smiled.

"Well," Danny said. "How much is it?"

"Yes."

"You don't really understand a word of English, do you?"

"Yes."

His sense of humor kicking in, Danny smiled pleasantly and asked, "Do you have camel dung for brains?"

"Yes," the man said.

"And your paternity is in doubt?"

"Yes," the man smiled.

"And you've been involved in all manner of crimes like forgery, fraud, and incest?"

"Yes."

"And you personally have cleaned the Shah's toilets?"

Going blank at mention of the Shah, the policeman glanced left and right and hurried away.

Seconds later, a group of European stewardesses hurried through the customs agents like they didn't even exist. "Pardon me," Danny called, but the beautiful women ignored him and rushed away into the evening.

"Excuse me," he asked a baggage handler. "Do you speak English?" The man raised his nose straight in the air and clicked his tongue insolently.

"I can't figure out what's going on here," Danny told Barbie as he handed her the tea. "These people are strange."

"What am I supposed to do with all this sugar?" Barbie said, ignoring his problem. "Do you want me to get fat?" Stowing the sugar cubes beside her on the cushion, she irritably began to read a brochure on Persian monuments.

"Do you have anything with Iranian numbers written on it?" Danny asked, looking through his pockets for a pen.

"Yes, I do," she said. "A student wrote the alphabet and numbers for me, but I can't figure them out."

As she continued to fuss beside him, Danny studied the numbers written on her paper. He could see now the two small teas had cost him the equivalent of 355 rials, for his change amounted to only 145 rials. There were 72 rials to the dollar, so he had been charged nearly five dollars for two tiny cups of tea. "I'll be back in a minute," he said.

"Where are you going? You're not leaving me again, are you?" Barbie wailed. "Those men are staring at me. They might rape me!"

"I'm going to get more tea. These little glasses don't last long." As he walked back to the bar, only the loiterer paid him any attention. He wondered if the man was one of the secret police, the so-called SAVAK. If so, he didn't blend in very well, but Danny figured that was the way to do the job. His sheer presence intimidated the guilty.

This time, the bartender hardly looked up. Danny leaned on the counter and said, "Hello, remember me?"

"*Chi dazam dareed?*"

Danny understood it this time, but he couldn't explain how. "*Chai,* please," he ordered.

"*Dota digeh?*"

"*Dota.*"

"*Digeh?*"

"*Digeh.*"

"*Dota digeh?*" the man asked, pleased to irritate the foreigner.

"*Dota digeh,*" Danny agreed, watching the man like one might watch a cobra rise out of the grass. Putting two glasses of tea on a saucer with more sugar cubes, the Iranian handed it to him without so much as a smile. Danny decided to test a theory. "*Digeh,*" he said, showing three fingers and indicating the sugar.

"*Seta?*" the man asked, wiping his nose with a sleeve.

"*Seta digeh*," Danny answered. The man placed three sugar cubes on the saucer. "How much?"

"*Char toman*," the man answered.

"How much...?" Danny asked again, letting it hang.

Reluctantly, the man translated, "*Chand mishe?*" He appeared tired of the game. Probably, Danny realized, tourists paid and walked away, not realizing the barman was in business to cheat them.

"*Chand mishe?*" Danny asked with a smile.

"*Char toman*," the man said.

This time Danny handed the man a hundred rials, and held out his hand for change. The surly Iranian sorted through his moneybox again and came up with sixty rials. "*Char toman.* Four tens or forty rials," Danny laughed. He had learned that "*dota*" meant "two of something," "*seta*" was "three," and "*char*" was four. His smile evaporated as soon as he gave the tea to Barbie.

"God in heaven," she swore. "You do want me to get fat."

"Barbie, I've been awake since five o'clock London time, whatever time that is here, but I know it's late. It's dark outside, and I'm in no mood for this. Drink the tea and use what sugar you need. I'm for getting out of here and finding a hotel."

"You can goddamn well do as you please," she said, "but we were told we'd be taken to a hotel courtesy of the Iranian Air Force, and I, for one, intend to wait."

Grumbling to himself, Danny unpacked the heavier of his two suitcases and located a duplicate of his contract. At the bottom, barely legible, was a telephone number of a "Duty Officer, Doshan Tappeh Air Force Base 732541." Using a phone on a dusty counter nearby, he dialed the number. Someone answered immediately but didn't say anything. "Hello?" Danny asked.

"Hello."

"Hello, may I speak with the duty officer please?"

"Yes."

"Are you the operator or the duty officer?" Danny asked in confusion.

"Yes."

"Are you the duty officer at Doshan Tappeh?"

"Yes."

Danny wanted to scream, but he had just learned when given a choice, Iranians usually answered in the affirmative if the last item mentioned was what they wanted. Thus, something simple like, "Would you like an apple or an orange?" would lead to the answer, "Yes," if the Iranian wanted the orange, and frustration if he wanted the apple.

Patiently, he tried again, "Hello, my name is Daniel MacCreary. I have a contract—"

"Contract instructor?"

"Yes, a new contract instructor. I am at Mehrabod—"

"We not expect you. Car will be there in one hour."

"Thanks. Didn't the Liaison Officer in Texas tell you we were coming?"

"No, they never tell us."

"But I have a contract!" Danny exclaimed.

"Contract no good in Iran. Renegotiation the contract tomorrow the morning."

"Didn't I tell you?" Barbie sneered as soon as he returned, "That they would pick us up? Someone's on the way, isn't he?"

"Yes," Danny said, not in the mood for more of her lip.

"I thought so. God, I just went to the little girls' room, and it's the filthiest I have ever seen. They don't have any toilets, just holes in the floor. How am I supposed to hit a hole like that? Squat? Just let it drop like a bomber on the fly? What if I get it on my shoes? And there was no toilet paper at all! Not a sheet, just a water hose to spray my butt and fingers with! You would think in a modern country—"

Ignoring her, Danny closed his eyes and slept. Well past midnight, a young Iranian presented himself to the two exhausted Americans. "Are you the contract instructors?" he asked.

"Yes, we are," Barbie purred, giving the man her best Miss Texas smile. "We are so tired."

"Of course you are. I am Mehdi Davarpanah. I am in charge of all contract instructors."

"How do you do? I'm Mr. MacCreary," Danny said, offering his hand. "This is Miss Hansen."

"Miss or Missus?" the Iranian smiled, eyes glittering.

"Miss," she answered pleasantly. "I understand we're supposed to go to a particular hotel?"

"Yes, the Hotel Atlantic off Takht-e-Jamshid Avenue near to the American Embassy. It's very convenient. Shall we go?"

Davarpanah was friendly, courteous, and even funny during the long drive, but Danny was too tired to care, having been on his feet for over thirty hours. Although Teheran was just a blur after the momentary glory of a marble tower called Shahyad just outside the airport, Danny formed a vague impression of a modern city with bright lights and high apartment buildings.

"You see? Very nice city," Davarpanah smiled reassuringly as he pulled up before the hotel. "You will be happy here in Iran."

"I'm sure I will," Barbie gushed. "I'm looking forward to this romantic country."

"I've already been introduced," Danny grumped, lifting their suitcases out of the trunk and walking stiffly into the little hotel. "See you tomorrow."

—5—

DOSHAN TAPPEH

"You must teach the SOP. It answers every the question."
—Mehdi Davarpanah, contract coordinator, Imperial Iranian
Air Force, Doshan Tappeh Air Force Base, Teheran, Iran

"Good morning," Barbie greeted Danny when he straggled into the hotel's restaurant for breakfast next morning. His long auburn hair was mussed, and he hadn't shaved or washed yet. His room didn't have a sink or a toilet, but it did have [an unlicensed] short-wave radio. "I'm having toast, eggs and tea," she said. "Look at this funny bread."

The toast, called *sangyak*, was hacked into crude squares with a dull kitchen knife; it was yellow, tough, and lumpy. The only jam available was made from carrots, but Danny found the bread quite good, and the jam delicious. The excellent tea was typically Iranian, made in a chromed samovar in the corner of the room.

"*Sobah khare.* Good morning."

They looked up to find Mehdi Davarpanah standing over their table. "May I see your contracts, please?"

"They were signed and notarized by the Liaison Officer in America," Barbie said. "I'm sure they're legal."

"You misunderstand," Mr. Davarpanah soothed her. "I must verify the information."

Danny spread his contract out on the table, but Barbie muttered threats under her breath as she fished through her purse. "I can't find it," she whined, dumping her handbag out. "I must have left it in my room."

"Ah, Mr. Mareery," the Iranian said, mispronouncing Danny's last name as he looked over the contract. "You were hired through the Liaison Office on Lackland Base, Texas." Pretending to draw a pistol from a holster, the man laughed, "Texas? I know all about Texas. John Wayne, eh?" His smile quickly fading, the Iranian announced, "This contract is invalid in Iran. You must renegotiate. Similar terms, of course, but now under Iranian law. Please take care of it as soon as possible."

"Well, I have the same contract!" Barbie announced irritably.

"Then we should have no problem putting you to work. Please locate your contract as soon as possible. Mr. Mareery, you will accompany me now. I will take you to the language school at Doshan Tappeh Air Force Base."

"What about me? I'm not finished with breakfast yet," Barbie complained.

"I will collect you tomorrow morning. Mr. Mareery, we go now," Davarpanah said, turning on his heel.

"Barbie, you sure know how to impress the locals," Danny whispered as he got up. He stuffed a piece of yellow bread in a pocket and swigged the last of his tea. He was hopeful today would be the start of his biggest adventure. He would meet the people who would determine his destiny.

But as he stepped out on the sidewalk, Danny's impression from the night before—of orderly traffic and modern apartment buildings—was destroyed. The street—Takht-e-Jamshid Avenue—was a bedlam of noise, dust, and traffic. Cars jockeyed for advantage in so confusing a fashion it was hard to tell what direction the traffic was moving. Mercedes trucks, small cars, expensive BMW's, Army troop carriers, donkeys with swaying cargoes on their backs, pushcarts, pedestrians, motorcycles, and flocks of sheep swarmed in every direction as far as he could see.

"Come, this is my car," Davarpanah waved. His car, parked half on, half off the wide sidewalk, was a red Paykan, the Iranian version of the British Hillman automobile. It had vinyl seats and no luxury features, but most Iranians paid cash for one and waited two years for delivery. Mr. Davarpanah's vehicle had been customized with a purple velvet dash cover and red tassels framing the windshield. A picture of a bearded saint, Ali, hung from the rearview mirror.

Stepping up beside the car, Danny missed a step and fell, badly scraping his left leg on the side of a ditch partially concealed under a concrete slab on which the car was precariously parked.

"You must be careful," Davarpanah cautioned. "This is the *djube*, the famous Iranian canal. It is exactly like those in Salt Lake City America, I'm told."

Although Danny would hear the analogy often, he couldn't see any similarity between this slime-filled ditch and anything in Salt Lake City. The *djube* was not really a gutter, but it was not a sewer either, since the city of Teheran didn't have a public sewage system, and it certainly was not a system of canals, as few *djubes* flowed, and even fewer flowed water. Instead, the *djube* was a cheap concrete ditch about eighteen inches wide, two feet deep, and only intermittently wet. In a city stretched to nightmarish failures of all public services, these festering gutters were used by the poor for bathing, drinking, trash disposal, and sewage.

Reminding himself to clean his scraped knee later, Danny got into the car. It smelled of Turkish cigarettes and exotic spices.

Davarpanah pulled into the street with nary a look at his rearview mirror; seconds later, sensing a hole in traffic imperceptible to his startled passenger, he made a U-turn and sped off in the opposite direction.

Along the way, they passed the American embassy with its high, liver-red brick walls and wide asphalt sidewalk. Unarmed Iranian police were stationed at every entrance and corner of the compound. Through a wide, wrought iron gate, Danny glimpsed trees, grass, and American normalcy inside the walls.

The street down which they were now traveling was one of the aging thoroughfares of central Teheran. Bustling with hotels, international banks, trade centers, and craft stores, Takht-e-Jamshid Avenue abruptly ended at Kouroush-e-Kabir, a busy north-south avenue. From that point on, Danny couldn't follow the route. Narrow streets, crowded intersections, residential neighborhoods, and outdoor markets all rushed by the window as Davarpanah raced through the traffic and confusion of east Teheran.

An hour later, they roared out of an alley into a traffic jam. Davarpanah maneuvered across the traffic, then turned onto a street only two blocks long. Narrowly missing a group of women dressed in black *chadors*, he parked next to a flock of fat-tailed sheep feeding on a pile of garbage in an empty lot.

"I don't have parking privileges on Doshan Tappeh," he explained. "We must walk from here."

Again they were exposed to the complete bedlam of Teheran. Two little boys ran out into the street after a soccer ball; not one car stopped. Deliverymen from a bakery were taking off into the traffic, having tied stacks of flat *barbari* bread on the backs of dirty mopeds, and they left chunks of bread on every bumper and outside mirror as they passed. Women in *chadors* swept by like shapeless tents in the wind, a beggar with a face deformed by smallpox grabbed Danny's arm, and an enlisted man wandered by aimlessly looking for excitement.

Overwhelmed by all the activity, Danny had to be led up the street to the high brick walls of Doshan Tappeh Air Force Base. He was ordered into a noisy gatehouse where a duty officer could examine his contract. Outside the window, a squad of the most slovenly dressed soldiers Danny had ever seen was standing in a ragged line. The men were looking in every direction except toward the gate they were guarding. Equipped with dented helmets and modern G-3 assault rifles, they were obviously not trusted with live ammunition, for they had plugged the empty magazines of their guns with Marlboro cigarette packages to keep the dust out.

After only thirty minutes, during which he read and re-read Danny's contract aloud, word for word, the officer grudgingly allowed the foreigner onto the base. Davarpanah was waiting outside the guard shack, and he led Danny past an old fighter plane mounted on a thick concrete pylon. Reminded of the static aircraft displays he had seen on Lackland Air Force Base in Texas, Danny, ever a tourist asked innocently, "What's that?"

A strange look crossing his face, Davarpanah claimed, "Perhaps it was the Shah's first plane...." Shaking his head at the unexpected question, he admitted, "I don't really know—" For an Iranian, it was an unusual admission of ignorance.

Doshan Tappeh appeared to be a clean, attractive training area. As they walked across the base, Danny noted neat brick classroom buildings, tree-lined asphalt streets, graveled parade fields, mess halls, and administrative buildings laid out in a logical, orderly military manner. The two-story headquarters of the language school faced a parade field where three formations of draftees were learning to do the goose step. A peasant boy seemed to be having a hard time of it, for rather than counting in modern Farsi (yek, do, se, char) like his more educated peers, he was counting in the traditional way "Yek! Do! Se! Cha-HAR!" and then he tried an extra hop to compensate for the added syllable.

Davarpanah waved his charge inside the headquarters. As they entered, he confided, "This is the only building warm in the winter and cool in the summer." Housing administrative offices, language laboratories, secret police offices, clean restrooms, a library, and an instructors' lounge, the building was the heart of the language school.

In a hurry to bring the American to the commandant's attention, Davarpanah took him directly into the major's office without even knocking. The commandant, in conference with several lieutenants, was, of course, not amused, so the interview was brusque and to the point: "Welcome to Iran," the officer snapped. "Start work in two days. Your contract is worthless here." Abruptly dismissing Danny, he ordered, "Renegotiate with my adjutant, Captain Tafafchian."

Without apology, Davarpanah ushered the crestfallen American into the darkened instructors' lounge. "Wait here," he said, rushing back to the major's office to make amends.

The lounge, a large room with heavily plastered white walls, was the only oasis in the noisy chaos of the school. A half-wall separated the snack bar from the rest of the lounge; comfortable booths lined the walls, and tables and chairs filled most of the highly polished tile floor. It was cool, dark, and private— three things Danny would soon crave—but sitting around the lounge with their backs against the walls was the strangest assortment of wasted human beings he had ever seen

The veteran instructors were all thin and pale, their eyes red and their skin dry as parchment. With long hair and patched, dusty clothes, they looked like miners coming off a shift. Some had small piles of books in front of them—mostly novels and how-to books—and others had a briefcase or shoulder bag filled with personal possessions. Like refugees from a war, these tired survivors of the previous contract sat resting in the peaceful darkness. Danny dubbed them the Gray Wolves, and he understood then that he and others soon to follow, were just replacements for these soon-to-be-departing veterans. And that was the first time Danny knew for sure he had made the biggest mistake of his life; he should never have signed the contract in America.

He decided to put on a brave front; walking up to the snack bar, he ordered a cup of tea and a sandwich. None of the dirty soldiers behind the counter spoke English—which he thought strange in a language school—but he pointed at a cheese sandwich in a torpedo-shaped bun. When he got a satisfying amount of change from the cashier, he said, "Khahesh mikonam," or "Thank you."

Minutes later, Danny went to look for a restroom. By chance, the first office he passed was Captain Tafafchian's.

"Doctor Mary, you are come to sign the new contract," the captain smiled, drawing himself up to full height. For an Iranian, he was quite large, well over six feet tall, but his uniform jacket barely buttoned over his belly.

"Oh ... yes," Danny agreed, though he was in a hurry to use the restroom. The morning's tea had worked its way through his system.

"In the American contract you are 'Mary, D. R.'?"

"Yes."

"So that is why Colonel Ahmadi, the Iranian Liaison Officer on Lackland Base offered you one hundred thirty thousand rials?" Thinking the captain knew about his successful bargaining with the colonel, Danny agreed.

"Good," Captain Tafafchian nodded. He handed Danny a contract, its spaces filled in except for MacCreary's first name.

"Excuse me," the captain apologized. "I forget your first name and middle the name."

"Daniel Rene."

Moments later, the contract was completed and ready for signing. Although there was no English translation this time, Danny was relieved when he learned his salary was actually higher. In this version, he was allotted one hundred sixty thousand rials a month—the same as what he had originally proposed in America—with a housing allowance that added another twenty-five thousand. Happily signing the contract, he thought no more about it.

Next morning, Davarpanah took Barbie to the base, but Danny was on his own. "How do I get to Doshan Tappeh?" he asked the hotel clerk. "Takht-e-Jamshid Avenue does not go there."

"Best way is to catch the taxi on Shah Reza Avenue down to the back, one kilometer. You must say 'Khiabun-e-Teheran-No.' When a taxi slows down, you say 'Istgahe Ferootgah.'" Within two minutes of trying it, Danny had a ride to Doshan Tappeh Air Force Base. Interestingly *istgahe* was from the English word "sky."

There was, of course, a mountain of paperwork to be done that day. Danny hurried to his first appointment, where he discovered that interminable waiting and foolishness alternated with periods of frantic activity during which he was accused of lagging behind. Even when he was admitted to an office to speak with someone, six or eight other people would rush in, shouting for attention. Anyone who stood in line in Iran was looked upon as gutless; loud and aggressive complainers were always served first. Since he would be working for the Iranians, Danny had to be as pushy as everyone else.

"Can I borrow your phone?" Danny shouted above the din in the Bank Markazi Iran where he had gone to open a payroll account. When a clerk nodded, he asked, "Do you have the Commandant's phone number?"

"The commandant?" the clerk spluttered. "Why do you want his number?"

"The Commandant wanted to see me at two o'clock," Danny bluffed. "I'm late now, so I wanted to reschedule—"

"There is no need for that," the clerk said, motioning to the bank manager. "We take care of you immediately. Don't call the commandant."

In minutes, Danny had a hefty advance on his salary, a bank account, and a voucher to pay the hotel. Even native Iranians were surprised he finished his paperwork the first day.

"Damn!" Barbie swore when she learned the Atlantic Hotel would not refund the money she had already paid for her room.

"You do not have a voucher," the manager sneered, hitching up his pajama bottoms like a badge of authority.

"That's too bad," Danny said as sympathetically as he could. He looked forward to the coming weekend. He wondered if he could buy alcohol in Iran. Anticipating a chance to see the famous Teheran Bazaar, he decided he wanted to do some window shopping, drink some beer, send a letter home to tell his family he had arrived safely, and unwind before beginning his new job.

–6–

THE NEW DOCTOR

"You are a doctor. I don't care what you say. The matter is settled."
—Muhmad Panak

From the beginning of his new job, Danny MacCreary learned there were distinct classes of instructors. At the bottom of the heap were Pakistanis, no matter their education or experience. Earning only 40,000 rials a month, certainly not enough to support themselves in such an expensive city, they lived in communes, six to ten in an apartment. Above them in pay and status were part-time instructors, most of whom were Iranians with high-school educations.

Next in rank were permanent, full-time Iranian instructors, most of whom had college degrees. Foreign wives of Iranians, many Americans, worked on annual arrangements, while other expatriates worked for six months as "temporaries." The true "contract" instructors, highest in status, were all hired in the U.S. at a base pay of 70,000 rials a month, plus allowances. The best paid were the American PhD's, including Danny MacCreary, for his first two initials, "D. R." had been mistaken for his educational level, hence his new title, "Doctor."

"Excuse me," he said to the commandant as soon as he realized the error. "There's been a mistake on my contract."

"Did you sign the contract?" the major asked haughtily.

"Yes, I did, but I didn't know—"

"Then there is no mistake."

"But there is a problem with my salary," Danny tried again, hoping to get it corrected before someone discovered the error and had it subtracted from his next paycheck.

"You signed the contract. You must work for that salary. It's too late to

–29–

renegotiate." The commandant spun on his heel and walked away. Danny had no luck elsewhere either. Luckily, in a country rife with corruption, there were no auditors.

To be an instructor for the Imperial Iranian Air Force, each candidate had to complete a six-week training course. Doctor or not, Danny had to attend this course. His fellow students in the class included poorly educated Iranians, Pakistanis, an Irish construction worker, an American woman married to an Iranian, an English girl of "proper" education, and an Australian couple. Only Danny was a contract instructor, hired for his experience. Due to his "credentials," Danny was considered the head of the class and an expert in language instruction.

"You must be the Doctor," the instructor greeted him the first morning. "Please sit in front."

"There's been a misunderstanding with my contract," Danny smiled apologetically, hoping to get off on the right foot. "I'm not really a doctor."

"Oh, I understand," the man said.

"You do?" Danny asked in relief.

"Yes, you are not a *medical* doctor, you are a Ph.D. Your degree is not in English as a Second Language, but you have a college education requiring a higher salary. Don't be apologetic. You must work harder than everyone else, for we expect more from a doctor than from common instructors."

No matter what else Danny tried, it never did any good. At first, he was embarrassed about his higher salary, but his classmates viewed his explanations as misguided humility. None of the Iranians or any of the foreigners were ever convinced he was anything other than a real PhD, a Doctor of Linguistics, so Danny decided to enjoy the privileges attendant to his new rank. Besides, he had to admit, he liked being called "Doc." His last name, MacCreary, was soon butchered to "Mary," and so he became "Doctor Mary" in Iran.

The training class consisted of a week of classroom observations on Doshan Tappeh Air Force Base followed by several weeks of intensive "microteaching." For the uninitiated, microteaching is composed of sample lessons in each of the three fields of the Iranian Air Force's slavish adherence to its official methodology. The lessons were Dialog, Reading, and Grammar.

Immediately, Danny posed the question, "How is this methodology adapted by the instructors to the books or the various levels of the students?"

"It is not your problem," the instructor answered, in Catch-22 fashion.

"You're telling me I'm supposed to take care of any situation that arises in the classroom without ever varying from your Standard Operating Procedure, the SOP?"

"That's correct. The SOP is our only method of exchange with the students."

Perhaps the system was the best way to teach a language under the circumstances. As Danny got to know his fellow instructors, he discovered the Pakistanis had a hard time speaking English without the disastrous effects of the rhythm of their native Urdu. Most of the other expatriates were minimally educated; many didn't understand English themselves. The lone Brit in the class prided herself on proper grammar, but whispered, "I can't imagine *explaining* it to anyone."

The strict methodology solved all of these problems. There was no time to get off the subject, no freedom to get lost in detailed explanations, no need to use any other method than the Standard Operating Procedure.

"This system," Danny's instructor explained, "is called 'lock-step methodology.' Our supervisors place students with similar ability in the same wing of a building, and every teacher there is expected to teach the same book, in exactly the same way, at the same moment as everyone else. Very simple! Any variance from the SOP is not tolerated by the supervisors or the students."

"I don't think I'm going to be able to do this," Barbie Hansen confessed when she spotted Danny in a hallway one afternoon. Only recently graduated from the University of Texas with a Masters Degree in teaching English, her head was filled with Chomsky's theories, jazz chants, "cloze" exercises, SQ3R, and all the cerebral paraphernalia so stimulating in college but with no relation to the blood and sweat of an actual classroom—especially in Iran.

Danny, however, was fascinated. Educationally weak in the field, to him the SOP sounded like a solid base from which to work. At the same time, he was swept away with the intellectual depth of the Pakistanis. For example, he met an expert in English grammar who was unable to speak a word of the language intelligibly.

"Look, I'll help you speak," he told the man one day, "if you'll help me learn my grammar."

"Isgudidea," the swarthy Pakistani answered shyly. "Tankyou eh-sir."

More than anything else about the class, though, Danny was enjoying the unashamed lust on the face of Nastaran, a young Iranian woman who sat across the room from him. The English woman, Deborah Barrington, wasn't pleased. Intelligent, funny, and sensible—something that Danny liked in a woman—Deborah was quick to judge.

"Look," she said one day on the bus ride home, "My mother and I are having dinner and drinks for a few friends. Would you like to come?"

"Great. What time?"

"Sevenish. There will be some interesting people there," she said. "You and Sandy Langarudi will be the only Americans. Have you met her?"

"Briefly."

"She has a mischievous sense of humor."

"I'm looking forward to seeing her again," Danny said.

"We'll also have Andrea Wilcox over. Do you know her?"

"No," Danny lied, though he had heard of her. She had a bad reputation. She was supposed to have powerful friends, and so one wasn't allowed to ask questions. "Shall I bring something?"

"Not necessary," Deborah said. "I think you'll enjoy our get-together."

– 7 –

THE DINNER PARTY

"I couldn't imagine passing such a thing around—"
                                                    —*Sandra*

"She's a prostitute," someone whispered in the men's room one day. Most of the foreign instructors, the ones the Iranians called "*farangi*," were careful to whisper such rumors behind the woman's back. Though Iranians sneered, "*Jende*" to her face, at the same time they seemed fascinated with her, and she appeared to wield a strange power over them. It was a sexual power...not unlike political.

Danny first saw the woman getting into one of the blue minibuses at Doshan Tappeh at the end of the day. She was well dressed and elegant. "Is that the blonde everyone's talking about?" he asked an acquaintance.

"Yes," the man answered. "She's rather honest about her position. The only reason she has to work here, I understand, is to maintain her residence permit. None of the students give her any problems in class. I think she has *parti bazee*."

While some of the women at work worried they might catch a social disease from sitting too close to "that bitch," or using the same (and the only) Western toilet on Doshan Tappeh, Danny wondered why such a beautiful and sophisticated woman would turn to such a sordid vocation. At the same time, he was curious how she managed to operate so openly in a Moslem culture. Yes, he decided, she must have powerful *parti bazee*, or political influence. She must have connections, and he wondered whom she knew and what she did for the favor.

On the twentieth of December, Danny eagerly prepared for a dinner at the Barrington's. The Barrington home, on the third floor of a new apartment building in Tajrish, was already one of his favorite places in Teheran, for it provided a respite from the constant profanity and stress around him. Despite being nearly unable to find what she needed in the markets, Sandra Barrington cooked proper English specialties. Danny often obtained recipes from her.

"Doc?" Sandra called as soon as her daughter, Deborah, announced his arrival. "I'm in the kitchen."

Sir David, Sandra's husband, nodded and smiled at Danny as he headed for the kitchen. Sandra's daughter, Claire, waved from the patio. Deborah, the youngest of the Barrington girls, was busy talking to her boyfriend on the phone, but she covered the mouthpiece and shot him a puckered kiss. Despite himself, Danny liked it, for Deborah was an attractive woman.

"Hi," Danny grinned, joining Sandra at the stove. Immediately to his left, he was surprised to see the dreaded prostitute dicing leeks at a small metal table.

"Danny MacCreary, otherwise known to his friends as 'Doctor Mary' or 'Doc,'" Sandra introduced rather ceremoniously, "I'd like you to meet Miss Andrea Wilcox, a fellow victim of the insanity we must endure in Iran."

"How do you do," he said, taking her hand. "I've noticed you leaving work in the evenings. You take *autobus char*, the new Mercedes bus; I ride *autobus yek*, the rattling wreck." Embarrassed to finally meet the woman, he smiled in what he hoped was a friendly way, and then turned to sniff the large pot bubbling on the stove. "This smells interesting. What is it?"

"It's an old family secret," Sandra confided, winking at the younger woman. "It's called water. Neither Sir David nor I drink the water in these primitive countries unless we *boil* it first."

"Really?" Danny grinned, dutifully picking up a spoon to taste it. "Excellent stuff. I must try this sometime. Could you give me the recipe?"

"He's been like this ever since we met," Sandra told Andrea in a stage whisper. "I think it has something to do with his being an American.

"Doc," she said, "be a good boy and collect all the empty bottles from the pantry and put them in the boot of Andrea's car. She's going to return them to the store for me."

"Do I need a key?"

"Of course," Sandra said, in much the same way she would speak to a child or an Iranian.

"Here," Andrea Wilcox said, grinning at the older woman. Fishing through an eel skin purse, she withdrew a large bundle of keys.

The prostitute was amazingly elegant and Danny had a hard time tearing his eyes away from her. "Thanks," he mumbled, almost gratefully accepting the warm keys from her delicate, slim fingers.

When he got back upstairs, Sandra was telling Andrea, "Two weeks ago, I had Doc to drinks and dinner with several of our friends. He showed up wearing those high-heeled boots like you see in the Western films."

"Cowboy boots," Danny said, as he joined them.

"Yes, I've seen Texas oilmen wearing them," Andrea laughed. Sitting nearby, Danny figured she had probably known plenty of oilmen in her time.

"I'd never seen the real thing," Sandra continued, "and before you know it, he took one off and passed it around! Can you *imagine* any of us taking off a shoe and handing it to someone during cocktails? Anyway, we were looking at this boot of his—and it was rather interesting, wonderful stitchery and so forth—and Richard Chatham, you know him?"

"We've met," Andrea nodded mysteriously.

"Richard asked Danny where he lived in the United States. Doc says he's from the West, just like in the cowboy films, you see. Of course, we asked about his home—"

"And I told them an interesting story about my cabin at Elk Mountain, Wyoming with an outhouse—I guess you Brits would call it a 'loo'—half a mile away. I told them about horses, rodeos, hangings, and shootings."

"We believed him," Sandra admitted, casting her hands up in the air.

"No!" Andrea laughed, giving Danny an amused look.

"Yes, unfortunately, we did. Doc had us hanging on every word! Finally, Richard asked when he planned to return to the States, and Doc told him as soon as he achieved something called a 'grub stake,' he would fly to New York, take the train to St. Louis, a stagecoach to Denver, and then would either buy a horse, or hitch a ride to his home in Wyoming with a muleskinner—and that's when Sir David began to laugh. You know how Sir David enjoys things that strike him as particularly delicious. I'm still not certain what was true, and what wasn't," Sandra said. "It's often hard to tell with Doc, but I think he's from a primitive place."

"You're a storyteller, eh?" Andrea laughed. "Well, Doc, put your coat on. We're going to the store, and you can tell me one of your stories during the ride."

"Who? We? Together?" he asked in surprise.

"Yes. Sandra's volunteered you to carry things," she said. "Do come along. We'll be back in time for dinner."

Andrea's car was the most luxurious Mercedes sedan Danny had ever ridden in, but she drove it like an Iranian truck driver. In no time at all, they had been to a bakery for fresh *barbari* bread, to a grocery, a liquor store, and a vegetable market. "Let's drop by my home," Andrea suggested, driving north on Pahlavi Avenue. "We don't need to be back before seven, and I have time to change clothes and pick up my boyfriend."

"You have a boyfriend?" Danny blurted before he could stop himself.

"Yes, I do."

She seemed to know what was in his mind. "I have a boyfriend. His name is Ali Nassiri. He's super rich, and he's got political connections. He's sophisticated and educated, but he's also quite impotent. As a business-man, impressions are important, so Ali and I have a pleasant relationship based on respect. When he entertains, I am the perfect hostess. We make appearances on the party circuit, we go to concerts, and we travel. We are close friends, and he leaves me to live my life as I wish. I don't pay rent, nor do I want for anything. I have a large swimming pool, a very nice home, servants, and luxury cars. I wear furs and expensive jewelry. I enjoy Ali's secrets and share his protection."

"Oh," Danny said, embarrassed. Moments later, he admitted, "I'm living in a cheap hotel, and I ride the public bus, so I can't talk, can I? Do people at work call you a prostitute because you're a 'kept' woman?"

"No. I am a prostitute," she admitted.

Looking him over appraisingly, she seemed to recognize Danny was curious, and would not, or could not, judge her. "I'm not your average street whore, though," she said.

As she pulled into a broad driveway, a gatekeeper rushed out to unbolt two huge, steel gates to let them inside a vast estate. There were fifty yards of paradise here—roses, trees, and real, untrampled, ungrazed grass. As Andrea drove around the corner of a palatial home to the servants' en-trance, they passed peacocks, fountains, marble sculptures, walkways, shrubs, and an Olympic pool. "Come along," she directed. "I'll show you around."

He obediently followed her into the stunning home, through dining areas large enough to seat a hundred, past a library with a pool table and a grand foyer lined with Italian marble. Taking his arm, Andrea led him up an immense staircase to her suite, where he sat waiting on a very ex-pensive French sofa near her bed while she showered and changed clothes in a separate dressing room. Precious carpets decorated one wall, while those that were merely antique layered the floor, one on top of another. On an elegant, vintage bookshelf nearby, there was a rosewood jewelry box overflowing with antique Turkoman gold and agate, modern Iranian silver and turquoise, and European diamonds, gold chains, jewels, and lapis lazuli, but the thing that attracted his eye in all this wealth and splendor was a smaller jewelry box of Japanese lacquer on a nightstand near the bed. To his surprise, it contained only cheap plastic bracelets.

"I charge a thousand pounds sterling a night," she said from her inner dressing room. "Come see my closet."

The walk-in was overflowing with clothes, furs, and shoes. "How much did you say?" Danny asked incredulously.

"A thousand pounds a night—that's about twenty-five hundred dollars at current exchange rates. Believe me, it's nothing for people who live like this, the upper crust of society. While they may have been educated abroad, deep down, they are only Iranians. I haven't met one yet that wasn't corrupt to the core, yet charming in the extreme. Money-grubbing hypocrites all of them, but they enjoy their pleasures, and they treat me with respect. It's not the dirty business you might think."

"I'm surprised they don't treat you like a whore."

"Not at all," she said. "The middle-class, on the other hand, is another story. They're every bit as corrupt as their betters and crave cosmopolitan pleasures too, but they hate restraint and are quite intolerant." Taking his arm, she led him back into the bedroom where they sat on the sofa facing each other.

Danny could hardly believe it. Small, with delicate bones and fine features, Andrea Wilcox was an extraordinarily beautiful woman. Two years older than he, she was neither booby nor flat chested, but her wonderful shapely breasts and her *breathing* were the type to stop conversation at parties. Her face had the gentle beauty of skin draped over fine bones, a beauty of class and what the British loved to call "good breeding." While her waist, hips, and legs were all minor treasures, and her fine blonde hair, nails, and make-up showed the extreme care with which she kept herself, it was her eyes that he couldn't stop staring into. Not the limpid blue of a beauty queen, her eyes certainly did not have the coldness of a burned-out whore either. They were the eyes of a calculating businesswoman, full of depth, yet curtaining her secrets, and there was something in them that scared him—she was looking into his eyes for secrets too! What could she see in him? His accursed innocence ... or his growing loneliness in this country?

Obviously, she had been testing him. He must not have been the first man she had brought to her suite. Some had listened for the start of her shower and then walked around the room casually appraising this, touching that to weigh the physical evidence of the woman. Some had surreptitiously crept to the open door of her dressing room to gaze at her blurred pink nakedness showering behind the translucent glass door; others had nervously gone onto the stunning terrace to gaze at the Alborz Mountains and beyond, but Danny had simply sat where she had indicated, patiently waiting for her return. Had he passed her test, he wondered?

She asked him a simple question. "Are you impressed by all this?"

"You don't happen to know any rich women who would pay a thousand dollars a night for a man, do you?" Danny answered, waving at the walls, the Matisse painting behind them, the antiques, and the carpets.

She shocked him by answering, "Yes, I do." Taking his hand, she pulled him to his feet and led him out of her bedroom and down the stairs. "But you're not the type. Come, let's find my boyfriend."

Ali Nassiri turned out to be a pudgy, sallow man in his early fifties, dissipated by a fast life and declining health. He had dull brown eyes, graying hair, a five-o'clock shadow from his cheekbones to his jaw, and a bad cigarette habit. Like many Iranian men who preferred perfume's sweetness to cologne, Ali used far too much. He was dressed in a lavender leisure suit, unbuttoned nearly to his navel, and he wore lots of gold jewelry. Impotent with women Ali Nassiri may have been, but Danny was fully aware of his Persian perversion by now, and his feelings were confirmed by the man's limp, wet handshake.

"Ali? This is Doctor MacCreary."

"A doctor!" Nassiri exclaimed. "Oh, you must visit me again, another time when we don't have social obligations. I have many things to discuss with you."

"Sure," Danny smiled agreeably, and Andrea squeezed his arm twice. "We'll do that sometime—"

"Come, we go!" Ali exclaimed in a high-pitched voice. Turning quickly, he shouted, "Ali Reza! Ali Reza*jun!*" and a little boy not eight years old appeared out of the deep cushions of a sofa near the library. After speaking to him in a soft, concerned tone that was not at all paternal, Ali patted the boy fondly on the derriere before reluctantly joining Andrea and Doc at the door.

"*Khodahafez,*" he sighed, waving at his little friend. Outside, Ali's chauffer-driven blue Cadillac waited, and as soon as they got in, the driver pulled away down the long driveway. Behind them, a garage door opened to admit Andrea's Mercedes, briefly revealing the fender of yet another expensive car, this one shiny black.

Ali angrily said something in French and petulantly turned to look out the window. "Doc? You didn't see anything just now," Andrea said. "Do you understand?"

"I only saw your car being put away. Any problem?"

"Not really. Ali doesn't know you're trustworthy. He's afraid of what you might say."

"Say?" Danny asked.

"There are only TWO Rolls Royce limos allowed in Iran, the Shah's and the British ambassador's. Last year, as *aid-e-shoma,* a New Year's gift," she smiled, touching her boyfriend fondly on the leg, "I gave Ali a Rolls of his own—trespassory importation, you see—"

"She means she smuggled it into Iran!" Ali accused. "I hate this language you use, Andrea*jun,* to cover up a crime. You do this every time you break the law to make it sound like something else. "Trespassory importation!' It means something far worse! The people you associate with are a bad influence. They never say exactly what they do, but Andrea*jun,* I know they are all criminals. Everyone who works for you, Andrea, is a criminal! Everyone you know is a criminal. You all use language to hide it from yourselves."

Patting his shoulder indulgently, Andrea sighed, "Yes, Ali. Anyway, I imported this car secretly from Saudi Arabia. We had it loaded on a *dhow* and brought it across the Gulf one night. Since then, Ali's been nervous about having it around. We've never driven it anywhere."

"You don't understand these things," Ali complained. "I will brick up the car in the garage. No one must find out about this Rolls Royce. If the Shah knew of it, it would be the death of me." Angrily sinking down in his seat, Ali pouted the rest of the way to the Barrington's.

"Ali, I think Doctor Mary can keep our little secret." Snuggling closer she took Danny's arm, then crossed her legs; he noticed she was wearing silk hose, held up by a lacey garter belt. He loved garter belts... and she smelled lovely. With a shock, he realized she wasn't wearing any panties....

"You mentioned rich women earlier, and I said you weren't right for the job. Would you be interested in making money another way?"

He didn't know what she was suggesting, but he thought about it only a moment before answering, "Yeah, I would. How?"

"How, rather than 'how much?' You don't trust me yet!" she laughed. "I need someone to deliver things, perhaps eight or ten times a month. I'll pay you a retainer of a five thousand tomans a week, plus your expenses, a private taxi, and bonuses."

"How much?" he gasped in surprise. That could be over $35,000 a year, plus expenses. What could his expenses be? Excitement showed on his face until the word "illegal" crossed his mind.

"Five thousand tomans a week. It's good money, and it's clean work. It's certainly NOT illegal," she said, anticipating his next question. "It's not dangerous, but I require three things."

"Is it drugs?"

"Certainly not!" she said, unconsciously glancing at Ali. "I told you it's totally legal."

"It's mostly business transactions..." Ali grumped, studiously looking out the window at the traffic.

"What are the three things?"

"Absolute personal loyalty to me. You take orders only from me, no matter how much money my competitors or clients offer you, and you will always tell me of these offers. Second, you must be scrupulously honest. You never accept one rial as a tip from my clients, and in fact, you cannot even drink a cup of tea from their samovar unless I approve it beforehand. Third, you must be discreet. You never reveal my clients nor keep written records."

"What kinds of things are delivered?"

"Information, contracts, money. Things like that. The point is, Doc, if there's a touch of larceny in your soul, I can't use you. I intend to start you off slowly, and if you're suitable, and if you're above-board, your reputation will get you into—and out of—snake pits alive. Naturally, I will reward you better as things progress. There are very few honest people in Iran right now, very few indeed. Almost everyone is here for the money, but you're not. I haven't figured out your motives yet, but Doc, you seem dependable. You must have a sterling character for my business."

Danny thought of his friends, his strict upbringing in Wyoming, his determination and moral convictions, but mostly he considered his intuitive ability to gauge another's character, and he decided he liked this unusual woman. "Okay," he agreed. "Five thousand tomans extra a week is more money than I hoped to make in this country. I'll do it." Hesitating just a moment, he reached over and took her hand out of her lap, shaking on the oral contract. In Wyoming, cattle are sold with a handshake....

That night, a strange undercurrent marred the Barrington's dinner party. Although trying to be friendly, Danny was withdrawn and spent much of the evening watching Andrea across the room. Sandra enjoyed Ali Nassiri, who was urbane, witty, and great fun. "Why, Ali," she joked,

"I expected you to bring your little boy friend. I didn't know you went anywhere without him...."

"Not tonight," he answered, misunderstanding her tone.

Andrea divided her time between Ali, the telephone, and Sandra's daughter, Claire. Sir David was moody and didn't feel well; he went to bed early. Deborah, the perfect hostess, was concerned with Danny's sudden interest in Andrea Wilcox. She watched him follow her with his eyes, wondering and listening at her every move, and she apparently mistook his fascination as romantic or sexual in nature. Taking him aside after dinner, she whispered, "Doc, don't be too interested in Andrea. She's not your type. She eats men for breakfast and spits out their bones afterward." As if in support of Deborah's warning, Andrea Wilcox left early with an Iranian businessman.

"Thanks, Deborah," Danny smiled, kissing her on the cheek as he shrugged into his coat at the door. "I find her interesting, but I'm not interested, if you know what I mean."

Outside, the night was cold. Danny put his hands in his pockets and looked up at the gray sky to see if any stars showed through the city's thick cloud of pollution. Deciding to walk home rather than catch a taxi, he felt he had just made one of the biggest decisions of his life, and he wasn't at all sure if it were a good choice or not.

– 8 –

THE SNAIL RACE

"Always get out of a taxi several blocks before your stop. Walk the rest of the way, or catch another cab. Better yet—steal someone's bicycle!"

—*Ali Ghorbani, a driver for Star Taxi*

A couple weeks after agreeing to work as Andrea Wilcox's courier, Danny felt her brush against him to leave a business card in his pocket as they were getting off a minibus at their new teaching assignments at Mehrabod Junubi Air Force Base. On the back, she had written: "Tonight. 9 P.M. My office. Call a taxi, they know where to go." The card was for a place called Star Taxi, advertising quick, discreet service.

Later that evening, Danny called the number. A man answered after the first ring. "My name is Doctor Mary," Danny said "I need a telephone taxi off Saltanadabad, on *Kuche Panj,* Number Forty-Six."

"Right away, Doctor," the voice acknowledged.

Ten minutes later, a driver rang at the door outside. "Who is it?" Danny asked on the intercom.

"Star Taxi," an Iranian said.

Hurrying out the door, Danny found the driver standing twenty feet to the side, his hand in his jacket pocket. "Are you the driver?" he inquired suspiciously.

"Yes, I am," the Iranian answered, pulling a pack of cigarettes from his pocket and lighting one. Moving to open the door of a new, gray Mercedes, the young man introduced himself, "Masud Pooinak. I will be your driver tonight." He extended his hand over the seat, and Danny shook it politely. He'd never shaken hands with a taxi driver before. Putting the car in gear, the man sped off, spraying the *kutche* with gravel. No one used seat belts in this crazy country, but as the driver careened through traffic, Danny was tempted to put one on. He couldn't find it in the back seat.

"I hear you are the new associate," the driver said, looking him over in the rearview mirror. Although the Iranian had a strong accent, he spoke English well.

"I'm sorry. What's that? An associate?"

"You work for Andrea Wilcox, the same as all of us. Welcome! I am Masud Pooinak, a driver, but not for Star. You will have other drivers later, but never me. Since Andrea has something special for you tonight, I volunteered to drive you there. You are our last associate. With you, there are eighteen of us. Star Taxi is one associate. They have an exclusive contract with Andrea, but they take orders from Dieter Mueller. You know him?"

"No," Danny said.

"Have you met him?"

"No," Danny said again.

None of this made sense, so he sat back in the comfortable leather seat and looked at the back of the Iranian's head. Longhaired and swarthy, this Masud Pooinak could pass for any young Iranian on the street, but Danny felt he had better memorize the driver's features.

"Dieter Mueller is the associate in charge of transportation. I am a driver for him. Tonight he called to say we are having a snail race."

"A what?"

"A snail race. You'll see soon enough. Tonight you meet Pamela, Ralf, Guenther, Carl, and Jamshid Busheri. Tonight, you will learn your business, Doctor Mary."

Danny wasn't sure what this meant, so he coolly watched the intense evening traffic rush by. Before long, Masud parked next to a dry *djube* on a lonely, dark *kutche* somewhere in north Teheran. Although Danny was certain they weren't far from Ali Nassiri's palatial home, the route they had taken was so circuitous he would have been hard put to say how far away the home was or even in what direction it lay. A steel gate nearby had the number 36 painted on it in Farsi script.

"This is it," the driver announced as he jumped out of the car. Ringing the intercom, Masud told someone inside, *"Deevar moush dareed, moush goush dareed."* A remote-controlled bolt banged open, and the heavy, steel gate swung inward. Inside, several luxury cars were parked in the yard of a simple, three-story apartment building. No lights showed from any of the windows, but there were many voices from within.

"Go inside," Masud motioned.

"Doc MacCreary?" an Englishman said, stepping out of the shadows in the darkness to his left. The man had a dancer's grace, but even in the darkness, Danny could see a boxer's scars.

"Yes?"

"I'm Carl Wolffe." He looked English; his manner and handshake were strong and manly. "I'm in charge of operational security. I must know everything that goes on outside those walls. Everyone except you reports to me. You'll work for Andrea, but if you need anything, ask, and I'll provide it."

Inside, just beyond the double wooden doors, an American jumped up from his seat at a heavy steel desk. "I'm Bob Fraser," he introduced, offering his hand and Kentucky friendliness. "I'm in charge of security."

"Doc MacCreary," Danny smiled. "I just met a man outside who claimed *he* was in charge of security."

"Operational security. Yes, he is. I provide internal security here at the office."

"Why is so much security necessary?" Danny asked, but his question was forgotten the moment a pair of doors opened to his left and an Oriental woman in a red slit silk skirt came out of a sitting room. So much of her leg showed in the slit that if it had gaped open two more inches, he would have been able to see her pubic hair. Thoroughly embarrassed at his own open-mouthed reaction, Danny had a hard time tearing his eyes away from the exotically lovely vision in front of him.

"Puff Omura, I'd like you to meet Doc MacCreary," Fraser laughed, clapping the younger man on the shoulder. "C'mon, let's go upstairs. I'm sure you'll see a lot more of the girls later!"

"Nice meeting you," the woman purred, her perfume clouding Danny's mind. He waved at her with his right hand and followed Fraser upstairs. Several more soft, sexy voices greeted him from the semi-darkness as he passed the door of a sitting room, and at the top of the stairs was another vision of lust, this time a tall, Teutonic goddess named Tephanie, who welcomed him as warmly as an old friend. Sitting demurely at a small receptionist's station nearby, an equally lush and carefully manicured Iranian woman named Shamsa Abedi Esfandiari spoke breathy Farsi into a phone. At the same time, she was writing something in an appointment book so big it could easily have contained five thousand names.

They entered another sitting room, this one brightly lit and arranged with comfortable chairs and divans around a blue Nain carpet. Andrea Wilcox, busy on a phone, merely waved hello. Masud Pooinak was already there, and so were Carl Wolffe and a very big, muscular German with wolfine, pale grey eyes and closely cropped hair.

"Hello, Doc," Andrea greeted him, as soon as she hung up. "Shamsa?" she called to the receptionist. "No more calls. I'm busy the rest of the evening."

"Okay," the girl replied.

"I think you've met Carl, Masud, and Bob," Andrea said. "This is Ralf Gruenewald."

The German nodded but didn't rise or offer his hand. Danny wasn't sure he wanted to meet him anyway. Ralf was huge—six feet, six inches tall and weighing two hundred-eighty pounds without an ounce of fat, but he did not seem to have the athletic grace that Carl Wolffe showed. Danny had never met such a man before, but he intuitively knew Ralf for what he was—a mercenary, a professional soldier, an assassin, a killer, a goon, a hired gun, a monster. Something about his sharp nose, the cold steely blue eyes, and the dark blonde hair cut in a severe flattop betrayed him. Although he was wearing a corduroy sport coat, Ralf would have looked equally comfortable in a butcher's apron splattered with blood.

"Welcome to Andrea Wilcox and Associates!" Andrea said. "You are now considered one of my men, yet you are separate from the others because you and I have a different financial arrangement. Everyone here shares in the net revenues of our organization, depending on their skills. We operate much like a corporation. We share the work, and we share the benefits. In Teheran, we're the new kids on the block, we're the *farangi*—the foreigners, but together, we have enough experience to take on the local establishment. All of our management expertise is European, certain essential elements are Iranian, and we intend to work both worlds for maximum gain. We plan to be nonviolent, we won't deal in drugs, and we absolutely will *not* become involved in the local politics. I suppose you have questions?"

"Yeah, I do," Danny admitted, crossing his legs, then nervously putting his feet back on the floor again. He didn't like the way the German watched him. "Just how do I fit in?"

"The chain-of-command," the German rumbled, his bass voice shivering the air. He seemed satisfied with Danny's question and leaned forward to watch his face.

"Doc, we are carving ourselves a niche in the local underworld. The Iranians have a sophisticated and active criminal subculture here, which is based on a long, historic tradition. All Iranians, of course, deal on two or three levels—never forget that. They are a devious and subtle people, but they are blind to new possibilities and reluctant to capitalize on them. Except for the intense political jockeying here and the espionage and intrigue found in any world capital, Iranians have delayed exploiting new ideas and talent.

"When I came from Beirut to escape the civil war," Andrea said, "I saw loose ends available for anyone with the resources. I've spent a year collecting experienced people. Ralf, for example, is a specialist in espionage; he has no loyalties and deals with everyone equally. We have another German, Dieter Mueller, an engineer, who is a specialist in surreptitious transportation and electronic surveillance. I have an Italian," she said, indicating a smiling, young man who had just entered the room, "Paolo Giaminelli, for copying and interpretation of business documents, and I use a photographer, Laurence Peters. I have the finest escorts—prostitutes, if you will—a doctor named David Faradi, a beauty salon, an office, a taxi company, an auto repair shop, a firm of attorneys...and you."

"Again, how do I fit in?" Reminded of Barbie's comment in London that he tended to attract the wrong kind of people, Danny felt sick, for he could see he was in with a fast crowd now. He wasn't sure what he had in common with such people. Why were they attracted to him, or he to them?

"You, Doc, possess the unifying skill, the one thing none of us have," Andrea said. "The most precious commodity in Teheran these days is *integrity*. No one trusts anyone. No one is honest—at least not among our sort. We are what some call 'rough trade.' The moment I saw you, I knew you were exactly what we need. We don't want you to get involved or even interested in our sordid businesses, but we need you to deal with our clients, to deliver things, to carry information, to pass secrets, and especially to carry money, lots of money. You, Doctor Danny MacCreary, will be our courier."

"I don't understand any of this," Danny countered.

"You will," she promised. "But before you begin, there are certain skills you must acquire. We will train you, but you are valuable to us and safe from others only as long as you remain uncorrupted. We're going to be your teachers, but you must do everything as we instruct."

"We start tonight," Ralf interrupted. "We will practice something we call a snail race."

"What's a snail race?" Danny asked, reluctantly.

Andrea let a moment pass without answer. Then, she turned and picked up a fancy briefcase from her desk. "Take this to Jamshid Busheri, my attorney. The address is on a piece of tape on the handle. Now, go!"

Of course, Danny wanted to ask questions, but he reached out instead for the briefcase; instantly, Andrea caught his hand and clasped a handcuff around his wrist, locking him to the case.

"Bracelets even!" Danny exclaimed, backing out of the room and hurrying down the stairs.

"Good luck," Shamsa, the receptionist, smiled "Where are you going?"

"Jamshid Busheri's office," Danny mumbled over his shoulder.

"Good luck and hurry back."

The girls in the lounge were laughing as he went past their door. "Where are you going?" one asked, giving him a look at her long legs.

"Jamshid Busheri's office," he said, dumbfounded by the sight.

Outside, the gatekeeper asked, "You go to the bazaar?"

"No, an office off Abassabad." The man pulled a heavy steel bolt and released the gate, ushering him out into the cold, dark *kutche,* then banging the gate closed behind him.

At the end of the block, Danny paused to get his bearings. Four blocks south, a pale neon sign beckoned—the office of Star Taxi. Hurrying toward the sign, he wondered who Jamshid Busheri was. Was he important? Why had everyone been so interested in where he was going?

"I'd like a cab please," he told the manager as soon as he entered the office. A half dozen unshaven drivers dressed in sweaters and sport coats, all twirling prayer beads, leaned forward eagerly. The room was filled with the smell of stale cigarettes and cold tea.

"Where you go?" the manager said.

"Abassabad. A thirty minute drive." Danny was, as yet only vaguely familiar with Teheran, but he knew he was now in a neighborhood called Mahmoudieh, so Abassabad was about six miles south, off Pahlavi Avenue.

"Thirty minutes, eh? What is the address of the place you want to go?" the Iranian asked, fumbling in his desk for cigarettes.

"Abassabad Street." Danny was eager to leave. This was supposed to be a race, wasn't it? A race in Teheran's intense traffic, where negotiating an intersection might take an hour— that's why it was called a snail race, but he still didn't understand how to goad the snail to go faster.

"Abassabad!" the manager laughed. "I don't think you know where to go."

"The corner of Abassabad and Farahnaz. Do you have a car or not?" Danny snapped. The information was written on a piece of tape Andrea had attached to the briefcase.

"I get you a Mercedes, thousand rials an hour."

"No. Three hundred."

"You are familiar with telephone taxis, but the time is bad. Traffic is terrible. Five hundred."

"Three hundred."

"Three hundred is fine," the manager agreed, waving his hands expansively. "Special for you, okay?"

"Shall we go?" Danny said.

"Do we take you to a house, a building...what?"

"The third floor of an office building. Now, can we go, or should I find another taxi?"

"No, no! I will take you myself. No problem," the Iranian grinned, picking up his car keys.

Minutes later, Danny understood why the man managed a taxi company, for he could drive very well. Drive or not, however, the Iranian got caught up in the traffic of Vanak Circle, then struck slow movement down Pahlavi Avenue to the impossible intersection at Abassabad. After an hour, he finally entered the slow, one-way flow on Takht-e-Tavous Street.

"Why didn't you turn left on Abassabad?" Danny grumbled from the back seat "That's where I need to go!"

"No problem. This is better for me. I take you to the corner of Farahnaz, then I can turn left on Abassabad to get back to Pahlavi Avenue. It's actually a shortcut for me."

Immediately after turning north on Farahnaz from Takht-e-Tavous, though, they were in big trouble. Two dark Paykans forced the taxi to the side of the road, and three Iranian toughs jumped out to drag Danny from the car. Instead of trying to help, the taxi driver jumped in the melee too, and started to kick his passenger, pulling on the briefcase and trying to get away with it. Danny did a body slam on one of his attackers, forcing the Iranian against the door of the Mercedes and then he gave him a hard, cupped slap to the ear with his left hand. The man crumpled in pain, but the other Iranians dragged Danny free and threw him down on the pavement.

Rolling quickly, Danny slipped between two parked cars and skipped across the concrete *djube*. The first Iranian to follow him got the full weight of the briefcase in the face, while the taxi driver, who had quickly circled around behind the cars, got kicked in the groin. The fourth Iranian turned and ran away, but so did Danny, for he took the opportunity to race up the street to a gray building, the only office building at the corner. On the register was listed Jamshid Busheri, Attorney of International Law.

Naturally, this being Iran, the elevator was out of service. Three flights of stairs later, a final horror awaited Danny, for just inside the sumptuous office suite, a proper English receptionist confronted him. "I'm sorry, we're closed for the day. Would you like to make an appointment?"

"I'm here to see Jamshid Busheri," Danny insisted.

"Mr. Busheri is not available," she said, looking out of the side of her face as she began to type. "We are closed for the day."

"I need to speak with him now." Danny hated to get rough, but he didn't know how far behind his pursuers were.

"Mr. Busheri is not here," the woman said. "Perhaps I can be of assistance."

"I need to see him personally." Danny stepped closer to her desk, resting his knuckles on the smooth walnut surface.

"Again, Mr. Busheri is not in. You can give me the briefcase, and I'll be sure he gets it in the morning."

"How did you know I was to deliver the briefcase?" Danny asked suspiciously. Turning suddenly, he burst past the woman's desk and stormed into the inner office. Somehow, he wasn't surprised to find Andrea, Ralf, Carl Wolffe, Bob Fraser, and Masud Pooinak already there, but he was startled to see that Shamsa, the Iranian receptionist, Tephanie and another German prostitute, Andrea's old gatekeeper, and an ancient Iranian woman he had last seen slumped in the corner of Star Taxi's office had also beaten him there.

"Hello, Doc," Andrea greeted him. "You owe everyone a hundred tomans."

"I didn't bet on the race," Danny grumped.

"You will learn your lessons the hard way!" she snapped.

"I don't have more than a few hundred on me."

"That's okay," she answered, "I'll put it on account.'" Pulling a red notebook out of her purse, she made a notation, then took out a handful of bills and paid each of the people in the room one thousand rials. Danny's taxi driver and the three battered attackers then entered the room and sat down. They each got five hundred rials. Finally, a distinguished Iranian in a tailored gray suit escorted his receptionist into the office. She got five hundred too.

"Doctor MacCreary? I'm so glad to meet you. We have needed you so badly! I'm Jamshid Busheri." Extending his hand, he shook Danny's warmly. "How much did the doctor lose?" the lawyer asked Andrea.

"Eleven thousand rials up front and two thousand for latecomers."

"Terrible, terrible," the Iranian laughed, shaking his head, "but there are things to be learned from this, and that's where I can help you." He seated himself next to Danny on a too-soft sofa, patted him fondly on the leg, and remarked, "Don't be discouraged." Turning to Andrea, he asked, "Who was the first to arrive?"

"Masud."

"Masud," the lawyer asked, "How much were your winnings tonight?"

"Nine thousand rials."

"And how did you get here?" the lawyer asked.

"Four taxis and some walking," the young Iranian answered proudly.

"How long have you been here?"

"One hour."

"A very good evening for you," the lawyer said. "Congratulations! Who was second to arrive?"

"I was," Shamsa said.

"How much did you pay?"

"One thousand rials to Masud," the receptionist answered.

"How much did you win?"

"Eight thousand rials," she smiled.

"And when did you arrive?"

"Forty minutes ago. I drove my own car to Pahlavi and Abassabad, where there was a traffic jam; I then caught a taxi."

"You see?" the lawyer said. "If you win, you are paid by everyone. If you're second, you pay a thousand to the winner and collect from everyone else. If you're last, like you were tonight, you pay everyone! Do you understand the rules?"

"Yeah," Danny remarked, feeling cool toward this strange group and their silly game.

"Now, let's look at your mistakes. Hamad?" he asked the manager of the taxi company. "How did you learn exactly where the doctor wanted to go?"

"He told me."

"And how did Mama Ghorbanifar, your aged mother, respected by all of us here, Allah be praised, how did she find out where he was going?"

"She was sitting in my office and overheard the Doctor."

"You see? You must be *very* secretive about your destination," the lawyer informed Danny as he fumbled in his pocket for a key to unlock the handcuff that attached Danny's wrist to the briefcase. "Be flexible about how you travel. Now, who," he questioned the group, "took more than four taxis to get here?"

"I did," Tephanie, the tall German prostitute laughed. "I took one to Vanak Circle, caught another to Pahlavi Avenue, one down Pahlavi, then another west on Takht-e-Tavous. I walked the rest of the way. Masud beat me by only twenty-one minutes."

"Very good," the lawyer congratulated her. "Andrea, when do we play again?"

"Thursday morning, ten o'clock. By the way, Doc, if you show up, it's payday—your first salary." She was bribing him, daring him, teasing him, for she seemed to sense how close he was to chucking this whole thing and telling them how stupid he thought they were.

"I'll be there," he agreed, but he didn't know why.

– 9 –

MEHRABOD JUNUBI
(Mehrabod South)

"I know this is a military school. That's why it's up to you civilian instructors to enforce discipline. If not, we're going to crack down on you!"
— *Major Rostam Ghollami, Commandant, Mehrabod Junubi*

T he night Danny arrived in Teheran, he had glimpsed Shahyad, an enormous marble monument the Shah had built to honor himself and his far-sighted "White Revolution." A squarish white tower on two flaring legs set in the middle of a vast *meidan*, or traffic circle, Shahyad had elevators to take the curious to an observation deck for a view of the smoggy city and the barren Alborz Mountains to the north. Although the poorly maintained elevators sometimes didn't work and the tower was surrounded by police in dingy blue uniforms, it was an impressive monument popular with picnickers, honeymooning couples, and tourists.

When she saw it bathed in the glow of golden spotlights the night they arrived in Teheran, Barbie Hansen had remarked, "That's the grandest thing I've ever seen."

"That?" Danny remarked in surprise. The grandest thing he had ever seen was down the front of a prostitute's dress in London. This monument was—what would be a good word for it? Inspiring? Enchanting? Impressive, maybe, but certainly not *grand*.

The traffic around Shahyad was intense. Several expressways and major streets fed into the circle. The airport's only major access, the slums of south Teheran and the gates of nearby air force bases were reached through it. In summer, automobile and truck exhaust and spinning clouds of brown dust hung over the *meidan*; slippery clay muddied the traffic in winter. Shahyad was never pretty, but Danny had to admit, it was memorable.

He soon grew familiar with Shahyad. The day after graduating from the training class at Doshan Tappeh, he took a telephone taxi to his new assignment, a base called Mehrabod Junubi. [It's now called Sattari Aerial University.] As he passed through the *meidan* this time, Danny saw Shahyad in a wholly different light. Sitting alone in the back seat of the telephone taxi, he was sullenly memorizing the way to work and, thus, the way home again, unmoved by Shahyad's impressive sight.

The crowds, the traffic—and the monument passed in a rush. They were driving south on a busy boulevard planted with hundreds of dead saplings which, in the Iranian fashion, were replaced every spring but were always dead by fall because they were never watered. To his right, Danny could see Mehrabod's runways; between him and the freedom the airport represented were high fences topped with concertina wire, jeeps patrolling a perimeter road, and, in the distance, the subterranean fighter bays and hangars of the Iranian Air Force. He noticed the base was camouflaged with a veritable forest of little pine trees. From the air, the regularly patterned planting was probably the only green visible for miles.

As he was to discover, however, Mehrabod was not just the hangars, jets, soldiers, guns, trucks, and other accouterments of a well-equipped military. It was also a dirty little secret that lay several blocks farther south, deep in the slums of Teheran.

"We are here," the driver announced as he pulled the taxi up at a blue gate set in high brick walls. Four heavily armed soldiers in gray greatcoats stood before the gate, but there was no one else around and no hint of what lay beyond the walls.

"Are you sure this is the right place?" Danny asked.

"Yes," the driver snapped. "This is the place you want. You owe me one hundred tomans. Pay now."

Reluctantly handing the man a thousand-rial bill, Danny said, "I hope you're right." In a country where he had discovered no one could give or follow directions, where laborers prided themselves on doing a shoddy job, where the stifling monarchy seemed to reward only mediocrity, he was learning to question every move by an Iranian. As the taxi drove away, he was not surprised to find that this was, in fact, the wrong gate.

"What do I do now?" he exclaimed.

"Go round," the guards demanded. "Go to main entrance."

"How far is it?"

"Half kilometer," they answered.

Danny converted it to a distance of about a quarter mile. Not understanding a quick five tomans would bend the rules, he shrugged and set off to follow the walls over slippery mounds of rotting garbage. "It looks like people throw their trash here on purpose," he said to himself.

With all the empty lots and junky corners available across the street, he wondered why civilians would dump garbage against the walls of a military base, the very symbol of authority in this country. The reeking filth was stacked nearly four feet deep, and in several places he had to scramble around the trash and into the busy traffic. He noticed there seemed to be sidewalks across the street, but a *djube* had backed up over them, spewing a sea of bilious discharge from the stoops of the homes to the middle of the roadway. Bloated bumps floating in the goo looked like dead cats but were, he decided after looking closer, probably rats instead. A shopkeeper was sweeping slop out of his door, while on the corner, a group of children splashed through the ooze as they played soccer. There was hardly a dry place to walk. He became convinced people purposely threw their trash here.

Fifteen minutes later, after an eventful trip around the garbage piles, he arrived at the main gate of Mehrabod Junubi. His feet were wet to midcalf, and he was sweating heavily. Hoping to make a better impression, he stamped his shoes to clean them off a bit, taking the opportunity to peek inside the narrow gateway. Ten officers and a dozen sergeants and draftees with assault rifles manned the gatehouse here. The senior officer—a haughty captain with a badly pockmarked face—was busy receiving and counting a herd of bleating sheep and goats bound for the officers' mess. Like any good haggler in a bazaar, the captain stepped behind each sheep to squeeze its pillowy tail to gauge the condition of the animal. Since the heavy tails were rendered for cooking fat, the captain rejected nine ewes as too scrawny, then accepted the rest of the flock.

Wiping his hands on a gray rag offered by an underling, the officer acknowledged the American standing before him. "I must see your orders," he said. He instructed a sergeant to call Doshan Tappeh to confirm Danny's status, then he examined Danny's ID and work permit and admitted him to the base.

"You are welcome. Contract instructors are badly needed here," he said, waving the ragged guards aside. "You will stand by this wall until the instructors' bus comes, and then you will ride into Mehrabod Junubi.

Never walk on the base if you can avoid it." (In other words, the base was dangerous....)

Moments later, an official, blue-and-white Mercedes shuttle bus arrived, packed with the same kind of unkempt, dusty instructors Danny had seen at Doshan Tappeh. Everyone studiously avoided the newcomer's eyes as he got on the bus. The bus was delayed by a large formation of grim-faced cadets circling the parade field as they goose-stepped ceremoniously to the tapping of an old drum. Several hundred students waited nearby, every eye on this, the latest graduating class.

"Watch 'em and weep, mate," an Australian chortled from behind Danny, who noticed the other instructors were studiously ignoring the ceremony as they busied themselves with reading, knitting, or doing crosswords in a newspaper.

"Why's that?" he asked.

"They're the last cadets to graduate from this shithole. From now on, all we'll see are *honarjoos* and *donesjoos*. Cadets will be trained on Doshan Tappeh in the future."

In Iran, all adult men had to give two years national service, but Danny had learned they usually had no responsibility and little to do. Though the remainder of the military were well-trained professional soldiers, Danny had noticed they tended toward arrogance and narrow-mindedness. Enlisting for thirty-three years, such men endured several years' training. Officers started as cadets, then moved automatically to the rank of third lieutenant. During the rest of their service, promotions were slow, and only a few would make *arteshbod*, a full general.

Enlisted men began service as *doneshjoos*, or trainees. As in most Middle Eastern countries, such soldiers could rise into the officer ranks, which provided some motivation for ambitious men. In the air force, nearly all the technical expertise came from *homofars*, or warrant officers, who did their training as *honarjoos*. Mehrabod Junubi, with its new emphasis on training enlisted men (*donesjoos)* and warrant officers (*honarjoos*) needed fewer officers on its staff to manage them.

The base itself looked fairly new. In fact, Danny shared in the first lunch served in the newly completed officers' mess. The technical buildings seemed new too, and barracks and the armory were still under construction. *Djubes* were being dug everywhere on the base, and young trees and roses were being planted to supplement older plane trees.

"This is it, mate," the Australian shouted as he and other veteran instructors stampeded off the bus the moment it jerked to a stop in front of one of the buildings. The teachers disappeared up a narrow staircase into the guts of a classroom building, but Danny followed at a more leisurely pace, unaware part of his future evaluations depended on his "enthusiasm."

He found his way down a dark, dusty, poorly ventilated hallway to the instructors' lounge where perhaps fifty people were seated around a dozen narrow tables. Conversation in the room stopped the moment he entered the brightly lit room. Across from the doorway, two larcenous draftees, or *sarbozes*, studied the newcomer from behind a dirty samovar set on a greasy lunch counter. Cigarette smoke hung from the ceiling in blue-gray clouds; there was a pervasive stench of stale sweat and old farts in the room.

The instructors stared at Danny as if he were an alien being from another planet. Brits, Pakistanis, Australians, and Iranians made up the bulk of the cadre. The only other Americans present were two women married to Iranians. Danny was to be one of three American men on the staff and among just a handful of contract instructors ever to work at the base.

Danny studied the other instructors as intently as they stared at him. After a minute of silence, he joked, "Belly up to the bar, boys. Drinks are on the house." Not a soul moved, but at least the veterans returned to their conversations, and the hubbub resumed. A *sarboz* pulled out a pack of Marlboros and lit one, grudgingly offering another to Danny.

"No thanks," he said, realizing it was some kind of test. "I don't smoke."

The *sarboz* grinned at his partner and whispered in Farsi. "No smoke, no man."

"Smokers die young," Danny responded sarcastically, thinking of his father. He was suddenly struck by a twinge of homesickness. The last time he saw his father, a World War Two veteran, he was coughing up blood, but he was still smoking. Would his dad live to see him come home someday? He wondered what would happen if his dad died while he was living in Iran. Would the Iranians allow him to go home for the funeral?

As if by magic, supervisors and officers poured into the lounge to greet the new arrival. "I am Captain Hamadi," the commandant introduced himself, stepping forward to offer a hand.

"How do you do," Danny smiled, taking Hamadi's sweaty fingers and giving them an American squeeze.

"We are well inform of Doctor Mary. You—"

"Excuse me," Danny interrupted, hoping to get off on the right foot. "That's MacCreary ... Muck-crair-ee."

"Is very difficult. I not proficient in American terminology. Doctor Mary is good," the commandant decreed, and Doctor Mary he would remain all the time he worked there, and at Doshan Tappeh later.

"Would it be possible to transfer back to Doshan Tappeh…?" Danny tried. This assignment clearly was not what he had hoped for.

"No transfer!" the captain declared. "You are our first contract instructor. We have more coming soon, but for now, your duties are critical to our mission at Mehrabod Junubi." Behind him, sycophantic supervisors and officers nodded agreeably.

Glancing unconsciously at the three stars on his shoulder to emphasize his importance, the captain explained, "Because you are a permanent contract instructor, you are responsible for more than term instructors. You are," he said, "expected to write curriculum, prepare homework exercises, write lesson plans, instruct remedial sessions, and substitute two hours a day in addition to your own eight-hour classes. You will share everything with the other instructors."

"You're kidding," Danny gasped. "No instructors in the world work so hard."

"You are responsible for ten hours work—"

"It's going to be a two-hour bus ride to get to Mehrabod Junubi," Danny countered.

"And two hours home again," the captain smiled. "Plenty of time to finish your work."

"You expect fourteen hours a day, five days a week…" Danny responded, a slow grin creeping over his face.

"Plus your own lesson planning," the commandant said. "You are expected to be an outstanding example for others to follow. As a contract instructor, you will provide continuity. The term people come and go every six months, but you will always remain. We require you to give us notice before taking a vacation so we can plan around it."

"How much notice?" Danny asked.

"One year. Your contract began in November. The earliest you can take leave is November next the year."

"I'd like to apply for leave in November," Danny said, playing along.

"I'm sorry, November through the following July are projected to be our heaviest student loads. No vacations will be granted."

"What about sick leave?" Danny asked.

"We have complete facilities to treat you here."

"But what if I'm too sick to come to work?" Danny inquired, thinking of the diarrhea to which he was susceptible.

"You must report at the beginning of your shift to the doctor in our clinic."

"You mean I have to work, no matter what?"

"Of course, if you are *really* sick, the doctor will certify you for light duty," the captain declared, smiling at the supervisors behind him.

Danny felt like he was being assigned work in a mental ward. "What's light duty?" he asked with a sinking heart.

"You will not have to teach any extra classes that day." Unfortunately, the commandant was not joking, and there were many rules he had not yet told the naive American.

Months later, in the heat of the dreaded summer, Danny discovered a copy of Joseph Heller's *Catch-22* in the Keyvan Bookstore downtown, and from it, he learned how to deal with the craziness. The day after finishing it, he marched into the commandant's office. "I want an extra month's salary," he said.

"Why?" the commandant screamed, jumping out of his desk and waving his arms like a Dutch windmill gone mad.

"Because my contract offers a month's leave for each year worked. If you want a year's notice before I can have a vacation, and you're not granting leave until July the year after next, that means I'll work far more than twelve months without a vacation."

The captain collapsed in his chair. "Never!" he declared, but soon thereafter, he relaxed some of the more ridiculous rules as they applied to Danny.

For Barbie Hansen, who was also assigned to work at Mehrabod Junubi—though on the day shift—adjustment never came. "I hate this fucking place," she claimed when she met Danny and other instructors for dinner one night. Suffering from extreme culture shock, she decided, "I'm going to fight them tooth and nail." It didn't work. Four weeks of confrontation followed, and after only three months at Mehrabod, she quit her contract and went back to Texas in disgrace.

Danny, however, remained. The facilities at Mehrabod Junubi, as well as the situation, were typical of the Iranian military. The buildings were poorly cooled and barely heated. The temperatures in the classrooms varied from well over a hundred degrees in the summer to near freezing in the winter. There was no ventilation at all—and the students ate raw onions with lunch and dinner. The floors, made of marble tiles, were always covered with dust.

The walls of the classrooms were "portable" plastic panels designed to interlock in various combinations to accommodate large classes or small offices, but workmen had permanently bolted them to the floor with little or no planning. Stepping off some distances in the hallway one evening, Danny became convinced there were rooms without doors, lost forever in the maze of walls.

Classrooms did not have doors, either, for the hinges had been stolen, so one of the duties of a class monitor was to lift a piece of plywood into place after break time and open the room again at the next bell. Student desks were adequate, but the rest of the rooms' furnishings consisted of only two items, a chalkboard and a podium. The chalkboard, a local construction made from plywood salvaged from shipping crates was green; the boards were always worn bare in the middle from the crude felt-and-plywood erasers. The chalk, a by-product of the marble industry, wasn't any good for writing, but it was great, Danny discovered, for throwing at sleeping students. The instructors' podiums were stout wooden structures weighing about a much as three big men; they were often useful as barricades.

"When you are in the classroom," Danny's supervisor instructed him one day, "listen for the bell. You are responsible for break time. In many rooms, you cannot hear the bell, so you must listen very hard."

"What?" Danny asked, shaking his head in confusion.

"Also, never forget, if the power goes off, you MUST move into the hallway immediately. This is very important. No students are allowed in the hallway in the dark. Supervisors will come with flashlights to collect instructors and escort them to the lounge."

In other words, Danny understood, it was not safe to be in the dark with the students. In fact Mehrabod Junubi was very unsafe—

Restrictions on the instructors were tight. There was never any excuse for an instructor to be out of his class except at break time. Since spy networks were an endemic part of the culture, every class Danny taught had a number of informers, some for SAVAK, the secret police, and others for the commandant or the supervisors.

The basic principle of the school was the students were always right. Any student was more powerful than his instructor. Foreign instructors, the *farangi*, were actually held in contempt by the commandant and his staff. The only discipline evident was that dished out to the instructors. Suspensions of Danny's fellow instructors were common, as were extra work, longer hours, and duty with exceptionally bad or stupid classes. Overall, it reminded Danny of a prison where the instructors, rather than the students, were the inmates.

Many of the instructors numbed the pain during break time by smoking hashish or opium in the restroom, and one man masturbated into a dry urinal every break of every day, five days a week for the entire two years Danny knew him. He called himself "Mr. Foot-long" and bragged of his endowment. Most instructors checked the claim out, but Danny never walked over to his urinal to see. (Mr. Foot-long was later stabbed by a fifty-rial whore in a straw-filled crib in the awful *Shahr-e-Now* district in south Teheran.) Among the other instructors, hysteria and panic were common. There was at least one instructor suicide at work that Danny was sure of, and perhaps a dozen attempts during breaktime, but despite the staggering human cost, the Iranians were proud of the base.

Nearly two years after Danny joined the cadre, a supervisor bragged, "Seventy percent of our graduates are accepted for technical school, and ten percent go to America for more training." Of the forty contract instructors eventually sent to Mehrabod Junubi, however, only two, including Danny, completed two-year contracts.

The problem was not just that the students were unmotivated, undisciplined, and rebellious. At forty to fifty students, the classes were simply too large for an instructor to manage. The rooms were blistering in the summer and frigid in the winter. There were numbing two-hour bus rides to and from work, incessant Iranian xenophobia with its informers, and worst of all, the deadening SOP lock-step methodology. Work became a horror, and though Danny became good at teaching on the base, there were many days in the next two years when he wondered if he weren't losing his mind.

– 10 –

MARVIN'S VILLA

"It's a nice fucking place to live, ain't it? Look at that goddamn pool! All we gotta do is fill it with water. Now, where the hell are we gonna get so much water? This is Teheran fucking Iran. We're in the damned desert out here. Where the hell are we gonna get so much water?"

—Marvin Roberts, ex-NFL, American businessman

O ne of the first shocks awaiting Danny in Iran was the difficulty of finding a place to live. The daily *Kayhan* newspaper advertised reasonable apartments for ex-patriates at a shocking $1,500 or more a month. In desperation, Danny tried word-of-mouth, but even so, he could not find anything cheaper. He was forced to move to a dingy room on the second floor of the decrepit Caravan Hotel in central Teheran. He had only one light bulb over his single room. For the next five months, he lived without a private shower, furniture, or even a sink. He didn't have a closet for his clothes; the restroom was at the end of the hallway. The rent was $1,400 a month. Downstairs, a Chinese restaurant provided much of his food, but its vented cooking exhaust was directly below his grimy window, and everything he owned was soon greasy and smelled of garlic and spices. The available women at work ignored him....

One day, he read an ad in the *Kayhan*, "Roommate wanted. Must be good with tools. Knowledge of Farsi required. Token rent in return for handyman skills."

The address was for a mansion in a residential area in north Teheran called Golestan. Built two years before, the palatial villa had never been occupied because the owner, a plastics manufacturer, had gotten into political trouble and was living in exile in France. Covered in expensive gray marble and surrounded by high walls, the mansion had thirty-five rooms, seven baths, two living rooms, a dining room, and servants' quarters. During the time it had been empty, it had been stripped of every electrical outlet, doorknob, screw, nail, and exposed bolt.

"Isn't it hot shit?" a gruff American asked as he showed Danny the palatial home. "Look at all the fucking possibilities!"

Once a professional football player, the man led Danny around the building to the so-called garden. A large swimming pool, dry but for a foot of muck in the deep end, occupied the center of the grounds. "What do you think?" the man grinned.

Danny was unimpressed. "It's a mess," he said.

The big American was like other businessman Danny had seen in Teheran, a man who wore cheap cologne, owned only polyester suits, and stank of sweat and cigarettes. On planes, such men drank all the free booze their tickets would allow, and in bars they argued over bowls of peanuts. He couldn't see himself living with such a person, even if the villa had been in good shape.

"It's got lots of fucking potential," the man persisted, his red-rimmed eyes glowing with the passion of someone who could already imagine grass growing in the barren yard and bikini-clad girls lounging around an azure pool. He obviously had no concept how much work was required to make the house livable.

"It doesn't have any possibilities. I don't know who talked you into this two-year lease but you ought to shoot him in the head."

"To tell the truth, I got it as part of a deal," the businessman admitted. "The son of a bitch who owns this fucked-up place owes my company, Homa International Shipping, several million dollars. We accepted this shithole as collateral on the debt, plus a villa on the Caspian coast at Chalus and a house near the ski area at Ab Ali. You'd have access to both of those, of course…. We could get somebody to fix the pool," the man suggested.

"In Iran?" Danny scoffed. "No one will fix the pool. No one will fix the pool! Where are you from?"

"Houston-fucking-Texas. I work for American Eagle Shipping."

"I thought you worked for Homa International," Danny said suspiciously.

"I do," the man sighed. "In order to do business in Iran, you have to be 51% Iranian owned. My goddamn company wanted a subsidiary, so they put up the expertise—me and another asshole—and found some camel-jockey to put up twenty million seed money. Last month, we finished port facilities in Ahwaz, rented offices here in Teheran—"

"Let me get this straight," Danny interrupted. "You're working for a multimillion-dollar corporation, you get this house free, and you want fifty thousand rials a month rent from me for the privilege of fixing this house?"

"Well, fuck, maybe that is a bit steep," the man said rather sheepishly. "How's thirty thousand sound?"

"How about putting me on the payroll, part-time," Danny suggested. "You pay me seventy thousand a month, give me unlimited money for hardware and help, pick up all the expenses, and let me live here rent-free."

"My name's Marvin Roberts," the big man smiled, holding out his hand. "It's a fucking deal. It's a good fucking deal for both of us!"

After agreeing on a few rules, the new roommates agreed that, with few restrictions, Danny could hire and manage servants, all of whom would be paid by Homa International. In addition, he would draw funds to restore the villa and landscape the grounds. Each month, he would be given an allowance for heating oil, cooking gas, water, electricity, phones, and the obligatory *baksheesh*.

Danny arranged two weeks off from work—which automatically extended his teaching contract by two weeks—then set out to make the villa livable. His first project was to hire help. Robert Hagh, an Englishman at work, had a hardworking *bargee*, or housekeeper. "You say this woman is wonderful," Danny said when he heard about her. "Do you think she'd like more work?"

"Perhaps. I overpay her, but she doesn't have much to do."

"How much do you pay?" Danny asked, though such a question was rarely asked in ex-pat society overseas. It was very personal....

"Eight thousand rials a month." That was more than a hundred dollars a month, Danny calculated, about average for a *bargee*.

At her interview, the woman ended up being better than average. Competent and businesslike, Mrs. Davood was exactly what Danny wanted. Physically, she was bigger than most Iranian women. When she came to the gate, she was covered in a black-and white-checked *chador*, but once inside, she chucked it aside and hung it from a welded window frame. Dressed in a black, frumpy shift whose hemline was a comfortable three inches above her nylon knee-highs, she was not at all motherly, something Danny was adamantly opposed to, for he had friends whose *bargees* had taken over their lives. As he came to know her, he learned she was taciturn, a desirable trait by those who wished to control their servants.

"My roommate has plans to fill this villa with young women in bikinis. Neither my roommate nor I live as Shi'ite Moslems do," he explained to her in Farsi. "We have different morals, a different culture, different religion. We're interested in hiring someone who would not be offended by—"

"It's not my business," the woman declared. "I don't care what you infidels do among yourselves."

"You might see things—"

"I no care."

An unusual Iranian, Danny decided. "There may soon be as many as twenty people living here, if my roommate has his way. Can you handle it?"

Looking at the mess around her, the woman nodded.

"How much?"

"Twenty thousand," the woman said, and Danny could tell by her eyes that she thought she was asking too much by half.

"I'll pay you six thousand tomans, plus you can have the servants' apartment to the left of the gate. All your food and utilities are free. Agreed?"

"*Chash!*" she said, and her eyes smiled, the only smile Danny ever saw her make in the next three years.

Pleased with the new housekeeper, Danny next hired a pleasant young man named Sadeq Donyadari to work as a gatekeeper. "I can do the electrical work and the painting," Danny told Marvin, his new roommate, not long afterward, "but I must hire a couple laborers. There's plastering and landscaping to be done."

"Go ahead," Marvin agreed, hardly listening. "Buy what you need, hire whom you want, Keep it within a half million rials a month."

"Okay," Danny said, though he knew the first project to restore the house was finding tools and enough supplies to do the job. Iranians were notoriously inept at maintenance projects, one reason being the sheer difficulty of getting materials. In Teheran's ancient bazaar, he found electric drills in a modern, brightly lit appliance store on Bazaar-e-Jomeri Street, but the drill bits could be purchased only at a supply house an hour's walk away. Nails were in nail shops, hammers were in hammer stores, electrical outlets might be sold by wandering vendors, and hinges were nearly impossible to find anywhere. But Danny found a modern hardware store on Abassabad Avenue, just across from the Super Shilon Supermarket. Stocked with everything Americans expected to find in their own country: tools, seeds, paints, glues, and hardware—all at twice the price of the same things in the bazaar–the store was an American's dream.

"What the fuck's going on?" Marvin demanded the day Danny drove up in a hired truck with eleven thousand dollars worth of tools and hardware. "Where'd you get all this shit?"

"I raided a hardware store," Danny grinned, waving for Sadeq to help the driver unload. "I'm appropriating the room next to the kitchen for a work area. It's my maintenance room now."

When he returned from work the next day, Marvin was pleased to find lights burning in the gatekeeper's apartment. Mysterious marks were on all the walls, and rusty water was running from taps in every bathroom and the kitchen. Taps! There had been neither taps nor water the day before. Beside himself with excitement Marvin ran upstairs to his personal bathroom and found that Danny had already replaced the Iranian toilet with a real commode and, next to that, a gleaming French porcelain bidet.

"I don't want no goddamned bidet in my bathroom!" Marvin complained. "When I shit, I want fucking toilet paper to wipe my ass, not that French toot up the butt!"

"Try it, you might like it. I hear they're nice," Danny replied.

By the fourth day, Marvin couldn't rush home fast enough to see the progress. Every room, all thirty-five of them, were soon restored, and the mansion began to take on an elegance unimaginable a short time before.

"Look at this," Danny chuckled one evening. "Here are two outlets. In Iran, male plugs use two round prongs to fit into the holes of a female outlet, but can you tell which of these two outlets is 220-volt electrical and which is a six-volt female phone jack?"

"Fuck, no," Marvin said, for the two outlets were identical. "Does that mean we could accidentally plug a phone into an electrical outlet?"

"Yep. It would blow the phone right out of your hand," Danny said. "I've marked all the phone lines with a T."

Marvin seemed happy about a new industrial refrigerator and stove Danny installed, but when he spied two dusty Kurdish tribesmen outside in the garden making tea over a smoky cardboard fire, he demanded, "Who are those assholes in the garden?"

"Diggers," Danny answered. "I need labor." Afghan and Kurdish peasants, attracted to the city by higher wages, had dirty, miserable lives squatting in the dirt of construction sites, eating dirt, moving dirt, digging dirt. Knowing that proud men were often the poorest, when he hired the diggers, Danny made a point of including two meals a day as part of the agreement. "I told them I'd pay five thousand a week."

"Five thousand!" Marvin complained. "We could hire a dozen dancing girls for that—"

"Yeah, but they can't bust dirt like these Kurds can," Danny said, grinning out the window at the two tall tribesmen. Dressed in gray pantaloons, black shirts, and brown turbans, each of the men owned a long dagger and an old, dented shovel, which made them look like out-of-work grave robbers. Neither spoke Farsi, but one had learned some English in the oil fields. The two Kurds seemed quite cheerful with their lot. Danny set them to landscaping the extensive grounds, and in two months he had blooming pink roses, trees, and green grass everywhere. Before long, he had filled the pool and fixed the pumps and filters. By early summer, the mansion was ready for girls.

"Where are you going to get them?" Danny asked one evening over dinner. He and Marvin were seated out on the patio, the swimming pool filled and inviting. A half-dozen servants hovered in the background.

"Stewardesses," Marvin answered. "That's where I come in! Most stewardesses are single. They stay only three or four days on layover. I heard most don't like renting an apartment they only use a week or two a month."

"Stewardesses!" Danny said, considering it. "Sounds like fun."

"Oh! Trust me," Marvin said. "Bring the honey and the bees will be beating a path to our door. The parties are about to begin! You and I are going to get fucked out of our skulls."

-11-

THE FEUD

"What the old bat needs is to get laid. How 'bout I give you a hundred dollars and you go rape her? Fuck that woman silly for hours," Marvin suggested drunkenly as he opened his twelfth beer out by the pool.

"Nah, I don't think so," Danny answered, lazily sipping his third beer. *"How about I give you two hundred dollars and you go do it? Take a couple hours and do a real good job."*

"OK, two hundred dollars. It's a deal. I'll go do it ... maybe tomorrow."

Six months after Danny took over the restoration of the mansion, it was known all over Teheran for its parties. Danny, who managed the servants and finances, learned by association most of the party people in Iran. Marvin cultivated women and set up the parties, which took place nearly every weekend. About thirty nubile stewardesses moved in, some only a day or two a week, some for weeks at a time. The women were never charged for rent, food, or booze; the pool was filled with bikinis—or even less—twenty-four hours a day. Of course, Marvin took credit for all that was done around the villa, but his only part in the restoration of the mansion was a petty war he was having with the neighbor, a widow named Mrs. Aryani.

Marvin's second-floor bedroom window faced hers across the garden wall, and only the wall itself and the narrow walkways on either side of the two mansions separated their bedroom windows. For modesty's sake, Marvin had taped newspapers over the windows and carried on, blissfully unaware everything he did in his bedroom was projected onto the yellowing paper like a movie screen by his bedroom lights.

The big American's tastes were exaggerated and kinky, and his wealth and lifestyle attracted women to him like flies to a blown corpse. Complicating this, the swamp cooler used to cool the house required a bit of draft, so his window was usually cracked open a few inches to vent air, with the result this prim and proper Moslem matron could see and hear his decadent "Western" sex life on display every night. Eagerly watching and listening, of course, so she could report its excesses to her neighbors and friends, Mrs. Aryani also plotted to put a stop to it as soon as possible.

She opened the war by parking her car in Marvin's spot out front, but that soon led to the two of them insulting each other in the street. Before long, they were slinging bags of trash back and forth over the adjoining walls.

"That fucking broad," Marvin complained one afternoon, "called me a *jarkash*. Do you know what that means?"

"It's not nice," Danny laughed.

"What should I call that cunt in return?"

"I think she'll enjoy your English cuss words more than any Farsi you could learn," Danny predicted, thinking of earlier that same month when three of his military students had asked him which was the dirtiest word in English: copulation, coitus, or fornication.

"Oh, goodness," Danny had told them, struggling to keep a straight face. The three young men had spent hours perusing their Farsi-English dictionaries for the words. "Those are all bad, but the dirtiest—"

"The bad-bad word?" the students asked eagerly, getting out their pencils and notebooks to copy it.

"Yes, the bad-bad word," he said, looking furtively over his shoulders in case someone was listening, "is coitus."

"Oh!" the students exclaimed happily. "We go to *Shahr-e-No* every month for coitus!"

Shahr-e-No, the New City, was a reputed den of sin in southwest Teheran, but Danny had heard its prostitutes were toothless hags in straw-filled stalls. Somehow the image was dirtier than the "bad" word he had just given the students.

Bad words or not, a few nights later, Marvin became so enraged by Mrs. Aryani's "spying" that he drunkenly clambered out onto the wall between their bedrooms, pulled down his shorts and mooned her. She responded by telling the local constabulary Iranian virgins were deflowered in the house of the *farangis* every night.

The next evening, when Danny straggled home from a long day at work, he found three police cars and a dozen officers raiding the villa. Outside, two neighborhood patrolmen leaned against the wall, smoking and talking excitedly.

"Alle shoma khubay?" they inquired pleasantly, when they recognized the young American who had paid such hefty tips whenever there was a party at the mansion.

"Merci. Chetoray?" he said amiably. Although he didn't smoke, Danny carried Marlboro cigarettes in his briefcase, and he now offered them one, waving for them to keep the pack. In Farsi, he inquired, "What's happening inside?"

"A perverted orgy has taken place here," one patrolman said. "Investigators from downtown have been called."

"From downtown?" Danny grimaced, thinking perhaps SAVAK, the secret police, might be involved.

Inside, Danny found the servants lined up against a wall in the dining room, two goons with G-3 assault rifles guarding them. Upstairs, Marvin—nude but for a sheet wrapped around his fat waist—was guarded by five policemen and three investigators; in the bathroom, a jiggly blonde had been cornered by six swarthy officers. The police were no fools—they hadn't allowed the woman so much as a washcloth to hide her lush body. Danny noticed her pussy was shaved. Nice. Good tits too, he noted.... She looked at him pleadingly.

"Danny! For God's sake—" Marvin tried, before he was cut off by a sinister look from one of the investigators.

"Your name, sir, and your relationship to this evil man?" a detective asked in Farsi, lazily brushing cat hair off the sleeve of his rumpled suit.

"MacCreary," Danny answered, producing his official Imperial Iranian Air Force identification card and blue resident's permit.

"Do you know the *Allemani* woman in the other room?"

"Of course, I do," Danny said, though he had never seen her before. "She is the German fiancée of my roommate, the division manager of Homa International Shipping, Mr. Marvin Roberts. Is there a problem?"

"No. What you *farangi* do among yourselves is our business," the investigator said, unconsciously telling the truth. "There was a report Iranian girls were participating in perversions here."

"Iranian girls?? Perversions?" Danny said, feigning horror. "What kind of perversions? I haven't seen Iranian girls here!"

"There was a complaint from an anonymous citizen next door to the north that sex had taken place ...with the mouth," the policeman smiled, touching his lower lip suggestively with a forefinger. Other police peeked into the doorway, more interested in the young *farangi's* reaction to the charge than even the booby blonde in the other room.

"Sex...with the mouth?" Danny choked, his face turning purple. The police smiled among themselves and winked knowingly. "SEX WITH THE MOUTH!" he shouted. "Get out of this house immediately!"

His reaction was not at all what they expected, and the Iranians' faces fell as they hurriedly backed into the hallway. "I will NOT have you people come into my house to say or insinuate such things! I pay taxes in this country; my roommate has business with the Shah's family! We have friends, powerful friends who will not be happy to hear how we've been INSULTED in our own home! To say such things! Get out of here this very instant! This perversion is almost unknown in our country."

"I thought it was common in America," the investigator apologized, backing down the stairs with his men, hand over his heart to show his sincerity. "I have seen it in X-movies we confiscation—"

"Pornographic movies?" Danny shouted.

"Yes, yes. We confiscation movies like these every day—"

"Why do you think they make such movies, you idiot? WE watch them too, you fool, because we can't believe it either! Do you assume everything you see in the movies is true? Do you DO everything you see in the movies?"

"No, sir. We Iranians would never have sex with the mouth! We make big mistake to bother you—"

"I'll say you did." Danny was shouting so loudly the halls of the big villa echoed. The veins stood out on his neck, and he was drooling and spitting like a wild man, yet the second the police drove away into the night, he returned to normal. Turning to go back inside, he saw the same two neighborhood patrolmen leaning against the wall, still smoking and talking. Politely, one asked if it had all been a mistake.

"Balle," Danny nodded, going on to tell them in Farsi, "That old biddy next door is an opium addict. She has ... hallucinations."

Addiction was one of the blights on Iranian society, and its effects were well understood. In an effort to control the illegal trade without hurting those identified as addicts, opium could be purchased legally in pharmacies with a government prescription, so the two policemen nodded knowingly and shrugged at the news. They were not surprised at all. The old woman was a known addict.

"Here," Danny said, giving each of them twenty thousand rials, a full month's salary, "Please don't be troubled by the old woman's fantasies again."

"We won't, sir. In the future, we will pay no attention to her complaints. We will never call downtown again."

– 12 –

THE MERCENARIES

"Trust only five people in Iran. All others are suspect. Everyone here lies."

—Andrea Wilcox

"D oc" MacCreary was what Andrea Wilcox needed: while not entirely naive, he was innocent enough to be trustworthy. Since she required him to be "available," it wasn't long before he began to spend his free time at her headquarters, a discreet four-story apartment building devoted to housing and managing her many girls. Because he never judged the exotic prostitutes nor exhibited moral superiority, he quickly became a favorite among the beautiful women. Shamsa and Masud, the two most prominent Iranians in the Wilcox organization, also accepted him because he made an effort to use Farsi with them.

Danny was reliable and did his job diligently. Called upon to deliver growing amounts of information and money, he was so honest, even to the point of politely refusing tiny tips, that he knew Andrea was pleased. It wasn't long before even the gruff mercenaries accepted the garrulous young American now in their midst.

At first, Ralf Gruenewald, a head taller and a hundred pounds heavier than Danny, was the coolest towards him. The huge German's wide nose, deep-set blue eyes, and close-cropped hair were in sharp contrast with the younger American's wholesome good looks and long auburn hair. No matter what Ralf wore, whether it was a tailored three-piece suit or a tight bush jacket and shorts, Ralf always reminded Danny of a butcher. Perhaps it was his smooth, pink skin, but more likely it was the look in his eyes— he seemed in the habit of looking at prostitutes and friends alike as just pieces of meat. Ralf, as far as anyone knew, had no past before Iran; he never spoke about home, family, or education, but he obviously hated black people passionately and often made disparaging remarks about Africa.

"I think he saw service in Angola," Bob Fraser confided one night over dinner. "I know for a fact he was in the Belgian Congo before it became Zaire." This surprised Danny. He had figured Ralf to be about ten years older than himself, but if Fraser were right, Ralf was probably somewhere in his early fifties.

Fraser liked to eat well. He and Danny began to share meals and explore restaurants together, meeting most often at Zarech's Restaurant off Abassabad Avenue for pizza or Mexican food. "I like Mexico," Fraser claimed, though all of his prior service was in Vietnam, the Middle East, and southern Africa. As an advisor, he had seen serious fighting in Yemen, and he had several ugly scars on his right arm to show for it.

"Awful intense," he said. "You couldn't sleep for a minute there. I don't think I slept for two years."

A typical American, he made very little effort to learn Farsi and even struggled with the simple password to Andrea's compound. Claiming he didn't want to get too close to the "natives," he suffered most the nights Masud Pooinak had control of the gates. "Diver mouse dairy, mouse goosh dairy," Fraser would whisper into the intercom.

"*Moush goush dareh, divar moush dareh*," Masud would correct him.

"Open up, you goddamn motherfucker," Fraser would shout in frustration. "Don't make me climb this damn wall again!" Masud, however, was strict about following procedures; he had been trained by Fraser himself. "Diver mouse dairy, mouse owse dahree," Fraser would try in desperation. Usually, Danny would have to step in to gain entry for them both.

"*Moush goush dareh, divar moush dareh.*" And in they would go.

Of the three mercenaries Andrea employed, Carl Wolffe had probably been through the worst fighting, but he never revealed where or when. His gray eyes were sad and hard, though, and he seldom smiled. Fraser believed Wolffe had been on the losing side in Biafra. In all the time Danny MacCreary knew Carl Wolffe, Carl would never live with anyone, never have sex with anyone nor was he seen in any other condition than alone. Wolffe always sat with his back to a wall, which made seating with him in a restaurant interesting, and he would wait an hour just to get a taxi to himself. "Never be the last person in a bar or loo," he often told Danny. "More good men have been killed while pissing in a urinal than in actual combat." Danny took note of this and remembered it.

"Carl's crazy," Ralf Gruenewald sneered in private, but Wolffe was the only person the German never tried to bully. Everyone else feared Ralf on sight; Iranians would step into the street to get around him on a sidewalk, Andrea's girls were cowed into nervous silence whenever he was around, and both Fraser and Masud avoided being alone in a room with him. Before long, however, Danny became Ralf's target, a natural "younger brother" to beat up on and tease. Several times Ralf punched him in the shoulder so hard Danny feared his arm had been broken. Bewildered at first by the man's odd jokes, the young American soon learned to dread them. He never knew when he would walk through a door at Andrea's place and find himself in a quick headlock, a sharp knife pressed to his throat. "Sharpens your senses," the German would laugh each time. "You must watch your back. You must anticipate anything. Nothing is obvious in this world."

The variations on the game must have been endlessly interesting to Ralf, for Danny was quick to learn and rarely made the same mistake twice. Fear, the best teacher, caused him to mistrust things out of place, notice people acting strangely, watch open doorways, and plan escape routes. He eventually learned to expect trip wires and not to run in the dark. Punches always seemed to await him around corners, and every time he fell or was hurt, the deep rumble of Ralf's laughter rubbed the defeat in more deeply. Even worse than that, however, Ralf soon broke every pair of glasses Danny had brought from America. Never able to obtain a suitable pair with correct prescriptions in Iran, Danny was forced to wear prescription sunglasses—his only pair—night and day for the next three years.

"I don't know why he's picking on you," Fraser once observed, "but I notice he isn't teaching you anything. I'll show you some things but you must never let him know. Ralf is probably the most dangerous man in Iran, and the only thing you can have over him is a trick or two."

Not long afterward, when Danny came to see Andrea about an assignment, Wolffe asked, "Do you carry a pocketknife?" A couple of the girls were leaning in the doorway of the lounge listening, but they left as soon as the Englishman jerked his thumb at them.

"Sure do," Danny said.

"Give it to me," the older man requested, extending his hand. Danny's knife was a good, stubby Barlow with years of use back in Wyoming and fresh oil on the blade. Carl took the knife in both hands, tested its construction, and then deliberately broke the blade. "It was a good knife to clean your fingernails with," he mused, folding the broken knife carefully, for he sensed it was a treasured gift from Danny's grandfather. "But it's not what you need in Iran. Never carry a knife like this again. Find yourself a lock-back with at least a four-inch blade. Don't get a serrated blade. They're sharp, but they can even catch cutting cardboard." As a demonstration, he flicked open his own knife without it making an audible click. "Buy some valve grinding compound and work it into the mechanism until you can open the knife this silently. Keep it very sharp and don't show it around."

Danny found such a knife in south Teheran. An Afghan peddling tribal carpets on the sidewalk happened to have a beautiful knife hand-made in Herat. Confident he had exactly what the young American wanted, the man laid the blade on a curbstone and struck it with a rock; it didn't even scratch the Koranic inscription on the blade, let alone shatter the steel! Smiling proudly, the Afghan then leaned over the *djube* and cut a thin sliver of steel and chrome from the bumper of a car parked there.

"*Chande?*" Danny asked, barely able to conceal his interest.

The tribesman probably thought he asked a fortune, but he was left wondering who had taken whom as the American walked away with the knife. Danny had paid him four hundred rials, plus two greenback American dollars, and a small silver ring that someone had given him.

"How much do you think it cost altogether?" Wolffe asked him later, hefting the big knife in his hands.

"Ten or twelve dollars, I suppose," MacCreary answered.

"It's a nice knife," the Englishman observed." "You got a very good deal. This is exactly the knife I was talking about. Men can be killed with cheap knives, but few are ever wounded with a good knife. Hollywood would have you believe you can jump through windows and glass doors without getting cut to hamburger, that cars explode in big orange fireballs, that the enemy can't aim a gun nearly as well as the hero, and that a knife is used in this manner—" and he spun Danny around and simulated drawing the blade across his throat. "That's not the way to do it. I'm going to teach you about gross anatomy and knife fighting," he said as he let go. "I understand you've taken to fattening sheep for your roommate out in back of his villa."

"Yeah. He's got a thing about the green meat in this country," Danny said. "I've been raising sheep, b*oogalamoons*, chickens, and other animals for the table."

"*Boogalamoons?*"

"Turkeys," Danny chuckled. He enjoyed using Farsi and its strange words, for they suited his colorful nature; besides, it was something he had over the dour mercenaries.

"How do you kill the sheep?" Wolffe asked.

"Hammer to the head."

"Try the Iranian method. Cut its throat. A human is about the same thing," Wolffe said, gripping the knife so the blade pointed back toward his elbow, the sharp edge along his forearm. "Reach around your customer and pull the point in. That way, if he fights or pulls away, you still get at least one jugular. If you're fast, you should get both jugulars and the windpipe, then you push the victim's head forward, and all the blood will flow down his esophagus. It's fast, quiet, and more importantly, this method always works."

He went on to show Danny how to kill by stabbing into the ear, the eye, the armpit, and the groin. Later, Wolffe demonstrated how to shift the knife to distract an opponent in order to unzip a ribcage or open a belly. What the big Englishman offered as simple lessons and an exercise of his own professional skills, however, Danny practiced with diligence.

One weekend a few months after Danny began work for Andrea, Wolff decided to teach him to shoot a gun. Together with Masud Pooinak, the Englishman drove Danny southwest of Teheran to an old, abandoned military post. The dilapidated brick roofs had mostly fallen in many years before, and the cold desert wind scattered grit and sand through the shattered doorways and windows. While Danny explored the interesting ruins, the other men unloaded several boxes from the trunk of a stolen Paykan.

"There was an Army garrison here a hundred years ago," Masud said, joining Danny in one of the empty rooms. "I think it guarded a caravanserai located about a mile to the south, but there's no trace of the caravanserai today." Guiding him through the compound, the young Iranian pointed out the ingenious brickwork used to make the domed ceilings. "Some of these construction methods are still used today."

"I've seen them during the restoration of my roommate's home," Danny commented. "In that whole villa, there's probably not a ton of cement between the bricks. Mud and straw—and the wedging of the bricks between steel floor joists—hold the place together. God help this country if there's an earthquake!"

"Yes, that's what would make it easy to take down anything with an explosive."

"That's for sure."

"Do you want something to drink?" Wolffe asked upon their return, offering a green bottle of Star beer as soon as Danny returned to the car.

"I don't care for this Iranian beer," Danny said, glancing apologetically at Masud. "It gives me headaches."

"It's all that glycerin," Wolffe answered "I think they rush the fermentation process with it. Personally, I prefer the Iranian wines, especially the Chateau Rezaye and Chateau Sardasht, but the local Pakdis vodka is good quality too. The best thing about Iranian booze, though," he said, poking Masud in the ribs, "is that it's cheap, eh?"

Masud nodded, then sighed wistfully, "I like Italian beer the best."

"Italian beer? I don't believe I've ever had any," Danny remarked.

"It's good. I lived four years in Milano, Italia. I always drank beer while everyone else drank the wine with dinner," Masud said.

"What were you doing in Italy? Were you working there?" Danny wanted to know.

"Not really," the young man answered, a shadow clouding his dark eyes. "I was married to an Italian girl."

"Really? I didn't know you were married." Although Danny liked Masud and was beginning to spend time with him, the handsome Iranian was a hard person to get to know.

"I'm not married now," Masud admitted sadly. "We lived together in Milano very happy. Her mother loved me, her father loved me, the family loved me. We had baby. I bring my wife and new son to Iran to live with my family, to live better than she lived in Italia...." He shook his head sadly and waved the memory away his hand. "After six months, she ran back to Italia and leave me with my son! I never see her again, but a year ago, she sends me divorce papers. I never signed them, but who cares? I got my son." Masud looked out over the desert, shook his head, and swigged the last of his beer.

"Were you ever married, Carl?" Danny asked.

"Three times."

"Divorced?"

"No, I just left the whores. It's a hard business I'm in," the mercenary laughed cynically, throwing his empty bottle onto a dune in front of a wall. "You may want some protection for your ears," he suggested, handing Danny a pair of earplugs and a handgun. "See if you can hit that bottle with this automatic."

Pulling the pistol out of its leather holster, Danny saw he had been given a nine-millimeter Browning Hi-Power. After manually chambering a shell, he leveled the pistol at the target and shot the sand an inch to the left.

"Not bad," Wolffe commented, surprised.

Danny's second shot was a bit low, but he broke the bottle with his third shot. "Not used to the gun yet," he apologized.

"That was good shooting for a novice," Wolffe declared, unintention-ally hurting Danny's feelings, for Danny had been shooting at home in Wyoming, America, since he was three years old.

Danny threw his own empty bottle skidding out into the rubbly desert dust and broke it with his first shot. He missed Masud's bottle with his first shot, then broke it too. "Where did you learn to shoot like that?" Wolffe asked.

"I have guns at home in Wyoming. My dad's even got a Browning just like this one."

"Try this," the Englishman offered, handing him a small pistol.

"What is it?"

"A Russian Makarov in nine mil, fairly common here," Wolffe an-swered. Danny didn't shoot as well with that pistol, but neither of the other men seemed to think he would, for they were partial to the Browning too. Next was a Heckler and Koch in 9mm, followed by a Colt Python in .357 Magnum. Danny also shot a Ruger Single-Six, a Llama .380, a Dan Wesson .44 Mag, and a Beretta, 9 mil. He broke bottles and bricks, shot holes through paper and boxes, and all Wolffe allowed afterwards was, "Not bad. You've got potential."

Privately, however, Wolffe told Andrea that Danny was a better shot than Masud. The only thing he lacked, according to Shamsa, who over-heard the conversation and reported it to Danny, was discipline; he usually shot before he was fully aimed, a mistake the young Iranian never made.

About two months later, Bob Fraser asked Danny to spend an after-noon with him. "Let's go on a picnic. I located an Armenian butcher that makes good ham."

"Ham? In Teheran?" Danny was surprised, for pork was forbidden for Moslems.

"Yep, right in the middle of Iran, these Armenians make damned good ham," Fraser said. "Anyway, lets get some ham sandwiches; I'll make po-tato salad, we'll ice down some beers and go exploring." Not surprisingly, the picnic was to the very same ruined buildings in the desert. "I believe I'm the only one who knows about this place," Fraser said seriously, and Danny pretended to believe it. "It's an old Army post that used to guard a caravanserai...." After dutifully exploring the ruins, Danny ate, drank a beer, and feigned surprise when Bob opened the trunk of his car and pulled out a gun.

"This is the Jee-Sat, a G-3 rifle, standard issue of the Iranian military," Bob informed him, unrolling the automatic from a blanket. "They call it the

Jee-sat here. It was designed by Heckler and Koch, but it's made in Iran under license. I have several. You can shoot this gun as a semi-automatic or as full auto. Its caliber is 7.62 by 51 millimeters. It has a muzzle velocity of about twenty-five hundred feet per second, with a range of 400 meters. It uses a twenty-round magazine, can fire grenades, be adapted for infrared or telescopic sights, or be fitted with a retractable stock. It's a pretty good infantry weapon—not the fastest available, but damned reliable."

"I see them at work every day," Danny said.

"Now you can fire one," Fraser grinned. Twenty minutes later, he leaned on the car rubbing the dust out of his eyes. Every target he had given Danny had been blown to hell. "Where'd you learn to shoot like that?"

"In Wyoming, my family's hunters. We've got guns."

"Shooting a bolt-action deer rifle doesn't teach you much about assault weapons," Fraser disagreed.

"I've never shot an automatic before, believe me."

"Well, you're natural-born," the mercenary decided. "Maybe it's your weapon of choice."

"What's that?" Danny asked. He had heard the term from Carl, but he had never asked what it meant.

"Some people are born to a certain style or a particular weapon. They take to it and never need lessons. My weapon of choice has always been a short-barreled .38 Special. I don't shoot the .357 well, which has the same diameter bullet, and I'm not much good with a nine mil, but give me a .38 Special, and I can hit anything."

Changing the subject, he remarked, "Ralf can hardly shoot a pistol, did you know that?"

Danny laughed. "I didn't know there was anything he couldn't do."

"You put him in a car with the windows rolled up, and he won't hit anything when he shoots," Fraser said. "Worst pistol shot I ever saw. He's good with an assault rifle, but his favorite weapon is the garrote."

"A what?"

"A garrote—a wire. He carries three or four all the time. He makes them out of stainless steel cable like salt-water fishermen use for leaders when shark fishing. Most of his garrotes are about three feet long with a handle on each end. He keeps them up his sleeves, in his pockets—-anywhere he can get to them in a hurry."

"What do you use them for?" Danny had seen Ralf playing with one, but hadn't known what it was.

"You come up behind your customer holding it in both hands so the wire's real tight. Ralf turns his wrists and brings his hands together to make a loop. He could throw that over someone's head, twist the wire to kink it, and it's done. That's that. There's no time for the customer to figure how out to untwist the wire. Ralf sometimes likes to hoist the customer onto his right shoulder so the man's feet don't touch the floor. The customer's own body weight kills him quickly."

"Have you seen him do this?" Danny asked in horror

"I've seen him play it," Bob replied evasively, "and I wouldn't want to be on the receiving end. He's so damned strong. Once the wire is around your throat, and he had you off your feet—well, there's just no way out of it. You're a dead man."

"What's Wolffe's weapon of choice?"

"Grenade. Hey, I got some here. You want to try them? They're great for booby-trapping cars."

"Sure!" Danny agreed enthusiastically. "How do you make booby traps with them?"

"Sew them into the headliner of a car right over the driver's seat and run a wire from the pin to the door. When the driver opens the door and sits down—Boom! He's headless."

"What a surprise."

"Yeah, aren't grenades great? These are Israeli fragmentation grenades, four-second fuse..." Later that afternoon, Fraser introduced Danny to the Uzi commonly used in Iran and a nine millimeter, MP-5 light machine-gun. "You're good," he told Danny afterward.

Danny learned from his friend Shamsa that Fraser had told Andrea he was becoming competent with a gun, "Yes, I know," Andrea had said, not even looking up from her accounting books.

The mercenaries, Ralf included, became confused. "Was Danny recruited for his shooting ability as well as his trustworthiness then?" they asked her, in private. When Andrea shook her head, they went on to report, "He's being taught other ways to protect himself."

"What kind of ways?" she asked. None answered.

"Knives, grenades, machine guns," Fraser admitted.

"Carl has taught him these very same things."

"What?" Fraser said, surprised. "That explains why he's a fast learner...."

"And Masud has shown him how to snail race," the beautiful woman told him. "Have you noticed he's been winning lately?"

"Yes, I had," Fraser confessed. "I owe him twelve thousand rials. Last

Friday, when we raced to Shahyad, he took seven different taxis and walked around four traffic jams. The kid is getting resourceful."

"Masud and Shamsa have shown him how to detect and shake a tail," Andrea said "They devised a game to teach him to elude pursuers. Shamsa calls it 'fox and hounds,' and she claims no one has ever caught him."

Danny was delighted to hear the mercenaries were accepting him as one of their own. Carl Wolffe began to teach him to stash things, and he became very good at it. Ralf decided to share favorite booby-traps, the manager at Star Taxi taught him to drive like an Iranian, and a mechanic at the Beste Body Shop instructed him in the finer points of unlocking and hot-wiring a stolen car.

"I didn't expect half so much when I hired him," Andrea told Shamsa privately. She also admitted she didn't like his sudden interest in the dark arts, so before long, she ordered her men to stop teaching him tricks.

Unfortunately, they didn't... and Danny would soon surpass anyone's expectations.

–13–

THE ROSE AND THE SCORPION

"A Persian carpet is the summit of human endeavor. It requires more technical skill to make, more culture to appreciate, more tradition, more work of little fingers, more love, more beauty, more appreciation than any other enterprise on earth... in all of human history."

—Benyamin Khodari, Jewish carpet
dealer, Ferdowsi Square, 1977

D anny MacCreary came from a town in Wyoming so small he knew all the faces and all the stories. Now, in a country far from home, isolated from his own kind and surrounded by millions of strange people, he thought everyone was staring at him. In fact, they probably were, for with his fair skin, sunglasses, and long, auburn hair, he stood out in every crowd. In this big city, it seemed like he never saw the same person twice! Out of sheer loneliness, therefore, Danny became a wanderer of the crowded streets. Walking for something to do in his free time, he explored Teheran with a camera and a notebook, which gave him a reputation among his fellow instructors for being both outrageous and eccentric. Curious and systematic, he studied the culture and people around him. Before long, he was wandering into and out of places a tourist or *farangi* would never go, and he talked to hundreds of unusual people, asking so many questions that, within a year, he could speak Farsi almost like a native.

One weekend, after a frustrating trip to the post office to mail a small box of souvenirs to his brothers in America, he found himself wandering north along Ferdowsi Avenue, a street famous for its carpet shops and antique dealers. Until only recently, he had browsed the souvenir shops in the bazaar, and he had avoided the carpet stores on Ferdowsi, for he heard prices were high and the dealers were as crooked as used-car salesmen.

"That one is just tourist crap," an Iranian leaning in a doorway commented as Danny paused at the window of a place called Emperor Carpet.

"Really?" Danny looked at the blue-and-cream carpet more carefully. He had seen thousands of carpets like this, hanging from balconies, laid out in streets for traffic to beat the dust out of them, or spread in the living rooms of middle-class homes. The tag identified the blue-and-cream carpet as a Nain, worth 170,000 rials.

Turning around, Danny noticed the stranger was big for an Iranian, perhaps six feet four inches tall and weighing well over two hundred fifty pounds. Although not much older than Danny, the Iranian was bald. Unlike most businessmen, he was dressed in a stylish, well cut suit, not the ubiquitous sweater and sports jacket. "How can you tell this one isn't good?" Danny asked.

"It's easy. It's *my* carpet. Come in, I will show you some good carpets and teach you what to look for."

"Perhaps another time," Danny stalled, having heard carpet dealers were better bargainers than any American salesmen. He hurried away and showed no more interest at any other windows along the street.

Two weeks later, after a mere three-hour wait at the post office for a few stamps, Danny again walked north along Ferdowsi Avenue, this time up the western side of the street on his way to Takht-e-Jamshid and the Keyvan Bookstore. Suddenly, the same friendly carpet dealer was leaning in a different doorway, smiling at him like he was an old friend. "Hello!" the man's voice boomed over the traffic noise. "How are you?"

Waving but not smiling, Danny doggedly continued on his way, but the man ran after him. "I was about to have tea. Would you join me?"

"I was planning to meet someone for lunch," Danny lied. He was always put off by Iranians assuming he had nothing better to do than spend time with them, and besides, he never knew how to deal with a stranger's aggressiveness.

"Just a cup of tea," the man begged. "Come this way."

Reluctantly, Danny allowed the man to usher him into a store called Royal Carpet. "I thought you worked across the street at Emperor Carpet," Danny grumbled suspiciously, cursing himself for being so easily persuaded.

"I do. This is another of my family's stores." In Farsi, the man greeted five old men sitting in the darkened rear of the shop, then imperiously ordered a young boy seated on a bale of carpets to fetch tea. "My name is Benyamin Khodari."

"I've never heard the name Benyamin in Iran. My name is Danny MacCreary. I'm an American."

"Benyamin is the same as 'Benjamin' in your culture," the Iranian grinned, taking Danny's hand in both of his. "I am Jewish."

"My formal name is Daniel. I don't care much for it, but it was a Jewish name once. My friends call me 'Doc... well, actually they call me Doctor Mary.'" Somehow, the Iranian didn't seem half bad now, and Danny squeezed Benyamin's hand three or four times in a vain effort to make him let go. Like most Middle Easterners, Benyamin seemed to believe physical contact showed sincerity, and he stubbornly pumped Danny's hand up and down like the handle of a dry well.

"Welcome," Benyamin laughed good-naturedly. "I have a brother in Tel Aviv with the same name."

Moments later, the errand boy returned with a large steel platter filled with tiny cups of tea and glazed pastries. Seating himself on a bale of tribal carpets near the old men, Danny relaxed for the first time in days. All of the men spoke English well, but Benyamin spoke with little accent. "I speak fourteen languages," he told Danny as he handed him a pastry, "but I can function in six more. In business, we deal exclusively with foreigners. Most Iranians buy their carpets in the bazaar, but on Ferdowsi Street, I do business every day with Japanese, Koreans, English, Allemanis, Italians, and Arab businessmen."

Impressed, yet suspicious of the man's hospitality, Danny drank tea for an hour and then accompanied Benyamin back to his own shop across the street, a place called Quality Persian Carpet. "My family owns Emperor Carpet, Quality Persian Carpet, Royal Carpet, Shahnameh Carpet, and Extreme Persian Carpet," Benyamin claimed, the last with distaste. Explaining his father and uncle thought the name sounded elite and so-phisticated, Benyamin admitted that Extreme did a lot of business with diplomats from the British Embassy just down the street. "It is because the name either appeals to their sense of humor or because they think the owners are simple-minded."

Emperor Carpet, with its huge windows and well-lit display space, was right on Ferdowsi Square. Royal Carpet, three doors south and on the same side of the street, had only one window; Extreme Carpet had lots of windows, stairs, and big doors. Shahnameh was a tiny walk-up on the east side of Ferdowsi Avenue, and Quality was a large, dark store just two doors south of the square. "We maintain our stores as a family enterprise; we aren't at all in competition. Each shop specializes in different types of carpets," Benyamin claimed.

With its excellent location and open style, Emperor Carpet attracted foreign businessmen interested in a quick investment to take home. "Its carpets," Benyamin confided, "are usually big, of fine quality, and moderately expensive. The store's windows are filled with intricately designed city carpets such as Nains, Isfahans, and Tabrizes. Tourists love that store," Benyamin said, "but I have not sold a carpet to an American there in six months. Americans are so suspicious. They think everyone wants to cheat them. No matter what price I name, they always offer half. I think this is because they do little bargaining in America except when they travel to Mexico. It is my experience Mexicans ask twice what they want, but we Iranians usually offer a fair price if we like you and much more when we don't. We like Americans—but the Americans halve every offer—and we don't do business very often."

Royal Carpet, he went on to explain, as he waved at the carpets around them, carried mostly bright, colorful carpets in lush blues, greens, and reds, most of which were fairly new. Extreme Carpet featured factory carpets at wholesale prices and attracted customers interested in a newer product. These carpets had never been walked upon, had only recently been manufactured, and were horribly overpriced. The Khodaris looked down on anyone who purchased a carpet here, but the store's open showrooms, four looms with actual carpets being woven in public view, sophisticated salesmen, and flashy advertising attracted a huge volume of business.

Shahnameh was designed to appeal to Iranians. Dark, difficult of access, cramped, and filled with the old men of the Khodari family, the shop was stacked to the ceiling with dusty, moderately priced carpets. People who shopped here were those who loved 'finds,' and they whispered its location to only close friends. It was, in short, the most profitable of the stores.

Finally, Quality Persian Carpet specialized in only the finest quality antique carpets. The Khodaris were well known at auctions in London, but they also bought carpets in Amsterdam, New York, Hong Kong, Johannesburg, and Rome. The carpets they purchased were the ones sold and lost to the *farangi* a hundred years ago, when Persia was weak and poor. Quality's carpets were national treasures returned home now with the abundance of oil money, and its customers were agents of the best Iranian families, including the Shah's. Carpets as thin as paper and hundreds of years old passed through Quality's showroom. While sales were few, profits were astronomical. The greatest carpet sold through Quality Persian Carpet was from a frozen royal Scythian grave more than 6,000 years old.

"Come upstairs," Benyamin said. "My immediate family lives in a second-floor apartment here." Taking Danny up a creaking metal staircase, he showed him the third floor of the building, a cramped, poorly ventilated storehouse stacked with many tons of valuable carpets; several small desks were crammed into alcoves, each with two or three phones to provide privacy for carpet deals, and in the back, two enormous safes were filled with a fortune in cash. The fourth floor was Benyamin's own apartment, which he shared with a deaf cousin, Mousa, and four Persian cats. Finally, the fifth floor—just a drafty garret—was filled with a library of precious Persian literature and miniatures. This attic was the home of Ibrahim Khodari, Benyamin's youngest brother, a haunted recluse, a sexually driven hermit, and an embarrassment to the Khodari family.

"Ibrahim hasn't left the store since he was twelve years old," Benyamin confessed. "He is terrified of the outside world." For over twenty years, the Khodari family had considered Ibrahim mentally retarded. Not trusted to make any sales, Ibrahim, nevertheless, had amassed a net worth of millions of dollars in books and rare drawings by shrewdly trading carpets *within* the family. Regularly buying carpets from his uncles and cousins, Ibrahim stored them away until the instant one of them couldn't convince a reluctant customer, then he produced the perfect carpet to clinch a deal. Of course, he always exacted a terrible price for his services.

"You are an American," Ibrahim smiled the moment he met Danny. Although he was a pudgy, sallow-faced homosexual, his handshake was the firmest Danny had encountered in Iran.

"Yes. How did you know?"

"All Americans dress alike. If you are cold, you wear a jacket; if you are hot, you roll up your sleeves."

"What's wrong with that?" Danny asked. "How do we Americans dress differently than ... say the English?"

"If an Englishman wants to wear a sport jacket on a cold day, he does. Of course, since it's cold," Ibrahim declared, "the Englishman wears ear muffs, a scarf, a sweater, and gloves. He will stand on a street corner looking for a taxi, shivering, his cheeks red as beets, miserable but dressed the way he wants to be. You Americans, on the other hand, will dress in a bulky ski jacket, big hat, yellow gloves, and fleece-lined boots. You are comfortable. You don't know how to be properly attired."

"So which is better?" Danny asked, enjoying the young Iranian's opinion. "Properly dressed but miserable, or warmly dressed?"

"Both are better," Ibrahim answered diplomatically. "I enjoy watching the street from my window. Come, I show you my view of the world, and you and I will drink tea while we watch the people and guess where they are from."

"I'll do that sometime," Danny promised, liking the gentle Iranian.

"Yes," Benyamin agreed, pulling Danny away. "You do not need to view the world the way my brother does. You do not understand yet. He ...how do I say this?"

"He's gay as hell, isn't he?"

"Yes, he is."

"He was nice, though," Danny laughed, going back down the narrow steel stairs.

"Oh, he is nice, but do not spend time with him. He can convince you trees grow with their roots pointing to the sky. Come," Benyamin said, pulling Danny's arm as he led the way down the stairs. "I show you a carpet more valuable than some Third World countries. Do you like Iranian food?"

"Yes, I do," Danny answered. "At work, I eat in the officers' mess hall. I've learned to enjoy everything except that breakfast soup cooked with a goat's head in it. The cooks try to give me the eyeballs as a treat, but it makes me nauseous."

"The soup is called gipa. It's food for working people," Benyamin laughed. "Those probably aren't eyeballs, but dried limes used for seasoning."

"No, they're eyeballs," Danny disagreed. "They wink at me while I'm cutting them with a knife."

"Really?" the Iranian asked. "And you eat them?"

"Not really. I can't bring myself to do it, but I've eaten a lot of good food here in Iran, like the khoreshes, especially bademjune with eggplant, and fesenjan with duck in pomegranate sauce. I love ghormeh sabzi too."

"Ah, chopped sabzi greens are good for you," the Iranian agreed. "In my family, we eat sabzi once a week."

"A Brit once told me if I ate the local food and drank the local water, I'd get diarrhea every forty days, and if I drank only bottled water and food I'd prepared myself, I'd get diarrhea every forty days," Danny laughed, "so I decided to go ahead and eat the food."

"There is truth to that," Benyamin agreed, turning to an old man lying on a bale of carpets behind him picking his nose with the long nail of a little finger. He translated the remark into Arabic for the old man then told Danny, "What the Brit didn't tell you is that forty days is probably the rule for us Iranians too."

"You mean you people get sick too? Why did you translate to Arabic?"

"Our family, the Khodaris are originally from the coast. Arabic is spoken there. Yes, sure. We all get sick. Diarrhea is the number-one killer of children in my country," Benyamin swore. "Let's go outside and get some air." Standing out in front of Emperor Carpet, watching the busy traffic inch by, the two new friends could hardly hear each other because of the honking. By now, Danny was so acclimated to living in Teheran, he thought nothing of the suggestion to take a walk—this despite exhaust fumes that could turn a baby blue in its mother's arms.

"Did you know in your country you are more restricted than we are in Iran?" Benyamin asked.

"That's hard to believe," Danny replied, thinking of the censorship, the secret police, and the tight government control of every facet of the economy.

"I am serious," Benyamin protested. "There are only two things forbidden in my country: membership in the *Tudeh* communist party, and criticism of the Shah." It was one of only two political remarks he ever made in Danny's presence. Most of the time, the Khodaris were quite circumspect, for there were only 80,000 Jews living in Iran.

Danny knew that of the minorities, the large, mostly middle-class, Armenian population was perhaps the best educated. The Zoroastrians, small in number, were regarded with distrust and some fear, though they were the original religion of Iran; the gentle Baha'i often were in the military or management, but the Jews were the best businessmen. Often vital in the ports as customs brokers, Jews were also prominent in the jewelry business and the carpet industry. Because of the repressive nature of the majority Shia Moslems, however, Jews and other minorities such as the Kurds, Sufis, and Sunni Moslems were clannish and distrustful of strangers.

"Here, look at this!" Benyamin exclaimed one day. "What do you see?"

"A carpet," Danny answered.

"Describe the carpet."

"It's a 'city' carpet. I think it's what you call a Kerman," Danny answered, getting down on his hands and knees to examine it more closely.

"Is that all?

"Its dominant color is red—or yellow." Danny was unsure which was more apparent, the background or the design. Just beginning to learn to choose a carpet for a particular room based on its complimentary hues, he recognized colors were still his weak point. "The carpet is wool with a silk warp and weft. It's old. "

"How old?

"Dunno.

"Touch it!"

He did, and it felt dry, yet slightly oily, while the pile, which was evenly worn, smelled dusty. "It comes from an old home ... in the south," Danny said intuitively.

"Aha!" Benyamin shouted, jumping up and hugging him. Across the room, the old men playing backgammon and smoking hashish from a water pipe nodded approvingly. "You are beginning to understand carpets. It comes from an old woman's home in Yazd and is a hundred and fifty years old. Its quality?"

"Fairly good." Danny measured a carpet by the number of knots per inch, something which he had read in a book. Benyamin, on the other hand, could pace a carpet for size, roll a corner back with his foot, and pronounce the price within a few hundred rials. "It's a *dozar* in size," Benyamin began. "It was made by two people working together," and he showed Danny distinct differences in the knots on one side and the other.

"It was made from several purchases of wool," Benyamin said, pointing out slight differences in color, "and it is made from wool of the spring and wool of the fall."

Try as he might, Danny could never learn the subtle textures of the wools; Benyamin, on the other hand, could easily tell whether the wool was cut from a living animal or a dead fleece. He could differentiate between wool from a sheep that had good grazing or ate only desert weeds, and he could often tell where the wool came from.

"Do you know why carpets are rarely stolen in Iran?" Benyamin asked over dinner one evening.

"I didn't know much of anything was stolen in Iran."

"Oh, many things are stolen in Iran! What's not nailed down or locked up disappears quickly, but rarely is there theft like in the Western cultures. Locks are seldom picked, houses aren't burglarized, and when there is a robbery, jewelry or money is usually taken. Carpets are not the commodities of crime here. An Iranian thief may walk over a carpet worth ten thousand dollars to steal a few hundred dollars worth of bracelets."

"Why is that?"

"Carpets are hard to carry without attracting attention, and they are eminently describable!" Nearby, a boy folding a bale of carpets nodded in agreement.

"Carpets are a form of wealth well understood in Iran. It is nearly impossible to borrow money for a car or purchase land, but you can finance a carpet anyplace. An exchange, a bank, a carpet store, or even a private individual will lend money to buy carpets, and all of this can be done by mouth. I think you call it a gentleman's agreement."

"Or an oral contract."

"I thought that was sex of some sort..."

"No, that's oral contact," Danny laughed, punching his friend in the arm.

Another time, Benyamin asked, "Do you carry a knife?"

"Yeah, I've got a good Barlow," Danny said, pulling out the treasured knife his grandfather had given him. (This was before it was broken by Carl Wolffe.)

"Today, I take you to a carpet factory."

The factory, in Qazvin, a hundred kilometers west of Teheran, was nothing like Danny expected, for there was nothing modern about it, not even electric lights. A brick structure built around a large, open court-yard, the factory contained a hundred vertical looms set in alcoves along the interior walls. Naturally ventilated, that is, very hot in the summer and quite cold in the winter, it was also naturally lighted, which meant work progressed only during daylight hours. A hundred young girls and boys worked at the looms, while a grossly fat, blind woman, the *ustad*, or master, chanted instructions in a monotonous tone, reconstructing a carpet from her youth entirely from memory, knot by knot, color by color, inch by inch. A typical *dozar* could take half a million knots, all from the *ustad's* memory. As she sang, the children followed her directions. It was nearly impossible to do it perfectly. For the first time, Danny could see how dealers found the mark of individual hands in the work. As he walked around the factory looking at a hundred carpets that were supposed to be the same, he saw differences in the wool, the dyes, and the workman-ship. Sometimes, out of sheer boredom, inattention, or individual creativ-ity, "mistakes" were made: the wrong color was slipped in, a detail added, or something omitted.

One loom was abandoned, its weaver discharged and sent home in dis-grace. The carpet hanging there was rattier looking than the others, since most of its pile hadn't been trimmed.

"What's the story on this one?" Danny asked Ahmad, the tall, dark man that owned the factory.

"Very bad piece!" the man answered in Farsi as he lit a cigarette. "Usually my workers can produce ten to fifteen thousand knots in a ten-hour day. We are regulated now by the government how we treat our workers. In the old days, many workers went blind by the time they were twenty, and always the best carpets were made by the little child! Today, in modern Iran, many carpets are made by women in the home or by contract workers like these, and all young workers must go to school each day before they come to work. Much better these days, eh?"

"Yes, much. When did it change?"

Glancing somewhat nervously at Benyamin, the man answered diplomatically, "During the White Revolution of the Shah. I don't know your years—I think it was 1963. Since then, the Shahbanou—the Shah's wife—has done much to improve conditions for workers in our industry. She has tried to stimulate the artistic revival of carpet making, but there is regulation by the industry, too. Quality standards control the dyes, wool, and silk."

"This particular design," Benjamin interrupted, "should have taken eight to ten months to complete. About every ten centimeters, the worker should trim the pile to see the picture and determine his mistakes. With a long pile, it's very difficult to see the design—that's why thick Chinese carpets must bevel a cut between the colors to show the picture. A Persian carpet emphasizes the intricacies of its design by cutting the pile very thinly. In your culture, a luxuriously comfortable, thick carpet is most appreciated; in Iran, a thin carpet is the most valuable."

Motioning for Danny to give him his pocketknife, Benyamin tested its edge, then asked permission to cut the carpet down. Waving his cigarette in agreement, the owner stood aside, pulling his sport coat over his shoulders like a cloak. Quickly, Benyamin slashed a hundred cords from the upper beam of the loom, and then paused. Unconsciously, the other man reached up to finish the cut, but Benyamin made him wait then finished rather slowly.

"This carpet is a disaster," Benyamin said. "The girl weaving it slept through several lines and never recovered the design. She didn't trim the pile, for she didn't want anyone to see her mistake, but Ahmad spotted it himself one morning and fired her immediately. This loom cannot be used for a factory piece until the other carpets are finished, so I have asked Ahmad to let a young man use the loom for a special design for a woman

in Brussels. He will begin tomorrow by stringing a new warp and selecting his wool and silk. It will take two days to set up the loom, weave the
selvage on the bottom, and then begin the knotting. The carpet will take
five months and should cost me seventy thousand tomans or about ten
thousand dollars."

"I'd like to see it when it's done," Danny declared.

"You will, my friend," Benyamin said. "Today I wanted to show you the
most critical part of carpet making, the cutting from the loom." Busying
himself clearing the mess from the bottom beam of the loom, Benjamin laid
the carpet out on the floor

"It's not square!" Danny exclaimed.

"Yes. When the cut begins, you must never hesitate. That's true in life
too. Remember this. Very true," Benyamin commented, indicating how the
warp had become deformed with only the first few inches cut loose and the
rest of the carpet still stretched on the loom. "This can never be corrected.
If it happens to a finished carpet, it is ruined."

"So when do the weavers get paid for their work?"

"Factory owners pay the weavers only after the carpet is cut and laid
on the floor. A specialist is hired to cut the carpets from the looms. Often
the families come to admire their children's work, and the cutting is a moment of drama and celebration."

After being cut from a loom, a carpet's fringe would be trimmed and
knotted, then the pile cut to its final length. Later the carpet would be carried to a carpet wash. The wash was surprisingly rough: carpets were man-
handled, often scraped with a hoe-like instrument, then rinsed, and laid on
a floor to dry. In the case of carpets with a wool warp susceptible to drying
unevenly, a toothed, shovel-like instrument was often used to stretch the
carpet before it was nailed to a wooden floor to dry.

"Finally," Benyamin said, "the carpet is trimmed one last time and
moved to the bazaars or shops for sale. A five-thousand-dollar carpet at
the factory can usually be bought for six or seven thousand dollars in
Teheran," though he did later admit that the Khodari family and others
with prime locations routinely doubled the costs of their carpets in order
to recover expenses. For this reason, despite becoming friends with the
Khodari family, Danny bought only one carpet on Ferdowsi Avenue, a rare
Sehna which Ibrahim sold at cost and which Danny treasured more than
any of the other 28 carpets he eventually acquired.

One day several months after the visit to the carpet factory, Benyamin
took Danny to Rey, a small town just south of Teheran, where they visited

the ruins of a Zoroastrian fire temple. Later, Benyamin drove to an enormous walled enclosure in the desert. The ancient brick walls were broken and tumbling down, but the fancy brickwork was still a marvel. "I wanted you to see this place," Benyamin said, waving his arm at the walls. "It is paradise."

"Paradise?" Danny asked, for the enclosure was just as dry and barren as anywhere in the vicinity.

"Paradise is originally a Farsi word," the Iranian commented. "This place was built as a *hareem* by a Persian shah. It protected gardens and was filled with fountains and flowers. The shah came here for relaxation. There were women and music, animals to hunt and every variety of fruit to eat, but now, like all paradises on earth...it is just desert."

"Oh my," Danny exclaimed, "Now I can tell people I've seen paradise. I didn't know the word came from Farsi."

"Many words in English come from Farsi," Benyamin informed him proudly. Although he lived as one of a distrusted, segregated minority, he was proud of his country's heritage. "Persians invented the spoon and the windmill. We domesticated the tulip and the rose—I know Holland is famous for its tulips and windmills, but they came from here first. In English, you wear 'pajamas' and sit on 'sofas' and 'divans'—those are Farsi words—and 'shah' is used to mean king. There are also words derived from 'shah' like 'check,' 'chess,' 'sheik,' and 'checkmate.'"

"That's amazing. Usually when I think of Iran I think of the rose—"

"Yes, Persian roses are everywhere. Every garden is filled with roses, and the great square, Meidan-e-Ferdowsi, has beautiful roses growing around the bust of our revered poet, Ferdowsi. The rose is in our carpets too, as the *gul* design."

"What we call a paisley design in my culture—what you call the *mir*—is what I consider Persian," Danny interrupted.

"The *gul* is typically Persian—but always, like modern Iran itself, a carpet design must balance a rose with a scorpion." It was only the second political remark Benyamin ever made, and Danny would often remember it in the difficult days that lay ahead.

— 14 —

THE MATCHMAKER

"Good Lord, she had hair all the way north to her navel...."
—"Doc" MacCreary

During the time Danny was teaching English, he was also mastering the tricks of the rough trade and becoming competent with his own specialty— couriering information in the late evenings. At least twice a week, Andrea sent him out on tricks in Teheran. Ferried interminably by late-night cabs from Star Taxi, he learned to deliver papers, money, letters, briefcases, cassette tapes, or sealed envelopes, but just as often, he carried verbal messages, Persian carpets, or signet rings. Although Andrea continued to pay him the 15,000 rials a week as she had originally promised, he heard her business had increased nearly 20% as a result of his work. She also gifted him with cash when something worked out well. The few nights he didn't go out, he went straight to bed after work.

He was exhausted most of the time, now, but before long, Danny learned a lot about the complicated world of Iranian business. Trusted by *bazaaris* and oilmen, military men and industrialists, by politicians and foreigners alike, he carried proposals between north and south Teheran, acting as the middleman between *nouveau riche* businessmen negotiating with established bazaar; Moslems trading with Jews; foreigners bribing government officials; and bureaucrats soliciting bribes. He usually didn't know *what* was going down, but he always knew *who* was dealing with *whom*.

One obscure member of the Pahlavi royal family was so frequently bribed by international corporations that he and Danny became quite familiar. "Ah, my friend, Doctor Mary!" the man would exclaim every time a servant ushered the young American into his study. "What do you have for me this time?"

The man was so greedy he often tore plastic bags full of money open on the floor, using the sharpened nails of his fingers like dirty little knives. Danny was often at his house for hours while the man counted and re-counted stacks of currency and gold coins; to entertain himself while the man was busy, he learned to carry a book to read.

Occasionally the man would express a perverted desire to meet a woman the Shah had enjoyed. "I understand Andrea has a new woman from France," he once observed.

"Yes. Her name is Monique the Unique," Danny answered. As instructed, he volunteered the information, "She smokes long cigarettes and takes her time."

For some reason, the phrase turned Iranian men on, and Andrea had instructed her people to use the phrase often.

"Yes, I understand that," the man said, practically drooling on himself. "Has the Shah requested this woman yet?"

Danny paused, not wanting to lose the man's business, yet unwilling to say too much. One of Andrea's strictest rules was never to reveal her clientele to anyone. The *Shah's* sex life was especially secret. If she ever supplied entertainment for him, she never told anyone, but Danny assumed the famous French businesswoman, Madam Claude, did not supply all the women for the royal family. In the world of prostitution, there was an understanding that most of the local business was Andrea's, whereas "imports" and "special occasions" were shared with others.

One of these special situations, Danny knew, was the island of Kish in the Persian Gulf, a luxurious resort for the very rich. Too hot for anything but indoor activities—summer temperatures were often in excess of 120°—Kish was a busy little island. For a time, Andrea maintained as many as a dozen girls on Kish, less than 10% of the women available there, yet she still managed to keep Teheran and the casinos on the Caspian coast supplied. At the same time, she regularly brought in "imports" on tourist visas for special parties or particular needs. It was possible, therefore, that she brought in women for the Shah too, but Danny was unwilling to talk about it.

Glancing at the Isfahan carpet at his feet, he hedged, "I don't believe Monique has met the Shah...."

"I must know the minute he has her," the man demanded, stabbing at his chest with a long finger. "I want her immediately afterwards. Within an hour! I want her still wet. Do you understand? I will pay any price."

"I don't believe that would be possible. She might leave the country," Danny opined. "But I hear she's very good."

"I will have her before him, then, godammit" the man smirked. "Make me an appointment."

As Danny's reputation for discretion spread, it wasn't long before Andrea decided to dispatch him on a trick into the dangerous Iranian underworld. "There are two important families here," she said one weekend afternoon, "the Sadeghi and the Hashemi, who control most of the criminal activity. The Sadeghis are a loose-knit group led by Manucherr Sadeghi. They deal in 'soft' crime—,,,

"'Soft' crime?"

"Extortion, fraud, *baksheesh*, inside information, smuggling of guns and radios, and perhaps support for various espionage services. Politics is very dangerous here, but they seem to be ... connected somewhere."

"Oh."

"The other clan is commanded by a patriarch named Sadjewi Hashemi. Their organization specializes in 'hard' crime: murder, robbery, drug smuggling, and kidnapping."

"They sound like rough customers."

"They are," she said. "Even in a country known for corruption and duplicity, the Hashemis are legendary. They're very rough."

"So why are you sending me to see the Sadeghis?" he asked.

"I've been asked to provide a go-between for difficult negotiations between the two families. Malek Amani, a Sadeghi lieutenant, needs to arrange a marriage between his daughter, Zara, and Sadjewi Hashemi's youngest son, Hussain. So, we're going into the matchmaking business," Andrea announced, rubbing her hands gleefully.

"Matchmaking?" Danny said. "There are professional matchmakers in Iran."

"There is an extreme need for tact and discretion here. Neither of the families wants to appear obligated to the other during negotiations. If you're careful on this one, Doc, we stand to make a lot of money."

Soon afterward, when Danny first met Manucherr Sadeghi in a dark, middle-class apartment in west Teheran, he had to listen to a two-hour soliloquy on the "historic" unity advantages of a union between the Sadeghi and Hashemi families. Nervously fidgeting throughout the harangue, Danny finally interrupted, "So what's the deal?"

"We will pay," Manucherr Sadeghi declared, "one million tomans for these negotiations, plus fifty thousand rials for each of your exchanges between our families until a contract is signed and the marriage consummated."

"One million tomans?" Danny said, trying to conceal his surprise. That was nearly twice what Andrea had estimated from the Sadeghis. "I believe that's acceptable," he bluffed.

"Good," Malek Amani, the girl's father, interjected as he rose out of a comfortable chair hidden in the shadows of the room. "I will match that million tomans." This time, Danny had to look at his shoes to avoid being dumbfounded. "You may use my Mercedes during the negotiations," Amani offered, handing Danny the keys to a luxurious new car.

"We'll give the car to Star Taxi to use as a rental," Andrea said when she heard it. "I'll split the rentals with you."

"Damn," Danny swore under his breath, for the only car at his disposal was an old Jyane that belonged to his roommate. Marvin's other cars, all fancy BMW's and Mercedes were loaned as favors to his many girlfriends.

Despite the unexpected terms he had been offered by the Sadeghis, the first meeting with Sadjewi Hashemi was anything but auspicious. Constantly interrupted by phone calls and visitors, the old man listened inattentively as Danny explained Amani's proposal.

"This is not unexpected," Manucherr Sadeghi told him over tea. "Arranged marriages, especially those complicated by love, are the most complex business deals in Iran. The dowry and financial guarantees in this particular case will be enormous." In fact, as Danny would soon learn, the money, real estate, precious carpets, furnishings, clothes, foreign travel, and other expenditures offered during the negotiations were greater than for the Shah's first marriage to an Egyptian princess many years before.

The negotiations would last a year but finally stall over two disputed points: the younger Hashemi's drug addictions and the dubious virginity of Malek Amani's daughter. At one point, anxious to break the deadlock, the Hashemis asked Andrea to have Danny personally check Zara Amani's hymen.

"You want me to do what?" Danny gasped incredulously. "A *man* to inspect the girl's virginity? That's unheard of in Iran, isn't it?"

"I understand," Andrea haughtily informed him, "that *mullahs* perform such duty, but in this case the families do not want religious interference."

Manucherr Sadeghi was outraged when he heard of it. "I will allow any of the Hashemi women to inspect the girl. I will permit a third party—perhaps even Miss Andrea herself—to see the girl, but I will not allow a man, especially an American, to do this."

Two months later, convinced the Hashemi family would not negotiate the issue further, Sadeghi reluctantly consented to the examination.

Summoning Malek Amani and his daughter into another room, he broke the news to them in private.

"If you touch my daughter, or if you have sex with her, I will kill you and everyone you know!" Amani swore at Danny as he stormed out of the building minutes later. Unsure if he meant sex in the Koranic sense, that is, even the thought as bad as the act itself, Danny was saved when he met the young woman for the first time and found he couldn't stand her.

Zara Amani was a spoiled, petulant, bubble-gum-chewing teenager dressed in the exaggerated fashion of a rich, pampered girl-toy. She was bored and boring, with hennaed hair and a nose job to reshape her Persian droop. Danny didn't like her on sight; it was obvious she didn't like him either. He was not surprised the only foreign language she spoke was French. Not trusting his own Farsi in such a delicate situation, he called Andrea, who sent one of her girls, Liza, to translate.

While Danny waited for the two women to stop talking, he watched the young girl carefully. Although she wore nearly a hundred thousand dollars worth of jewelry, she smoked the cheapest Turkish cigarettes, the kind Masud Pooinak claimed tasted like tar. The end of the cigarettes was stained with hashish oil dripped into the tobacco prior to smoking.

"She tells me," Liza said, "that she is a virgin, in the technical sense."

"What does that mean?"

"She has had her hymen restored by a surgeon in Paris."

"More than once?"

Again, there was an extended conversation. "She tells me," Liza said, "four times ... plus an STD."

"STD?"

"Sexually transmitted disease."

"Mary, mother of God!" Danny knew hymen restoration was common among Middle Easterners, especially in the case of arranged marriages. Virginity was important. A bloodstained sheet was used to prove a marriage had been consummated. Considering how much money was involved in these particular negotiations, however, Danny figured this was dangerous information, especially since he was dealing with violent people. "Does her father know?" he asked.

"No, he believes she's been a good girl while away at school in France."

"So she has had sex then?"

"Only four times in the front. She says she's enjoyed sex from behind in order to save her virginity."

"Geez," Danny said in dismay. "Did she have sex only with *French* boys, or has she indulged among Iranians too?" He worried too many people would know about the girl's illicit activities.

This time, the women spoke for nearly twenty minutes. Finally, Liza told Danny, "She claims the only Iranian man to enjoy her in front was Hussain Hashemi. He has had her perhaps a dozen times in the back."

"God in heaven!" Danny swore. In Iran, a man could get killed for this kind of information.

"That's not all," the woman said. "She also learned about other girls in the French boarding school. She likes to go down on other women."

"Does she understand," Danny asked, looking the young girl in the eye, "that if her father or any of the Hashemis ever learn of this, she's dead? Does she understand that? They will kill her to protect their family's honor. Does she understand this?"

"Yes, but she says she loves the boy."

"Okay," he said, in disgust. Waving his hand, he waited while the girl undressed, sat in an armchair opposite him, and nonchalantly raised her knees to her shoulders, giving him what was literally a million-dollar view. She had black pubic hair all the way to her navel.

For months afterward, Bob Fraser joked, "Inspector of Virgins! How do you qualify for a job like that?"

Even though the situation may have been a bit funny at the time, however, the other side of the coin was not. Manucherr Sadeghi now demanded Danny pay a surprise visit to Hussain Hashemi to verify his condition. "I want to be sure he is not using drugs again," Sadeghi said.

"Impossible," the old man, Sadjewi Hashemi, refused when Danny proposed it. It took quite a few meetings before Danny finally persuaded the old gangster to allow a visit, but Sadjewi tried to control the timing.

"*Farda, farda,*" he kept saying. "Tomorrow, tomorrow."

One day, however, Danny popped in and asked the old man to produce his son. "He has been very sick all this week," Hashemi apologized. "The doctor has him on the penicillin."

"No matter. I need to see him," Danny countered. "The Sadeghi insist on it."

The boy was brought in supported by two brothers, one of whom was practically breaking his arm to keep him standing upright. Very high, Hussain's head rolled around on his neck like a tetherball on a pole.

"Do you speak English?" Danny asked.

"Yeah, I do," the young man snapped. "Do you, you motherfucker?"

Danny knew Hussain had spent two years at Tulane University in the

United States. Brought home in disgrace after failing, the boy was rumored to be worthless. "Are you stoned right now?" he asked the young man.

Hussain ignored the question even when one of his brothers twisted his arm. "What drugs have you been taking today?" Danny asked.

"Fuck you," the young man answered.

"I don't think I'm the one who's going to get fucked," Danny sighed, calling an end to the visit.

Soon thereafter, negotiations between the two families ended, and tensions between them increased dramatically. Sending Liza home for her own safety, Andrea totaled her accounts. She had made nearly eight hundred thousand dollars, including rentals on the Mercedes, while Danny had earned about fourteen thousand dollars and was graciously allowed to keep two gifts: an expensive carpet from the Hashemis and an elegant, engraved brass samovar from the Sadeghis.

"Quite a job you've got," Wolffe remarked. "Easier than what we do, but it's so close to the edge between danger and thrills, I wouldn't trade shoes with you if you paid me in gold."

─ 15 ─

THE PROSTITUTES

"That was the best fuck you'll ever have in your life, wasn't it?"
— *"Loulou" Chantain, Teheran, Iran, October 1976*

"Not even close to the truth."
— *Danny McCreary, sitting on an Appaloosa as he
waited to choosh some cattle out of a draw south
of Saratoga, Wyoming, September 1992*

As they were getting on the bus at Mehrabod Junubi one evening, Andrea whispered, "You haven't earned your salary for two weeks. I'm sending you out tonight with one of the girls."

"An accompaniment?" Danny asked in surprise, for it was the first time she had asked him to do one, though Masud, Ralf, and the other men in the Wilcox organization did them regularly. Andrea nodded subtly, then turned away lest anyone on the bus notice them talking.

The bus was crowded that night, as it was every night after work now, since several of the buses, including Danny's, had been canceled due to new austerity measures by the Shah's government; nevertheless, Andrea took her accustomed seat alone behind the driver. Danny stood far back in the bus with about twenty other standing instructors. Traffic seemed angry that night, and he swayed back and forth,

A discreet four blocks past her stop, he waved for the driver to let him off. "Where you going, Doc?" one of the new teachers asked sarcastically. "Going out to eat again? At this rate, you'll never save enough money to go home. It's expensive eating out every night in Teheran...."

"I'd like to know how he affords all his carpets," another joked as

Danny hurried down the aisle. "He told me a couple months ago he has over twenty Persian carpets. He must deal in drugs."

"Really?" another asked with interest.

"I came on to him real hard a couple months ago," a busty German woman whispered. "He wasn't even interested...."

"That's a sure sign. Drugs, for sure!"

Moments later, the bus out of sight, Danny doubled back to join Andrea in her latest Mercedes. "Home," she told the driver and then twisting around on the seat beside him, she undid the tight bun in back of her head, letting her long blonde hair fall over her shoulders. Although they had just finished a hot April evening shift at work, she still smelled soft and clean.

"I haven't anyone to send out with the girls tonight except you and Ralf. You will accompany Puff Omura. Upon arriving at the appointment, identify yourself with our gate call, go inside, find out how many participants, and collect 35,000 rials each."

"You mean there might be more than one guy?"

"There shouldn't be," she answered, smiling cynically. "Sometimes we meet smart fellows who try to slip friends in on the action for the same price. The major portion of Ralf's work is collecting for such unexpected situations."

Danny knew Ralf and Masud often acted as muscle; the big German frequently bragged about how he extracted money from cowering tricks claiming the girls had "asked" for it. Ralf would come back to the office bloody; Masud never did. He simply threatened. Both were effective.

"The whores never ask for it," Ralf would laugh in private. "They just tell you what it will cost."

"As long as my clients know what to expect," Andrea said, "they are gentlemanly. If they don't pay right away, or if there are any problem at all, don't argue. Cancel the appointment and leave as graciously as possible. Get my girl back safely. Don't ever haggle. We don't haggle in this business. I know we live in a country where you can bargain over utility bills, but we don't do that. Also I want you to wait nearby—in the living room perhaps or just outside the door. Most of the time, Iranians are charming, but in fact, they're not fully civilized. Most of them think because they've paid for sexual services, they own the girl the night. If they know you're waiting nearby, they'll treat the girls with respect."

"I think I can handle it," Danny replied. Philosophically, he had accepted prostitution for what it was, a business, but accompanying a woman he knew while she sold her attentions—well, that was a different story.

"Let's see, I collect thirty-five hundred tomans...." he said, hoping Andrea wouldn't see the conflict in his face.

"Plus more for special services."

"Special services? What are they?" he asked.

"I'm sorry, Doc. My business is full of euphemisms. I rarely say what I mean—except in the bedroom, of course." She smiled, touching him on the knee. Danny liked it when she was affectionate. She often touched people she liked, and she never walked with him that she didn't at least link arms. Ali Nassiri, who blushed when she unexpectedly put her arms around him, seemed to enjoy being touched too, but Ali never touched her back—his affections were reserved for young men, the younger, the better. Danny figured Andrea might be starved for attention. His arm was always available.

"Special services," she explained, "include anything out of the ordinary. For the most part, our clients are interested in just two things: straight and anal. Straight is in-and-out sex in any position the client requests."

"Ah," Danny nodded uncertainly. Although Andrea was careful to call her customers "clients," the girls usually referred to them as "tricks," a term Danny had borrowed to describe his contacts as a courier as well. "So the client gets what he wants...."

"The client," she said, "may want to be on top, on the bottom, doggie style, in a bedroom, a bath, or in public, but it's all straight as long as it's vaginal. Anal intercourse is popular in Iran. We charge fifty thousand for anal or for a combination of straight and anal."

"Why is it more expensive?"

"It is not particularly healthy. A combination of straight and anal can introduce yeast to the vagina and put a working girl out of action for a couple of weeks. Because of this, the girls will want to take a shower and douche afterwards, so be careful not to let a client rush them out the door. All of the girls except Carole Barber will do an anal scene if the money is right."

Andrea hesitated, unsure what else to say. She and Danny rarely talked about sex. Although he was interested in the girls, he had spent little time learning about their business.

"Special services," she continued, "include French, Swedish, B&D, S&M, e-stim, fetishes, and everything else you can imagine. This is usually taken care of over the phone so you will know what to collect, but if the client springs a surprise on you, charge the maximum he will pay and then check with the girl. Most of my girls haven't any inhibitions as long as the money is good, but a few draw the line somewhere."

Since he came from a small town background, Danny had a hard time imagining the beautiful and sophisticated women he met in Iran doing such kinky— yet somehow sexy—things for money. Puff Omura–for example—what a thought! She was better than hard-core porn—she was real! Danny had experienced backseat quickies back home, for he was never able to pass up a date with the town sweetheart, but the things he was learning while working for Andrea were beyond his understanding, and he was beginning to enjoy them.

"Oral is an attraction for Iranian men," she answered. "That's because it's not common in this culture. Many find the idea of using the mouth for sex repulsive. While some of our clients want to receive it for the first time, few will return the favor to the girl for two reasons. One, they believe it's easier to catch venereal diseases that way, and two, they think because the girl trades sex for money, she's dirtier than other women. The truth is, most of the gonorrhea in this country is transmitted anally by all these teenage boys buggering each other when they could enjoy one of my medically certified girls—well, I just don't understand it."

"What about the other kinds of sex you mentioned?" Danny asked.

"As you know, homosexuality is common here, but other forms of sex are unusual. Fetishes and masturbation are common. Iranians are morally repressed, so items of sex are often more important than the act itself. Touching, voyeurism, fondling undergarments—all of these are such safe, passive forms of sex that we charge only the flat rate."

"You mean a trick might just watch the girl strip?" Danny asked in disbelief.

"Not unusual. Merely playing with a woman's panties or garters, or watching her shower—common here. One thing you will notice about most of our clients: they are almost exclusively rich, upper class. We deal with few middle-class clients. It's the middle class, in every country and culture that are the carriers of a society's values. What the middle class does is copied and refined in the changing attitudes of both the upper and lower classes later. Here in Iran, the middle class is increasingly educated and sophisticated, but they cling to a romantic ideal of Islamic fundamentalism and Sharia law. So, because we are not dealing with the typical Iranian, we must be circumspect in our activities. We will never change Iranian society; we only cater to an active minority."

"But I thought all Iranians were interested in the pleasures you offer," Danny said.

"I think our clients are more open about their desires, but what we're profiting from here has no effect on the nation of Iran," she said. "You hear people blaming the deterioration of Persian values on the influence of the decadent West, but in actuality we haven't corrupted them in the least. The fundamentalists decry the spread of Western pornography, for example, but look at the old Persian miniatures sometime. The religious leaders blame us for the evils of alcohol and drugs, but read Omar Khayyam. No, we haven't corrupted the Iranians in the least. What we offer is an illusion, the Western, technical perfection of sex."

They had arrived at the richly painted gates of Ali Nassiri's mansion. "Remember, Doc," Andrea cautioned as he opened his door and got out of the car, "You're going out with my Japanese girl, Puff Omura; she's experienced in all this and will help you with details, but you must be careful. Bring her back safely."

"Oh, I will," Danny laughed. "This'll be interesting."

"Let's hope it's not *too* interesting," she warned, her voice quite cold.

As the car pulled into the driveway, he waved goodbye, then stood wistfully looking through the gate at the beautiful garden beyond. He had never been invited back to Ali Nassiri's home since his first visit, but after all the dust, traffic, and congestion of Teheran, he felt a growing desire to lie in cool green grass, listening to peacocks. Sighing as the gatekeeper closed the gate and the wonderful vision of paradise disappeared; he turned and walked around the block to Andrea's drab office building. In the lounge of the boring building, the beautiful Japanese woman was already waiting.

"Oh, Doc. I so glad you are to take me out tonight," she said in a high-pitched voice. Collecting a shoulder bag, she lifted her long black hair for him to help her with her coat. She wore a tight orange silk sheath and very high heels with ankle straps, but no jewelry. Danny rarely saw the girls with jewelry except at parties, because it was too easily lost when they were working.

In the taxi, he found himself overly enjoying her wonderful perfume and the sensuous way she cuddled up to him for warmth in the back seat, but every time he pulled away, reminding himself she was not *his* date, she moved even closer. Only a short ride later, they pulled up before the gates of a large, marble-fronted home in Elahieh, in north Teheran. Although the home was dimly lit, a timid voice answered the intercom the instant Danny pushed the buzzer.

"*Balle?*" the man asked nervously.

"*Moush goush dareh, divar moush dareh,*" Danny answered in Farsi, and the gate swung open immediately. A sweating Iranian in his late forties met him at the door.

"No, no! Not this time. I ask for a *woman* tonight," the man protested, trying to close the door in his face.

Embarrassed by the man's mistake, Danny quickly corrected him, "Your date is here, in the car! I'm her bodyguard."

"In that case, you are welcome. You take the money, of course," the man said with relief, and Danny was left wondering if Andrea employed homosexual prostitutes. If so, he had never seen one around her office. He was sure Wolffe or Fraser would have said something if she did have gays working for her, but instead, no one mentioned them. Intuitively, he realized that meant either Andrea had nothing to do with that part of the business, or, more likely, they were housed and managed elsewhere. Perhaps Andrea's operations were doubly large and more secretive than he had imagined.

"Yes, I collect the money," Danny told the nervous Iranian. "It's 35,000 rials, fixed price."

"Yes, yes, I know that," the man snapped, in a hurry to conclude the business and get on with his date. "It's 75,000 rials altogether for my special services tonight. Here is the money."

Danny counted it and went out to the taxi to collect Puff and her shoulder bag. Alone now, the driver, one of Star Taxi's best, settled in for a long wait with a pack of French cigarettes for company. Inside, exaggerating her shyness at first, Puff had to be encouraged to shrug off her coat, but after she did, she was thoroughly in charge. Her tight dress was cut up to her waist and down to her navel, and even Danny had a hard time tearing his eyes away. Legs and boobs and inviting shadows beckoned; her softness and perfume tempted the very air. The Iranian trembled expectantly, nodded for Danny to wait in the living room, and waved Puff into his bedroom. Minutes later, haunted by the sound of moans from the other room, Danny got up and went out on the balcony to gulp the cool air.

An hour later, Puff touched his arm. "I ready, now, Doc. We go?"

She smiled sweetly, but her eyes were deep, black, and mysterious. "Hussain give me a big tip. Here is three thousand—my *baksheesh* to you."

"Oh," Danny said rather stupidly as he accepted the money, but his hands shook when he helped her into her coat. He escorted her out to the waiting taxi, his mouth as dry as the Desert of Bones, in eastern Iran.

"How you like to make another five thousand tonight?" she asked.

"Doing what?" he asked.

"I know someone," she smiled, "an Englishman, very kinky. He pays sometimes after we girls have dates." Seated next to him in the taxi, she crossed her legs seductively, exuding the musky smell of sex. Danny noticed she wasn't wearing anything under her dress. In the dim light, there was a shadow between her legs as she crossed them.

"I don't understand," he told her.

"He masochist. He wants spanking for being naughty. It takes only fifteen minutes." Surprisingly, Danny wasn't as put off by the idea as he thought, perhaps because he was learning that passive forms of sex were safe money for the girls.

"What about Andrea?" he asked.

"She doesn't know—and we don't give her a cut, do you understand?"

"I don't like it."

"Stay in the car then," she snapped petulantly, turning to look out the other window. Without being told, the driver drove straight to another house, this time in Tajrish. Puff rang at the gate and was gone only twenty minutes. When she returned, she gave the driver a wad of money and handed Danny two thousand rials. "There could have been more, Doc. He likes to be watched. Next time, you watch, maybe get five thousand."

"Not interested."

"You will. After all, you took the money," she laughed. "Maybe you come home with me tonight?" Taking his hand in hers, she slipped it up the silky slit of her dress, cupping his fingers in her warm, wet pubic hair.

"What? Do you think I'm interested in another m-man's—?" he stammered, his head saying no, but his fingers curving deeper into her wetness. She began to hump hungrily against his palm. She hadn't cum during her appointment, and she humped his hand eagerly—at least that's the way it seemed. Ralf once joked whores never came; it was an occupational hazard. Cumming involved an emotional attachment, and a whore couldn't risk that, he said.

"I douche for you," Puff told him huskily, knowing she'd won.

"Okay," he said, taking her in his arms. She had wonderfully firm breasts, larger than he expected. He eagerly cupped them, and she caught him by the back of his head and guided his mouth to her nipples. Moaning lightly, he gave a moment's thought to the taxi driver, then realized the Iranian had probably seen much worse while accompanying girls on their dates. Throwing caution to the wind, Danny thrust his hands under her dress and pulled her legs around him, lost in an open-mouthed kiss.

Danny MacCreary was a one-woman man, though it was hard to tell the next few months. As the girls gossiped among themselves, his "luck" with them increased, and he slept with a number of them. An Arab woman—perhaps Egyptian, Lebanese or Libyan—named Shalah Shahlu—was an intense attachment of his for a couple months. He was nuts about her, but she left … suddenly … for the sex markets in Nigeria, and he never saw her again. Puff Omura, however, would maintain his interest for a year, for she was an incredible woman. She was Japanese; she had smooth, wonderful skin and a great touch. It was her deep, deep black eyes that—Did he ever please her, he wondered? It was impossible to tell. Her eyes watched him without sign.

One day, however, Andrea asked, "Do you enjoy fucking my girls?"

"Yeah, I do," Danny answered honestly, though he knew there was something missing. Perhaps it was the secret in Puff's dark black eyes, or the wry smile she allowed when they finished having sex, but he knew he didn't like the way she and the other girls jumped out of bed after sex to take a shower. He also realized he didn't want to hear shoptalk in bed or their comparisons of his cock and style to dozens of other men's. Though his masculine pride would never have allowed him to admit it, deep down he was tired of the prostitutes.

Andrea intuitively understood his dilemma. She said, "I'm going to cut you off, Doc. You'll have to pay for it from now on."

"How can you do that? The girls have been going to bed with me of their own free wills!" he exclaimed.

"Perhaps, but there's something you don't understand about them. They go to bed with you for selfish reasons, none of which have anything to do with sex. They're interested in you because you're nice. The girls talk—they always talk when you men aren't around. They're fascinated with the men of my organization. You think you've been seduced? Some of my girls have left wet trails across Carl Wolffe's desk trying to seduce him, and he's never shown any interest in them at all. There's a competition of sorts to get him to unbend.

"Ralf, as far as I know, has only gone to bed with the black girls," she confided, "and he's been very rough, almost scary. My photographer, Laurence Peters, has been the rounds like you, and Roberto Viera, my electrician, can't keep his hands off anything blonde. Paolo Giaminelli has kinky tastes, Dieter Mueller is hung like a horse, and some of the Iranians—like two of Carl Wolffe's soldiers, Alireza Rostgoo and Mohammad Balourchi—have actually fallen in love and proposed marriage. And you, oh, how they talk about you! All good, of course, but you're … how can I say this without being harsh? You're so goddamned *innocent*. For your own good, I'm cutting you off."

Of course, Danny didn't believe she could, but afterwards, though all of the girls were just as friendly as before, none ever had sex with him again. As the months passed, he had to find girlfriends elsewhere: stewardesses staying at Marvin's villa, secretaries, a married German fooling around on her husband, and a horny English nurse. Although there would come a time when Shamsa, Andrea's receptionist, would pursue him, he never indulged with her or with any other Iranian woman. Shamsa wanted more than he had to give, which was odd because the prostitutes somehow offered less than what he needed. In the end, he had to admit, he didn't really know what he wanted from a woman, or whom to give his all to. And he certainly did not understand the beautiful women around him.

Once, Danny asked Andrea about the girls. "I know how they think," she said. "I've been a prostitute since I was thirteen."

"Good Lord, you are kidding!"

"No, I'm not. It was an economic necessity."

"I don't believe that." Danny was amazed someone so sophisticated could have been so desperately poor.

"I know what you think," she laughed, "but I am not what you imagine. I never found out anything about my father. My mother was a clerk in a store; she drank everything she earned. Two months after my first period, she put me on the street. When I was fourteen, a man came to our door, offering 'protection,' and when I was fifteen, I was introduced to heroin by another pimp. I worked the streets on my own after that. Twice, I've been in hospitals after being beaten, and I've been arrested twelve times, but finally, I learned something about this business I'm in.

"A good prostitute's got to plan for the day she retires. She's got to improve herself, or she'll wind up doing penny-ante mouth jobs in alleys the rest of her life. I was fortunate to have spent time in the pleasure markets in Beirut before the civil war destroyed that wonderful city, and I learned class is not inherited, it's earned. While other girls practiced jiggling their tits during line-up in the brothels, I learned a proper accent and grammar. I taught myself to think, to plan, and to manage. The destruction of Beirut and the good money here in Teheran gave me an opportunity to develop something on my own, to become someone I had planned for all these years. Today, I am my own creation. I have proper accent and appreciation of fine wines, dancing, socializing, and couture, but I have never read a newspaper article or a single book in my life or learned anything about science or mathematics...."

"Where does it all lead?" Danny asked. "What happens to you after Teheran? This has got to end someday."

"Of course it will! I dream I'll find a rich man, or someone to accept me as I am, past and all, but in truth, my future depends on the money, Doc. Just like it does for all us working girls."

$-16-$

The Fifty-first State

"I felt so lost. I couldn't even recall simple details about my own country."

—"Doc"

"Lockstep methodology," Danny explained to his roommate as they sat out by the swimming pool listening to the neighborhood *muezzin* sing the call to evening prayer, "is the most perfect method for numbing a teacher's mind that was ever invented. Teaching a language this way is an exercise in mental survival."

"Then why do you do it?" Marvin asked.

There was no simple answer. "The money's good," Danny said, but deep down he didn't understand what was happening to him. He hated to admit the Imperial Iranian Air Force's version of teaching English, the dreaded SOP, was cheap, utilized mostly nonprofessional teachers, and graduated enough students to fill the military training slots in America. The waste was not an important consideration. Everyone in the Iranian Air Force had to learn English, the instructors had to teach it, and between these two purposes lay a hell of angry classrooms.

"The building is arranged," Danny's supervisor had told him his first day at Mehrabod Junubi, "according to the books. The first floor of the building is devoted to the low books—400 through 1100. Only native Iranian instructors teach these books so they can answer all the students' questions in Farsi. On the second floor, the instructors teach books 1200 to 1400. On the third floor are the advanced series of books, the 2000s."

"You're telling me that as long as I'm in your section I'll be teaching the same three books—twelve, thirteen, and fourteen hundred?" Danny blurted out, having a terrible vision of going stale, then burning out like all the other losers he saw in the instructors' lounge.

"Oh no," the supervisor laughed. "My section only teaches book thirteen hundred."

"So I'm supposed to teach the same book over and over for two years?"

"Yes! You will get very good at it!"

Unfortunately, that wasn't the worst. The school was arranged so the classrooms on each wing of the building would be on the same lesson at the same time. The supervisor had a desk at the head of the hallway so he could listen. If the first instructor was teaching a dialog from lesson 1301, the supervisor expected every class in that wing to be working on the same dialog in the very same lesson. Absolutely no deviation was allowed.

"That sounds awful," his roommate laughed. "What are the teachers like?"

Only a few instructors were professional language teachers; the rest of the staff were only minimally educated. One of the teachers on Danny's hallway was a retired Icelandic fisherman. At one time or another, an English laborer, an Australian house painter, and a Belgian pipe fitter taught English across the hall. The lockstep methodology reduced the chance of their making an error in the classroom. In theory, Danny had to admit, "Students don't have time to ask involved grammatical questions. They're to listen and repeat until English becomes comprehensible and comfortable."

"Does it?"

"Become comprehensible?"

"Yes."

"Yeah, it does," Danny said. "Anyone with normal intelligence can learn another language when exposed to it. We have more ability when we're children, but we can still learn a language, even as adults."

"I haven't learned any Farsi," his roommate grinned, swilling down the last of his twentieth beer.

"You've gone out of your way *not* to," Danny laughed. "But if you wanted to, you could learn Farsi without having anyone translate for you."

"Not me," Marvin declared. "I'd hire me some big-titted dancing girl to do all my translation. Fuck no," he said, thinking better of it, "I'd hire me *two* fucking dancing girls, one to translate and one to teach me more...."

Chuckling, Danny punched his roommate in the arm. Every time he tried to discuss something serious, Marvin had a way of turning it sexual.

There was another problem, though, in the business of teaching

English besides the strict methodology. As springtime came and the class-room buildings began to warm up, senior instructors searched for rooms with better cooling systems.

"You must move out of your room at the end of the shift," the supervisor told Danny at lunch one day.

"Why?"

"Ah, the question."

Why? was an unacceptable question in the Imperial Iranian Air Force. Every supervisor enjoyed telling students and instructors alike that there was no "why?" in the military.

"I have decided to give your room," the supervisor smirked, "to Mr. Jaffari-Nejad. His room will be too hot this summer."

"But I've been in that room for four months," Danny protested. "It's *my* room. I spray the room with Pif-Paf bug spray to keep the students' body odors down. I fixed the door myself so it actually closes, and I painted the chalkboard so the students can see what I'm writing."

As he spoke, he realized he should have saved his breath. He was learning it was better not to fight such a hopeless system, but several months later, after he had endured a horrific summer in a one-hundred-ten-degree classroom with no ventilation at all, he was again bumped by the same instructor and sent back to his original classroom, since it had no heat for the winter.

"Hey, you can't keep pushing me around," Danny complained, but actually the supervisor could. Danny was trapped in a peculiar Iranian arrangement called *parti bazee*. *Baksheesh* money, of course, could always smooth the way, but the true operating system in Iran was *parti bazee*, or influence peddling. A foreigner could never understand the complexities of this ancient system.

Danny learned, for example, that a *sarboz*, or lowly draft soldier, might have more influence over the language school than the commandant, who was a captain, because the *sarboz's* father was the landlord of the captain's cousin. The commandant might defer decisions to the *sarboz*, and in fact, the *sarboz* might even sit behind the captain's desk and sign papers. This same draft soldier, however, might owe favors to a second sergeant on the gate detail who was the brother of his wife's employer. The second sergeant might, in turn, have financial obligations to the master cook who was taking kickbacks on his commissary supplies, but as befitted his lower rank, was paying a percentage to the commandant, who had to share with the *sarboz*, and so on. Iranians seemed to sort out *parti bazee* with a minimum of effort; a *farangi* like Danny could not. As he was soon to discover, foreigners tended to overrun the delicate system.

After twenty months on Mehrabod Junubi, Danny thought he understood the lay of the land and planned his own *parti bazee* to get a transfer back to Doshan Tappeh Air Force Base. One of the men he had come to know through Andrea Wilcox was an Air Force officer, General Jahanbani, who was trying to arrange a marriage for one of his relatives. Danny had carried message after message between the two families only to have negotiations break down in the end, but then the general asked him, "Is there some favor I can do to repay your discretion in this matter?"

"Yeah, I'd like a transfer to the day shift on Doshan Tappeh," Danny said. He was sick of the late afternoon shift at Mehrabod Junubi and was tired of teaching the same book over and over. He imagined Doshan Tappeh would solve all his problems, and that working with cadets would be less stressful than working with enlistees.

"Oh," Jahanbani remarked in surprise. "You could have asked your commandant for a transfer, but I take care of it for you."

The general was a good and true Iranian, a regular Prussian compared to his peers, and he made good on his promise the very next day. Danny was transferred to the day shift on Doshan Tappeh so smoothly that even his salary wasn't messed up, which was a miracle in Iran. It was, however, an example of over-doing *parti bazee*, for the incident left Danny forever marked as having dangerously powerful friends.

He soon noticed that while his new supervisor on Doshan Tappeh avoided him, fellow instructors openly despised him, and his bus driver often "didn't see" him and drove right past his stop on the way to work. Worse than that, however, was the fact Danny was usually assigned the "best," meaning the most obstinate classes of arrogant cadets, each with his own *parti bazee.*

One day, while teaching book 1200 for the first time since coming to Iran, Danny started a reading lesson on the geography of the United States. The lesson's objectives included vocabulary for basic industries, natural resources, and geographical concepts, but he got hung up on the opening sentence.

"The United States of America is a very large country consisting of fifty-one states," he read aloud to the class. Fifty-one? At first, Danny suspected that another state had joined the Union while he had been in Teheran. District of Columbia? Guam? Did Texas split in two? California finally did it? He knew he was seriously out of touch with his own country, although he read the Kayhan newspaper every day, but the news was so heavily censored in Iran he didn't know what to believe. Even so, he doubted he was that uninformed.

"I think there's a mistake in your books," he told the students.

"No mistake," the class monitor corrected him.

"Excuse me? I'm the instructor here," Danny snapped. It always irritated him when a student presumed to know more than he, and it appeared to be growing more common lately. Taxi drivers, waiters, and passersby seemed to go out of their way to challenge him. He was wasting more time every month in petty arguments. Was it the stress of urban blight, the mental deprivation brought on by the never ending meddling of the central government, or just the phases of the moon?

"Yes, sir," the student replied contritely.

"Anyway, I'm there are only fifty states in the United States," Danny informed the class.

"No, sir, there are fifty-one. It says so in the book," another student insisted, a superior look on his face. This came from the Iranian conviction: if it is written, it's true.

"I know, but the book is wrong," Danny said.

"No, sir, the book is correct."

"Look, I'm an American, it's my country, I know how many states there are, and there are fifty," Danny declared.

"No, sir, there are fifty-one. Here it is in the book. We can see it."

"The book is wrong," Danny said, grinding his teeth in frustration. He hated this Persian obstinacy, for he rarely won, but this time at least, he was 99% certain the book was wrong...unless Texas had split in two without his hearing about it.

Next period, he returned from his break to find an empty classroom. There were no chairs, no podium, no chalkboard, and his briefcase sat abandoned in the middle of the floor. Angrily, Danny took out a novel and sat on the floor near the door reading, intending to outlast the students, but instead, his supervisor came running down the hallway "Where are your students?" the man demanded.

"Dunno," Danny mumbled, hardly looking up from his book.

"They are in Miss Fougulet's room! She now has eighty students. What did you do, Dr. Mary?"

Danny tried to explain the situation to the Iranian, but there was a strange reluctance in the man's eyes that caused him to stop. "What's wrong?"

"You are stupid. If the book says there are fifty-one states in the United States, there are fifty-one!"

"No, there aren't," Danny insisted.

"Do you dare argue with me?"

"Wait," Danny smiled, trying to defuse the situation before it got out of hand. "I'm an American. There are only fifty states, not fifty-one."

The supervisor ran out of the room in a rage. Ten minutes later, General Compani-Tabrizi, head of the Air Training Command of the IIAF sent a third lieutenant and an armed sergeant to summon Danny to the instructors' lounge. The general often had tea here to practice his English with the instructors; Danny had talked with him at least twice. Sitting at a large table in the center of the dark room while a dozen military officers and enlisted men hovered nervously in the shadows and five worried civilian supervisors and two Iranian secretaries sat nearby, the general, who was a round, short man, looked his most impressive.

First, the general questioned the supervisors in Farsi about Danny's attitude and teaching. He was impressed that "Dr. Mary," as they called him, was a two-time winner of the Instructor of the Month Award.

"Dr. Mary," the general said in English, turning to Danny, who was seated at the opposite end of the table, "I know the strain you are laboring under. It's very difficult to come to this country to teach our students. I'm sure there is a misunderstanding here. Would you cooperate with these men in an investigation of this matter?"

"Sure," Danny agreed, for he was just as eager to clear up the problem as they were. He liked and trusted General Compani-Tabrizi, an unlikely man to have such a rank, for he was gentle and always polite. "I'll cooperate fully, but I believe there is a typographical error in the book."

"That is not for me to decide," the general smiled. "I have other duties. I leave this matter to Major Faradji and Captain Rafi'i."

Major Faradji was a hard faced, hawk-nosed terror with a reputation for an agile mind. Captain Rafi'i, on the other hand, was a typical *falawi*, a man who had bullshitted his way up the ladder. In America, he would have been called an ass-licker. Between them, the two officers decided Danny should take pen and paper to list the American states. After discussing the decision with their underlings—who generally praised it as the greatest legal decision since the time of King Solomon— they posed it to the lone American.

"Okay," Danny agreed, "that sounds fair."

He began to write. Florida. Georgia. South Carolina, North Carolina—and as each name went down on the paper, the assembled officers looking over his shoulder whispered aloud, "Oh, Alabama! Oh, Nebraska! Oh, Oregon!"

In his mind, Danny tried to picture a map of the United States, and he listed the states in order from one coast to the other but it didn't work. He could list only forty-seven, but since he was a Westerner, he was sure only that the Rocky Mountain, West Coast, and Great Plains states were accurate. His errors had to be among the piddling little states on the east coast.

Maryland! He quickly added it to the list. He thought hard for several minutes, and realized he had skipped Kentucky. Forty-nine ... forty-nine ... forty-nine.

"Doctor Mary, it is hopeless," Major Faradji finally declared. "Second Sergeant Hosseini has been sitting at a table behind you writing down the states as he remembers them. He was in America only two months ago, as you know, and he finished listing all fifty-one already."

"Fifty-one?" Danny groaned.

"Do you still insist the book is wrong and you are right?"

"YES!"

"You are suspended for three days for insubordination."

That night, Danny sat on the verandah of Marvin's home trying to list the states by name. Out by the pool, two buxom German stewardesses were splashing in the water, naked, teasing him to come join them, but he refused and continued to write. It was distracting. Both of them had great boobs, though Inge was hairy top and bottom.

"Marvin, can you do this?" he asked. His roommate was sitting out by the pool, drunk.

"Fuck, no!" Marvin laughed.

"C'mon, I'm serious..."

"There ain't but one fucking state that matters, and that's Texas," joked the other American. Marvin was a graduate of Texas A&M, and he had played professional football in Dallas.

"I help you," Hilde, one of the German women volunteered, emerging from the pool, wet and naked. "What do you need?"

"Can you list all the American states?" Danny asked.

"Sure, no problem," she said, and she quickly wrote down, from memory, a list of fifty-seven names.

"Oh God," Danny groaned. Scanning her list, he scratched Los Angeles, the Ozarks, Chicago, and Mexico, but he hesitated on New York City. Had it become a state in the two years he had been out of the country? What about Quaker State? Wasn't that a brand of engine oil?

He was frustrated, and he looked across the table at Hilde, and she looked across at him and smiled—and they went upstairs for the night, the conundrum put aside.

Of course, the first thing he did next morning was to go to the library of the Iran-America Society on Abassabad Avenue to look up a map of the states. He had forgotten Delaware in his original list, but he was right, there were only *fifty*, not fifty-one states.

Although it was a silly controversy, Danny had begun to feel his sanity was slipping away after two years teaching in Iran. Finding out he was *right* reassured him he was okay. He practiced writing the fifty states until he could do it without a mistake.

"I'm reporting back for work," he told his supervisor after his suspension expired.

"You stand there like you still believe you are right," the man told him, leaning back in his chair and crossing his arms over his fat belly.

"I am right. I looked it up."

"So did we," the supervisor smiled superciliously. "You know we buy some of our books from the DLI school in America?"

"Yes, so?"

"And you know we copy these books ourselves to save money?"

"Yes, I know."

"Here is one of the original books from America."

Not surprisingly, the book clearly said fifty-one. Danny knew it was a typographical error—or someone's insane joke on the Iranians that had been copied *ad infinitum* and was now firmly entrenched in the IIAF's mythology. Not one of the hundreds of instructors working for the Iranians over the years had ever called it into question!

"Will you now apologize to your class and explain that you were wrong?" the supervisor asked.

"No."

"You are suspended for another week."

"Marvin," Danny told his roommate that night. "I'm beginning to think that this country is the most perverse place I have ever been."

"Fucking amen," his roommate agreed.

Eventually, though, Danny had to think about eating and paying his bills, so one day he swallowed his pride and endured a humiliating public apology to his former students. "I'm sorry," he told them in front of the general, the school's staff, a hundred other instructors and a *sarboz* holding the Iranian flag. "There are fifty-one states in the United States. I will not make such a mistake again."

Strangely, in an Iranian way, the students warmed to him after his defeat, and he became the most popular instructor at Doshan Tappeh Air Force Base.

"I don't understand this country," Danny told friends afterward, "but I know I won't ever win here."

Several weeks later, Danny spotted Second Sergeant Hosseini walking near the lab building. "Excuse me," he said, running to catch up with the squat little soldier. "I'd like to ask you a question." He hated Hosseini for being "smarter" than he was, but convinced he was still right, he felt he had to ask.

"*Balle?*" Hosseini replied.

"Do you mind if I ask which state I forgot to put on my list? You know, the fifty-first state?"

"Oh," the Iranian smirked in triumph. "You forgot Puerto Rico. Better luck next the time."

-17-

MARILYN THE PISSER

"You pissed all over my bed!"

—*"Doc" MacCreary*

Having been raised poor, Danny's roommate, an ex-professional football player, had a hard time adjusting to his new wealth. Working for an Iranian shipping company right in the middle of the oil boom, Marvin Roberts found himself at the fulcrum of money interchange: those who had, and those who wanted; those with goods, and those with needs, so no matter who was dealing, Marvin benefited.

"Hell, I run this country," he boasted, and it was true. No one else had the sense to decide if a reefer ship loaded with frozen chickens could dock before a ship loaded with dry rice, but Marvin did, and his decisions were determined by who gave him the most cash under the table.

His nominal salary ranged from about $7500 to $10,000 a month, depending on the volume of trade during that period, plus all the perks: a luxurious house, cars, a generous expense account, a long vacation, and a huge Christmas bonus. He also received *baksheesh* in the form of goods, services, and cash; not infrequently, he generated some of his own investments at the expense of others. Since Danny had charge of only those funds that went through the household accounts, he had no way of accurately measuring Marvin's worth, but he assumed it was over two million dollars a year, quite a sum.

In March 1977, however, Danny got a good idea of his roommate's potential. It was the custom during the Iranian New Year, *No Ruz*, a sentimental holiday somewhat comparable to the family get-togethers of an American Christmas, to give tips to the postman, the neighborhood cops, the trash collector, and the servants. There was an endless stream of people popping up at *No Ruz*, especially when it became known that this was the home of a rich *farangi*.

By chance, Marvin had to go to a meeting in New York that season, so rather than have his tires slashed, his mail delayed for months, and the trash never picked up, he told Danny, "Here, you take care of the tips this year."

He left a large sum of cash to be administered as needed, and in a little over a week, Danny disbursed nearly $200,000 in tips. At the same time, Marvin's secretary handed out an even larger amount to business associates. Weeks later, the big American confided during a commode hugging drunk, "Shit, I raked in three dollars for every one spent." Most of this money was, of course, illegal, untraceable, and untaxable.

Times were good. The house was full of women, liquor was cheap, hashish and opium were available, cars were fast, and motorcycles even faster. In the middle of a monumental mid-life crisis, freshly divorced, and free of kids and a mortgage for the first time in his life, Marvin did business with the powerful, made friends among the famous, pursued his unfulfilled desires with lowlifes, and indulged his appetites for drugs, sex, and alcohol.

Andrea finally stopped doing business with him. "His tastes, if such they can be called," she informed Danny when asked, "are becoming too much for my girls. We're used to better treatment, faster tricks, and more money."

As the months passed, Danny watched his roommate go through stages of depravity. He had a B&D stage; next, he went through an S&M phase. He often jeered at Danny for taking his own pleasures privately.

"Hey, let's share," he'd shout as Danny led a new girlfriend upstairs to his third-floor room.

"Nope."

"In that case, let me watch!"

"Find another hobby," Danny would answer in disgust, though he knew his roommate probably would.

It was inevitable Marvin's appetite for excitement would go beyond excessive; he simply had too many personal problems. Usually drinking a liter of vodka a day, he often partied on two or even three. The only man Danny ever met who could drink so much alcohol he could become sober again, Marvin sometimes binged on sex and drugs. To his associates, he bragged he could screw for hours without getting off, but with Danny he admitted, "I can't cum anymore. I don't know what's wrong. I get hard as a brick, but I can't cum. I haven't cum in eight weeks..."

"You're trying too hard," Danny advised. "Try relaxing."

"That's why I drink so much...."

"Then maybe you should stop drinking—"

"Don't say that," Marvin interrupted. "I've got to do something I enjoy."

Through all the depravity, Danny paid the bills, kept accounts, and minded his own business. Luckily, he was gone a lot too. What with work, tricks for Andrea and his own dating, he didn't see much of what was happening at the villa.

Marvin's parties had become legendary, as did his largess. If someone went to dinner with Marvin, Marvin picked up the tab. If a woman flashed cleavage, he would reward her with jewelry and a proposition. Clinging homosexuals became his trusted advisors, procurers and druggies his best friends. Wild people flocked to him like hornets to meat hanging on a hook, and it was surprising to what extent Danny's own friendship with the "rough trade" of mercenaries, prostitutes, military, and criminals began to overlap his roommate's licentious crowd.

About twice a month, Marvin would decide, "Let's have a blast," and fifty or sixty of his friends would be invited over for a bacchanal. Sometimes it was a pool party, a costume ball, or an open-house reception with Marvin providing all the food and most of the liquor and hashish. Occasionally, he would have a "rip-snorter" for business purposes, to which two or three hundred guests would be invited. This being Iran, where an invitation customarily included friends and family too, there was no way to predict how many would actually show up for such parties, so Danny had to plan for as many as five hundred people.

Normally, Danny stayed at these parties for only for an hour or so. Prior to the festivities, he would have done all the planning, assigned the servants their duties and made sure the drinks and food were adequate. By the time the decorations were ready and the Persian carpets rolled up and locked in his bedroom upstairs, he was already tired. The drinking, drugs, vomit, sex, noxious smoke, music, fist fights, and the same old gossip got on his nerves after three or four hours—and these parties could last all night! Usually arranging to spend the evening at Andrea's office while she and the girls circulated at Marvin's party to drum up business, Danny would enjoy a quiet evening of gin rummy with Shamsa, who wistfully talked of becoming a prostitute herself someday. Shamsa never let on that she was willing ... with Danny ... if only ... but he didn't figure it out. She was a natural match for him, but he never saw it.

Sometimes, though, Danny would play host at a party for a few hours.

Nursing a gin and tonic, he would circulate among the guests and flirt with the women; even so, he always left early and alone. Still, there was one party in the summer of 1977 that everyone in Teheran knew would be the biggest and wildest of all. Even Danny wasn't going to miss a minute.

"How much is it costing?" Marvin grumbled the morning before the party.

"Three hundred and sixty thousand tomans," Danny answered without even consulting his account books. He was busy fixing a leaky toilet and didn't appreciate his roommate's intrusion.

"Shit, fifty thousand dollars."

"C'mon," Danny grumped back. "You get plenty of business from these parties. You charge your company for all the expenses, yet you still deduct them from your taxes. Get real!"

Danny was increasingly frustrated with his roommate's questionable financial dealings. Marvin was becoming excessively petty. Just two weeks before, he had ordered his company auditor to go over the household finances because he suspected Danny of embezzlement. "Hey," Marvin shouted as they went over the books, "What's this goddamned tube of toothpaste for the third-floor bathroom doing here as a fucking household expense? Pay for personal items yourself, asshole!"

Questioning a two hundred-rial tube of toothpaste from a budget of several million a month was too much for Danny. "What do you mean a personal item? We needed it for the guests."

"Listen, if we need it so fucking bad, let the guests pay!" Marvin shouted.

In answer, Danny pulled some coins from his pocket and threw them at his roommate's face. As he walked away, he noticed Marvin picked the money up and was even counting it.

He was unable to talk to Marvin for a week afterwards, but it taught him generous people could also be the greediest. While Marvin footed the bills for all his friends, he remembered the costs to the rial. His new cocaine-smuggling operation—in which he used a few stewardesses to carry the product for him through customs—was dropping rapidly now that the Hashemi family was moving into that lucrative business. Even so, the day before the big party, he settled into his old self again and got on the phone to invite two hundred more guests. Andrea and her girls were coming; Masud, Carl, Bob Fraser, Ralf, and even Shamsa were invited. Amazingly, he also asked Sadjewi Hashemi and ten or fifteen of his family and goons to come. The rival Sadeghi gang was invited too, as were government types from the American embassy, Iranian military men, and dozens of foreign expatriates and businessmen.

That night, Danny found himself leaning against a wall talking with a fat American woman whose husband worked for EDS, a firm trying to computerize the vast Iranian social services system. "There's some weird people here tonight huh?" she said, pointing at the crowd.

"Yeah, a lot of weird people," he agreed absently.

Just then Ralf passed by and patted his shoulder affectionately. "Good evening, Doc," the lumbering German greeted him. Dressed in a tweed sport coat, flared trousers and expensive cowboy boots, Ralf looked as uncomfortable in fine clothes as a schoolboy going to church in a suit and tie.

"Hi, Ralf," Danny answered.

"Where do you know him from?" the woman asked, as she pulled the collar of her blouse tighter around her neck.

"We sometimes work together. We're friends."

"But he's supposed to be a mercenary! He's killed people, they say!"

"How do you know that?"

"I saw him at a party a few weeks ago. Someone told me about him."

"Technically, you could call me a mercenary too," Danny said, "because I work for a foreign military."

"Well, he's the first real mercenary I ever saw," she answered. "He's a dangerous man."

Danny looked around the party at his friends. Across the room, Andrea was sipping a drink, a hairy Iranian sitting beside her with his arm around her waist. The girls were everywhere. He noticed Puff Omura seated on the pillows lining one wall, languidly smoking opium from a brass *hookah* and watching him with her dark eyes. It had been over a year since they had slept together, yet she still eyed him seductively. He never knew what she had on her mind, but he really liked Puff. Those eyes always attracted him; did she ever really want him? In another corner of the immense room, Sadjewi Hashemi and three of his bodyguards were talking to their counterparts among the Sadeghis. In a different part of the room, Carl Wolffe was discussing helicopters with an Iranian Army colonel. One of the Shah's relatives sat nearby, deep in discussion with a Korean shipbuilder. Both were smoking opium. Drug addicts high on hashish, coke, opium, or all three flitted around the room while Ali Nassiri fawned over his latest conquest, a young teenaged Adonis in tight blue pants. The Russian neighbors were practically taking notes on the conversations. The CIA and SAVAK were well represented, and Israeli and other intelligence operatives were working the crowd, too. As he looked around, Danny realized he knew all these people, some rather well, some not so well, some too well.

"Yeah, there's some weird people here tonight," he repeated, but the woman had already turned away to talk to one of her friends, a housewife married to an American diplomat, who ate commissary food, shopped in the embassy PX, used her APO mail privileges exclusively, and proudly asserted she would never mix with these "damn Arabs." Danny shook his head at the women's ignorance and walked away.

Late that evening, he encountered a woman like none he had ever seen before, a creature of the night. She had long, waist-length black hair, an alabaster complexion, and black eyes. She was introduced to him as Marilyn the Pisser, and apparently, she had no other name. People assumed from her accent she was English, but as the rumors said, several years earlier, her mind seared by a drug overdose in Isfahan, she had lost her money, her passport, her identity—everything but her life—and she had been screwed ever since. Marilyn had survived through the kindness of strangers, but she had become a welfare whore who had been fucked in every combination by nearly everyone. Taken in by businessmen, foreigners, and Iranians for a night, a week, or a month, she frequented parties, each time on the arm or arms of strangers. She was passed from man to man like a white elephant.

Characteristically drunk and stoned after such parties, she was practically limp when some stranger carried her home like a door prize. She had become a standing joke, someone to laugh about with the guys, while legend had it she had been screwed so often she had lost control of her bladder, hence her nickname. Out of curiosity Danny watched her over the top of his drink, then turned his attention elsewhere.

"Heinz Reibach just told me to check out the bathroom on the second floor," Marvin whispered excitedly as he joined Danny at one of the bars. "There's some Iranian girl getting it up there. Shit, I was going to go up and watch, but Heinz told me to wait. Hey, did you meet Marilyn the Pisser yet?"

"Yeah," Danny said with a grimace "A scuz, isn't she?"

"Maybe," Marvin grinned excitedly, "but Heinz took her home from a party last week, and he told me I could fucking well have her tonight. He owes me for all the business I've steered his way!"

"You're not that desperate," Danny grumbled. His protest was half-hearted, though. After Marvin's recent escapades, Danny was not sure his roommate wasn't incurably bizarre.

"Hell, I ought to try her out at least once," Marvin countered, "just to say I did! She's famous."

Next morning Danny wasn't surprised to find Marilyn still at the house. Returning home from a late-night trick that involved a veritable suitcase full of money, he found Marvin and Marilyn curled up naked on a beanbag chair in the middle of Danny's expensive Turkoman treasure carpet, smoking opium from a brass hubbly-bubbly.

"Don't you two burn my carpet," Danny shouted. He was pleased the servants were busy cleaning the house after last night's extravaganza. Most of the floors were already clean, and the carpets were down and swept. There was a tinkling of dishes from the kitchen and a rustle of linens being snapped onto the beds.

"Fuck you, asshole!" Marvin called after him as Danny went upstairs to bed. "I pay the rent on this house, and I can fucking well sit where I want."

Two hours later, Danny was nudged awake by a naked woman. "I'm c-cold," Marilyn chattered dismally, cuddling up to him for warmth. In truth, she <u>was</u> cold, colder than any living human Danny had ever felt, and she gave him the willies. Disgusted by the clamminess of her skin, he rolled away to avoid touching her and tried to go back to sleep. Though she was naked and willing to have sex with him, he figured she was riddled with diseases.

Moments later, however, he was startled awake by a childhood memory. "What?" he mumbled, reaching down to feel the sheets. "What in the world? Oh, GODDAMN!" he howled, jumping out of his bed. "You whore, get out of my bed. You're wetting the sheets!"

"Sleep," Marilyn moaned, clutching his warm pillow to her naked breasts as she rolled over, completely unconscious. Furiously, Danny ripped a spare blanket from his closet and made himself a bed on a pile of carpets across the room. The long party, followed by an overly long trick with a greedy businessman had made him tired; he wanted a couple of hours sleep. He hoped he would wake up to find Marilyn's visit a bad dream.

"I see you had a good time this morning," Marvin roared angrily, poking him awake an hour later. "I can't even bring a girl home to fuck without you fucking her too. First the toothpaste, now my woman!"

"I didn't fuck her, Marvin," Danny said grumpily, putting on his glasses. "Go feel what your whore did to my bed."

"I don't give a flying fuck what she did to your bed!" Marvin screamed.

"Listen, moron, you better care what she did!"

"Fuck you. I own this house," Marvin bellowed. "I can do what I want!"

"She pissed my bed!" Danny screamed. "I'm going to have to clean it. The servants won't touch it! I'm the only one that ever does anything here. I always have to clean up your messes—"

"Damn you," Marvin yelled, yanking the woman out of Danny's bed and dragging her from the room. "I want you out of this house by tomorrow."

"You'd starve to death, you loser," Danny shouted after him, feeling like an idiot for getting into such an inane shouting match. He was reasonably certain Marvin couldn't get along without him, but he was disgusted with how badly the living arrangements were turning out. After dressing in a pair of old jeans, he stripped his bed, which was actually just a foam pad laid on a plywood base. Marilyn probably didn't weigh a hundred and twenty pounds, but the mattress was saturated with urine. Dragging it out onto the balcony, he dumped it into the courtyard below, intending to hose it down later. Amazed such a tiny woman could have so much fluid in her, he was absolutely horrified by the mess downstairs. Marvin's beautiful, ten-foot French sofa was similarly saturated, and a trail of sickly sweet urine led into the living room, where a puddle of piss glistened from the middle of Danny's two hundred-year-old Turkoman carpet. Though they continued to live together as roommates, and Danny still ran the house and its accounts, Danny and Marvin hardly spoke to each other ever again.

-18-

THE HASHEMI MURDERS

"It is sometimes necessary to exact justice in our business."
—*Andrea Wilcox*

Like a pattern on an extravagant Persian carpet, morning sunlight dappled across Danny's bed while a light breeze rippled through his tawny Isfahan-cloth curtains, but he only screwed his eyes shut more tightly and rolled over, trying to get a few more minutes' sleep. Since he had escorted Andrea's girls and worked tricks of his own every night during the last month, now, with nothing on his schedule and temporarily without a girlfriend to spend the day in bed with, he only wanted to sleep until noon and then go swimming in the pool outside his window. His lazy weekend plans were shattered, though, when one of the stewardesses threw open his bedroom door to announce, "Doc, you've got visitors downstairs."

Padding barefoot across the hall dressed only in a wrinkled bathrobe, he was not surprised to find one of the many new women living in the villa had splashed make-up on the commode and counter top of his bathroom again. He ran some cold water anyway, washed his face, and brushed his teeth while absently staring at his blurred image in the mirror. He was tired of all the strangers in his life. By the time he learned the names of the women staying at the villa, they would leave, only to be replaced with a fresh crop of stewardesses.

Few of these women stayed more than two months now. Since most of the international airlines were concerned with the rising political tensions in Iran, flight crews were limited in the length of their assignments in Teheran. Normally, pilots and stewardesses worked two days on, three off, but the women at the villa appeared to spend most of their time sleeping, smoking, or gossiping. None of them made any effort to learn Farsi or explore the country, so Danny had little sympathy for the so-called hardships they were suffering. Recently, there had begun to be routine electrical blackouts, and there was never more than twelve hours' of power a day. Up on the mansion's roof, a stewardess and her Iranian boyfriend were laughing as they hung out wash to dry on a clothesline. Clotheslines! Was this why he had put in heavy-duty wiring for a big American clothes dryer? God, Danny thought bitterly, if you couldn't have the perks of a luxury lifestyle, how were normal people coping?

"*Sobah kher.* Good morning," Masud Pooinak greeted him as soon as he stumbled downstairs.

Danny's shirt was only partially tucked into his pants, but he didn't care. "*Alle shoma khubay?*" he answered, somewhat less warmly. Scratching his scraggly face, he wondered if he shouldn't start growing a beard. Shaving was irritating his skin during the summer's heat; besides, many Iranian men were growing beards now, though theirs filled out much thicker than his since their facial hair started at the cheekbone.

"This morning we will go for a ride," Masud announced. "Andrea is waiting in the car."

"Tell her to come in. Have some tea while I take a shower," Danny yawned, unconsciously tucking in his shirt at mention of her name. Not a morning person, he resented her deciding to drive somewhere so early on a weekend, but if that's what she wanted, that's what she got. Andrea always got what she wanted. Suddenly wishing he had brushed his teeth better, he thought how strange it was this beautiful English woman had come to mean so much to him. Her other people made better money, Danny knew, but every time she snapped her fingers, he jumped like everyone else.

"Good morning, Doc," she smiled, lightly kissing him on the cheek as she breezed into the house moments later. She shed her floor-length fox coat and draped it across a chair in the foyer. She wore an expensive wool skirt and a Persian silk blouse, and, as usual, high heels. In fact, Danny remembered her in tennis shoes only when she was playing tennis, sandals only at garden parties, and barefoot when in a pool. The rest of the time she wore high heels. It was one of the things that set her apart from other women. It was part of her *persona*. And the higher the heels the better.

"Roommate home?" she asked, pressing her hands together in front of her face, a peculiar prayer-like thing she'd been doing lately. It played well with both Moslems and Oriental clients.

"Yeah, he's upstairs. I'll make some breakfast," he responded, stifling a yawn. What he really needed was a tall, cold bottle of Coca-Cola to wake him up. Too bad they hadn't had reliable refrigeration in two months. Perhaps if he threw all his remaining cokes into the evaporating swimming pool, they'd be cooler—but no, probably not. They would just get stolen by the servants. The servants were doing that a lot lately, but what made him most angry was that one of them had poisoned Khanoom, his two year-old female guard dog, the day before. She had been born wild in the streets. Danny had knelt beside her mother at milking time; the bitch had allowed him to take the puppy. An Iranian would have been attacked, but Danny was a "dog person," and Khanoom grew up to be a very special dog. She was smart; she understood English and Farsi—but, of course with accompanying hand signals.

Suspecting it was Sadeq, the gatekeeper who had always hated dogs, Danny resolved to lower the boom. In the last few months, Sadeq had moved his mother-in-law and a cousin to Teheran. Together with Sadeq, his wife and their four children, there were now eight people living in the gatekeeper's tiny quarters, a space not much bigger than an average bathroom in America. It was time Sadeq found another job, Danny decided, or moved most of his family back home to Shiraz. Danny had planned to take care of it this weekend, but now there was an interruption. The same thing was happening all over Teheran lately. A city of six million just two years before, now was estimated to have ten million.

"There's no need for breakfast," Andrea informed him. "I've already eaten. Tea is nice, but we must hurry."

"Where to?" he asked, leading her toward the kitchen. She always seemed to have plans for those around her, but he had never been able to decipher them beforehand.

Ignoring his question, Andrea paused at the door of the living room appraising the furnishings. Marvin's cheap rugs were all garish Pakistanis, but Danny's Turkoman and Balourchi carpets, and his enormous Kuwaiti dowry chest showed real taste. "Going native are we?" she asked, cynically.

"I like tribal carpets."

"So do I, but I would never buy one," she laughed. "They're not good investments."

"Sometimes you think too much about money," he criticized, taking time to open his brass-covered dowry chest to lift out a heavy red carpet. Unfolding it in the living room, he showed her his greatest treasure: a real Russian Boukhara from Samarkand more than three hundred and fifty years old.

"There's more pride in tribal carpets, though perhaps not so much technical skill," he explained. "This particular carpet was woven on a floor loom. My friend Benyamin Khodari can see five different hands in it and four seasonal lines where the colors are different. It probably took an entire family two years to make."

"I've never seen a better Boukhara," she admitted, "but Boukhara or Turkoman, they're all just faded red carpets. I prefer a Nain or an Isfahan for the monetary gains."

After carefully refolding the huge carpet, Danny put it in the chest, patting it fondly before closing and locking the lid again. He led the way through the house to the kitchen. The cook was busy plucking ducks for *fesenjan*—duck boiled in pomegranate juice, topped with ground walnuts, and served over rice—but she quickly put the dripping birds down and moved to make breakfast.

"*Nakhare*," Danny stopped her. "*Chai.*"

"Got anything for munchies with the tea?" Andrea asked. "For Masud, I mean. He hasn't eaten yet."

"Yeah, Mrs. Davood gets fresh pastries from a bakery on Saltanadabad every morning," Danny said. He opened a large white box on a nearby counter, laid out a selection of pastries on a silver platter then found some saucers and teacups for his friends. The steel samovar on the counter was hot and heavy; there was plenty of tea. Thank God cooking gas was still available or there would be rioting in the streets...well that was stupid! There already was rioting in the streets...!

"Do you mind if Ralf, Bob, and Carl come in too?" the woman inquired. Marvin had never liked Carl and had forbidden Danny to have him in the house; Ralf and Bob were *personae non-gratiae* too, since drunkenly trashing the pool area at the last party. Ralf had actually unzipped and pissed in the pool that night to insult Marvin. Standing at the edge of the pool in a turquoise leisure suit, Ralf's piss streamed into the water noisily; Marvin didn't stop him. He was scared of Ralf, but he forbade him to be in the house after that. At the moment, though, Marvin was taking a bath with one of the stewardesses and wouldn't know they were here.

"I'm sorry. I should have asked who else was with you. Sure, bring them in," Danny apologized. "This is my house too, and my friends are welcome here. Mrs. Davood will get tea for you. I'm going to take a shower."

When he came back downstairs, he found his friends scattered awkwardly around the kitchen. While Andrea sat with her back to the open doorway, the three mercenaries perched nervously on gray metal kitchen chairs facing the open glass of the garden door; Masud stood guarding the doorway to the rest of the house. Little things like this always set these men apart from everyone else he met, Danny realized, but in modern Iran, there was no need for such precautions. There was a strong king, a bustling economy, a powerful military, an effective secret police, and a fairly low crime rate. Why were they always so worried about security?

It was funny how his friends had ended up being not the gentle language instructors at Doshan Tappeh but, instead, professional soldiers, prostitutes, smugglers, and hired guns. Thinking back to the time he had been accused in London of attracting only the wrong kind of people, he realized he had learned a lot since those innocent days. That things had worked out this way made him strangely happy. He was actually one with these people. He cared about them.

"What's up?" he asked.

"We'll tell you in the car," Fraser answered, jumping to his feet. Masud stuffed the last of a sweet pastry in his mouth and led the way outside. They were to ride in Andrea's new Range Rover; Masud drove, Danny sat up front with Ralf, and Andrea sat in back, flanked by Fraser and Wolffe.

"This is not a good day," Andrea said as soon as they pulled into the busy traffic of Saltanadabad Avenue. "The Hashemis have invited us to an object lesson in the mountains. I must go, of course, and I chose Ralf, Carl, and Bob to go with me. Neither you nor Masud has to go," she declared, putting her hand on Danny's shoulder, and he turned around in his seat to look at her. "But I wanted you to come along. Forgive me, you don't really need to get involved in this part of my business, but I wanted ... well, I feel better with you along."

Uncharacteristically, she was fumbling with words, yet somehow, Danny understood the significance of what she was trying to say, and he was glad in his heart. There was something indefinable about his relationship with this woman. Never was she anything but polite and professional towards him, but once in a great long while an honesty crept into their comments to each other that told him she favored him. She was too high-maintenance for him to hope for more to develop between them—and the thought never even occurred to him—but it pleased him when he noticed a spark of feeling in her.

"Another thing," she continued, "Bob says that since you deal with the Hashemi family nearly every week now, it's best you know what you're up against. Having you along as a courier makes us less participants and more the observers. I don't like it but I do understand the necessity of this in a business like the Hashemis'."

Actually, Danny didn't understand what she was talking about, but the others seemed off in their own little worlds, looking out the windows in every direction. Danny noticed all of them were heavily armed, so there was no use talking about it. He sat back, stared out the window, and watched the crowded streets roll by.

An hour later, they parked along the curb near a warehouse in south Teheran. Several cars filled with men were already waiting there; nearby, a dozen burly men paced alongside the high wall of an old brick building. Obviously Hashemi guards and hired guns, all of the men looked armed.

Ten minutes later, Mohsen Hashemi, one of Sadjewi's younger sons, emerged from a steel gateway and approached their car. "Miss Wilcox," he smiled, greeting her through the open passenger window. "Who do we have with you today? The Allemani, Mr. Fraser, and Mr. Wolffey. Ah, good morning, Doctor!" he smiled as soon as he spotted Danny in the front seat. "You too? My father is inside. Would you like to come in and say hello?"

Andrea reached up and put her hand on Danny's shoulder to forbid it, but Wolffe pulled her hand away. Danny knew he had to meet the challenge.

"Yes, of course I'd enjoy seeing your father again," he replied, troubling Ralf to let him out of the car. Just the sight of the German getting out of the Range Rover made the Iranian finger his pistol, yet Danny walked right through a group of heavily armed Hashemi soldiers like they didn't even exist. "And how is your father today?" he asked as they entered the strongly fortified gate.

"He is in good health, thanks be to God!" Stopping abruptly, Mohsen instructed a guard with a G-3 assault rifle to frisk Danny and escort him across the compound. Several men were standing in the courtyard with machine guns and drawn pistols, and more waited inside the building, a dry, dusty warehouse with a dirt floor and an ancient, broken roof which admitted pigeons and shafts of sunlight. The warehouse smelled of delicate bazaar spices and baled *hashish*, gun oil, dust, and stale urine. Three men were on their knees in the middle of the floor, their hands bound behind their backs with baling wire, but no one seemed to pay them any attention. Aside from Alireza, Sadjewi's oldest son, who was talking with three Kurds in an office, Danny didn't see anyone else he knew.

"Doctor," Sadjewi Hashemi called from a dark corner. "Come, my friend. Sit with me over here."

"*Alle shoma khube?*" Danny asked, feeling his way into the darkness and sitting down beside the old man on a three-hundred-year-old Isfahan carpet hastily thrown onto a bale of *hashish* the size of a small refrigerator. He noted the aging gangster, one of the wealthiest men in Iran, was wearing the same threadbare brown sport jacket he wore every time Danny saw him, but today he had added a dirty gray sweater underneath. Sadjewi always looked and acted like a common *bazaari*, though his tastes and businesses were anything but ordinary. Brown-skinned and wrinkled from a childhood laboring in the fields, Sadjewi was crippled with arthritis but still agile-minded. Somewhere over seventy years old, he was rumored to speak ten languages fluently, and he had recently hired a tutor to teach him Japanese. The year before, he had made the obligatory pilgrimage to Mecca, and he now wanted to be called "Haji Sadjewi," a term of religious respect, but no one outside his family bothered. He was too evil to be a "haji." At first, Danny had tried addressing him as "Mr. Hashemi," but there were so many other Hashemis to deal with that he finally just settled on, "Sadjewi."

"You haven't come to my house in two weeks or more," the old man complained, twirling his prayer beads irritably. "Have you been well? Is business good?" Sadjewi never mentioned the failed wedding negotiations between the Sadeghis and Hashemis.

"Yes, Sadjewi, thank you. I've been very busy."

"I understand your Jewish friends, the Khodaris, have purchased an extraordinary antique carpet at an auction in London. They have returned this remarkable piece to Iran, its true home, to have a torn corner restored. When this work is completed, I would like you to represent me to them. Of course, I will pay you five percent of the final purchase price to bargain for me. That's between me and you only."

"Okay," Danny agreed. "Is this a carpet for your collection?" Sadjewi's home, an apartment on the top floor of a five-story building he owned, was filled with expensive but unremarkable carpets. Often bartering with these carpets, the old man was as likely to pay employees and soldiers with a rug as with money. For this reason, he seemed to have mostly Nains, Tabriz' and Isfahans, all easily convertible to cash.

"No, this carpet is not my personal taste. It's a wedding present for my nephew who is getting married at the end of the year. The carpet is an investment for these young people, especially in these uncertain times."

Having said this, Sadjewi rattled his prayer beads and sat quietly, lost in thought. Danny noticed the old man's left little fingernail was recently stained black. Mexican tar or Thai black opium. Sadjewi was said to be able to taste the purity and origin of every shipment he received.

Alireza concluded his business in the office and began to shout to men in the warehouse. Someone started a truck across the courtyard, and steel doors banged outside. "It's time to go," the old man announced suddenly, hopping off the bale of *hashish*. "It was good to see you again, my friend, Danny. *Khodahafez*."

"*Khodahafez*," Danny nodded. "And I will do what I can about the carpet."

"Thank you, Doctor. We will speak of it again at my home within the week," the old man muttered, scurrying off into the darkness; the armed guard reappeared at Danny's elbow to escort him back to Andrea's car. Another appeared and whisked the carpet away.

"You okay?" Ralf inquired, scowling at the ten guards around the Range Rover as he let Danny back in.

"Yeah, I'm fine. The old man wants me to buy a carpet from Benyamin Khodari."

"The old man himself?" Bob Fraser asked incredulously.

"Doc has a friendship with the old crocodile," Andrea interrupted. "I see no harm in it. Doc is a courier. He can walk into and out of snake pits without being harmed."

"But is it safe?" Fraser persisted, a look of genuine concern on his face. "A snakepit is one thing, but Sadjewi Hashemi's own warehouse is another! There's no way we can offer protection in there."

"I think it's safe. Doc's learned to separate business from his personal life," she declared. "It's all right to be friendly up to a point. Besides, Sadjewi just might prove useful someday."

At that very moment, the outer steel gates opened, and a big truck burst out of the drive, its back covered with a piece of dirty gray canvas. Turning right, it hurtled away down the narrow, crowded street, quickly followed by six or eight other cars— Mercedes, Paykans, BMW's, and a Fiat. Masud pulled the Range Rover into the street and joined the convoy. It was hard to tell in the traffic how many cars were following the truck, but by the time they got on the Karadj Freeway headed west of Teheran, Ralf guessed there were at least a dozen vehicles, most of them packed with armed men.

The small town of Karadj was just a blur. About ten kilometers farther west on the Qazvin Highway, the truck slowed, then turned north on a rutted farm road toward the mountains. Thirty minutes later, the convoy crossed a cobbled stream and entered a high, dusty plateau. Another ten minutes passed before the truck pulled over and stopped. It was high noon.

Danny knew somewhere in the mountains west of them was the hideout of the *Hashshashin*, history's legendary Assassins. Far out in the desert south of them, dozens of mounds marked the sites of lost, dead villages, but here on the plateau, there was only rock, dust, and wind. What a miserable place to die, he thought, shivering against the cold.

Masud had parked in such a way they could leave quickly, and Carl ordered Masud to stay by the car and keep the keys in the ignition. Then, flanking Andrea on either side, Wolffe and Fraser escorted her to a slight rise overlooking the desert. Ralf followed twenty feet behind them to the left, while Danny walked alone to the right as he had been taught. Watch everyone but walk alone, he remembered Fraser instructing him. He looked about, memorizing the faces. There were about forty men waiting there in seven distinct groupings in the dusty wind, but none of them complained at the delay as Andrea picked her way over the rocks in her high heels. A man Danny knew to be a *bazaari*, clad in the usual dirty sports jacket over a gray sweater, dispatched one of his retainers to a car to fetch a folding chair for the woman. The only other sounds were the crunching of gravel underfoot and the whine of the desert wind.

About fifty feet downslope, a shallow hole had been scraped into the rocky soil. Two rusty shovels were stuck in a mound of dirt nearby, and guards armed with machine guns were scattered everywhere around the crowd. A couple of peasants were making tea over a smoky fire near the hole, while a hundred meters south, fifty sheep were grazing on a small hill.

There was a shout, and the three men Danny had seen in the warehouse were brought out of the truck and hounded to the edge of the hole. As they were forced to kneel, one wept openly, another looked dazed or stoned, and the last stared into the open grave stoically. Alireza Hashemi and several gunmen surrounded the prisoners, waiting patiently while Mohsen Hashemi escorted his elderly father from a car. There was complete silence while the old man struggled up the slope, but when he finally made it to the group by the hole, he seemed uninterested in the execution.

His son, Alireza, launched into a long monologue in Farsi detailing the sins and offenses of the three prisoners. It was not important the speech be translated for Andrea and her associates since its purpose was already understood as a lesson—a warning among competitors—but Danny, who knew Farsi well, understood only some of the frantic monologue pertaining to times, days, *hashish*, and money. It didn't make sense. He waited patiently for it to end.

Moments later, Sadjewi interrupted his son, and they conversed in harsh whispers for nearly five minutes. Apparently satisfied, the old man abruptly turned his back on the cowering prisoners to make his way unsteadily up to the little knoll, every eye but the prisoners' and Alireza's following him. When Danny realized the old man was coming straight toward him, he froze in terror. What could the old man want so badly he would interrupt an execution?

"Doctor, my friend," the old man wheezed, putting his gnarled hand on Danny's arm. "I have thought about this carpet some more. It is very important these damned Jews do not know whom you buy the carpet for. They will charge me double the price. You must promise to conduct the purchase with discretion."

"Of course," Danny agreed, amazed Sadjewi could be worried about business at a time like this.

"That is good, my friend. I do not want to spend more than a million, five hundred thousand tomans for the carpet. [About $200,000] This is a decent profit over what they paid for it in London."

Meanwhile, Alireza motioned for his henchmen to back away from the doomed men, except for Reza Malek-zadeh, his personal guard, who stepped forward and pulled the slide on a .22 automatic to chamber a cartridge. After making a brief concluding remark, Alireza called out to his father.

Sadjewi, however, was still grappling with the complexities of the carpet deal. Turning deferentially to the beautiful blonde woman, he said, "Miss Wilcox, earlier I asked your courier to arrange the purchase of a carpet for my family. I offered him a five percent commission, but my son says this should be a professional courtesy between us."

"Of course. I'll take care of it," Andrea answered coldly. "It's probably best it's handled through me anyway," she said, glancing at Danny, "rather than through a private commission."

"Very good. *Motchakeram.*" Rather apologetically, the elder Hashemi turned towards Danny again. Speaking in a hushed tone without ever looking him in the eye, Sadjewi whined, "Doctor, my son does not understand commitments like this, but it will be no problem for you. You are on retainer to Miss Wilcox, and the obligation is hers. She is a rich woman. You understand? You will get your money from her."

Danny was too disgusted to respond, but there was actually no need. The old man had welshed on the deal and put Andrea in the uncomfortable position of paying the commission. It was so typical of what Danny had learned to expect of an Iranian. Knowing he would never see any money from Andrea either, he swore in his heart to negotiate a premium price for the carpet. Fortunately, his reply to the old man was preempted by a final, shrill summation from Alireza, followed by a great sigh, whether from the desert wind or from the prisoners he could not say. Hardly looking at the drama downslope, Sadjewi waved his hand gaily.

"*Khodahafez*," Alireza shouted at the prisoners.

Reza Malek-zadeh stepped behind the first victim and placed the muzzle of the pistol to the back of his neck. Pop! The man's body fell forward; his head snapped back, a surprised look on his face. As the body fell into the hole, there was another Pop! And another Pop! The job was done; the three were dead. The peasants by the fire rushed over and began to fill the pit with gravel and broken rocks. When they were done, all three victims' feet protruded from their rubbly grave. Meanwhile, the killer, who had hardly glanced at his victims, looked up to meet the eyes of Ralf, then Carl, and finally Bob. It was a look of professional recognition. Rather deliberately, he looked then at Masud and winked. Pointing his finger like a gun at Danny, he said, "Bang!"

Danny smiled and genuflected.

"I can't believe it," Danny mumbled thirty minutes later during the silent drive back to Teheran.

"I can't either," Ralf agreed, deeply depressed. "Two years ago, when I first came to Iran, this was not possible. People disappeared, and business went on. What the Hashemis' purpose is now, I cannot say, but it worries me they are changing the rules. A public execution. There is no reason for that, except to warn us. Mark my words, hard times are coming, Andrea. The Hashemis are playing a dangerous game, and we must be careful."

"No, that's not what I meant," Danny interjected. "Can you believe the old man was worried about a carpet deal at such a time?"

He didn't understand why his friends broke out into laughter, punching and tickling him mercilessly, but at least the tension of that terrible morning was broken. Together, they returned to enjoy what was left of their weekend. Andrea had recently discovered a Chinese restaurant on Takht-e-Tavous Avenue, where they all got drunk and ate like pigs. She paid the tab, a first for her. Danny's innocence was gone forever.

~ 19 ~

SANDY

"She was a friend of mine, but I couldn't help her...."
—"Doc," sitting in the lobby of the Wolf Hotel, Saratoga, Wyoming

Although she had a tendency to put on weight, Sandy Langarudi was one of the most attractive women Danny MacCreary ever met. With her flawless complexion, candy-blonde hair, big blue eyes, curvy body, and ready smile, she, like many American women married to Iranian men, had met her husband in college, in her case the University of Texas at Austin. To her, Parviz Langarudi was an exotic, charming engineering student with an accent, a very hairy burly chest, and a man who had courted her for more than two years. He seemed like a kind, considerate gentleman—though in fact, he was probably nothing of the sort.

With little knowledge of the Middle East other than childhood tales about Aladdin and Ali Baba, Sandy was a romantic masochist, and she never knew it. Parviz was everything she had ever dreamt about: swarthy good looks that exuded sex, flashing black eyes, and such a hairy, barrel chest. Unlike the American *boys* she had dated, Parviz wasn't shy about his assets either. He wore tight pants to show off his nicely rounded buns and strong legs, and he sported three gold chains around his neck—how European, how chic! He even carried a man-purse, something the Texas hicks refused to do. He gave her flowers and recited romantic poetry from his country, and he positively drooled when she went braless or showed cleavage. He always noticed when her breasts flopped when she walked.

As he wormed his way into her heart, though, Parviz became demanding and bitchy. As much as he charmed her, however, she was suffocated by his control, and Sandy grew restive. "Maybe we should see less of each other," she suggested one night.

Never a fool, of course, Parviz reluctantly promised, "I will do better. Perhaps you're right. I will graduate from college soon and I have been thinking about going home to my country, Iran, the Persia of old! There are many opportunities there."

"Home?" she said in surprise. "But that's so far away!"

"Yes, it is. We might never see each other again."

"Parviz, I don't know what I'd do—"

"Of course, I would stay in Texas if you really wanted me to, but Sandy, Iran, the Persia of old, the romance, the roses, the carpets, and the oil money beckon me. Let's get married and move back to my country."

And so, to the chagrin of her father, a retired Army colonel who didn't like "that damned Arab," Sandy and Parviz were married by a justice of the peace in Austin, Texas in July 1975. Sandy was twenty years old and wanted a life of her own, a family, and a man to take care of her forever.

The reality hit as soon as they stepped off the plane in Teheran. Showing a complete disdain for the details of their arrival, Parviz walked away from the luggage, swept through passport immigration control alone, and ran off into the welcoming arms of his family. Thirty minutes later, after Sandy had cleared the luggage through customs, found a porter to help her, and presented herself to the family, she was greeted with cold stares. Attempting to look her best, she had worn a bright flowery blouse over black slacks, sunglasses, Mexican sandals, and a big straw hat. She knew she looked good, but the entire family—including Parviz— gawked at her like she was a deformed cripple.

Obviously, Parviz had never told the family about his American wife. Giving them her biggest Texas smile, she introduced herself, "I'm Sandy ... Sandy Langarudi, Mrs. *Parviz* Langarudi."

Strangely, the family broke out into hysterical laughter at this unexpected surprise, then swarmed excitedly all over Parviz, congratulating him. A few minutes later, the father and a younger brother broke away long enough to take charge of the baggage, even insisting on carrying Sandy's purse. Since none of the family spoke English, Parviz acted as translator during the long drive across Teheran, but oddly, only for his family's questions to her and not for her questions to them. Later, he complained privately, "Button your blouse. You are showing too much tit. You are acting like a whore!"

"But darling," she said in surprise, "you know this blouse doesn't have a top button. You never minded before...."

It was a scene acted out thousands of times by thousands of foreign wives, but undoubtedly, the most naive were the Americans. For most of these women, their worst depression came when they had to convert to Islam, give up their passports to their husbands, and accept Iranian citizenship.

For Sandy, it was worse. Parviz demanded she learn Farsi "just like he had learned English." He neglected to mention he had spent five years studying English in formal classes in Isfahan and then had a private tutor for two years in Teheran; he remembered only those first painful years in college in Texas, isolated and lonely in a new culture. Parviz also never admitted he spent every spare moment in America with other Iranians so he could speak Farsi and satisfy his desire for Iranian food. Now, however, he demanded Sandy have nothing to do with Americans. She was expected to spend her time with her domineering mother-in-law in order to learn the proper skills of a good wife. She must learn to make Persian rice.

The preparation of rice, the basis of Iranian cuisine, was both an art form and a litmus test for a young wife. First, the rice had to be sorted by hand, and the gravel, chaff, and discolored grains discarded. Believing each grain had to be separate and flaky, Iranians often soaked the rice to eliminate all the surface starch. It was then cooked in a pot of boiling water with some oil, and then steamed until done. Perfect dry rice with a slight nutty flavor was the result, accompanied by an added treat—the crunchy, crusted rice from the bottom of the pot. Iranians ate their rice plain, topped with raw eggs (in Farsi, "*tokhm-e-morgh*," or literally the seed of a chicken) or delicately seasoned with expensive *saffron* or *soumakh*.

The rice was difficult to make to everyone's satisfaction, and Sandy just didn't have the aptitude to please her fussy mother-in-law. "What do you mean they don't like my rice?" she screamed one night after Parviz hustled her out of the dining room to confront her in the kitchen. "I worked hard! Do you know that? I worked all day with your mother bitching at me, just so you and your cousins, grandparents, and acquaintances can sit out there and pass judgment. 'It's too salty.'; 'It's too dry;' 'It's too moist.'!" she mocked.

"My family is particular—"

"I don't give a damn about your family, Parviz. What about *me*?"

"You disgraced me—and you are embarrassing me now! My family can hear this what you say. You think they are stupid?"

As hard as she could. Sandy flung a metal platter against a wall and screamed, "I don't care if they hear us! I don't give a shit what their opinion is. I only care about you, Parv—"

He hit her and not just once. He knocked her down, he kicked her, he threw her against the stove, he bent her neck until it popped, and then he slapped her repeatedly. The beating lasted fifteen minutes, and when he allowed her to scrape herself off the floor and run for their bedroom, she caught a glimpse of the family sitting at the table, smiling that order had been restored.

Months later, when Danny MacCreary arrived in Teheran and began his training at Doshan Tappeh, he noticed the pretty blonde sitting alone in a corner of the lounge. Although he didn't get an opportunity to speak to her, a few days later he found himself standing next to her in line at the cafeteria. "Hi," he nodded, giving her his best smile.

"Hi."

"My name's Danny. Danny MacCreary."

"Sandy Langarudi."

"Langarudi's an Iranian name."

"My husband's an Iranian," she replied, looking away.

"Lived here long?" he asked, disappointed to hear she was married—especially to an Iranian.

"Yes, I have. A long time...."

"A few years?"

"No, just since July."

Three weeks passed, and every day they had a similar exchange. One day, on the way home on the crowded bus, he found himself sitting quite alone. He was feeling lonely and sorry for himself. People were avoiding him, though he didn't know why. Suddenly, the pretty blonde got up from her seat and came down the aisle. "Is this seat taken?" she asked.

"No," he said. "How are you doing today?"

"Okay."

"You look tired."

"I am. I'm..." and she looked at him with the most soulful expression on her face, a look of lost hope, the look of a Wyoming beaver, its foot in a steel trap knowing it would drown. It was the look of the captured. "I'm pregnant," she said.

"Oh," Danny said, smiling awkwardly. Like many single men, he was at a loss dealing with pregnancy and often found himself making a fuss over pregnant women and new babies. "Is this your first child?"

"Yes."

"Congratulations!"

A half hour later, she announced, "It's a boy."

"How do you know?"

"It kicks so much."

"Is it kicking you now?" he asked, looking at her belly in wonder.

"Would you like to feel him?" she offered.

"Yes, I would," he said, breaking into a grin.

Taking his right hand in both of hers, she placed it firmly on her swollen belly. "There. Did you feel that?" she asked.

"Yeah!" he chuckled.

They were friends ever afterward, though it was difficult for a man and a woman to be friends in Iran. After he was sent to work at Mehrabod Junubi, the only chance Danny had to see Sandy was on the weekends, but at least once a month, they would meet at Quality Persian Carpet and sneak away to have lunch somewhere.

"This is not a good thing, this friendship with that woman," his Jewish friend, Benyamin Khodari, complained. "I know you think you are just friends, but friendship between a man and a woman is not natural to a Moslem. It says in the Koran just being alone in a room with a woman implies sex. Sex in the mind is sex in the body, and don't fool yourself, Danny, you have imagined sex with her."

"C'mon, Benyamin. She doesn't have anybody to confide in."

"If you ever get caught together," the carpet dealer warned, "her husband must kill you to get his honor back. He would never be arrested for such a crime. Look around you. This is Iran, not America. Family honor is everything here."

"I know," Danny laughed, for he had been in the country long enough to understand some of its peculiar laws. "The police would probably congratulate him for murdering me, but she doesn't have anyone else."

But Sandy did have other friends, and they were all sad wives married to Iranians like her. After she gave birth to her first child, one of them warned, "Watch out for your mother-in-law and the other women of the family."

"Why?"

"The Langarudis are village people recently moved to the city, aren't they?"

"Yes."

"Well, they might still follow some of the time-honored traditions of this fucked-up country."

"What do you mean?" she asked.

"You see that woman, Myra, in the back of the instructor's lounge? Just ask her."

"You mean that old gray-haired lady?" Sandy asked.

"She's not old. She's early forties."

Myra'd had five children and was content in a sad way now that she and her family had a home of their own. "So what do you want me to say?" the wasted woman asked, stubbing out her twentieth cigarette and peering through wrinkled eyes. "Do you really want to know? I don't think they even do it anymore, except in the villages down south."

"Do what?"

"Salt dildo."

"What?" Sandy asked in horror.

"It's an old custom. You know how these guys always want it nice and tight? After you have the first baby, you're all stretched out and don't give enough 'satisfaction.'"

Sandy looked away, realizing for the first time she was not alone. "Last night, Parviz raped me."

"I don't doubt it," Myra said, bitterly pursing her lips. "Anyway, it's usually the mother-in-law's duty to do it in order to keep it in the family. She buys this dildo made of salt in the bazaar; the women of the family tie the young mother down and cram it up her for a couple of hours. It tightens her up with scar tissue, her husband gets more 'satisfaction,' and he doesn't wander, so everyone in the family is happier."

"That's terrible."

"Yeah, you get numb down there after a while," Myra sighed, "but after your second or third kid, sex doesn't matter anymore."

Shocked, but not surprised, Sandy whispered what had happened to her the night before. Parviz wanted to turn in early, she told the older woman, but she still had homework to do and offered to join him later.

"Now, Sandy," he ordered, undoing his pajama bottoms.

Smiling tiredly, she ran her fingers through her hair "Look, Parviz, not tonight. God, I just had a baby three weeks ago. "

"Let's go."

"No."

"Let's go," he insisted.

"No!"

He grabbed her arm and roughly marched her to the bedroom, throwing her facedown on the bed. "Yes," he said, undoing his pajamas.

"No. I don't feel good, and I'm not going to—"

Parviz never paid any attention to her objections. He forced her face into the blankets and pulled her dress up to her waist.

"Don't! Let go of me. NO!" she screamed, as she felt him jamming his finger up her. "Leave me alone!"

"No, baby. You know I need … *relief*." The word never sounded so dirty. Afterwards, Sandy sat on the floor and wept.

"Danny?" she asked a few days later. "You know a lot of Iranian men, don't you?"

"Quite a few," he answered.

"Do you think most of them are queer—I mean deep inside?"

"Yep."

As a heterosexual American male, Danny'd had adjustment problems of his own in Iran. The hand-holding, the grab-ass games of teenage boys, the surreptitious close contact on a crowded bus, the ubiquitous little tea boys mincing around, the rich and famous old men with their youthful paramours—even the fondness of Ali Nassiri, Andrea's dear friend—were very threatening.

Iranian teenagers up to the time of marriage seemed to prefer the company of other boys. The men were supposed to be great fucks after they were married; Danny had met several Western women who claimed the average Iranian man could get it up several times a day, but it didn't last long. Sometime after the births of their second or third child, many of the men began to consort with their male friends again, until by old age they spent all their time in tea shops making kissing sounds at young, round-assed boys walking past.

As a result, Danny had little respect for the sexual preferences of Iranian men. Even his friend Benyamin exhibited tendencies that sometimes put him on the defensive, and Benyamin's younger brother, Ibrahim, had the most extensive collection of homosexual Persian miniatures that he had ever seen. Despite Ibrahim's homosexuality, however, Danny liked the gentle Iranian and often spent afternoons talking about carpets with him. Ibrahim's cluttered apartment, upstairs from the family's carpet store and warehouses, was one of his favorite places, and he often went there to sit and read while Ibrahim played the *santur* or talked with his many friends on the phone.

"OH! Look, look!" Ibrahim once exclaimed, holding up a magnifying glass to analyze the details of a tiny new miniature he had bought recently. "Look, the stallion's rod. It push through the woman's … how do you call this in English?"

"Vagina, pussy, cunt, snatch, twat," Danny said. "And that's not a stallion. A stallion is a male horse."

"Oh! Yes, and the man in this painting is such a *horse!*" Ibrahim laughed gleefully.

Two years later, Danny was surprised to learn Ibrahim was in love with him and had written hundreds of verses of romantic poetry about him. By this time, he had so well adapted to the culture that he was not horrified; instead, he put his arms around the tearful Iranian and hugged him. "Thank you, Ibrahim. I'm deeply touched—but you know I've never thought of you that way."

"Yes, it is unrequited love!" Ibrahim wailed. "You will never understand the passion one man can have for another."

"Perhaps someday," Danny suggested, "you could copy your best poetry for me."

"Doc, I'll make you a deal," Ibrahim said. "You often wear this hat, this fishing hat you say brings you so much luck. Give me this hat, warm from your body, and I will copy my finest verses for you."

Reluctantly, Danny took off his favorite hat, a tweed ascot he sometimes wore, held it his hands for a moment, then gave it to his friend. Three months later, Ibrahim presented him with a leather-bound, engraved edition of his own careful calligraphy, a volume of hot, homosexual lust Danny was glad had not been translated into English. He gratefully accepted the beautiful, leather-bound, handmade gift, and though he never learned to read Farsi, it was, ever afterwards, treasured.

"Yeah," Danny told Sandy Langarudi, "I think there are a lot of strange things in this country."

Sandy had a second child just eleven months after her first, then a miscarriage followed by a hysterectomy. Her marriage was now a disaster. Tensions within the Langarudi family escalated; she even found it best to dye her hair black to attract less attention when shopping in her neighborhood. She took to wearing a *chador*, as her once attractive figure evolved into the shape of a lumpy potato. Her skin went bad, and one eye watered from an injury. Later, Parviz knocked out two of her front teeth, one on the bottom and the other on the top.

"Why don't you just leave him?" Danny asked soon after he was transferred back to Doshan Tappeh to teach.

"I can't," she admitted. "I don't have any money. He takes my paychecks as soon as I walk in the door. I have two kids to think about now and besides, I can't leave the country on an Iranian passport without my husband's written permission."

"Why don't you go to the American embassy and get another American passport?"

She looked at him like he was simple-minded. "If it were that easy," she said, "the embassy would be mobbed by thousands of American women. As it is, consular officers just shrug their shoulders and swear they can't help."

"I think my roommate can get people in and out of the country. Let me ask him," Danny offered.

"Twenty thousand dollars," Marvin bellowed through the bathroom door when Danny asked that evening. Marvin had had a Western toilet installed, and he was determined to christen it with something solid, brown, stinky and long that evening, though all he seemed to get was gas. "Dammit," he yelled. "I'm not eating enough! Order me a couple of pizzas."

"What about the woman?"

"Twenty thousand dollars. Payable in advance."

"Where am I going to get twenty thousand dollars?" Sandy hissed when she heard the news. "Doc, promise me something? When you get back home, you will rescue a naive woman from an Iranian man for me. Just one. Do you promise?"

"Sure," Danny agreed. Two days later, he told her, "Marvin says he'll take a promissory note. When you arrive in the States, deposit the money in his bank in Houston."

"And what about my children?"

"Darn, I forgot to mention them. I'm sorry," Danny apologized. "I'll talk to him tonight."

"KIDS!" Marvin exclaimed when he heard it. "No fucking way. I don't want to get involved. You know how these Iranians are about their children, especially sons!"

Months passed, but one day, Sandy greeted Danny with great excitement in her eyes. "My father died."

"Oh, I'm sorry," he said, puzzled by her glowing face.

"No, no, you don't understand. I've been notified by a probate attorney in Killeen, Texas, there's an escrow account waiting for me with a quarter of a million dollars in it. My father's money—enough to start over. Oh blessed Jesus, it's a gift straight from heaven! Tell your roommate I'll pay him fifty thousand for me and my two little boys."

"Where'd she get fifty thousand all of a sudden?" Marvin wanted to know. He was predictably suspicious of a good thing.

"Tell him I had an inheritance," she instructed.

"How much?" Marvin demanded when he heard that.

"Tell him a hundred thousand," she reluctantly decided.

"Two hundred forty-eight thousand, seven hundred and sixteen dollars and fifty-two cents as of last Wednesday at close-of-business at 5 pm," Marvin announced proudly when Danny came home from work that day.

"How'd you find out?" Danny asked, not really surprised.

"A company lawyer researched it for me. I want 60% off the top," the big American said. Marvin had certainly learned to do business like an Iranian, Danny thought, but he passed the offer on to Sandy anyway.

"No chance," she fumed. "Thirty percent."

"Thirty percent barely covers my expenses," Marvin countered.

And then she disappeared for five months. Danny hoped she had gotten away, gotten free of Parviz and Iran, but instead, she reappeared on his bus one day, sitting alone as usual.

"Hi," he smiled warmly, taking a seat beside her.

Completely ignoring him, she looked out the window at the traffic. Thirty minutes later, she sighed and turned to face him. "Hi. *Alle shoma khubay?*" she asked.

There was something odd about her eyes. "Haven't seen you in some time," Danny said, reaching over to cover her hand with his own.

"I've b-b-been in th-the h-hosp-p-ital," she stuttered, tears springing from her eye and flowing down her cheeks.

"Oh, my God. What did he do to you?" Danny asked, his own eyes watering as he realized the truth.

"H-he b-beat me. I had to have an o-operation." Pulling back her chador she showed a long pink scar along the side of her skull.

"God damn him straight to the fires of hell," Danny swore, squeezing her hand tightly. He felt completely helpless. Unable to say anything else, he silently promised himself to talk with Ralf about Parviz Langarudi, and if it cost him a year's salary, he would get justice for Sandy.

"Tell y-your r-roommate I'll p-p-pay him the s-sixty percent," she stuttered as the bus pulled to a stop in front of the school's headquarters building. "Parviz knows about the m-money. I haven't got m-much t-time. He w-wants m—me to go to Texas without my b-boys to get the m-money."

"I can't do it, Doc," his roommate told him later that night.

"What do you mean you can't? You cannot keep holding this woman up for more money," Danny objected indignantly.

"Things have gotten tighter in the ports with these recent political troubles. Fuck, I don't understand what's going on lately, but suddenly every asshole's on the take. I'd do it just for expenses, let alone a profit, but there's just no fucking way. Look, I feel as shitty about it as you do."

Andrea was no help either, nor Ralf. "She could smuggle herself over the mountains into Turkey or down across the Gulf," Fraser suggested, "but she could just as easily get her throat cut for her cash. That's a money-up-front, take-your-chances proposition. Right now, I'd say it's impossible, especially with two little boys."

Sandy's face fell when she heard the news, and she sagged from some-where deep in her chest. "Do you know what they have me t-teaching?" she cried. "Air c-cadets! And it's payday—I've only made 70,00 rials this month, due to my absences."

Cadets were the most critical group of unforgiving arrogant bastards in the whole Imperial Iranian Air Force. The cadets laughed at her the first two or three days and began to jeer at her openly in class. After a week, they refused to put up with her handicap any longer, so the four-time win-ner of the coveted Instructor-of-the-Month Award was fired.

"Sandy? I'm so sorry," Danny told her on the bus ride home that eve-ning. "Give me a little more time. I'll find you a way out of Iran yet."

Though she squeezed his hand, she didn't look at him, and she re-fused to answer, nor look at anyone else on the bus. Instead, she got off at her usual stop and walked slowly away. Danny wanted to do something, say something magical to make things better, volunteer a new idea, but there was nothing he could do. Perhaps one of his tricks, a man who was a smuggler with contacts in Kuwait, could arrange something next week. He knew it would be expensive, but he hoped something—even a ride across the Gulf in a leaky *dhow*—might be arranged for her and her sons. As the bus pulled into the traffic, he half rose in his seat to wave goodbye, and he caught sight of her walking up the narrow street, dragging the back of her ragged black *chador* in the dust.

A few days later, he learned from sympathetic friends Sandy Langarudi had walked home that evening, given her *bargee*—the housekeeper—her entire salary, and fired her. Alone in the house for a couple hours, she filled the bathtub with cold water and drowned her two little boys. She then gathered up every photograph of herself and her children from throughout the house, set them on fire in the kitchen sink, and hanged herself from a closet rod with an old, cheap belt.

— 20 —

THE *DJUBE*

"You did good, my friend. We couldn't find the body."
—*Masud Pooinak*

In the days following Sandy Langarudi's suicide, Danny MacCreary was fundamentally changing. No longer in the mood for rollicking fun with his many friends—though his naturally carefree spirit did reassert itself occasionally—he realized his usual mood now was one of introspective, focused thought. A realization of his own mortality crept around the edges of his conscious mind, but it wasn't just the result of Sandy's death; it was the knowledge he had eternally *failed* someone. Someday, when he returned to America, he resolved to honor his promise to save at least one American woman from an Iranian man, though he knew in his heart it was the least he could do to expiate the guilt he felt.

Of course, the news was all over the front pages of the newspapers, but Danny knew the true story wouldn't be told. The guilty party was not some poor, lost American woman brutally murdering two innocent Iranian babies and then killing herself; it was the abusive husband now looking for another woman, probably blonde and busty like Sandy. When Parviz Langarudi allowed himself to be interviewed on NIRT national television one night, something snapped inside Danny.

"Yes, a tragic thing, this sordid crime against my family and my honor, but I must go on with my life," Parviz Langarudi claimed in Farsi to an interviewer. He went on to blame all sorts of behavior on his insane American wife, then he said, "A change of scenery will do me good, so I am thinking of leaving Teheran. I, as her heir, must go to Texas, America, to recover her estate. I have applied to the Texas A&M University in the College Station to pursue a master's degree in electrical engineering. In two months, I will go back to America. Perhaps I will find a better woman."

Upon hearing that, Danny became quiet as death, and he would remain so for days.

At work, he sat during break time, lost in thought. On the few evenings when there were no tricks for him at Andrea's place, or even a simple accompaniment with one of the women, he would sit in the darkened lounge, his chin in his hands, not even bothering to lift his eyes to watch TV or chat. He no longer took pleasure in his former activities: he stopped dropping by the Khodaris for carpet-talk and tea, declined to go to dinner with Fraser or his English friends, quit joking with Ralf, and wouldn't discuss anything with Andrea. He was inconsolable; his cheerful nature was so overshadowed by impenetrable depression and grief that his normal facial expressions varied from a scowl to a vacant stare. Even Shamsa couldn't get him to play gin rummy anymore, and his roommate avoided entertaining guests when he was at home.

"What a fucking sourpuss!" Marvin complained behind his back. "When is he going to get the hell over that woman so we can have some goddamned fun around this place again?"

"I don't like it when he broods," Masud whispered to others one evening. A few feet away, Danny stood staring out a window, oblivious to the conversation behind him.

"Stay the fuck out of his way," Ralf whispered back. "I've seen this many times before...." Wolffe and Fraser looked at each other over their newspapers, shrugged and went back to their reading. They'd seen it too.

It was strange, Danny thought, without turning around, but lately, all of the mercenaries were curious about Iranian politics and culture. They studied the newspapers every day. Wolffe had even gone so far as to pin a map of Iran over his desk, and finally, after two years in the country, Fraser was attempting to learn Farsi.

For Danny, however, grief was not enough. In frustration, he felt he needed time to reflect on the meaning of Sandy Langarudi's suicide. He wanted to glean truth from this affair to prevent him making further mistakes in his lifetime, but the ultimate moral lesson wouldn't come. He didn't have a clue how to prevent this in the future, but ... maybe there *was* a way he could save an American woman from an Iranian man—at least this particular Iranian man. Seized with a new resolve, Danny began to walk the narrow, crowded streets of eastern Teheran at night after work. He was looking for a particular car, a red Paykan he had seen Sandy drive.

He found it just twelve blocks from her old bus stop. Which house did it belong to? he wondered, for like all little *kutches,* the street was hemmed in by high, blank garden walls. All the houses were uniformly ugly.

By chance, a toothless sugar vendor was walking down the street shouting, "*Shakare! Shakare!*" The man was good enough to stop his heavily laden donkey to help Danny read the names on the rusted gates along the street. "Langarudi," the man wheezed, squinting through cracked spectacles. "It is a family name. You want go in?"

"No. No I don't. I just couldn't read the Farsi names. Thanks for your help. *Motchakeram,*" Danny said, handing the old man a hundred rials. "I needed to know who lived here."

"You want *shakare?*" the vendor asked.

"No, I don't need sugar," Danny replied. Since rock sugar was much harder, sweeter, and therefore better for sweetening tea than refined sugar, many Iranians valued the gritty crystals sold by such street vendors. Danny had seen men like this sugar-pounder all over Teheran; the tap-tap-tap of their wooden hammers on blocks of hard sugar as they pulverized enough for a sale was one of the ubiquitous sounds of the big city. This particular vendor was better equipped than most: his donkey sported a flat piece of wood tied atop the load where the sugar block could be hammered. The over-burdened donkey, however, wore a permanently pained expression on its face from the heavy hammer tethered to its load swaying against its calloused left flank.

"If you look for carpets here at this house, or maybe *hashish,* you could ask a different person—?"

"No," Danny said, giving the vendor a wry smile. "I'm not looking for anything in particular. I just thought it was a pretty house—" Pretty house? he thought in disgust, looking up at the stained concrete stucco exterior. Couldn't he come up with a better reason than that to allay the old man's curiosity? Reminding himself he mustn't attract attention, he added, "I wanted to take a photograph of a typical Iranian home, but this one is too big. Yes, it's too big. I'll try another street." Thanking the old man, he turned and hurried away to wait for another night.

Like most *kutches,* the Langarudi's street was narrow. High concrete stucco walls lining the street on both sides were broken only by rusted steel gates at the entrances to driveways and gardens. Deep *djubes* in concrete-walled ditches ran down either side of the street, the dark, dirty water flowing in them as black and cold as witch's piss. Leafless trees were set in the dirt every twenty feet or so along rough, clanking sidewalks made from concrete tiles. Dozens of typical middle-class cars were parked next to the *djubes*: Paykans, Jyanes, and Fiats. Except for a bare bulb over a driveway across the street, there was no light for at least a block. In the distance, the cold, blue line of the Alborz Mountains rose high above the city of Teheran. The *kutche* was perfect for what Danny had in mind.

There was, however, nowhere to hide at night. Selecting a piece of wall twenty feet from the Langarudi's driveway, Danny stood in the darkness for two hours, but Parviz never showed. It was the first of twenty-six such nights Danny spent there, nights of winter cold, boredom, and harsh winter wind.

"Hell, I wish I knew what the fuck was wrong with you," Marvin shouted from the kitchen one evening. Trying to make Mexican enchiladas from ground mutton, he seemed irritated they didn't taste the same as those he had eaten in Texas.

Upstairs, Danny was putting on two pairs of socks, a shirt, two sweaters, and two pairs of jeans to go out in the cold again. "I'll be back later," he announced as he ran down the stairs and headed for the door.

"Shit," Marvin shouted, running from the kitchen to catch him. "I want to talk to you, asshole!" He was too late. Danny had already gone. The two of them rarely talked.

Outside, Danny looked up at the cloudy Persian sky in satisfaction. He removed a brick from the gatehouse wall, retrieved a bundle wrapped in plastic from inside the hole, then got in a waiting telephone taxi. Quietly unwrapping the plastic in the back seat lest the driver see what he had, Danny slipped a Russian Makarov pistol in 9 mil by 18 into his pocket. "Let's go," he told the driver.

There was a lot of traffic on the Langarudi *kutche* that night; a party was going on across the street where a single light shone over a driveway. Couples and families parked their cars and walked by, but Danny concealed his face, pretending to be waiting with a purpose. There was a wedding reception going on there. After a while, it grew quieter along the narrow street, and fewer people hurried to join the party. The cold, winter wind whistled drearily through the leafless trees.

The only other sounds were a muffled hum of music from the party, and a scurrying of dry snow upon the ground. Danny pulled the pistol from his pocket and checked its action. The gun—what Fraser called a "throwaway"—was a Soviet automatic, double-action with a range of fifty meters. The slide was stiff and difficult to work in the cold, so he removed the magazine, ejected a round from the chamber and worked the slide back and forth until it loosened up again. How many times had he cleaned Cosmoline from guns Fraser had acquired? he thought bitterly, but now that it really counted, he hadn't even taken the time to do it for himself! Pulling a handkerchief from his pocket, he wiped the gun as well as he could, then snapped it three times to make sure the hammer and trigger worked freely. Shaking his head at his stupidity and inexperience, he put it back in his pocket, gripping the gun tightly to warm the cold steel.

An hour later, a door opened somewhere behind him. There was a glow of warmth and television noise, then squeaking snow as someone crossed a garden in slippers. Was it from the Langarudi house or the neighbor's? Danny wondered. His mind was clear, his nerves steady, his body coiled like a tight spring. The Langarudi gate opened. A large, broad-shouldered man stepped out onto the sidewalk. His back to the wind, the man hunched over against the cold and crossed the snowy sidewalk. As he bent to open the door of a red Paykan at the curb, Danny recognized Parviz Langarudi in the light.

Carefully sliding down the wall so he wouldn't make a clatter on the loose tiles of the sidewalk, Danny pulled the warm gun from his pocket. Parviz was fumbling in the glove compartment looking for cigarettes, but he seemed to sense a presence approaching him from behind. As he straightened up beside his car, Danny slipped the safety off and raised the pistol.

"Parviz Langarudi, please think of Sandy from your pit in Hell," Danny hissed, stepping within six feet of the man's vulnerable back. Aiming the gun at the base of the Parviz's neck, Danny squeezed the trigger. CLICK. Reacting immediately, he pulled the trigger again to chamber another round, thinking he had forgotten to do it earlier, but there was only another CLICK, and then the Iranian turned around.

"*Shoma!*" he exclaimed in surprise as he recognized the American behind him as one of his late wife's co-workers.

Frantically starting to work the gun's slide by hand again, Danny suddenly realized why the gun wouldn't fire—he had forgotten to reload the magazine after checking the pistol earlier! Gnashing his teeth, he threw the gun down at his feet and angrily launched himself against the Iranian. Parviz met the attack with a solid blow to Danny's left side, then a glancing blow to his neck. As Danny clawed his way upward, trying to get a grip on the Iranian's throat, he suffered another blow to the head, but he answered it with a sweeping Irish roundhouse that carried both men off their feet and into the side of the car.

Scrambling for their footing on the very edge of the crumbling *djube*, the two men fought for their lives. Danny was again knocked on top of his head—an unscientific blow that nearly drove him to his knees—but pushing back with all his might, he caught Langarudi under the arms, and they sprawled into the open door of the Paykan, where they became wedged between the front seat and the dash.

Parviz's greater size and bulk easily matched his younger opponent's strength; the Iranian got a long fingernail hooked in Danny's ear which he tore open. Desperately pressing his thumb against the Iranian's throat, Danny twisted violently and somehow levered himself up onto the seat, his own blood splattering all over his glasses, temporarily blinding him. Parviz struggled up off the floorboards too, but the American's berserk power forced him back against the steering wheel, shattering the windshield. "You goddamned motherfucker," Danny swore. "I'm gonna kill you in revenge for Sandy—"

In answer, the Iranian shouted, *"Allah-u-akbar!"* and he shoved Danny outside, where Parviz lost his footing on the icy, crumbling concrete just as he struck Danny, but this time, Danny bent at the knees and swiveled as Parviz' blow sailed past his head, and they both fell headlong into the watery *djube.*

The *djube* here was eighteen inches wide and two feet deep, its bottom slimy and bumpy with untold horrors flushed down from higher in the city. Now, wedged on their sides in the narrow channel, with filthy water— black, cold, perhaps a foot deep and as thick as thrown-up soup—washing over them like a flood, both men fought with only one arm and a leg. Danny began a strategic move to lever his body on top of his opponent's; Parviz fought for tactical advantage, frantic with the desire to draw blood—and blood he got! He clawed Danny's face hysterically, then one of his long, dirty fingernails caught in Danny's left eyebrow, and he used the nail like a scalpel to rip the American's forehead open.

Gushing blood, Danny pulled his right arm out from under Parviz and delivered his first clear blow of the fight, an elbow straight in the face, which momentarily stunned the Iranian. Trying to pull himself on top, Danny found he was too exhausted to do much more than pummel his opponent repeatedly.

As they grappled and splashed in the *djube*, partygoers emerged from the gate across the street. There were noisy good-byes, doors slamming, headlights flashing, and cars driving past as people left the party. Langarudi made an effort to shout for help, but Danny drove a fist into his jaw, breaking teeth.

Tightly gripping him between his legs, the Iranian repeatedly slammed his right fist into Danny's left side, but then Danny's long-term strategy paid off: he was finally able to lever himself on top of the struggling Iranian. For the first time, the fight became a contest of skill and strength against desperation and bulk. Stunned and increasingly helpless, Parviz fought on as best he could, although he was injured.

A child paused on the other side of the car, apparently questioning why the light was on and a door open, but at the last moment, it was called away by its mother. "*Bia inja,*" she shouted, snatching at his hand. In Teheran, she told him, one must never see what one didn't need to know.... Angrily, she pulled the child towards her car, although she did allow herself one last, curious look back across the street.

There were more goodbyes, more partygoers preparing to leave, but the struggle in the *djube* went on. Fighting now only to lessen the injuries the American was inflicting on him, Parviz made a subtle shift on his part to defense. Quickly taking advantage, Danny forced the man down into the black, filthy water, pummeling him in the chest to knock the air out of him. Sensing victory, he then wrapped both hands around the Iranian's neck and forced his head underwater. Frantically, Parviz fought his way back up to breathe, banging Danny again and again in the left side until he broke ribs.

"Allah—" he panted whenever he got his head above the filthy water, but God was not with him that night, only the Devil, waiting his due. After Sandy's suicide, God would never help someone like Parviz....

Meanwhile, the furious splashing had attracted a woman who approached the car from the party across the street. This time, the two fighters were beyond caring; Danny clenched his teeth, trying to strangle the Iranian or at least drown him. Parviz splashed noisily, fighting desperately to keep his head above the water. The woman looked in the window, spoke in question marks, then shrugged and walked away. Langarudi made another surge to catch his breath or to shout for help, but Danny forced him back into the water, driving his knee into the Iranian's rib cage. This time, there was a bubbling from beneath the water as Parviz lost his breath. Desperately, he began to rip through the sleeves of Danny's jacket with his long fingernails. In seconds, Danny's forearms were shredded and bloody.

Again, Danny drove his knee into the Iranian's gut. This time, there was bubbling, followed by a long sigh and an unusual sucking sound; the Iranian's hands relaxed for the last time and finally slid down Danny's arms and into the dirty water. Sandy Langarudi had been avenged.

Weakly, Danny rolled over the crumbly side of the *djube* and sprawled in the cold, dry dirt beside the sidewalk, panting like a dog. Across the street, yet another group was leaving the party. Quickly reaching over the *djube* to slam the car door shut so the light wouldn't attract more attention, Danny reached down into the dirty water to take care of the body, but Parviz was already twenty feet downstream, slowly being washed away. As he retrieved his glasses, knocked off in the struggle, Danny knew the corpse would catch somewhere under the streets and be hidden in a flood of filthy black *djube* water for several days. Relieved, for he didn't have the strength to carry the body anywhere, Danny got unsteadily to his knees, swept his hands over the dirt until he found the fallen pistol, then staggered away, dripping blood wherever he went. Unobserved by any of the partygoers, he disappeared around the corner and limped away to catch a taxi.

——◆——

"Andrea?"

Awakened an hour later by her private phone, she answered, "Yes?" though she was not in a mood to talk to anyone. Why did the most important calls of her life come when she was sleeping most peacefully? she wondered.

"I need Ralf."

"Ralf's in Isfahan," she said.

"I need help."

"Who is this?"

"Doc."

"Doc!" she exclaimed, sitting up and turning on the light next to her bed. Why would he call in the middle of the night? A fat, hairy male figure with hair on his back like a goddamn gorilla grumbled at the intrusion, but she irritably pushed him over on his side, and the man went back to sleep. "Are you all right?"

Dead silence at the other end of the phone told her something had happened. "Where are you?"

"Kouroush-e-Kabir. I need help. I need somebody. Can you send someone?"

"I'll be there in thirty minutes," she said. "Tell me where you are." Damn! Ralf was gone, Wolffe had the night off, Masud and Fraser were both out on tricks with the girls. What rotten luck! For the first time in weeks, there was no one trustworthy around. Making a mental note to hire more help, she grabbed a pen off her nightstand and began to copy.

"I'm a mile north of the Blue Mosque. Grocery store, two doors down from a carpet shop," Danny whispered. "I'm near Stephan's house," he added, referring to one of her tricks.

"I know the area," she said. "I'll be driving Ali's gray BMW."

A thousand thoughts raced through her head. Would she need a gun? Money? Medical kit? He had given her no clue—standard procedure for her men, for they knew SAVAK, the secret police regularly monitored their phone calls—but now she was left wondering what to do.

True to her word, Andrea pulled up half an hour later. Danny was sitting behind a meat cooler in a tiny grocery store, a piece of cardboard under his chair to absorb his dripping blood. Taking in the situation at a glance, she ran back out to the car to cover the expensive leather upholstery with a blanket, and then hurried back to help Danny outside, wrapping him in another blanket. He could hardly walk he was so stiff. He couldn't talk. "I'll be back in a moment," she told him as she closed the car door and went back into the shop.

"*Arghah*," she said, summoning the scruffy storekeeper. "My friend had trouble tonight because he was sleeping with another man's wife. He is not Moslem. He is a tourist and doesn't understand your culture. He was badly beaten by an angry husband, but he has learned a valuable lesson. Do you understand? He is only a tourist…. He will go back to his country tomorrow."

"Yes, miss," the man said, barely able to suppress a giggle, though he shook his head sympathetically.

"It's a terrible thing, really," she lied. "I am so sorry this happened, but really, it's not your problem. I'd like to offer something so you will not be offended by this or think of it again."

"I forget it already."

She gave him twenty thousand rials and ran back out to the car. Whatever had happened, Danny was badly banged up, and though she listened to his story as she drove, she had a hard time making sense of it all. First thing, she had to find Masud, Fraser, and Wolffe—they would know what to do!

Much later, in a secret apartment in Tajrish, Danny moaned and acted like he wanted to get up. Standing nearby, a couple of bloody shirts and sweaters in his hands, Fraser mumbled something about his young friend's arms looking like hamburger, but Andrea growled, "Isn't that damned doctor on his way yet?"

Fraser had been the first to come to her aid, but where was Masud and that doctor of hers? She paid the doctor thirty thousand tomans a month for discreet medical attention for her girls, but the doctor was rarely fast enough, and now she wondered if he were discreet enough for her tastes. She would have Ralf tail him for a week, and—she promised herself—if the doctor stepped out of line, she would have him killed. Masud could find another doctor who hurried.

One of the girls soothed Danny's forehead with a damp cloth. Nearby, another was setting up a coffee table with alcohol, cotton balls, gauze, and tape, but Andrea just sat nearby, worried. What had Danny done this night—and how well had he done it? My God, she agonized! If any of her other men had aced someone tonight, she would only be worried about fixing his wounds, but Danny was another story. He was an amateur at this sort of thing. Had he left a trail of clues that might implicate them? Had he slipped up somewhere? Were the police or SAVAK already on their way? None of the others seemed concerned, though Fraser did check his pistol periodically. Rather nervously, Andrea lit a cigarette, something she rarely did, and she got up and paced the floor.

An hour later, Wolffe entered the room. "I don't know how the fuck he did it. We found the Paykan with the broken windshield easily enough, and I got rid of it, but there was no trace of a body anywhere. It was a very good hit— very good hit—a bit rough, but good. No body anywhere to be found."

Sighing with relief, Andrea buried her face in her hands. "Thank God! Thank God he killed him clean!"

The big mercenary walked over to the couch and looked down at his unconscious friend's naked body. "He's pretty cut up," Wolffe said. "Fifty or sixty stitches on his hands and forearms, maybe twenty in his forehead, ten in his left ear. He has a lot of contusions and welts. Four busted ribs. We must dose him up for infections, for if he really fought up to his chin in *djube* water, there's no telling what kind of germs he's been exposed to." Smiling proudly, he added, "I think he must have strangled his customer with his bare hands. I'd say Doc did all right tonight, didn't he? He's one of us now—"

"No," she disagreed. Joining the Englishman beside the couch, she looked down at Danny. "His was a crime of passion, not profession. "He may have killed someone tonight, but he's not as bad ... or as good ... as we are. He would never kill for money or politics."

"Perhaps you're right," Wolffe agreed, "but I'm proud of him. All those things I taught him must have made an impression."

"No one must hear about this," Andrea decided, reaching up to put her delicate hand on his big, tattooed arm. "Not any of our contacts or tricks, and certainly none of our competitors. If anyone thinks he has learned from you or Ralf, his credibility as a courier will be finished. His safety relies on his innocence. Do you understand?"

"Of course. We'll tell no one. Besides, you're right," Wolffe grinned. "One murder does not a killer make."

–21–

THE ONION RIOT

*"Who cares about this fucking revolution? None of us care a god-
damn thing about anything except eating once in a while!"*
                                    —*An anonymous voice on the bus*

Toward the end of his first two-year contract, Danny had to admit not
all his hardships in Iran resulted from the insanity around him; some
resulted from his own decisions to stay. He had made up his mind to sign
another two-year contract with the Imperial Iranian Air Force, his second
tour.

"The benefits are substantially better than the first contract," he told
Andrea one evening. "I hear they're having a hard time recruiting English
teachers in America, so they're paying a premium to keep us experienced
people here."

"How much are they offering you?" she inquired in a curiously detached
way.

"A hundred and ninety-five thousand rials a month, plus ninety-five
thousand for housing, a generous bonus of three hundred thousand for
signing the contract, and they'll even give me the money they would have
paid for my plane ticket home," Danny grinned, wondering why she was so
indifferent. The terms seemed generous. Under the new contract, he would
be making nearly four thousand untaxed dollars a month and not paying
rent either. "It's pretty good, don't you think?"

"Perhaps ... if you want to be an English language instructor all your
life."

"What's that supposed to mean?" he asked irritably. Lately, she seemed
to enjoy throwing a wet blanket on all his ambitions.

"I'm quitting as soon as my current six-month contract is finished."

"But how will you stay in this country?" Danny objected. The Iranian government was strict on residency requirements, so for more than two years—on a part time basis—Andrea had put up with conditions at Mehrabod Junubi in order to keep her resident's visa current. How could she afford to throw it away now?

"Everyone takes bribes," she replied. "I found someone to issue me a permanent residence permit. I could do the same for you, if you'd agree to work for me full-time—"

Thinking how bored Wolffe, Fraser, Ralf, Masud and others were during the daytime, Danny answered, "No, I'm glad I have a full-time job, even if it is with the Iranians. Since I've been working at Doshan Tappeh, things have been bearable. I think I'll stay as a courier on a part-time basis, if that's okay."

"Sure," she snorted in disgust. "If that's what you want. And, to be competitive, I'll give you a rise to thirty-five thousand per week, plus a bonus of fifteen thousand a trick if you handle more than three tricks a week. How's that?"

Danny knew her business had expanded rapidly in these uncertain times; he would probably earn the bonus many times over. What he didn't know was what she charged for his services. Shamsa had hinted that his courier services were a lucrative business.

"Twenty thousand each trick," he countered.

"Okay."

"And forty thousand a week."

"Okay."

Danny enjoyed working for her. Without a moment's hesitation, he agreed. Besides, he thought, he had actually come to enjoy the adventures of his strange life in Iran. He never knew what was going to happen next. Just crossing a street in traffic gave him more heart-pumping excitement than anything he had ever done back in the States. Perhaps what Andrea joked about was true after all: that after the intensity of his life in Iran, he wouldn't be able to readjust to a simpler, quieter life in his native Wyoming.

Several days later, Danny found himself sitting in the instructors' lounge, drinking a Coke between classes. He was staring at the new contract on the table in front of him, his pen poised in mid-signature while he entertained a last doubt. Halfheartedly wondering if he were making another big mistake in his life, he was considering quitting now while he was ahead, but then the door opened and a large, noisy group of strangers came into the room. As they stood there in the semidarkness, blinking to adjust their eyes to the gloomy lounge, he realized he was staring at them as though they had come from another planet.

Dressed in bright, fashionable clothes, the newcomers looked strong and flushed with health. They were the new contract instructors, fresh from America, their heads full of college methodology and their eyes bright with self-confidence and classroom ambitions. Filled with pity for these naive fools, Danny looked away lest they catch him watching them. And then, with a start, he remembered it had been exactly this way when he himself had entered the lounge two years before and seen the previous contract's instructors lining the walls like old, gray wolves. As he looked around, he saw his fellow instructors sitting alone or in pairs along the walls, staring at the noisy group in the doorway. There was a resentful mood Danny had long since come to know well. Perhaps he could break the cycle.

"Welcome," he croaked, trying to clear the desert dust from his throat. Welcome them to what? he wondered as soon as he said it, then he declared rather mysteriously, "Welcome to the darkness of the instructors' lounge."

The recent arrivals, of course, stared at him in surprise. Welcome them to the darkness? Turning away, they chattered among themselves, bubbling over with enthusiasm, totally oblivious to the horrors that awaited them in the classrooms of the Imperial Iranian Air Force.

For Danny, however, the moment was a turning point. Reluctantly, he had become a gray wolf at last. He picked up the pen and signed the contract on the table before him. Thereafter, Danny, who had never attended any of his fellow instructors' parties or had time to travel or drink with them, could count on his table in the lounge filling with other tired instructors like himself. Never again would he sit alone on a crowded bus. In addition to Marvin's crowd and Andrea's hardened people, he now developed another circle of friends, the ESL instructors from work, and he was much happier.

It was a strange time to come to peace with his daytime job. Ever since the early spring of 1977, there had been power outages. At first, they were unpredictable and mysterious in origin, but as they increased in frequency, the government felt obligated to explain. The newspapers reported a hydroelectric plant designed to meet Iran's burgeoning needs had been delayed for technical reasons.

One of Danny's regular tricks, a construction materials supplier, explained, "The turbines at the heart of the generating station burned out because they were badly seated in second-rate concrete. The concrete contractor has fled Iran."

"Shit, it's going to take *years* to sort out the legal mess," his roommate chortled when he heard it. "The Iranians will spend more time assigning the *blame* than they will in fixing it. A lot of engineers are going to the shithouse over this. Generators have got to be balanced in good concrete."

In the future, the newspapers said, electricity would be rationed. Though voluntary conservation was suggested, the recommendation was soon abandoned. The undisciplined Iranian masses, with their "me-first" mentality, had little concept of personal sacrifice or cooperation on a national scale. In fact, one of the first things Danny learned in Iran was that Farsi had no word for "team" or "teamwork," so the people around him continued to consume electricity based on the assumption that they themselves were not included in government restrictions. Rules were for the other guy, not them. Consumption of electricity increased, despite the blackouts. Shortages escalated, and tempers flared.

There was a persistent belief the use of modern traffic signals was responsible for the shortage of electricity. In true Iranian fashion, the government turned the signals off for several days. After chaos and a near gridlock ensued in Teheran, the government next attempted to solve the problem by shutting off power to certain districts at specified times. Shopkeepers, many of whom had grown used to hanging hundreds of light bulbs along the sidewalks to attract attention, grumbled loudly when the mandatory outages began, but then they hung gas lanterns outside their stores instead. Soon, there was a shortage of lantern fuel, wicks, and candles.

Neighborhood after neighborhood was blacked out on a rotating schedule, with the result that, for Danny, there was almost no electricity at all. For twelve hours at a time, there was no power at work, and at night his neighborhood was out too. At first, few hospitals had generators, so patients died by the hundreds. With frozen and refrigerated items becoming impossible to store, restaurants could not maintain menus. Cold drinks were in short supply, a serious problem in a desert country. With little radio or TV available and almost no news or music, the public's boredom escalated dramatically. By late 1977, Danny began to hear a new name on the streets.

"Who is this Ayatollah Khomeini?" he asked Benyamin Khodari one afternoon as they were sitting on a bale of tribal carpets. Ibrahim Khodari and the old men of the family looked up anxiously from a carpet they were repairing, but when Danny glanced at them, they turned away and began to whisper among themselves.

"He is an old man living in exile in Iraq," Benyamin replied grimly.

"Saddam Hussein has him under house-arrest. Khomeini is a Shiite traditionalist, a troublemaker left-and-right for many years, but he is a symbol of resistance to the Shah and the modernization of Iran. Khomeini is a romantic. He is eloquent, and he dreams of Persia five hundred years ago. Many of the Shia Moslems listen to him and hope the Ayatollah can do something about the Shah."

"An exiled old man in Iraq trying to do something about the Shah?" Danny laughed. "That's unlikely, isn't it?"

Unlikely it may have been, but someone took Khomeini seriously. In January 1978, a newspaper attacked the Ayatollah's character, charging him with low birth and questionable morals. The slander caused a protest in the religious city of Qom, and twenty people were killed in a stampede.

"What the fuck!" Danny's roommate swore in early February 1978. Small protests in the ports had disrupted his business all week, and some agitators had been killed in other cities. In sympathy, the nation's communication workers went on strike, so telephone and telex lines were down. Marvin was literally out of communication with his bosses in Tampa, Florida, America. "Of all the shit-ass luck! Are these goddamned people biting the hand that feeds them? The Shah's the best fucking thing that ever happened to this country," Marvin shouted. "Without the Shah and oil, this country would be nothing but desert and shit."

Smiling at his roommate's way of putting things, Danny predicted, "The police will get this under control."

"SAVAK'll get it under control," Marvin declared. "The Iranians fear the secret police more'n they fear the military. There're two thousand political prisoners in this country. I bet they'll take it to five thousand over this—"

Perhaps it was true, Danny thought, for in a country without a democratic tradition, the mandatory two-year draft was the only shared national experience. Persians, Kurds, tribal peasants, and educated Armenians alike were required to serve two years. Every adult male in the country had handled a G-3 rifle and drilled with the professional soldiers. Among such men, respect for the military was low. Refusing to follow an officer's orders was a Persian art form. Because of this, only a few disciplined, pro-Shah units were truly feared: the secret police (SAVAK), the Imperial Guard, some elite military regiments, and a variety of police companies.

"Yeah, SAVAK can deal with the unrest," Danny said, pursuing this train of thought, "but what's the government doing about these shortages?"

The crisis soon had a benefit: even though he had signed a new contract just three months before, he soon received a hefty 20% raise at work, due to the madly spiraling inflation. Shortages of everything from bricks to heating oil, drastic cuts in public spending, and rapidly rising rents concerned everyone in the country. Somebody, he thought grimly, was going to have to do something soon.

Unfortunately, no one seemed to know what to do, and it wasn't long afterward the riots started, not the political demonstrations that seemed to happen far away, but the ones closer to home—the ones that mattered to common people.

Danny had been having a hard time keeping things running at Marvin's villa. Shortages of cooking gas, *naft* for heating, and even gasoline forced him to hoard dangerous amounts of these flammable fuels out behind the swimming pool. He was thankful for a good summer's yield from his garden, and he had managed to store quite a few vegetables, but the one thing he hadn't planted that year was the basic staple of Persian cuisine: onions. As important to the Iranian psyche as apples to the American, they were impossible to find anywhere. There were rumors of landowners hoarding veritable mountains of onions, but even Marvin, with his underworld contacts and unusual friends, couldn't find onions for his table.

One day, while Danny was standing at his usual corner waiting for a blue military bus to work, a dusty stake truck loaded with sacks of onions pulled up before a vegetable market across the street. The driver got out, took one small bag from a man sitting on top of the load and then sauntered into the store to make a delivery. Danny was halfway across the street when the first housewives surrounded the truck and demanded more. Quickly joining the group, Danny was soon involved in a mob of five hundred angry people.

Someone punched the driver, and an assault on the truck began. By the time Danny looted one measly five-pound bag, the truck was on fire, the driver probably dead, and the man who had been sitting on the load was running for his life. Two thousand people converged on the scene for three hundred bags of onions, and only Danny's superior strength and speed, plus a good Samsonite briefcase used as a battering ram, enabled him to escape with his life.

An hour later, he managed to flag down a passing Air Force bus on Shah Reza Avenue. Jumping aboard, he shouted, "*Boro*, go!" at the driver as four youths ran up behind him and began banging on the door. Hiding the bag of onions as best he could under his jacket, he slunk down the aisle to an empty seat. Glaring at the other instructors to leave him alone, he had lost his hat and a glove, his jacket was torn in four places, the back pocket of his trousers had been ripped off so that his blue undershorts were exposed, his glasses were bent, and his hair mussed. Despite his condition, however, he cradled the bag of onions under his jacket like a first-born.

"What's happened to that guy?" a new instructor a few seats away asked a veteran.

"Nothing, why?"

"He's sitting there trying to hide a bag of onions under his coat!" the greenhorn laughed.

"So? He's got a bag of onions, and we don't," the veteran said, shaking his head at the newcomer's naiveté. "Things are tough here in Iran. You'd better get with the program if you're going to survive."

Danny, who overheard the conversation, looked at the gray faces of his friends, nodded knowingly, and hugged his onions all the tighter. Looking out the window as the angry traffic rolled by, he now turned his attention to *eggs*, something he hadn't been able to find in months.

The Iranian Revolution was on....

22

THE WOMAN IN RED

"When you last did eat?"

—*Benyamin Khodari, carpet dealer*

A study published in another country claimed Iran had a higher inci-
dence of mental illness than any other nation on earth. For months,
the heavily censored Iranian newspapers discussed this mysterious report
without ever quoting from it or identifying its source. Conversation on the
street seemed to be about little else; likewise, the subject dominated social gatherings. The controversy was so prevalent Danny MacCreary found
himself wondering how an entire nation could be so obsessively defensive.
He had much to learn about Persian xenophobia—an ancient Greek word
used to describe the Persians.

Nevertheless, Danny knew someone who *was* mentally ill, and she was
so well known for her eccentricity she had become famous. A gossip magazine once carried her story, and nearly everyone had seen her at one time
or another; even so, common people shrank away from her, and decent
women spat at mention of her. Most people seemed to feel she should die
and go away.

Her name was probably Leila, though she sometimes identified herself as Nastaran. Her last name, of course, was lost forever, for she was a
fallen woman who had dishonored her family. Her story was so romantic,
and oh, how Iranian men loved romance! [Iranian men are as romantic as
American women. They love flowers; they love music; they love poetry.]

Long ago, Leila had loved someone. Her family had disapproved of
the match as socially beneath them, but Leila's suitor persuaded her to
elope with him. He claimed her family was unimportant; their eternal
love would overcome every obstacle. One thing Danny had learned in Iran

was no matter how horribly mismatched they might have seemed at the time, things probably would have worked out just as the lover had said, for Iranian families were very forgiving after the birth of a grandchild. Arranging to meet her in Ferdowsi Square, the young man told Leila to dress all in red so he would be sure to recognize her in the crowds. Instead, he was probably killed by her family in an "honor-crime." She never saw him again.

Twenty years later, she still waited for him in Ferdowsi Square.

In a Western culture, Leila might have had a tearful reconciliation with her family, perhaps been punished or even cloistered in a convent for the rest of her life—but it would have been kinder than the abandonment she experienced at the hands of her family in Iran. She lived in Ferdowsi Square, surviving by the kindness of strangers, mostly Jewish. In the summer, she sought shade in the doorways of their carpet shops, in the winter, just an occasional warm draft when a door opened. All her needs were met as they arose. She never asked for food, yet they kept her comfortably fat. What little money she had went for red clothes. She had red dresses, red coats, red shoes, red purses, red suitcases, and red hats. In the winter, Danny never saw her but she was dressed warmly in red wool, and in the summer, cool, red cotton. Unconcerned with the future, she did not maintain stashes of clothing; as the seasons passed, she obtained new clothes and discarded the old. Her small suitcase contained only a few tattered photographs and a broken hairbrush. Her purse held, at most, a hundred rials.

She was a favorite of the gentle recluse, Ibrahim Khodari. Rarely would he approach the first-floor windows of his family's carpet store to look out on the traffic, for he was desperately afraid of being arrested as a draft dodger. For more than twenty-five years, he had lived in the shadow world of the store, spending his time hiding in the attic, studying books, writing poetry, and collecting erotic miniatures; nevertheless, he would always stop whatever he was doing to rush to the windows to see the woman in red as she passed by on the street.

Perhaps it was the romantic in him, or maybe his wonderful compassion, but the only time Danny ever knew Ibrahim to reach out on the sidewalk was to hand the woman money, in that case a thousand-rial bill. In a way, Ibrahim Khodari and the homeless Leila were both trapped in Ferdowsi Square—one outside, forever searching for a lost lover; one inside, forever watching the world from a little window.

Meidan-e-Ferdowsi was the worst, yet best, place for this woman to live. Shah Reza Avenue from the east and Eisenhower Boulevard from the west joined at the great square, and Ferdowsi Street and Sepabod Zahedi met north and south. Named after a revered Iranian poet, whose marble bust sat among rose bushes in a small park in the middle of the square, Ferdowsi was the true heart of Teheran. Traffic was orderly, for police were nearly always obeyed here; the Jewish carpet dealers to the south and the Moslems to the north were only competitors, and the night clubs of Laleh and the conservative merchants of Eisenhower were somehow kept in balance here.

The queen of Ferdowsi, the only street person to inhabit the great square itself, was Leila. Perhaps twenty percent of Teheran's population of five million were street people. Leila was the only woman living on the streets that Danny ever saw in Iran. On the way to work, he saw Kurdish tribesmen squatting over smoky fires in rubbly lots; Afghans and Balourchis packed twenty at-a-time under rude awnings; and *cigarees* slept on sidewalks beside their portable cigarette stands, but Leila proudly claimed the doorsteps of Ferdowsi Square as her fiefdom.

"Esm-e-shoma chiye?" Benyamin Khodari would ask her whenever he saw her.

Sometimes she would look away at the traffic and absently brush her unkempt gray hair away from her brow, and then she would sigh, *"Esm-e main Leila."* Benyamin would hand her fruit, *chelo kebab*, or hot *barbari* bread.

"Why do you always ask her name?" Danny once asked.

"She must know it," his friend answered. "It is her only touch with reality...and our world...where she lives."

Another time, while looking over a recently received bale of Persian carpets, Benyamin announced, "Vegetables!"

"Excuse me?" Danny asked, not understanding how vegetables had anything to do with Qaskai workmanship.

"She needs vegetables," Benyamin said, and off the two friends would go to find green *sabzi* to share with the old woman.

It wasn't long before Danny got into the habit of buying pastries on the way to work and offering them to her from his briefcase. If she suspected he had only bought them for her, she wouldn't pay attention, but if he pretended they were part of a precious treat for himself, she would grudgingly accept half. It was the sole reason Danny ate Iranian pastry, since its dreadful sweetness gagged him. When the winter arrived, he shared hot *labu* (beets) with her; in the summer, he fed her *sangyak* bread and carrot jam or pistachios from a box. Finally, after two years of cultivating her, she "recognized" his face.

"Alle shoma khube?" she would ask, her hair blowing madly in the exhaust of passing double-decker Leyland buses.

"Merci. Chetoray?" he would answer, looking for a treat in his briefcase.

"Bahd nist," she would smile, her eager brown eyes searching the crowds for a certain friendly face. Sometimes he would find her a few blocks down the street, but only rarely did she go far. Ferdowsi was the center of her world, her entire universe lay there; she felt safe in the great square that nurtured her.

———◆———

But there were terrible winds approaching, great desert winds full of grit and sand. Shah Reza Avenue was a pathway toward the heart of the revolution. The Sepah, or government area, lay to the south, the effete decadence of Laleh to the east, the wealth of Pahlavi Avenue to the west, and the American Embassy was only a few blocks north—

Angry crowds marched through Ferdowsi Square before anyone knew a revolution had begun. Shouting, "Death to the Shah!" the marchers seemed to think it was a protest like those in scattered provincial capitals, or maybe an afternoon of fun and mayhem in the streets. Forty days later—the traditional mourning period—after all the shooting had died down and a dozen bodies buried—much larger crowds swept through on the way to Shahyad—and more shooting. Leila was helplessly swept away by this second demonstration, and she never returned to Ferdowsi Square. Undoubtedly lost, she vanished somewhere to the west in the maze of narrow streets around Teheran University. She was alone—and probably died alone...in a *kutche* in west Teheran.

Her disappearance weighed heavily on the simple mind of Ibrahim Khodari. "Where does the woman get food now?" he would ask, shaking his head in sorrow.

"She's dead, Ibrahim. Forget her," Danny would advise each time. "You know there's no one to look out for her like the carpet merchants of Ferdowsi."

As a comfort to his friend, however, Danny haunted the gruesome morgues of Teheran looking for the old woman's body. In horror, he witnessed the bribes, the cool—but not cold—rooms, the wet slabs, and the mangled bodies of the revolution—more and more with every protest. Every forty days, every time there was a riot, Danny pressed his way through crowds of weeping women and somber police; he watched bloody bodies sewn into cotton shrouds. It was the beginning of an awful deathwatch, though he didn't realize it at the time. In the early days of the Revolution, the Iranian people were shocked by death tolls of a dozen or more. Soon, however, death would become quite common; the cemeteries would swell by the thousands.

In utter disbelief, Danny saw men learn to sew shrouds—for just a hundred and fifty rials, payable in advance—and he listened to the peculiar wailing of women and families as they suffered their losses. Though he endured weeks in the morgues and saw it all, he tried to deny what was happening. He told himself they were after just one body— Leila's. All these others were some terrible mistake. People would come to their senses, he hoped. Surely, this would end. How could common people dream of overthrowing the Shah, and what kind of life could they expect if they succeeded? Iran was nothing without oil, and who had made Iran the dominant voice in OPEC? Who was pulling Iran into the modern world almost single-handedly? The Shah, of course! For that reason, Danny found it impossible to accept the people believed they would be better off with an elderly cleric in some other country as their leader, a man so set in his ways he wanted to return them to the Fourteenth Century.

After several fruitless weeks of searching the morgues and hospitals without finding any trace of Leila, Danny and Benyamin had to admit defeat. It wasn't long after that, however, that the biggest protest of all, nearly a quarter of a million people, swept through Ferdowsi. Huge banners bearing the scowling image of the Ayatollah Khomeini appeared for the first time above the marchers. Depressed by Leila's disappearance and perhaps seeking some diversion, Ibrahim Khodari stepped out of the carpet store for the first time in twenty years to see the demonstration better. From his door, it was only a hundred feet to the edge of Ferdowsi Square, but he never came back.

"Danny, my friend, can you help me? My brother is missing all the day," Benyamin wept over the phone that evening. "My brother Ibrahim is gone—"

"I'll be right over," Danny promised, pulling on a field jacket. Hurrying downtown, he hoped Ibrahim was smarter than Leila; the gentle carpet dealer would be able to keep his sense of direction and find his way back. Still, he knew the gentle Ibrahim must be terrified out there, all alone in the shooting and the burning night.

Together, Benyamin and Danny searched Eisenhower Avenue all the way to Shahyad Square and back several times. Walking until his feet were bloody, Danny explored every *kutche* on either side of the avenue. He then went with Benyamin to the morgues, the newly crowded prisons, and the teeming hospitals. He talked with hundreds of people, including military men, for heavily armed soldiers could be found anytime now, especially near Teheran University. Suspecting his simple-minded friend wouldn't know how to ask directions home, Danny sought out foreigners and taxi drivers who might have seen him, while Benyamin grilled the street people.

The two friends were so busy running down leads, they had no opportunity to work together. Depressed by Ibrahim's disappearance, Danny grew lonely without his sidekick Benyamin, but the time for friendship was finished now. Teheran was going wild. The streets were more dangerous every day. Danny took to carrying a gun, an S&W .357 Andrea had given him the year before. Benyamin spent a fortune in bribes at the gates of hospitals, morgues, and prisons. Though their friendship grew stronger during the search, in the end, they never found a trace of Ibrahim Khodari.

— 23 —

FIRE IN THE SKY

"Shithead, you ain't going near Ferdowsi Square, not tonight, not never fucking again. I guarantee it!"

—*Marvin Roberts*

There were rumors, misty movements, and muted sounds out on the restless streets, but they were only as real as nightmares viewed through lidded eyes. Since the loss of Ibrahim Khodari, Danny MacCreary's life in Iran had become quiet. There was no music and little news, yet there was a noise of a sort: a muffled undercurrent of revolution in the streets as monotonous in sound and activity as the scurrying of mice in a bedroom wall.

During breaktime at work, he sat in silence, a lonely wolf lost in memories. At home, the villa was deserted; many of the stewardesses had fled Iran. The swimming pool hadn't been refilled. It was two feet low, and there was a scum line around its edge. Mehrabod Airport was closed more often than it was open, and the airlines were pulling their people out. Danny's friends at work were gone too, and even Marvin's cronies were finding jobs elsewhere in Saudi Arabia, Venezuela, or Nigeria—anywhere the oil bubble had not yet burst.

There was nothing new to see and even less to do. Danny walked the streets untouched, unmoved despite the hustle and bustle. Traffic had grown particularly ferocious. Fistfights, arguments, thrown stones, insults, and fear were all around him. Women in *chadors* scurried home with groceries, and *cigarees* hawked newspapers from every corner. The diabolical image of the Ayatollah Khomeini glowered from shop windows and walls, and the cleric's quiet, dry voice urged the people to strike, to confront the military and the police, and to die as martyrs....

Teheran had become a plague zone, the dense black smoke from burning tires clinging to the city like a pall, yet Danny walked like a ghost through the hysteria, unable to believe he had been so overtaken by events. Torn by the desire to leave Iran but struck helpless by grief, he couldn't decide what to do. He was not yet personally involved, though he suffered the shortages, the blackouts, and the confusion like everyone else.

The quiet was almost sepulchral at Andrea's. The phone still rang upstairs, but the girls rarely came down to the lounge to gossip. Drivers came in; girls went out. Bob Fraser was often too drunk for conversation, and Andrea spent her time entertaining for Ali Nassiri, as there was political hay to be made in these troubled times. As a result, Danny spent long evenings sitting in the dark lounge, thinking.

He did a lot of sitting at home too, on the roof with Marvin and the few remaining stewardesses, rarely more than five in number now, and never with boyfriends. At night, he drank warm beer and watched the darkened city; the others listened to tapes or kept their eyes on a battery-operated TV. Nearby, neighbors had taken to living on their roofs too, and their anonymous calls for revolution and vengeance echoed in the night. In the darkness, far from the prying ears of strangers or fruitless searches of the police, there was that ominous voice on the cassettes, telling the people it was okay to kill a father or murder a friend, if by doing so, the course of Allah's intended revolution was furthered. This dry old man—this Ayatollah Khomeini living in exile in Iraq—urged his people to die as martyrs, to fill the prisons and the morgues to overflowing, to sacrifice their family and their loved ones, to march in the face of the army's guns, and to give their very lives to establish something he romantically and idealistically called an "Islamic Republic." Many Iranians embraced this message.

Understanding the appeal of Khomeini's orders to the Iranian people, Danny was, at the same time, fundamentally terrified by the cold-blooded horrors the old man suggested. Fathers sacrificing their children in order to waste the bullets of soldiers trying to regain control of the streets? Never in a million years! Mothers dressing their sons in death shrouds so their bodies could be identified after the rioting? No civilized people in the world behaved this way, but Danny was seeing it every day. It was happening all around him! Caught up in the hysteria, the people were listening to the Ayatollah's most insane suggestions as though they issued from the mouth of God himself; indeed, Shi'ites believed God would not allow a man to say such dangerous things unless they were God's will, not understanding, of course, the Devil also speaks through men. As a logical person, Danny only heard the Devil speaking now. How could these people believe any of this crap? But even Iranians educated overseas bared their hairy chests in the face of the Army's guns.

One night, two months after this quiet moodiness had seized him, there was a noise from downtown: a rhythm of crowds and clanking tanks, the sizzle of burning tires and swirling smoke filling the streets between the high buildings. On the rooftops, there were shouted rumors of shooting and frenzied running in the dark, the hysteria of sweaty fear and terrible risk. For the first time in weeks, Danny raised his eyes and actually looked out over the anxious city of Teheran. He could smell the fear of women and children locked in their homes and feel the hush of dead streets after frantic crowds had run through. At last, he was able to feel the excitement that gripped the people of Teheran.

"What do you suppose that is?" he inquired, rising from his creaky lawn chair on Norman's roof. A glow lit the sky to the south of him. Clouds of pink smoke billowed above the blackness. No one answered him when he turned around; he could tell they were keeping something from him.

"What are they burning?" he demanded. "What are those fools up to now? What the fuck are they destroying?"

He checked all the landmarks. The American Embassy? No, he decided, the angle wasn't quite right. Was it Laleh with its garish nightclubs and gold merchants? Shahreza Avenue or Kouroush-e-Kabir? No, too far to the left. This fire was—

"Ferdowsi?" he asked the night.

"I'm sorry," one of the Lufthansa stewardesses croaked, looking at the others in embarrassment. "They started looting the carpet shops this afternoon. Things got out of hand."

"Ferdowsi?" he screamed, the truth dawning on him at last. "Of course! They're after the Jews. Benyamin and his family are down there."

"Forget it," one of the women said, "There's nothing you can do," but Danny was already rushing downstairs to his bedroom.

"You stupid sonofabitch," Marvin shouted, jumping to his feet. "It's too fucking late! They're all dead."

Hollering, "No!" as if their protests could keep this horrible thing from happening, the women rushed down the stairs too. Someone dropped her wine glass on the roof's concrete tiles. It bounced three times before shattering into pieces, but no one paid it any attention.

Marvin was the first to start after his roommate but the last to arrive. Danny had already thrown on a pair of cowboy boots and was shrugging into a field jacket when the first stewardesses burst through his bedroom door. As he coolly pocketed a knife and gloves, Marvin and another woman piled into the room. Moving through his friends like a tornado, Danny fished a Smith and Wesson .357 out of an air duct and then retrieved two boxes of shells from a hollow book.

"Where the hell you think you're going?" Marvin demanded, forcing his way through six frightened women.

"Don't mess with me, Marvin. Not now. Now's not the time to do this."

"Listen, you're not going downtown," the big man snapped, drawing himself up to full height. "In fact, shithead, you're not going anywhere near Ferdowsi, not tonight, not never fucking again!"

His threat lost its power, however, when two more women pressed into the room, pushing him aside as if he weren't even there. There was a palpable fear in the room, and wonder, too, for something about Danny MacCreary had changed forever. Behind his sunglasses, a new resolve shone in his eyes. His indecision and apathy were gone at last. The Revolution had changed him forever.

"Marvin, I don't like to cuss, but you get the fuck out of my way," Danny ordered. "All of you get out of my way." Flipping the cylinder of the .357 open, he methodically dropped six shells in, then slipped the pistol into a pocket and put his gloves on. "Mind your own fucking business for once. It's too late to start minding mine—"

The first to hit him was Inga, a German stewardess. In seconds, Danny was buried under a pile of women's bodies. His friends seemed convinced that if he left them now, he would never return. Struggling to get loose, he found himself pinned under their bodies. An English stewardess straddled his chest, then Inga, screaming in rage, cocked her arm back and hit him in the nose as hard as she could.

He woke up an hour before sunrise, sore, swollen, and tied to a bed. His nose was broken for the third time in Iran. Ralf had been the first—a deliberate elbow in a simple tussle. Masud was the second, with his head, as he straightened up unexpectedly and caught Danny leaning over him, but this third time was from a woman. Danny was embarrassed. Using tricks Fraser had taught him, he worked his way out of the bonds but discovered his gun and boots were gone; after a short search, he found them hidden in Marvin's closet. Fortunately, the pistol was still loaded, though his spare bullets weren't anywhere in sight. He looked in the mirror. His nose was very bloody, and his eyes were already black; he straightened his nose in pain, using two Bic pens to align his nostrils. He would have sinus problems the rest of his life.

There was a buzz of conversation upstairs on the roof, but nobody was downstairs except the maid and the gardener. "Have you fed the animals yet?" Danny demanded, getting a warm Coke from the refrigerator. The electricity had been off for over eighteen hours, yet the cook had managed to make breakfast by candlelight again. She was a good woman, Danny thought. Despite bottled gas being hard to find and refrigeration next to impossible, she fed over twenty people a day at the villa. He made a mental note to give her a raise, but he vowed he would never hire back her worthless husband, a coward who had run away to their village at the first sign of trouble in the city. Fucker!

"I no feed the animals yet," the gardener answered. "I no do nothing this morning."

It was this spark of belligerence that was spoiling the country, Danny thought. Fools! They were ruining the best Iran they would have in their lifetimes. The Shah might not be perfect, but at least he had a dream and the will to make it happen.

"Go do it," he told the servant, "and have Sadeq help you clean the pool. Do you think life's stopping because there's a revolution going on? While you're at it, water the garden— we've got to eat, you son-of-a-bitch!"

"I go now," the man replied impudently, glaring at Danny as he hurried out to feed the sheep and rabbits fattening in cages behind the swimming pool.

Outside, the streets were deathly quiet in the dawn. On Saltanadabad Avenue, traffic was subdued, and there were no cops to be seen anywhere. Women hurried from shops wrapped in *chadors*, for it was unusual now to see a woman in western clothes, even near the boutiques of Pahlavi Avenue. Old men in pajamas strolled home with fresh, hot *barbari* bread. *Cigarees* were opening their stands and arranging their cigarettes and gum stands for sale. Whatever had happened to the national lottery? He had been in the habit of buying tickets every week from the *cigarees*, but it had been months since he had seen the tickets offered for sale at the cigarette stands.

At first, Danny couldn't get a taxi, "Shahreza Avenue! Shahreza!" he shouted again and again in the open windows of empty taxis. A few dozen cabs passed him by, unwilling to pick up a *farangi*, but finally a friendly businessman in a BMW gave him a ride.

"I can only take you to Pahlavi Avenue," the man apologized.

"That's fine."

"I think it is a good time for you to go home," the man suggested. "Things are becoming difficult here—"

"No," Danny smiled. "Not yet," and he wondered when, exactly, was a good time to go back to Wyoming? If it weren't now, with all the violence and shortages, when would he finally make up his mind? Everyone else was packing up; the American community was shrinking by the hundreds every day the airport was open, but when would he decide to go?

Downtown, traffic on Shahreza seemed choked off somewhere to the east, so Danny had to walk again. Groups of hostile young men in field jackets and angry soldiers in full combat gear were everywhere. Once, he was badly scared near Teheran University by running youths, but he managed to avoid trouble, probably because he pulled his gun whenever anyone got too close.

There were crowds near Meidan-e-Ferdowsi, and soldiers prowled the side streets to the north and south. In the great square itself, he could see the grassy park around Ferdowsi's bust was torn up, the rose bushes stripped of their leaves, and garbage strewn about. Slipping like a shadow into the square itself, Danny was overcome at the sight. Smoke hung in the *meidan* like a pall. Broken signs and pieces of clothing were scattered everywhere. Near his feet, someone's eyeglasses were crushed on the sidewalk among broken bricks. A dead man lay across the square, his stiff hands reaching in agony toward the sky, exactly where Leila used to stand, long ago.

Emperor Carpet, Benyamin's uncle's store, was burned out, its windows gone and its display rooms stripped and smoky. A burned body lay across the main entrance, and there was an awful barbecued smell coming from inside. Running quickly now, Danny turned the corner and crossed Ferdowsi Avenue, nearly slipping on piles of broken plate glass lying in the middle of the street.

Quality Persian Carpet, Benyamin's shop, was no more. The whole front of the building had vanished, and every floor had collapsed into the fiery interior. All along the glass-littered street were piles of smoking debris, the remains of a king's fortune in precious Persian carpets and cash. Half buried in the smoldering ruins was a blackened hulk, all that was left of the Khodaris' big safe and many, many millions of dollars in foreign currency.

Not interested in the fire and smoke rising from other Jewish shops along Ferdowsi, nor in the soldiers shooting into the air near the British

Embassy a half mile south of him, Danny stood on a smoking pile of junk near the front of Quality Carpet and wept.

"Benyamin!" he screamed in grief, but the only answer he received was a bony clatter of bricks cascading from inside the blackened interior of the store.

$-24-$

DISAPPOINTMENT

"I thank you for your honesty. I know you are afraid. You think it is dangerous to tell the truth, but the information is appreciated. Your safety is guaranteed, though you must never tell anyone about this conversation."
—The Shah, Shahanshah Aryamehr, Mohammed Reza Pahlavi

The phone rang unexpectedly one weekend. After answering, Danny pulled on his pants and looked for a clean shirt, a rarity now that there was no electricity to run Marvin's American-made washer. By now, he was used to being awakened late, but he didn't like it. Even so, he snapped awake the moment he recognized Andrea's voice. "Get dressed, Doc," she'd said. "I'm coming over now. This is big...."

Squinting nearsightedly at the clock—two o'clock in the morning—he retrieved his sunglasses from a bedside table and then brushed his long hair and new, scraggly beard. In the dim light of his cluttered bedroom, he looked like some kind of beatnik in the mirror, but tired as he was, he felt more like a bum. The only thing Teheran never lacked during the Revolution was water, so at least he showered regularly; articles like soap, razor blades, toothpaste and deodorant, however, were hard to find, so he always felt grubby and smelly. All of his socks had holes in them; many of his shirts were missing a button or two. Having brought new clothes from America three years before, he discovered his clothes were now wearing out all at once, yet the revolution prevented him from taking care of his simplest needs. Brushing his long, straight hair away from his face, he realized a barber hadn't cut his hair in nine months.

Just the other night, when his roommate tried to treat him to the national dish, *chelo kebab*, there had been no fresh mutton available, no eggs, and no spices—so they had settled for white rice with no *soumakh*, mediocre tea, and no sugar to sweeten the tea. The waiter just walked away from the table after serving them. He didn't expect a tip; no one tipped anymore. What were the common people eating out there? Not only were the strikes hurting the upper class—the revolution's intended target—they were devastating the economy, and the poor were suffering the most. Rice was difficult to find; meat nearly impossible, and there was no refrigeration anyway. The supply of vegetables or "greens" (*sabzi*) was erratic. The only thing the Ayatollah and his "strikes" seemed to allow without restriction was rice and bread. *Sangyak* and *barbari* bread were commonly available. As the Revolution consumed Iran, Danny's diet devolved into Cheez-Whiz™ slathered onto hot *barbari* bread. His stomach—like millions of others—was full, but there was minimal nutrition. People couldn't drive without gas, nor could they dine without meat and vegetables, yet the revolution dragged on and on with a life of its own.

Every day, the Ayatollah's followers were urged to destroy Iran's economy until the country was theirs, and every day the fanatical mobs became more shortsighted and dangerous. Once, the Ayatollah advocated the closing of pharmacies; there was no telling how many people died or were hurt. Last night, it had been close: the liquor store two blocks away from the villa had been firebombed and the owner burned to cinders on the sidewalk outside. No one collected the body, and sixteen hours passed. People were afraid. Funny, Danny thought as he tucked in his shirt in his bedroom, how one couldn't drive a car, but there was no shortage of gasoline for Molotov cocktails—

Something about Andrea's tone had jarred his senses alive, causing him to hurry downstairs. He had begun to feel anxious lately, though most of his friends advised him to treat the crowds of demonstrators as he would packs of wild dogs: if he didn't look anyone in the eye, they would pose no threat to his safety. Still, these were extremely dangerous times in the streets of Teheran, and no one knew where the disturbances were leading. Resisting the temptation to load a gun, he sat down in the kitchen to wait. Mrs. Daryani, (bless her!) got up and made him a cup of coffee, two spoons of sugar, but he didn't touch it. It was coffee from Uganda, the only kind he could find now, and it was bitter. It needed lots of sugar—or whiskey—to make it palatable. The steaming cup sat in front of him on the table until it went cold. He appreciated the warmth, but he couldn't drink it. How could he repay that woman? It was coming up on three o'clock in the morning, yet she got up to serve him. He had fired her husband two months before....

Twenty minutes later, Andrea arrived in the back of a Mercedes filled with dark-suited SAVAK secret police. Danny was escorted to another car, this one filled with men in suits not quite so nice as the SAVAK men's, indicating they were military officers. Why would SAVAK and the military cooperate on a pickup assignment? Puzzled, Danny glanced out the window to see if there were anyone following them, then checked out the men with him. He decided this wasn't a routine assignment. Something was up, and he recalled Fraser telling him opportunities often come disguised as disasters. Andrea and he were being taken somewhere—and it wasn't a prison.

The darkened streets flew by as the two cars raced higher and higher in the city towards the mountains and the neighborhoods Danny knew best—past the beautiful homes of the powerful, the rich, and the dangerous—and then along a twisting route down narrow *kutches* filled with expensive cars. Neighborhood police on patrol became more common. After a lengthy drive, the two cars parked beside a towering, whitewashed wall. Branches of large plane trees overhung the wall, which showed no bumps or ripples in its construction, indicating this was either a military compound or a palace. Prisons always had lumpy walls, Danny had observed, as did government ministries, since no worker felt pride in their construction. The military, on the other hand, supervised its own projects, so the lines of its buildings were usually straight, the floors level, and the roofs leaky only in a rain.

A few steps from the curb, a strong steel gate was guarded by two crack soldiers armed with loaded G-3's. Inside the gate was another gate and walls where there were more disciplined soldiers. Danny recognized them as the Imperial Guard, the so-called Ten Thousand Immortals. It was the only branch of the military he had never encountered in Iran, and it still instilled fear in the streets of Teheran.

Twenty yards ahead and surrounded by armed men, Andrea led the way up a sidewalk toward a low marble palace while Danny followed at his own pace, four soldiers and two officers bringing up the rear. A lone SAVAK officer waited by the gate.

Their destination was an airy wing of Niavaran Palace, the least opulent but most hospitable of the many homes available for the royal family's use. They were whisked past guards standing in the snowy gardens, and directed through a glass door and down an empty hallway. The palace, which had a good central heating system—a rarity in Iran—was suffocatingly warm inside. Notable, but not extraordinary works of art hung from the walls, and loyal servants moved silently across the fine, but not precious, carpets covering the floors.

Ushered into a small room—a room that had no real function, a luxury only the truly rich could afford in their homes—Danny and Andrea were told to wait. A working desk near a window was cluttered with papers and a man's eyeglasses. Opposite the door, two small oil paintings by Impressionist masters accented the creamy, but otherwise empty plaster of the walls. The room was a private area where conversations could take place and be forgotten, a retreat from public pomp or the family intimacy of the rest of the palace.

They had barely sat for what they thought would be a long wait, when the door opened and a man entered the room. "Miss Andrea, we meet again," he acknowledged in a mellifluous, but not altogether warm tone. Taking her hand, he kissed it lightly, his black eyes glittering with excitement.

"We meet again," she agreed, but Danny could see no joy in her eyes as she pulled her hand from the man's grip. Where had she met the man before, Danny wondered?

The man turned, nodded and said, "Doctor Daniel Rene MacCreary of the Imperial Iranian Air Force ... and the Wilcox Organization."

"How do you do?" Danny nodded, unsure if he should extend his hand or not. The man was a dangerous courtier. Thinning hair, beaked nose, medium build—he could be anyone.

"Let's get to business," the man said. "You are both well known here."

Questioning whether "here" meant in Iran or within the palace walls, Danny wondered how much these people could know about him. Was he in danger? Was he among friends? He couldn't guess, and the man gave no clue.

"On occasion, Miss Andrea has been of value to us," the Iranian proceeded. "As a source of advice and information, she has provided a medium of communication far beyond what was available prior to her coming to Iran." The man paused, smiling without showing any teeth. Dubbing him "Lizard Lips," Danny observed that unlike most of his countrymen, the man spoke English without much of an accent.

Andrea responded with a smile of her own, but she was pale, and a vein in her neck pulsed. Why was she so afraid? Danny watched the man carefully, noticing he spoke almost without words touching his tongue—a practiced, veiled way of communicating without saying what he really meant. He was probably a diplomat, Danny decided, a man used to conveying the thoughts of others.

"Doctor Mary," the man said, turning an expressionless eye on him. "You are a man whose honesty is a marketable commodity—a sad comment on modern Iran, but true, nonetheless. You, too, have been of use to us, for you have carried treasures far beyond your comprehension. If it were up to me," he declared, "You would both be richly rewarded for your valuable services to Iran ... and then I would have you shot in the garden. Do you understand my position?"

Gulping audibly, Andrea faltered, her cool, practiced facade slipping, but Danny knew the man was playing with them. While teaching English as a Second Language, he had learned to interpret body language, the non-verbal signals used to communicate a person's true meanings. Now, as he watched the man speak, he decided this messenger boy was toying with them, and he casually reached out with his right foot and flipped the corner of a beautiful Isfahan carpet below him, noting its quality and appraising its value. Benyamin Khodari would have been proud of him, but Andrea stared in disbelief. Suddenly understanding the action as a signal, she recovered her icy composure. By the time the Iranian looked up from Danny's shoe, she had restored her aristocrat's facade, her temporary weakness gone.

Still the man persisted. "We have volumes of material on each of you. Miss Andrea, for example, has done business with the enemies of society and the laws of man."

What had happened to Islamic rhetoric? Danny wondered. The man was bold, if nothing else, for even the Shah gave lip service to the precepts of Islam in his speeches. What was this "laws of man" business? The pock-marked man had obviously spent too much time in the West, for no real Iranian believed in human rights or the "natural" laws of man. Perhaps this was the reason President Jimmy Carter, with his calls for human rights, was scaring Iranians every time he spoke righteous words out of a naive mouth. He seemed every bit the radical that the Ayatollah appeared to the Western world! The enemies of society? Danny allowed himself a cynical smile. Was the man referring to the drug smugglers, the prostitutes, the mercenaries, and the killers, or did he mean the religious clerics who were trying to destroy the order and modern progress of the Shah in order to restore an outdated feudal society?

The door opened again, and a thin man stepped in to look over the guests. Evidently he was a senior servant of some sort, for the other Iranian hardly looked at him; the tension in the room increased noticeably when the stranger stepped back into the hallway and closed the door. Outside, there were whispers and the thump of rifle butts on the floor.

"And the Doctor," the Iranian continued, "a man who specializes in paper. You have carried the cassettes and messages of religious fanaticism, and you have delivered promises and obligations against the State and the Person of His Majesty, the Shah. You have compromised the rich, you have bargained with power in Iran, you have dealt with the cream of Iranian society and profited from it, yet you have also moved among the worst sort, doing business north and south."

Ah, "worst sort," Danny thought. The man had been educated in England....

Quite bored now, Danny decided the paintings on the wall must be lesser Monets, the frames more ornate than the heavily painted canvases. He promised himself that after he got out of this miserable country, he would take a leisurely trip through all Europe's finest art museums. Art, movies, literature and music—he wanted to indulge them all after the cultural vacuum he was living in Iran—

Suddenly the door opened again, and a man came in, nodded to the servants and guards outside, and quietly closed the door. Once, long before at Lackland Air Force Base in San Antonio, Texas, Danny had seen this man in a photograph. He had seen him again—in the flesh—at Doshan Tappeh as he got in a helicopter at some distance, dressed in a uniform resplendent with medals and gold sashes while hundreds of ramrod-straight officers and soldiers stood at attention. His photograph was literally everywhere in Iran. Although the Brits enjoyed calling him The Shit of Iran, or Himself, or Ralph, his real name was feared and respected throughout Iran and the entire world. The Shah, Light of the Aryans, king of kings, Shahanshah Aryamehr, His Imperial Majesty, Mohammad Reza Pahlavi, the real royal "We" now stood before them in this little room. And he breathed air, like they did....

Beyond the myriad photographs and far from the shouts of the raging mobs, the man who took a chair at the desk and faced them was dry, proper, and small-boned. Dressed in a plain business suit, he could have been almost anyone else except for those penetrating eyes. Danny felt his heart hammering as he realized he was in the presence of one of the most powerful men on earth.

The Shah sat at his desk, but he was not directly involved. The interview belonged to the other man, and it was apparent that something was to be proven here, something that was not being asked, but confirmed. "Miss Andrea Wilcox," the other man said, by way of an introduction.

The Shah nodded imperceptibly, barely moving his eyes in her direction.

"We are familiar with Miss Wilcox." His English was not as comfortable as the other man's. Danny had heard the Shah's French was much better.

"Doctor Daniel Rene MacCreary," the other Iranian added. The Shah did not acknowledge Danny with even so much as a glance. "Doctor MacCreary is the courier of the Wilcox organization," the pockmarked man announced, his eyes glittering again with the excitement he had shown earlier. "He delivers information and money—under the strict control of Miss Andrea herself, of course."

Again, the Shah nodded slightly at mention of her name. "To business," the Shah ordered in a quiet voice.

"Yes." The other man jumped out of his chair and opened the door. A secretary and a guard brought in three stacks of files tied with velvet ribbons, which they placed on a table beside the man's chair. Another, much thinner folder, bound in sumptuous blue cloth, was laid on the desk near the Shah's hand, after which the servants withdrew.

Almost as if he realized their presence for the first time, the Shah raised his eyes and asked, "Would you like something to drink?"

"That would be nice," Danny answered. If he lived through this adventure, he promised himself to never forget speaking to the Shah. For him, it was like an autograph to a collector, a treasured moment no one could take away from him. He was to talk with the Shah himself!

Their questioner, frustrated by the interruption, let it be known he was displeased; nevertheless, the Shah summoned a servant to bring tea, coffee, and pastries. Although she was used to being served at the homes of the rich and famous, Andrea seemed horrified at the imposition yet morbidly fascinated with the goodies to be offered. For his part, Danny helped himself to a generous piece of a twenty layer raspberry tort and an American-sized cup of coffee. While the others sipped small cups of tea in awkward silence, he munched and drank, thoroughly enjoying himself.

"On to business," the Iranian said when Danny finished and wiped his mustache and new beard with an Irish linen napkin. "You have been asked here to provide an accounting of some of your activities. Specifically, we will inquire as to the frequency and nature of some of the transactions you have had with certain individuals."

"Our service has always been confidential," Andrea interrupted, looking the man in the eye.

"Yes, but in these circumstances, your confidentiality is a commodity like ... your trust." He used the word like a whip, apparently hoping to taint it, but it didn't work. The Shah didn't even look up from his files.

"Confidentiality," the Shah decreed, "is not a commodity here, nor is trust." Although his voice was small and quiet, there was enough fire and power therein to chasten his adviser. "This interview is based on mutual trust and confidentiality."

"Of course," the man agreed, momentarily stifling his anger. Obviously, he hated the two foreigners. Danny wondered how he could jockey for Byzantine bonus points while his country was burning in the streets outside. As he swallowed his pride, however, Danny again caught that glitter in the man's eyes, a lust for power, whatever power there was—or whatever power remained. "I have … that is—we have a need for information both reliable and factual," the man said, regaining his composure.

Their interrogator would as soon be pulling their fingernails out along with their secrets, Danny realized, but at the moment, they were safe sitting under the Shah's protection. Danny smiled at Andrea, and after a thoughtful moment, she smiled back. She was pale. The Shah was not really so bad—

Taking the first bundle of file folders from the stack on the table, the man untied a ribbon and asked, "Do you deal at all with this man?" He held up an 8" x 10" photo.

"Yes, that's Prince Hamid. We have done business with him on occasion," Andrea answered.

"Regularly?"

Danny looked at Andrea, then answered for himself, "I've seen him four or five times in the past two years."

"And you?" the man asked, nodding at Andrea.

"I had business with him perhaps twice or three times a year," she answered.

"Personally, or just your girls?"

"Neither," she answered. "I supplied escorts for a party hosted by Prince Hamid. Some entertainment was, of course, provided, but I do not remember the Prince as being involved in any way."

The man's eyes were cold and disappointed. "Very well," he replied through clenched teeth. "He is the Shah's younger brother, you know."

"Yes, I know."

"Hmm," the man continued, apparently trying to inflict damage. "Can you tell me of any interests this man is known for?"

"I'm sure your intelligence services have more information than I could supply," Andrea snapped. "Such information is nothing but gossip anyway, since I've already stated I have not dealt with him more intimately."

"Yes, I agree," the Shah said, much to the chagrin of the questioner.

"Then you," the Iranian said, turning to Danny. "You've had business with him too? Have you carried things from him or to him?"

"That I can recall," Danny answered, "both."

"What did you carry to him?"

"A few proposals of some sort, suggestions for business."

"From whom?"

"Bazaaris, if I remember correctly."

"That's it? Just legitimate business proposals?"

"That I can remember, that's all."

"And what have you carried from him?"

"Do you remember a kidnapping case a couple of years ago? A girl from a rich family, the Mahmoudieh, disappeared and was said to be held for ransom?"

"I heard of it. She was never found...."

"She was, sir," Danny countered. "Some time later. Raped and strangled...."

"I did not see a police report...."

"I have it from—" Danny stated, "Creditable sources," he finished lamely.

"I am saddened to learn of this," the Shah said honestly. "She was from a good family."

"I carried money from Prince Hamid to the Hashemi family," Danny said, "to ... ah ... finance ... a discreet inquiry into the condition of the girl. I don't know if the money was from the girl's family or from the Prince himself. The girl was found south of Qazvin, her throat cut all the way to her backbone. She had been raped ...well, she was real bloody."

"But the Prince had dealings with the Hashemi?"

"No. I dealt with the Hashemi," Danny answered. "The Prince did not want to be involved with them, which is why I was contracted for the trick."

"That is not my view on the matter," the man said, and the Shah didn't correct him. Emboldened, he unwrapped a larger bundle and took out another photograph.

"The Princess Ashraf," Andrea offered, recognizing the Shah's twin sister, who was, in many ways, more feared than her brother. Andrea often dealt with her, and Danny, who was friends with one of her nieces, knew much of the Princess' court and personal business. They had much to discuss, almost an hour's worth.

"Do you know this man?" the Iranian asked later, holding up another photograph.

"Not personally—" Andrea muttered.

"Yes," Danny said. "This is Amir Abbas Hoveyda, the former prime minister."

"How do you know him?"

Embarrassed, Danny said, "I met him once, when I attended a dinner with friends. He was there to see a precious carpet for sale after the meal."

"He bid on this carpet?" the Shah asked incredulously. A year before, the Shah had lost faith in Hoveyda's government; he had dismissed Hoveyda and replaced him with Jamshid Amuzegar, a hard-liner who had only compounded the difficulties and shortages plaguing the country.

"No, I think he was there just to view the carpet," Danny said. "I believe Ali Nassiri's brother bought it."

"Did you see the carpet yourself?" the Shah asked.

"No, I couldn't get closer than twenty meters," Danny replied. "I believe it was just a carpet fragment...."

"Yes," the Shah said. "It was offered to me for one hundred million tomans. I was told the carpet was looted from a frozen Scythian tomb deep in the Soviet Union. The artifact is thought to be the oldest carpet fragment ever found—perhaps six thousand years old—but I felt the costs of buying it were too high for the Iranian State. I advised the agent to donate the carpet to the Hermitage Museum in the Soviet Union."

The pockmarked man appeared disappointed he had failed to uncover any real dirt on Hoveyda's character; the Shah, however, appeared torn between personal loyalty to Hoveyda and political uncertainty. After a moment's hesitation, the Shah looked away rather sadly.

"And this woman?" the man asked, holding up another picture, "What about her?"

"I often supplied girls for her parties," Andrea admitted. "She used the girls as favors for her business partners, but she also slept with a few of them herself."

"What about you?" the man asked Danny.

"I've dealt with her many times," he answered. "She has control over the ports and customs."

"She does not!" the Shah snapped. "She does not! She has never had control!"

"I'm sorry, sir, but she does," Danny disagreed. "Do you remember the hundreds of White trucks that were imported to Iran but were never cleared through customs? They're nothing more than rusted hulks in the ports now, but I carried at least a dozen proposals and lots of money to this woman to allow or not allow the trucks into this country."

"What did it cost?" the Shah interrupted.

"A truck full of money, foreign currency, not to allow the trucks into the country. I heard later the woman was involved in importing another company's trucks into Iran."

"We know that," the Shah said, disappointment showing on his face. "We did not know about her connection in the ports."

"I believe she's also involved in the manufacture of automobiles here in Iran, the Paykans, and she gets ... um ... consulting fees from the drivers' license bureaus."

"Enough. Perhaps I allowed her too many concessions," the Shah admitted. "I did not set enough limits on her." He looked at the floor, and his right hand twitched.

Other photos followed, mostly members of the Shah's family, though some were businessmen or members of the court. Generally, the interview painted a picture of corruption and cynicism. A few of the Shah's family and advisors were revealed as truly unscrupulous, but most were merely opportunists who had profited from Iran's incredible oil wealth.

During the interview, Danny realized for the first time the Shah himself was incorruptible. He was someone who had given his all to his country, who had expected much and gained much in return, but who had never presumed to take what he could grab. But the Shah had shown a blind side where his relatives and friends were concerned, and great was his depression as the interview progressed. Somehow—though neither Danny nor Andrea understood it—the interview was a turning point in the Shah's attempts to counter the revolution. From this moment on, he would only grow moodier and more disillusioned; his actions would rarely be strong enough or conciliatory enough to win popular support from the people.

After four hours, the interview was over. Danny and Andrea had identified and commented on nearly thirty of the Shah's family and perhaps as many of his advisors. Only two or three actual surprises were revealed, but the Shah's face aged considerably as he learned of the unethical and illicit activities of his own people.

"Thank you. You have been of great personal service," he said, extending his hand. Andrea took it and curtsied. When he offered it to Danny, the way thousands of courtiers had received it to bow over and kiss, Danny shook it gravely, an American to the last. Americans don't kneel, he reminded himself. They shake hands. Like other Iranian men, The Shah's handshake was weak and a bit wet.

"I have noted your interests in Persian handicrafts. Please accept gifts for your services tonight," the Shah said, disappearing into a ring of servants and guards waiting for him in the hallway.

It was nearly light outside. The guards and secret police were gone, and the grounds of the great palace were empty and covered with fresh snow. Together, Andrea and Danny walked unaccompanied across the wintry garden and through the gate to a waiting car. On the seat next to the driver were gifts from the Shah: an expensive silk carpet for Danny and an inlaid box containing antique Turkoman earrings for Andrea. Although it did not mean much at the time, Danny soon prized his new carpet above all the others he acquired. Running his hand over it on the drive back into the city, he noted that its ancient pile was so closely trimmed it resembled felt. Very nice, he thought to himself, looking out at the traffic and smiling.

Not long afterwards, the Shah laid down a strict code of ethics for his family, but its terms did not become public until much, much later. Missing the chance to act forcibly against some of the excesses that had contributed to the unrest among his people, the Shah again appeared indecisive, but it really didn't matter, since most of his family had already fled the country.

−25−

THE REVOLUTION

"[Iran is] an island of stability."
—President Jimmy Carter, December 31, 1977, Teheran, Iran

Ask an Iranian what he remembers about the Revolution, and he is likely to mention pictures of the Shah and President Carter on the lawn of the White House wiping tears from their faces after tear gas used to quell demonstrators drifted the wrong way. The Shah had feet of clay; he could weep tears with real salt, like a normal human being. The pictures were shown on international television—and endlessly viewed in Iran.

The first act of the revolution, however, was a newspaper article accusing the Ayatollah Khomeini of homosexuality, communist tendencies, foreign birth, and a mother who worked as a professional dancer. On January 7, 1978, five thousand people gathered at a mosque in Qom to protest these insults to the Ayatollah. The army dispersed the crowd, but about a dozen people were killed.

Forty days later—the traditional mourning period—there were more riots and a few more fatalities. On March 28th, a hundred demonstrators were killed in Tabriz when the provincial governor ordered tanks to disperse a crowd. With power outages and shortages of commodities beginning, the people became hysterical, started hoarding, and openly grumbled about censorship, repression, and the Shah's avaricious family.

On May 7th, 1978, there were small riots throughout the country; before long, the bazaars closed, bringing trade to a halt. Even so, tensions did not become unbearable until the month of Ramadan. Moslems were irritable enough that month, since they were to refrain from eating, drinking, smoking, or having sex during daylight hours, but the result was a populace exhausted by eating, drinking, smoking, and screwing all night with precious little sleep. On the sixth day of Ramadan, there were riots in Isfahan. Armed with Molotov cocktails, the mobs burned vehicles, banks, theaters, hotels, police stations, and liquor stores. The military opened fire, killing about a hundred.

"I treated two hundred people for burns in Isfahan," a German doctor told Danny later that month. "The majority of the injuries were self-inflicted."

"You're kidding," Danny said.

"Nope, troublemakers playing with gasoline bombs for the first time!" the man laughed.

Soon, however, an underground movement, supported by the PLO, began training people for urban warfare. As a result, the rioters became adept at fighting in the streets. With the country in chaos, civil servants went on strike, paralyzing the government. Danny was put on indefinite furlough at Doshan Tappeh Air Force Base, and the language school quietly folded. It would never reopen.

"Damn!" he complained. "Now what do I do?"

"Work for me," Andrea offered. "Two hundred-fifty thousand rials a month, plus five thousand for each trick."

"Great," Danny said enthusiastically. "I'll do it. What about my work visa?"

"I'll take care of it. I have contacts."

There were explosions nearly every day now, little ones and great big ones. Airline offices were destroyed and stores blown up as an expression of anti-Western sentiment. Like Jesus' disciple Peter, Danny found it safer to deny who he was; he began to identify himself as a Canadian.

On August 19, 1978, the Cinema Rex in Abadan was torched with a full audience inside. The arson was so obvious everyone chose the most unbelievable explanation: SAVAK must have done it to divert attention away from the Shah. Over four hundred screaming people were burned to death that day, and everyone in Iran claimed to know someone killed there.

The revolution had begun in earnest.

"I'm convinced," Danny told his roommate one night as they sat on the roof listening to the raging city below, "the revolution started with a movie."

"How's that?" Marvin asked, swigging the last of his sixteenth beer.

"You know how Iranians wanted their country to be in the forefront of movie making?"

"Yep. I knew an English asshole who came and tried to finance the *Shahnameh*, the Persian literary classic. Later, when someone made *Caravans*, I got to meet Anthony Quinn."

"You met Anthony Quinn? Did you have him over to the house?" Danny asked incredulously.

"No, I met him at Heinz Reibach's place."

"Good," Danny joked. "If you'd had him over here, and I hadn't met him, I'd be very upset!"

"What does a fucking movie have to do with the revolution?"

"You know most of the movies shown heren have been Italian films or romantic Indian musicals," Danny said. "The Teheran Film Festival was the only bright spot for serious moviegoers. It brought in movies from the world. I had a devil of a time getting tickets; I was starved for something from the outside world, something fresh and interesting. A couple of years ago, the most popular American entry was a Robert Redford film called 'Three Days of the Condor.' I believe that movie started the revolution in Iran."

"How?" Marvin asked. "I saw the movie too."

"Most Iranians suspect their country is manipulated by superpowers. The Shah promised the people the rise of OPEC and the control of the oil weapon would lead to dominance over the Western world, but here was a movie that mocked that fantasy. You remember at the end of the film where Cliff Robertson talks about destabilizing regimes as a weapon to regain control of worldwide energy production? The movie seemed to say the sovereignty of any oil-producing nation could be interrupted at any moment. That's what happened here in 1953 with the Mossadegh government. The CIA and others influenced Iran, and a lot of intellectuals have talked about that afterwards. I think Iranians believe nothing can be produced in Hollywood that's not condoned by the American government. They think everything must be officially approved. I believe it caused people to question Iran's future for the first time."

"But the movie was fiction!" Marvin laughed.

"I haven't met an Iranian yet who believes in fiction," Danny laughed. "They're so used to censorship and propaganda, they believe anything produced for public distribution must have a political aim. A movie you and I would see as fiction would be interpreted by them as a warning. I think they believed the movie "Three Days of the Condor."

"I don't think so," Marvin said. "I believe this Ayatollah Khomeini had this fucking revolution planned for years..."

"I don't," Danny said. "No one has planned this thing. It's been building. People have been dissatisfied. They're tired of seeing the Shah's picture everywhere, and they're fed up with his constant harping about development and the corrupt morals of Western democracies."

"And they're tired of SAVAK, too," Marvin added.

"Sure," Danny agreed. "But after my experience here, I've become convinced a couple thousand political prisoners, a little censorship, and some repression are inherent in any Third-World country with no tradition of democracy. Even so, you have to admit there's been a lot of personal freedom and opportunity here."

"Opportunity creates its own tensions," Marvin said. "Look how Iranians hate foreign influence—particularly the influence of American mass culture. We're blamed for everything that has eroded their traditional values."

"Yeah," Danny admitted. "The lack of housing, haphazard industrialization, uncontrollable spending, big projects never completed, traffic and more traffic—none of these resulted from American influence—but it's been convenient to blame us for all of them."

Helping himself to another beer from the ice chest Marvin had brought from work, Danny reminisced, "The Shah bragged Iran's industrial production would exceed West Germany's within twenty years; he was wrong, of course, but he was only guilty of pride. I remember Prime Minister Hoveyda declaring, 'Iran now ranks among the advanced countries of the world,' and I laughed at the time, but he and the Shah really believed it. Iran has never been a great country, but it might have become one. As things stand now, this place won't ever be the country it was when I first came here. They're destroying it right now in the streets in front of us."

"Ain't that the truth," Marvin agreed, throwing his empty bottle over the fence into Mrs. Aryani's back yard. "Shit, I'm heading for bed. It's depressing thinking about this goddamn revolution."

"See you tomorrow," Danny said, putting his feet up on the parapet. He hadn't had a good night's rest in over a month. He spent most of his free time listening to the city. His salary was good, and Andrea kept him working nearly every day, but with the fighting in the streets escalating, her other businesses had dwindled. Sa'ad Behbahanian, a regular client, was off in Europe on "business," Bijan Rahim was in Japan, and the party boys, Hamid Fardousti and Manucherr Shabazi, had fled to America. One by one, the good customers were disappearing overseas, and there were rumors vast fortunes were leaving the country. Carpets, gold, and jewelry commanded premium prices, for they were easily transportable wealth.

"Doctor," one of Danny's Iranian friends asked one evening, "Do you still own that small silk prayer carpet you bought in Isfahan last year?"

"Sure do," Danny replied.

"You paid seventy thousand tomans for it, I think?"

"Yes I did," Danny admitted, something he rarely did when talking about carpets.

"I will give you two hundred thousand tomans for it. A deal?"

"A deal," Danny agreed. The carpet would be out of the country within the week, perhaps even headed back to Europe where it had been purchased three years before for a tenth of that price.

"My friend," another advised him a few weeks later, "It's a good time to ship your carpets to America."

"Thanks, but I shipped most of them two weeks ago," Danny replied. "I sent them to my brothers in Cheyenne, Wyoming. I still have three small silk carpets left."

"Bring them to my house. Now is the time to convert them to cash."

Danny later discovered Andrea had shipped her jewelry to England, especially the clunky items she treasured more than gold and precious stones. At the same time, several million dollars disappeared from her accounts, and Shamsa gossiped Andrea had talked to someone overseas about a large purchase of land somewhere.

Ali Nassiri, whose fortune lay mostly in real estate along the Caspian coast, was liquidating too, as were most prudent Iranians and Europeans. Ali took three quick trips to France to bank suitcases of cash, jewels, gold, and carpets. By coincidence, one of his recent purchases was the antique silk prayer carpet Danny had only recently sold.

One night, very much under the influence, Ali Nassiri told Andrea, "I have put all of my overseas accounts in your name so they can never be traced back to me. I will give you the pins, passwords, and account numbers."

"I appreciate the trust," Andrea said, "but if you are leave Iran, you'll need the money. It might be easier to collect if it's in your name—"

"I will never leave Iran," Ali Nassiri predicted. "I cannot leave. Too many people depend on me. If I need cash, I will send you to get it for me."

One by one, the prostitutes disappeared overseas as the money dried up. Puff Omura didn't say goodbye. One day she was there; the next she wasn't. Although effete Iranians were becoming more discreet with their pleasures, the girls that remained did a roaring business in desperation. Iranian girls—Kabri, Ratna, Behnaz, Fusie, Farah, Nilufar, Sahar, and finally even Shamsa, the receptionist—were suddenly in demand, though there was beginning to be trouble in the business too. One day, Danny learned a customer had beaten Kabri to death. A week later, one of Andrea's soldiers, Sa'ad Pourafkari, disappeared while waiting out by a car during a trick, and then Farah was found a few days later with her throat cut.

— 26 —

THE TURNCOAT

"Bert's dead? You cannot be telling me this! He was just an accountant. He wasn't important to anybody on this planet."

—Andrea

"Ralf?" Andrea shouted from the top of the stairs one afternoon. Danny and the big German were sitting together in the darkened lounge of the office, talking about the Shah and his problems. Danny and Ralf often had conversations now. Ralf had a lot of experience in Africa and was skeptical about everything; Danny had a lot of insightful thoughts and had met a lot of influential Iranians. There was so much to be discussed and digested, yet the more Danny learned from Ralf, and the more Danny shared with him, the more concerned the two became. Danny moved all of his stashes; Ralf converted everything he could to foreign currency.

"Yes?" Ralf answered Andrea's distant voice.

"I've thought it over. Can you arrange a touch for me?"

"Farah's last client?" he asked, his voice shrill with excitement.

Not liking the tone of the conversation, Danny got up to leave. Even so, he heard Andrea declare, "It's got to be him. He's been violent lately. He's erratic—on drugs—I'm sure he killed Farah. I'll pay four thousand tomans for a clean touch."

"Done," Ralf agreed, smiling with as wolfish a grin as Danny had ever seen.

The murdering of clients was one of the dirtiest sides of Andrea's business, but it indicated the opportunities possible in revolutionary Iran. With the police impotent, the Hashemis were hiring private soldiers all over the country in a bold attempt to take over the criminal underworld. If someone needed gasoline, the Hashemis had it. What about cooking gas, rice, flour, or sugar? The Hashemis could provide. Onions? Yes, the Hashemis had an unlimited supply. Inevitably, the thin line between what was Hashemi and what was Sadeghi blurred. Sadjewi Hashemi moved to take over the black market in guns and radios; Hashemi gunmen began to work extortion, kidnapping, and ransom rackets too, infuriating Manucherr Sadeghi further. With hardly any warning, the fifteen-year truce between the two crime families was broken.

Sadjewi Hashemi's youngest son, Hussain—the one Danny had found unsuitable for marriage with a Sadeghi girl—was mysteriously murdered and his body dumped outside an abandoned construction site in Tajrish. In revenge, Khani Abbassi, Sadjewi's most trusted lieutenant, was killed two days later while inventorying six tons of newly-delivered hashish, and then four Hashemi soldiers were shot to death when the minor warehouse they were guarding was torched.

Two days later, a massive assault took place on the Sadeghi headquarters in the Teheran vegetable market. A truck loaded with explosives drove through a steel gate and exploded in the central courtyard. Thirty gunmen dressed in police and army uniforms burst in and shot up the facade of the building while a lone European placed an explosive charge against the door and another in a stack of cooking gas cylinders.

The explosion vibrated dust off rooftops two miles off, and windows were shattered a quarter-mile away. The resulting fire was far worse than the explosion, for it spread from rooftop to rooftop, ultimately burning the entire vegetable market to the ground. In a city suffering severe shortages of fresh food, this was the worst catastrophe yet. Nearly a hundred innocent people died in the blaze. Manucherr Sadeghi lost all his sons and two of his four lieutenants: Malek Zimani and Khosrow Nejad. Sixty of his soldiers were killed too, including three that were friendly with Danny: Mohammed Mohammedi, and the cousins Abbas and Ghassem Jaffari. The people of Teheran blamed "terrorists" and SAVAK for the fire; inevitably, even the Shah himself was accused of the arson.

"You must help me," Manucherr Sadeghi begged Andrea and her assembled associates later that week. "Let me contract the service of your best, especially the Allemani, Ralf Gruenewald."

"No," Ralf snapped before Andrea could answer.

"But Andrea, you have the only men who can stop the Hashemi!" Sadeghi begged. "You have the best private soldiers in Iran today. You can hardly—"

"Not for hire," Ralf said from across the room.

"Ralf, we don't know the offer yet," Andrea chided, trying to be reasonable.

"I've been involved in things like this before, in Africa. I prefer commitments to one-time contracts."

Guenther and Dieter, two mercs who spent very little time at Andrea's office since they were married men, plus Bob and Carl, all mercenaries to the core, stared at each other in surprise over Ralf's sudden obstinacy. They smelled money in this Sadeghi offer. Never before had the huge German turned down such an opportunity. Nearby, even Danny was amazed. Lately, Ralf had been acting mysteriously, changing apartments twice in the last month and trading cars every few days; even Danny didn't have his phone number now. Since this proposed contract was worth a lot of money, Danny simply couldn't understand why Ralf would turn it down so hastily.

"I want someone to take Sadjewi Hashemi in his headquarters in Qulhak," Sadeghi confessed. "I will pay cash—"

"In Qulhak?" the mercenaries laughed. Instantly, Sadeghi lost his audience, for none of the men was foolhardy enough to undertake such a risk. After an hour trying to convince them, Sadeghi stopped, angrily determined to gather his soldiers and do it himself. His first assault, however, on a major smuggler's warehouse in Karadj west of Teheran, was so poorly executed that he lost his two remaining lieutenants. Alireza Jaffari, the last of Danny's friends among the Sadeghi, caught a bullet in the throat and was decapitated. Rahim, Mohammed, Sa'ad, Mehdi, Parviz, Reza, Dariush, Hamid, Farzad—the names dripped away in blood when the Sadeghi got caught in a crossfire between a regular army unit and Hashemi gunmen. No one, not the Sadeghi, the Iranian Army, or the Hashemi could put together what had happened.

Two days later, Paolo Giaminelli, Andrea's business advisor, was surrounded by three Paykans driven up onto the sidewalk. Although he fell to his knees and begged for his life, he was shot to death right on Pahlavi Avenue in broad daylight.

More of Andrea's people soon died. Laurence Peters, a photographer who often took photos of the girls—for advertising purposes, of course—caught a bullet behind the ear the next day. Two of her newly hired soldiers, Alireza Rostgoo and Ali Bahadin, were found by police with their hands wired behind their backs and their heads blown off. Mansour Mansouri, another of Andrea's gunmen/drivers, was strangled outside his home. His wife discovered his body on the sidewalk outside their home when he didn't return that night.

Andrea's New York accountant, Bert Rosenstein, had the bad luck
to arrive in Teheran two days after Sharif Emami was named the new
prime minister. All the principal hotels and restaurants were closed, and
Princess Ashraf's pet interest, the Women's Ministry, had just been abol-
ished. The country was returning to the use of the Islamic calendar, and
the Ayatollah's pictures were being published for the first time. Earlier
that day, a slaughter had taken place near Jaleh Square when a crowd of
worshipers emerged from a mosque to confront army gunfire. Sixty people
had been slaughtered in the street.

Alarmed by the growing violence, Andrea sent two of her best men,
Mohammed Balourchi and Bahram Ghelikhani, to meet Rosenstein at the
airport. In a second car, she dispatched two gunmen, Ahmad and Sa'ad, to
cover them, but all these men were ambushed at a stoplight on Shahreza
Avenue just east of Teheran University, resulting in what became a famous gunfight.

Rosenstein was hit by so many bullets the doors flew off his Mercedes.
Although Mohammed Balourchi was cut in half by automatic gunfire,
Bahram Ghelikhani made a good account of himself: he killed seven
Hashemi before falling face down in a flowing *djube*. Sa'ad and Ahmad,
who caught Hashemi gunmen from behind, were in turn shot from the
rear. Army units, police, and troublemakers poured into the area from every direction, with the result that more than a hundred people died in a
confused melee before the army regained control of the street.

"We should have helped Mr. Sadeghi when we had the chance," Bob
Fraser told Andrea later that day.

"Well, we didn't! And now they fucking can't help us!" she snapped.

"But now we have to do something," Wolffe said. "Worse that that, we
have to do it alone." He was obviously unhappy with security, more so since
he had discovered Andrea had directed Danny to steal gas pipe. "I would
like to know if there are plans afoot to insulate this building from attack,"
he complained.

"Yes, Carl. You, yourself, designed a protective grid around our headquarters several weeks ago when you went to dinner with Doc," Andrea
lied. Actually it had been Danny's idea all along, but she had not endorsed
it until the day before, finally realizing the need for it.

The plan was simple. For the last two years, gas lines had been labo-
riously laid all over Teheran. Deep trenches had been dug beside many
streets, traffic diverted, and pipe welded, all to no avail, since only limited supplies of natural gas were ever delivered. Danny had suggested

an artificial gas line trench be dug from the Star Taxi office, on Tavanir Street, six blocks north to Shiraz Street. The trench was to be five feet deep and two feet wide, backed up with a four-foot embankment of earth topped with a heavy, welded, immovable gas pipe several blocks long. The trench would completely isolate the eastern end of the streets to Andrea's office (*kutche char*) and Ali Nassiri's home (*kutche panj*). Furthermore, the western end of *kutche char* was to be blocked by a stolen dump truck filled with liquid concrete so heavy it would collapse the *djube*, causing the truck to roll over and dry into an impenetrable wreck.

"You were drinking that night," Danny soothed Carl, "and you told me your plan. You must have forgotten it."

"Oh ... " the big mercenary said, embarrassed into thinking maybe he had come up with the idea after all.

"Of greater import is what we are going to do about the Hashemi," Andrea reminded her men.

"We must hit them where it hurts," Fraser contributed

"Yes," Mueller agreed. "The drug trade. It is the basis of their cash flow."

Snapping his fingers, Guenther Hauser suggested, "Hey, what about hitting the Hashemi warehouse near the railway station? Isn't that where they store most of their opium and hashish? Has anyone been inside it?"

"I have," Danny admitted from across the room. "I've been there several times." That wily old goat, Sadjewi Hashemi, stored bales of precious antique carpets in the warehouse, and Danny had gone there to pick up or deliver "gifts" and bribes. Carpets were an untraceable form of wealth; anyone could just scoop one off the floor to close a deal. Sadjewi liked to brag he had enough carpets in the warehouse to supply Ferdowsi's Jews for months, but Danny knew enough about carpets to estimate less than ten million dollars' worth was kept there at any time.

"What's it like, Doc?" Wolffe wanted to know, pulling out a sheet of paper to take notes.

Danny described the high walls, the double steel gates, the courtyard, the truck barns, the warehouses, and the offices. He told them how alert the guards were and what kinds of guns they carried. Whenever he hesitated, the mercenaries knew just the question to get more information from him. Feeling stupid at having observed all these details without understanding the use of such information, Danny again appreciated the technical skill of Andrea's professionals.

"How long will it take?" Andrea inquired.

"Two days," Ralf suggested a bit too quickly.

"Just one," Wolffe disagreed. "I can fix a charge tonight that will level the place."

"I mean two days to plan for any ... eventuality," Ralf said, looking him in the face.

"Fine," Wolffe agreed. "It's a bit conservative, but let's plan on seven o'clock in the morning, two days hence."

"Agreed," Andrea said. "Doc? You can go now. We have much work to do, and your part in this operation is done."

"Okay," Danny grinned, unwilling to get further involved, for he did not relish killing like these mercenaries did. Besides, he still had to hire a crew of Kurdish diggers and to steal a pile driver to cut the streets for the trench.

———◆———

Wolffe, who was placed in command, adopted a modified frontal assault through the gate followed by a laying of charges and a quick withdrawal. He knew from past experience that a massive explosion was better than risking lives needlessly, especially since they were so heavily outnumbered. He assigned Ralf to cover the rear with Roberto Viera and four soldiers. Bob Fraser would create a diversion, while he himself covered the operation to the north, leaving Masud Pooinak responsible for the south. Guenther and Dieter would take the assault in with twenty private soldiers, two Army trucks, and five cars. Guenther would simply crash the gates in a stolen 2 1/2 ton Army truck, followed by Dieter and the armed men, who would flood in and lay explosives. It was simple.

A couple hours later, Andrea was confronted by seven smoky men sitting in her office. Masud Pooinak slumped in a corner in shell shock. Wolffe, nursing a forearm that had taken a bullet through it, was dripping blood all over his boots. Bob Fraser was limp with exhaustion. Four of her soldiers were bleeding on a silk carpet nearby. She would have to have that washed professionally....

"Where's Dieter? Where's Guenther? Where's Ralf? Where's Roberto?" Andrea demanded. "What happened?"

"I think the question should be: where's the Doctor?" Wolffe asked, looking her in the eye. He had never approved of shielding Doc from the dirty side of their business in order not to taint his credibility, but now, Danny was the most conspicuously absent member of the crew.

Masud nearly collapsed, stunned by the suspicion, but Fraser just looked up and echoed the question, "Yeah, where's Doctor Mary?"

"He's been out since last night, arranging the trench," she replied as a dreadful possibility struck her. "Where's Dieter?"

Dieter had been killed when his truck hit the reinforced gates of the Hashemi warehouse. Concealed charges blew the vehicle back with such force it stood on end for a moment before collapsing upside down in flames. He never knew what hit him.

Guenther Hauser and most of his men died in a hail of bullets. He never got a single explosive into place, let alone detonated them. Roberto Viera was dead, and Ralf was missing. Andrea had lost thirty good men in ten minutes. Obviously, the Hashemi had been expecting them. Someone had warned the Hashemi about the impending attack.

"Where's the Doctor?" Wolffe hissed. "Only one of our men knew the Hashemi—especially the old fox, Sadjewi Hashemi—on a personal basis."

"He—" Andrea wept bitterly. "He couldn't have. He couldn't have done this to us. Not Doc!"

"He was the only one of us who'd been in their warehouse," Masud said, rousing from his shock.

"He was the only one of us who didn't go on this raid. He was the only one that knew all the plans," Wolffe declared, looking around for confirmation from the others.

"Doc knew exactly when we were going to do it!" Bob exclaimed in surprise.

"Where is he, Andrea?" Carl asked again.

"I don't know. I don't know...." she sobbed, hugging her chest in horror.

"He's turned against us," Carl concluded. "Why the fuck did he...?"

"I understand what he's done," she cried, wiping her face. "It's *my* fault. I'm the one who hired him."

Suddenly, Ralf entered the room, tattered and smoky but still in one piece. Looking around to see who had survived, he shook his head sadly.

"It was the Doctor," Masud told him, seemingly unable to believe it himself. "Danny MacCreary betrayed us to the Hashemi."

"My question is, what the hell are we going to do about this?" the big German asked the anxious faces around him.

"It's my responsibility," Andrea admitted, wiping the tears from her face. "I created him. I hired him. I discovered more than three years ago he was good with guns. I supplied him with a couple pistols and several radios. I trained him to shoot out in the desert at an old *caravanseri*.

He has several hundred rounds of ammunition. He's very good with a pistol—"

"No," Wolffe disagreed. "I trained him to shoot. He wanted to know more about explosives too. I taught him everything I know." Looking at the others in embarrassment, he sighed, "I knew Andrea used him to make stashes, so I had him hide my explosives for me. He has eighteen pounds of C4 and a dozen grenades. And I showed him how to make a concussive bomb with a grenade and C4...."

"Me too," Ralf claimed. "I taught him personal defense. I taught him to think, to live among his enemies, and to conceal himself. I gave him two Russian RPG's and four rockets. He also has 8 pounds of C4 from me."

"And I gave him six handguns, two G-3s, a thousand rounds, and ten thousand American dollars, plus four pounds of C4," Masud admitted, shaking his head in horror.

"Oh, hell!" Fraser shouted. "He's got all of my explosives too!"

"I taught him to use a knife."

"I taught him to use his hands to kill."

"I gave him an Uzi and a silencer—"

"I gave him four landmines, a hundred thousand tomans cash, and two thousand rounds of ammunition."

"Do you see what we have done?" Andrea laughed through her tears. "Each of us, in his own way, shared something dangerous with Doctor Mary. We've created this *thing* out there, this monster, this horrible, horrible monster...."

"You know what we have to do," Wolffe said, looking each of them in the face. "We can't let Danny MacCreary work against us. We've got to take him down."

Trembling, Andrea regained control long enough to declare, "I'll pay two hundred thousand tomans for a nice quick hit on Doctor Daniel Rene MacCreary. I want him dead. I don't mean blown-to-hell dead, bits of brains and skull all over the walls from an explosion. I don't mean shot-through the head dead, blood all over a goddamn linoleum floor in an empty kitchen somewhere in south Teheran. I mean fucking dead. Cold and bloody dead! Body on display on a marble slab in a fucking wet morgue some place downtown where I can go see it, dead, stiff, and cold as hell. Totally dead! I want Doc MacCreary dead. And I want him dead soon. Do you understand what I'm asking of you? Please tell me you're going to kill him!"

It was done. Although they understood the necessity of it, they still could not look each other in the eye as they filed out of the room.

Masud was the first to recover. "Two hundred thousand tomans. That's about twenty-eight thousand dollars!" he exclaimed. "Easy money. Danny is an easy hit."

———◆———

An hour later, Ralf told a mysterious voice on the phone, "They think the doctor is the traitor."

"Very good."

"Andrea placed a contract for two hundred thousand tomans on his head."

"Even better! Then no one suspects you at all?" the stranger chortled, enjoying an evil joke.

"No."

"And we get rid of the doctor at the same time. Too bad for him. He was too innocent for us anyway."

"I don't think they will get the doctor yet," Ralf hedged. "I called to warn Doc about the others. I told him I'll meet him at seven o'clock in Abbassabad. And then I will kill him myself."

Laughing wickedly, the stranger ordered, "As soon as you collect your reward for killing the doctor, then you work for us, the Hashemi?"

"Yes, as long as the price is right," Ralf agreed. "That's really all I'm interested in...the money."

"Good," the other man laughed. "We've got plenty for you to do. By the way, have you completed the radio-controlled car bomb yet?"

"No. I have the explosives, but I need some electronics," Ralf informed him. "It's been difficult to find things with this revolution going on."

"When you get it put together, let me know. I have the perfect target."

_27_

OPEN SEASON

"You have been a friend to me. It is dangerous for you now. Let me do a favor, then you will leave, and no one will see you again."
—_Hilde Rasmussen_

The most recent little boy was quite a snoop. Fascinated with the beautiful foreign woman who would leave the palatial home of his benefactor to walk the connecting walls to an apartment building on the opposite side of the block, he began to spy on her. Once, he saw her by a window on the fourth floor of the other building, and he frequently heard her voice coming from a dining room on the third floor. She didn't seem to understand Farsi like everyone else he knew; she spoke one of the strange _farangi_ languages, and it hurt his ears. It was a perfect mystery for a curious boy. Although she fondly fussed with his hair as she passed, she made no attempt to talk to him.

One day, he heard her raging at someone upstairs, and he crept closer to the apartment building than ever before. Suddenly, a huge man snatched him from his hiding place on the wall and flung him into a rose bush. As he struggled to free himself, a big blonde man grabbed him by the leg and dragged him into the open. He was barely saved from being beaten by the man when the beautiful woman herself ran into the garden to stop the _farangi_ from slapping him around.

"Carl, let him go!" Andrea ordered. She nodded for Shamsa to take the boy, who was badly scratched from the rose bushes.

"I caught him spying on you again," Wolffe accused, his dangerous blue eyes glittering like those of a hawk when it sights a rabbit in the grass.

"He is just a boy," Shamsa snapped, sweeping the child off his feet and carrying him into the kitchen to wipe the blood from his face.

"He's Ali's boy," Andrea explained.

"And Ali's a disgusting butt-fucking fag. Tell him to keep his—"

Her slap was so unexpected, it knocked the spit right out of his mouth, and though he was unhurt, his face turned crimson.

Looking down guilty, Andrea apologized first. "I'm sorry," she said. "I had no right to do that to you. You're entitled to your opinion."

"No, it's me that's sorry," Carl said, stepping forward to hug her. He was surprised by the wetness in her eyes. "Ali *is* a fag, but he's your friend, and he's been good to all of us."

"Yes, Andrea agreed, her eyes bright with unshed tears. "He has been a good friend, one of the few who have been steadfast."

"I'm sorry Doc didn't work out," Carl consoled her, understanding the source of her disappointment. It was the first time anyone had mentioned Danny since the manhunt had begun. "I thought he was a friend myself."

"Times are difficult," she said, heading inside. "People change. Money can change people."

Alone and lost in thought, Wolffe paced irritably in the garden, then checked the wall again, smiling at the secret booby trap he had laid several days earlier. He remembered Danny once mentioned the drainage pipes bolted vertically on the walls of most buildings.

"You could climb such a drainpipe?" he had asked the younger man.

"Sure," Danny answered. "I'm a good climber. I used to climb mountains in Wyoming. I can go up anything vertical."

"It might come in handy someday. Roofs are the least protected part of a building in Iran," Wolffe had joked, but he wasn't laughing now. The idea was out there in Danny's head, and it was a dangerous idea. The booby trap was insurance. If Danny dropped in unexpectedly, a light explosive charge wired midway up the wall along the drainpipe would blow him clear to Isfahan and all the way to Hell itself. Fuck him for turning against them!

———◆———

The manhunt had gone badly. Eager to get the sizable reward for themselves, Andrea's men hadn't worked together. The first to reach Marvin's villa looking for Danny, Masud had thoroughly ransacked the place, searching for weapons and questioning the servants. Minutes after his departure, Bob Fraser climbed over the wall, armed to the teeth. While he was still there, Wolffe arrived, similarly armed. Khani Nassiri, the manager of

Beste Body Shop and Hamad Ghorbanifar, the manager of Star Taxi, were next, and in the next hour, four more killers showed up.

The men broke into all the rooms and searched every nook and cranny in the villa and on the grounds, but all they could find was a cheap .25 caliber Raven pistol that Danny sometimes carried. Though Fraser and Wolffe both fancied themselves great stashers, neither could find a trace of the antitank rockets, the explosives, weapons, cash, or ammunition they had given Danny to hide. Most feared of all, however, was the .357 Smith and Wesson Andrea had given him for his birthday and another .32 that Fraser had fitted with a silencer so Danny could practice without attracting attention. There were several thousand rounds of ammunition missing too.

Kicking an armchair so hard it slid out of the living room and rolled across the patio, Carl swore, "We were damn fools to ever trust him."

"Yes, we were," Fraser agreed. "If any of you see him," he warned the stewardesses huddled in a sobbing mob in the living room, "don't tell him we're looking for him. If you help him in any way, we'll look for you, too. Here's my card. I'll put it by the phone. Call me. There's money in it for you."

He knew it was a futile effort. The women would never turn on Danny MacCreary without coercion. There was nothing like being *nice* to a woman to ensure her loyalty, and Danny was always that. He must be a goddamn sociopath, Fraser decided, which explained how he, too, had been so taken in by the young American. He stormed out of the villa and sniffed the night air. Someone was burning trash down the street, a common thing in Teheran now, but the acrid smoke stung his eyes more than usual. It was probably someone burning a body. It smelled like Varanasi. As he wiped his face with a handkerchief, he felt someone looking at him. Surreptitiously glancing in the mirror-like reflection of a car's fender, he spotted Ralf sitting in a BMW across the street, looking frustrated.

Minutes after the dangerous gunmen had gone, the phone rang in Marvin's study, and Hilde Rasmussen, a German stewardess, answered.

"Yes?" she said.

"Hilde?" She recognized the voice.

People looked at her curiously. She tried to act casually as she stalled for time. "Yes, we missed your call. We were busy when you called earlier. Some people were here looking for … da Doctor.

"Is someone in the room with you now, Hilde?"

"*Ja … Ja*, the power is on, Mrs. Aryani." The eyes watching her turned away, satisfied she was only talking to a nosey neighbor.

"Was the visit friendly...or unfriendly?"

"I thought so, *ja,* but you know that man is so unfriendly all de time."

"Is it safe now?"

"No!" she laughed, though heartbroken to tell him. "I don't think so."

"Will it be better later?" the voice asked.

"Never, I'm afraid. Never again."

"I was supposed to meet Ralf at seven o'clock, on Abbas—"

"Not a good idea," she interrupted. "With the revolution...."

"Thank you, Hilde. You have been a friend. Wish me luck, huh?"

"You have my blessings, dear. Enjoy your trip home," she said. Later, in the privacy of her bedroom, where no one could see her, she wept, for she knew in her heart Danny MacCreary was a dead man. His own friends were going to kill him, probably after other friends betrayed him for money.

In the coming weeks, numbers of hired guns would invade Marvin's home. One of the Swedish stewardesses was beaten and violently raped by an Iranian looking for Danny, and from that time on, the girls drifted away. Having missed the excitement because he was at work, Marvin took to drinking and sitting on the roof. Hilde, one of the last to leave, knew that spendthrift though he was, the big American carried two hundred thousand tomans in his wallet, which he planned to hand to Danny MacCreary if he ever saw him again. It was travel money, for Marvin was convinced his roommate had to get away in order to survive the revolution.

$-28-$

THE BLUE MERCEDES

"I love you."

—*Andrea Wilcox*

Brooding over how badly she had misjudged Danny MacCreary, and how events were so quickly spinning out of control, Andrea Wilcox now spent a lot of her time sitting in the dark on the balcony at Ali's house, drinking gin by the bottle and watching the sullen city below. There were no mixers; there was only sporadic refrigeration. She drank her gin warm, straight from the bottle. There were always shouts from rooftops in the neighborhood now, both anti-Shah slogans and taped revolutionary messages from the Ayatollah. Strikes crippled the country; one day the oil workers would go on strike, the next day, government workers would walk, followed by baggage handlers at the airport, and then the bus drivers.

The country was rocked by demonstrations. Martial law was declared in Teheran. In Yousefabad, a neighborhood just a mile or so from Ali's home, inexperienced conscripts captured six taunting youths, lined them up against a wall, and shot them to death before an officer could intervene. The incident was endlessly exaggerated by the foreign press as an example of the Shah's "repression."

Meanwhile, at the request of the Shah—and goaded by a naive President Jimmy Carter in America—the Ayatollah Khomeini was expelled from house arrest in neighboring Iraq by Saddamn Hussein and sent to France. There were rumors of an attempt to buy him off, but with unlimited access to long distance phone lines, the vengeful cleric succeeded in organizing his supporters for the first time, thus establishing himself as the head of a revolutionary movement.

On the eighth of September 1978, dozens of demonstrators were killed in the streets of Teheran. President Jimmy Carter phoned the Shah to pledge American support, including tear gas. Intended to stop the bloodshed, this humanitarian gesture confirmed what many Iranians believed: the Shah was a stooge of the superpowers.

Alone and not fully informed, yet arrogantly assuming he completely understood the situation, the Shah allowed himself to be talked into following a harder line. The Commander of the Imperial Guard was appointed the administrator of martial law. Troops poured into the streets, and fighting raged all over Teheran. There were calls for blood and bandages in every hospital in the city. The wailing of ambulances announced the end of each confrontation. Public taxis carried eager young men off to the demonstrations and were filled with wounded and dying afterwards. Masud Pooinak's teenage brother, hurrying out in a new field jacket to get in on the excitement, was killed near the university. It was days before his mother succeeded in recovering his body from the morgue. He'd been shot eighteen times. Shamsa's brother disappeared too; his nude body, badly beaten and burned by cigarettes, was found two weeks later. He had been killed by other revolutionaries—but not in his faction.

And then, the hand of God: there was a massive earthquake in Tabas that killed twenty thousand people. The Shah rushed to give aid, empowering millions of dollars in relief. Although he was photographed personally extending his hand to the victims, it was widely viewed by the people as a public relations gesture. The Ayatollah belittled the Shah's generosity, though a lot of the king's fortune was spent to help the injured.

"Andrea? May we talk?" Manucherr Sadeghi asked over the phone the night after the earthquake.

"Yes?"

"We must do something about the Hashemi."

"What do you mean?" she inquired, not trusting anyone outside her circle of friends.

"I understand you are looking for the Doctor. I know where he is. I know where the Doctor has been hiding all this time. You will never guess. He is not with the Hashemi, but he is in their pocket, so to speak. I will give him to you, but I think only *you* can get access to him. None of your men can do it. None of your men has the access you need. Ha, ha," he chuckled mysteriously, "You will have to kill the Doctor yourself."

"How much do you want?"

"Satisfaction."

"What do you want?" she asked again, unsure Danny MacCreary would be worth the price.

"My enemy is the Hashemi," Sadeghi declared. "You have a traitor among you, and you do not know whom to trust. You can trust me. I am preparing an action with the Hashemi, and I need the services of Carl Wolffe for two hours."

"And for that you'll provide us with Doctor Danny MacCreary?"

"Yes," Sadeghi laughed mysteriously.

"Why?" she asked.

"You do not want to know the details?"

"Of course not!" she snapped. "What do you need?"

"I have explosives I do not know how to use. My experienced people are all dead. I have hired many gunmen, but they are green around the ears."

"I understand," she said. "All right, I agree. How shall we arrange it?"

"I will meet you on Farah Shomali Street across from the pastry shop. Seven o'clock. I will have three men."

"And I will have three men too," she promised, wondering how Sadeghi had found Danny when none of her men could. And why did he think it was so *funny*? Why was *she* the only one able to gain access to Danny? Why was she the only one who could murder him? Was Doc hiding right under their noses, or was there something *else* about his disappearance that Sadeghi found so humorous? What did he mean by getting *access* to him? She couldn't figure it out, but she consoled herself with the thought she would soon have the information, and Danny MacCreary would be dead at her feet at last. (And she'd save some money, to boot!)

As soon as he heard about the new deal, however, Carl Wolffe threw the magazine he was reading against the wall and shouted, "You foolish bitch! What a stupid arrangement, and on a public street no less! Anybody could salt you. What a stupid thing you've agreed to."

"Nevertheless, Sadeghi has his back against the wall," she reminded him. "He has no quarrel with us."

"Well, I don't fucking like it."

"Nor do I," Fraser agreed. "If it works, great. We kill two birds with one stone—no, three! If the Doctor is an 'independent,' we take care of him. The Hashemi might be neutralized, and the Sadeghi might become allies in dangerous times, but if anything goes wrong, we all get killed, Sadeghi loses, the Hashemi win, and the Doctor—who knows?"

"What do you suggest?" she asked. "Do we have any other options?"

"Here's what we're going to do," Bob suggested. "Carl and Masud will take over the pastry shop three hours early."

"Sounds good," Wolffe nodded in agreement.

"We have two boys who're good with snipers' weapons. We'll put them on the roofs across the street."

"Good," Wolffe said.

"Andrea will take three of Ghelikhani's best men—"

"I know just the men." The two mercenaries grinned at each other wolfishly.

"Alireza Rostgoo's brother ... and Rostom and Mohsen?" Andrea asked, proud of herself and her two mercenaries. For the thousandth time, she appreciated how much these men were worth. When Danny was dead, she resolved to give each of them a bonus of ten thousand dollars.

"You know these men?" Carl asked in surprise.

"I watch all of you. True killers are easy to spot," she laughed, jumping up to change clothes. "Most men can pull a trigger, but only a few can kill...."

At precisely seven o'clock, she pulled up beside the curb, where she was instantly cut off by three Paykans. Hashemi gunmen poured onto the street, firing wildly at everyone that moved. Andrea hit the floorboards, then kicked open the driver's side door as glass and bullets splattered all around her. One of her men opened up with an Uzi but was killed seconds later when he was hit in the eye. Rostom never got off a shot: he died bloody in the back seat. Mohsen couldn't unjam his G-3 and died in frustration as tears rolled down his cheeks. With Hashemi dropping all around her from the sniper-fire from across the street, Andrea crawled across the sidewalk, put her back against a brick wall, and shot her 9mm Beretta until it was empty.

A dead Hashemi covered her lower legs. Another lay dead just beyond her. Four more were running toward her when Carl and Masud cleared the street with 12-gauge Winchester shotguns. In seconds, it was over. Carl grabbed her by the shoulder and threw her into a nearby Paykan. "DRIVE!" he shouted, and she punched out the shattered windshield and sped away bleeding from a hundred glass cuts.

<hr />

"Hashemi," Carl declared, as Fraser rushed up.

"Hashemi," Bob agreed, glancing up the *kutche* to their left. "Look there!" he said, grabbing Wolffe's arm.

A Mercedes parked at the curb a few cars up had bullet holes in its back window. Inside, they found three dead men bleeding all over the seats. Across the street, Manucherr Sadeghi was slumped against the wheel of his BMW, a wire wrapped around his neck. Fraser poked a pocketknife under the garrote to cut it loose. Holding it in his hand, he analyzed its construction. "No," he denied.

"No, it's not," Wolffe agreed. "Garrotes are common enough among professionals...." Tossing the wire over a wall, the two mercenaries hurried away, quickly disappearing into traffic to the south.

———◆———

Andrea was so shaken when she got home, she drank Scotch straight from a bottle to calm herself.

"Andrea*jun*," Ali Nassiri soothed her, taking her delicate hands in his own soft mitts. The little Iranian boy hung onto Ali's pocket, but he, too, reached out and touched Andrea sympathetically. "You must not worry about this anymore. It has gone too far. You have not asked for my help, but the time has come to stop this madness. The violence is too much. I have great *parti bazee* in the Ministry of Justice. I will come up with a surprise for the Hashemi no one can predict. Times are difficult, but my family is very powerful. I will arrange something tomorrow. Do not be upset anymore."

"Ali, I wish you could take care of it," she cried, burying her face in his burly chest, "but it's too dangerous. Everybody's getting killed! This is much worse than Beirut was. I should have left Iran weeks ago. The police have lost control; the military are barely holding their own in the streets. I'm afraid the Hashemi—"

"Don't worry. *Farda, farda*—tomorrow, tomorrow—I will take care of everything," he smiled tenderly. "Go take a hot bath and rest. Sleep peacefully. I will take care of everything! You need not worry."

"Thank you."

Next morning, when she met him at the breakfast table, still puffy-eyed from a sleepless night of crying, Ali announced, "I have an appointment at ten o'clock with the Minister of Justice. It's all arranged. We will discuss courses of action. I may go to the Shah later this afternoon. He always sees me—even without an appointment."

"Thank you, Ali."

"*Chash*—"

"No, really. You've always been so good to me. I have never told you how much I appreciate your help."

"Dear Andrea. You and I are friends. You have helped me too, more than I ever admitted!" he exclaimed, giving her a confident smile. "I will do this little thing for you. No problem. It's a small favor."

"Thank you."

"You are very welcome," Ali said. Collecting his handbag, he arranged his hair before an antique French mirror in the hallway. "I think I need a haircut. I will ask Shamsa to cut it for me later. Do you think she would mind? My hairdresser, Ali Hamadi, was raped by a gang of revolutionaries and killed last week. He was put up against a garden wall ... naked... and shot."

"Oh, no! I knew him! No...Shamsa wouldn't mind at all. She'll cut your hair. Please be careful," she said. "There are demonstrations everywhere. I saw military trucks in Abbassabad yesterday. Hundreds of soldiers."

"Of course! I am always careful. Hamad*jun*!" he shouted to the little boy. "*Bia inja.*"

Hamad ran to Ali's outstretched arms, and Nassiri bent down and tongue-kissed the little boy's mouth passionately. Patting him fondly on the ass, Ali fussed with the child's suit. "He looks especially nice today, don't you think?" he asked. "I should send his mother another ten thousand tomans. A nice boy, don't you think?"

"Yes, very nice," Andrea agreed, making an effort to smile at the seven-year-old boy. "You look nice too."

"I do? Thank you. Do you like my new pants?"

"Yes, I do," she said, accompanying him and his little friend through the house. Pausing in the patio doorway, she looked out over the expansive garden and driveway, appreciating how wonderful it was to have such an oasis in the middle of a shooting revolution. Thank God for Ali, she thought. He had always helped her.

"I will take the new Mercedes you bought me," Nassiri announced, kissing her on the cheek. "Powder-puff blue, my favorite color, my favorite car from my favorite friend!" He held her hands tightly, and she was impressed with how warm, strong, and confident his grip was. He was good at this kind of thing. Politics were his specialty. If anyone could convince the Shah to help her, Ali could.

"It's time to go," he said. The boy had wandered away again, so Nassiri clapped his hands playfully and called, "Hamad*jun, bia inja!*"

And then, as the driver opened the door of the expensive limousine and the little boy clambered inside, Andrea could stand it no more. Wishing he didn't have to leave, she said, "Ali? Wait."

"Yes, dear."

"I ... love you." It was true. She loved this gentle homosexual more than any man in her life. He had been her most loyal friend, and she wanted him to know how deeply she appreciated his willingness to get involved in her troubles now, especially since it would have been convenient not to.

"Oh! And I love you too, Andrea*jun*...!" he said in surprise, his eyes misting over.

Including his own mother, Andrea was the only woman who had ever told him such a personal thing. Smiling to himself, Ali glanced out the back window, waved confidently with his left hand, and then told the driver to go on with his right.

The car pulled down the driveway and disappeared through the gate, but Andrea couldn't bring herself to go in the house just yet. A male peacock with spread feathers called from the garden to her right, and she walked out into the peace of grass, flowers, and fruit trees. Soon, she hoped, the Hashemi would be history, Danny MacCreary would be dead, the revolution would end....

But minutes before his meeting at the Ministry of Justice, Ali Nassiri was dead. A radio-controlled bomb hidden under the car blew the blue Mercedes completely off Pahlavi Avenue in a fireball, killing Nassiri, little Hamad, and the driver instantly. Except for the Shah and his immediate family, Andrea's best friend was the last aristocrat left in Iran.

$-29-$

Rabbit in a Hole

"Where the hell did the doctor go? Why can't any of you find him? How hard can this be? I don't think he left the country. He's still here! He is dangerous. You are the best. Find him. Please keep looking until you kill him. I want him dead."
$\qquad$ *—Andrea Wilcox*

O n the first of October 1978, a haggard-looking Danny MacCreary presented himself to the Captain of the Guard, Lieutenant Khosrow Assadi, at the main gate of Doshan Tappeh Air Force Base in Teheran. "I need a place to stay," he informed the startled Iranian, trying to hide the desperation he felt. Now that Andrea's men had turned on him, he had nowhere to go, no money, and no friends he could trust. Under his ragged field jacket, he carried an S&W.357 Magnum, a .22 Colt fitted with a suppressor, a 1911 .45, a length of chain, three knives, eight grenades, and a pair of gloves with the knuckles weighted with lead shot and wrapped with duct tape.

"ID?" the lieutenant asked. Once one of Danny's favorite students, the Iranian showed not a glimmer of recognition in his eyes.

"Doctor Mary," he read aloud from the identification card and blue work permit Danny handed him. "You have clearance to Doshan Tappeh Air Force Base, but the language school is closed. Why are you here? State your business."

"My apartment has been burned," Danny lied. "I don't have anywhere to stay. My friends are leaving Iran, and I don't have any money because my bank, the Bank Markazi Iran, was blown up. I can't get food, the Air Force has my passport in a safe in the headquarters building here on base, and the airport's closed all the time anyway, so I can't leave the country. Heck of a predicament, isn't it? No place to stay and I can't go home."

"It is not my problem," the Iranian concluded.

"No, it isn't, but I'd like to earn enough money to go home."

"The language school is closed. I told you that already."

"There are a lot of *homofars* and officers who were scheduled for training in America that have been delayed by this fighting. I'm sure they are not getting enough practice with their English. These are military contracts that must be honored. When the political troubles are over, these men will go to America unprepared. Let the Iranian instructors stay out on strike, but perhaps I could teach an informal class for whomever wants to—"

"Where will you stay?"

"I don't know," Danny answered uncertainly. That was his biggest problem. He couldn't trust anyone not to kill him. He couldn't go anywhere. He couldn't sleep, couldn't eat, couldn't continue walking the streets, couldn't dawdle. He was exhausted.

"You can stay in my office," the lieutenant offered magnanimously, changing his tone. "What will you eat? The officers' mess is closed."

"I'll have one of the *sarboz* draftees bring me *chelo kebab* every day," Danny said. He knew there were small restaurants and a bakery just outside the main gate of the base.

"I'm sure there are few students for you, but perhaps I can arrange private tutoring until things improve or the strikes are over," Lieutenant Assadi offered, his eyes glittering rather strangely.

Moving aside, he opened the door of the guardhouse and waved Danny onto the base. Dispatching three armed guards to escort the *farangi* to his office in a book warehouse west of the administration building, Assadi gave strict orders the American was to be totally restricted to the classroom buildings. Although Danny was to live here safely for the next four-and-a-half months, he would be virtually a prisoner, living without heat, electricity, water, a bath, hot food, news, or any clean clothes. It was a miserable existence, much like living in a prison.

In effect, he completely vanished from the streets of Teheran. Both Andrea's men and the numerous freelancers drawn by the bounty were stymied in their hunt for him. At first, the Hashemi were intent on finding him, too, but then, for reasons of their own, they mysteriously abandoned the effort, instead focusing their energy on the remaining Sadeghi organization. For her own part, Andrea seemed relieved Danny had gotten away. She told her men he was probably among the Hashemi in Isfahan or somewhere else. She ordered them to redouble their efforts to find him. His roommate, on the other hand, appeared just as certain Danny was still in Teheran, for in his bedroom at the villa, Danny had left three silk carpets worth twenty thousand dollars. Marvin was sure Danny wouldn't leave them behind.

It was a good time, however, to get off the streets. The Ayatollah, now operating openly in France, urged his followers on with renewed fervor. As the undisputed head of the many fractious revolutionary groups, Khomeini mercilessly ordered general strikes throughout the economy. Every day there were shutdowns: the refinery workers went on strike and there was no gasoline, diesel, or *naft*, then the transportation and communication workers struck, followed by the civil service, and with each new strike, Khomeini tightened his stranglehold on the country's economy. Whenever anyone disagreed, the Ayatollah countered it was Allah's indisputable will. God Himself spoke through the Ayatollah's mouth. Who could resist the Almighty voice of God? Anyone who disagreed must be killed ... and so they were! Hundreds of executions took place every day.

Bored, lacking electricity or gas, unable to travel, and hardly able to get enough food due to Khomeini's maniacal calls to ruin the economy, the people perversely began to believe only *he* could rescue them from the mess they were making of their own country. Convinced Allah would not allow a religious leader to suggest anything counter to God's will, families sacrificed their children to the revolution, believing the Ayatollah's promise God would open the doors of Paradise to receive them. Mothers dressed their boys in death shrouds before sending them out to demonstrate, and fathers grieved for their martyrs as children left home for the last time.

To defuse the hysteria sweeping the country the Shah announced a partial amnesty for political prisoners and even released fifteen hundred of them on his birthday, but there were riots in Hamadan, Mashad, Qom, and Kerman anyway. Although the military proved effective in stopping the demonstrations in the major cities, no one seemed capable of controlling the strikes now paralyzing the country. In despair, the Shah fired his cabinet. The military withdrew from the streets to demand control of the government.

Before long, millions of people were demonstrating in the cities, but bad weather unexpectedly stabilized the shaky political situation. November 1978 was the coldest on record, the freezing weather complicated by severe shortages of gasoline, diesel fuel, and *naft*, or kerosene. This was in a country that was one of the leaders of OPEC. Moving to end the suffering, the United States and other countries actually sent oil to Iran in an attempt to cover the worst shortages, but the Iranian people grew angrier at the outsiders' interference. On the fifth day of the month, the largest mobs ever burned the remaining movie houses, airline offices, liquor stores, government buildings, and part of the British embassy.

The following day, the Shah established a military government. Soldiers retook the streets, and fighting raged everywhere. Fires started in the streets were fed with abandoned tires. Black smoke obscured everything for miles. Wildcat roadblocks were set up by revolutionaries; people were dragged out of their cars and executed against garden walls for no reason. Thousands of people died.

Danny, however, without TV or radio and rarely able to find even so much as a newspaper, was insulated from the outside world and knew little of this. For those instructors willing to work, there were 100% pay raises, so he was making more money teaching English than he had ever made before, but there was nothing to buy. Finding it necessary to spend most of his free time pacing the width of Lt. Assadi's office to keep warm, he sent a soldier to find him several cheap turtleneck sweaters and gloves. At night, he slept under three carpets on the lieutenant's desk. One of these was a moderately priced silk Tabriz. How could a lieutenant afford such a luxury at his office—and why wasn't it stolen by a lesser soldier? In the end, the carpet was the warmest…. When there was electricity, which was rare now, he read, and when there was nothing to read, he paced endlessly back and forth in front of the window.

There was little news from anywhere, and what there was, was uniformly awful. General Azhari, who had been appointed the head of the military government days before, collapsed from a heart attack [like many other senior officers, he was murdered by revolutionaries]; former Prime Minister Amir Abbas Hoveyda was imprisoned. The Shah's failure to review his troops on November 17, Armed Forces Day, put morale among the military at an all-time low. Robbery, burglary, rape, and vandalism escalated wildly as police protection and investigation virtually ceased. People were no longer safe in their homes from gangs of punks in looted field jackets and beards roving the streets in search of trouble and excitement. Fear ruled the cities, especially Teheran.

The economy was on the verge of collapse. Banks were only open occasionally, cash was short, perishable imports stacked up at the borders due to a strike by customs officials, and slowdowns paralyzed the country.

In desperation, the Shah canceled several big development projects and began to preach fiscal restraint, but there wasn't any money left in the treasury anyway. On the third of December, when the Shah visited the air cadet training center at Doshan Tappeh, Danny was stunned by how gaunt and sick the man appeared, even at a distance.

Finally, the beleaguered king took the bold step of appointing Shahpour Bakhtiar, one of his long-time opponents and probably the only man in the country able to compromise, as the head of an interim government, hoping thereby to short-circuit moderate dissent and reduce violence in the streets. It was not to be, however, for the military, which was the mainstay of the Shah's power, was too divided. Loyalist units like the Imperial Guard refrained from supporting the new government, and there was talk of overthrowing Bakhtiar and instituting a stronger military government. With Bakhtiar's strength eroding and the military wavering, street fighting grew more violent. Demonstrators flooded the streets. As many as 700 people were killed in a two-day period in Teheran.

In Lavizan, enlisted men broke into an officers' mess, killing twelve officers in the first reported mutiny. Shock waves from the incident further eroded military leadership. On Ashura, the tenth day of the month of Moharram, 680 A.D., a day of mourning and flagellation to commemorate the tragic death of the Imam Hossain—a million people marched quietly and without incident down Shah Reza Avenue to Shahyad Square, establishing the Ayatollah Khomeini's control over the mobs.

It was impressive.

Trying hard not to embarrass the Shah, President Jimmy Carter refused to order an evacuation of American civilians from the country. Wiser foreigners, however, were fleeing by the tens of thousands every day Mehrabod Airport was open. Street fighting was continuous; the sound of gunfire could be heard at all hours of the day. In Teheran, tens of thousands of fires stained the sky with black smoke. While all this was happening, Danny quietly taught English to small, nervous groups of officers on Doshan Tappeh.

And then, on January 1, 1979, not a single student came to his class. Although he didn't know it yet, Danny MacCreary's career as an English language instructor had ended forever.

"Did you hear the news?" Lieutenant Assadi asked, rushing into the office after sunset and waking him from an uneasy sleep. The officer was hopping from foot to foot he was so excited.

"No, what's happened now?" Danny asked, sleepily putting on his sunglasses. He never knew what to expect anymore, but he had learned to take news stoically.

"The Shah has left Iran!" Assadi announced, so excited by the news Danny was unsure if he were happy or sad. The lights flickered on momentarily, a teasing gesture by one of the Ayatollah's followers, then switched off again, and the blackness seemed more intense. "Did you hear me?" Assadi asked quietly.

"Yes, I did, Danny answered, relieved the Iranian couldn't see the conflict of emotions on his face.

"The Shah has left Iran!"

"Incredible news."

If the Shah thought to defuse the situation by exiling himself from his beloved Iran, he was wrong. While he spared the country a bloody civil war, he had, in effect, abandoned hundreds of thousands of his supporters. Iran went wild at news of his departure. That night, millions of people pretended to see the face of the Ayatollah Khomeini on the moon, the largest mass "hallucination" in recorded history. In Hamadan, people sacrificed sheep, while in Teheran; the rooftops were filled with people howling like animals. The Japanese, West Germans, and British ordered their citizens to evacuate the country.

"Put hands up!" several enlisted men shouted at Danny the next night, after they had kicked in the door and poured into the room, brandishing assault rifles and knives.

"Sure, but I'm one of you guys," Danny said, lying behind his smiling teeth, for he didn't have the slightest idea where their loyalties lay. "Look, I felt exactly the same way when the Shah left."

While the men ransacked his few belongings and trashed the officer's desk, Danny prayed he could talk his way out of this. He knew he couldn't understand how these men felt, although he was personally saddened by the Shah's decision to leave. In a way, Danny had actually come to like the Shah and was sorry things had worked out this way. Perhaps, he hoped, the revolution would lead to a more constitutional monarchy, and the Shah would abdicate in favor of his son Reza, perhaps in a constitutional monarchy. Maybe then the people would be satisfied and return to work, but even so, Iran would never be the same again.

"Shut up," one of the armed men ordered. "We don't want to listen to you *farangi* anymore." Danny recognized two of the men as former students, and he knew he was in deep trouble. He allowed the men to wreck the office, having nothing of his own there except a broken toothbrush and a clean turtleneck sweater with an unusual metal insert sewn into the collar. His guns, cash, and most of his belongings had been carefully hidden in anonymous boxes in the vast book warehouse.

"You are lucky," one of the gunmen said after the search. "We find nothing. It is good for you to leave Iran soon!"

"Don't worry, I will," Danny promised with a smile, "just as soon as I save up enough money for an airplane ticket home."

After they had gone, however, he sat down at the desk and shook uncontrollably. There was no way to tell the various factions apart. Were those men pro-Khomeini, pro-Shah, pro-Bakhtiar, or simply hoping for a military takeover? Worse yet, were they just mutineers looking for trouble? Hiding out on Doshan Tappeh was no longer safe. The time had come to go back out onto the streets, out into the violence and the shooting, out into the murders, rapes, and assaults, out into the fury of the street demonstrations, out to face the bounty hunters, the Hashemi, the Sadeghi, his friends … and his own destiny in the violence of the Iranian Revolution.

— 30 —

ZARECH'S RESTAURANT

"I can't tell you any more about it. I'm so sorry. He was my friend."
—Doc

"**D**octor Mary! Come sit with me. It is time we spoke freely," called Mohammad Hashemi, Sadjewi's eldest son. He waved magnanimously at a seat opposite him in a darkened booth in Zarech's Restaurant, just north of Abbassabad.

Across the room, Danny saw two Hashemi soldiers, Ali Rezaee and the dreaded Reza Malek Zadeh, but undoubtedly there were other gunmen scattered among the tables, for there were three cars parked illegally outside, and none of the tables had women or children. Knowing he was in the midst of vipers, he seated himself across from the dangerous mobster, careful not to show any sign of fear.

"What's new, Mohammad?" he inquired in Farsi, his voice warm though he felt frigid inside. "And how is Sadjewi, your father and my respected friend?" Since earlier that day, when a mere *child* had walked up and handed him a note summoning him to this meeting, Danny had realized the Hashemi were close. There would be no refusing their invitation to meet.

"Fine, Doctor Mary, thanks much. All of my family is good, thanks be to Allah. All praise to Allah."

"Allah," Danny nodded deferentially. And business?"

"Not bad. And your roommate?" the Iranian asked amiably.

"Marvin's not my roommate now. We had a falling out," Danny answered. It seemed like everyone was hunting him; he didn't know whom to trust, but he still felt loyalty to those who had once been friends. It was dangerous to be too closely associated with him. Out of concern for

Marvin's and the stewardesses' safety, he decided to minimize any association. "I moved out of the villa months ago," he said. "Everyone is so tense now."

"Yes, the political crisis is affecting all of our society in so many ways. Demonstrations, strikes, propaganda! My family has seen it all before. It's part of the eternal class struggle which Karl Marx first theorized about."

Danny recalled Mohammad had a degree in history from a French university; he was the only Iranian Danny had ever met who was fascinated with the American Civil War. Danny was not prepared, however, to get into a political discussion with the Iranian now, for he had crossed intellectual swords with this man before and not won. Like many of his countrymen, Mohammad Hashemi had a closed mind; he firmly believed *his* opinion was the last word on any subject. Even worse, he was incapable of critical thought: the first account he studied was the last, and anything conflicting with his original ideas was viewed as revisionist. Though he spoke eight languages fluently, Mohammad Hashemi was a superficial reader who often confused important details. He was familiar with Karl Marx's writings about the American Civil War as an example of a populist struggle against federal tyranny, but he couldn't grasp the federalists won, and America was one country unified afterward. He still thought of the United States as a divided territory, those pro-slavery versus those anti-black versus those ... well, on and on. He was conflicted in his understanding and preferred thinking his way. It was so much clearer than in terms of 1860's populism, to Karl Marx's writing, to early communists, and to finally Mohammad Hashemi.

At one of Marvin's parties, Mohammad had bragged, "I have a mind like a sieve. I sort through all the bullshit to get my facts." And yet the facts were those he preselected.

No, it was not time to get into a discussion with such a man, Danny decided. "Have you ordered?" he asked, pointedly changing the subject. He knew the menu by heart, for in the old days, he and Bob Fraser had often eaten here. The restaurant, located just a short walk north of Abbassabad Street, was one of the few places in Teheran that offered both pizzas and passable Mexican food. With all the demonstrations lately, Danny was surprised the place was still open, let alone able to produce a semblance of a menu. It was probably owned or protected by someone powerful, perhaps even by the Hashemis themselves.

"I ordered a pizza with the works. You want one?" the Iranian offered politely. "It's on me. I bet you hungry, huh?"

"No, no pizza, thank you. I'd rather have a plate of spaghetti," Danny said, waving at the waiter, who turned his back and busied himself brushing imaginary crumbs into a nearby customer's lap.

"*Arghah!*" Hashemi shouted, angrily snapping his fingers. "My friend would like to order. Whatever he wants—put it on my tab."

"Spaghetti, green vegetables if you have them, garlic bread, and two cold teas," Danny ordered as soon as the waiter sauntered over. It was customary to order everything at once, including dessert, since in Iran, waiters often didn't return to check on their customers.

"*Balle*," the waiter replied sullenly. Many times before, he and Danny had visited in English; now, because of the revolution, the man appeared to look down on the American as just another *farangi*.

"Never mind, my friend," Mohammad said, reaching across the table to take both of Danny's hands in his own. In a Western culture, this gesture of sincerity would have been mistaken for something else, but Danny had learned much in Iran, so resisting the urge to jerk his hands away, he sat there calmly, albeit a bit woodenly.

"You and I have so much in common," Mohammad continued glibly. "We have similar minds. We are living at a critical juncture of history; only political minds like ours can appreciate the forces aligned on the streets today. A lesson of history is that only those prepared to profit from the past can inherit the future.

"A time of national renewal is upon us as the common people throw off the unwanted chains of foreign domination. A new era of Islamic fundamentalism, combined with modern technology will usher in a period of growth, prosperity, and purification in our country," Mohammad gushed. "It has happened time and time again in Persian history.

"What we are witnessing now," he said warming to his subject, "is a military drawn from the lower and middle classes protecting the corrupt pleasures of the Western-educated aristocracy. What the soldiers face in the streets today are their own kind. Soon, my friend, the military must balance its own interests with the national good. History teaches us that military force can only be used successfully in the early stages of a revolution. As blood flows, the military discovers it must protect the nation against the interests of the privileged class. Later, of course, if not protected against by civilian control like in your own country, the military itself emerges as the new ruling class. That possibility will not happen here."

"Why not? I think a military takeover is inevitable," Danny countered, sweeping his napkin across the table to clean it as the waiter arrived with a basket of garlic bread and two small glasses of warm tea. Wine with dinner in revolutionary Iran was too much to ask for, though Danny's mouth watered in anticipation. He hadn't had anything alcoholic in six months.

"No, my friend, it is not so simple. At this very moment, there is an American general sent here by your President Carter to foment a military takeover of the Bakhtiar government in the interests of your country. His mission will not work."

"How do you know about this?" Danny asked between bites. Despite the dangerous gunmen on every side, despite having been frisked and prodded by additional gunmen outside—amateurs, Danny discovered, for though he had stashed his weapons in a wall down the block—he had concealed his Afghan folding knife lengthwise in his underwear, and they had missed it, too embarrassed to touch him in the groin.

"The general has the wrong approach, and, besides, in the last two weeks, other men representing different political interests have preceded him. The military," Mohammad said, waving his hands expansively, "has already decided on a policy of nonintervention in the clash between the people's traditional values and the realities of the modern world."

"Let me ask you," Danny asked, wiping his face with a paper napkin. He was sweating, yet he pulled the collar of his bulky turtleneck higher. "How do you know what the military feels about this revolution?"

"Ah, my friend," Mohammad exclaimed, "You do not understand. We Hashemi have maneuvered ourselves into a long-range program of growth and domination of our business. We've been doing this for over eighty years. Let's face reality."

Squeezing one of Danny's hands firmly, Mohammad smiled as one would to a wayward child. "Crime is here to stay. There will always be *hashish* in Iran. There will always be opium in Iran. There will always be extortion and professional murder in Iran. There will always be kidnapping, blackmail, *baksheesh*, influence peddling, and smuggling here. And there will always be Hashemi control of these enterprises long after the *farangi* are gone and the country rules its own destiny."

"That means that no matter who wins the revolution, you do?" Danny was not surprised. As a courier, he had witnessed much jockeying in the last year but hadn't grasped its long-term significance until now.

"You understand after all. I knew you would. The others in my family had given up on you, but not I. I knew you would come around to our way of thinking."

Assuming Mohammad was thinking negatively of Andrea and her people as the *farangi* corrupting Iran, Danny asked, "Is prostitution a natural element of Iranian society?"

"Aha! I knew you'd understand! Yes! Prostitution is one of the oldest foundations of our culture, long predating Islam. It is part of our national character—"

Recalling the simple cribs and open legs of the whores of the "new city," Shahr-e-Now, in southwestern Teheran, Danny said, "In Iran, prostitution tends to be cheap and quick. Is that all your culture will allow?"

"Yes and no," Mohammad chuckled. "We still crave the essence of sex and the romance of your Western culture. The 'X' movie, or a liaison with a sweetly scented woman of the night who will drain you of your juices and your cash is a fantasy of modern Iran. There will always be a market. We Hashemi hope to control this market."

"Perhaps you're right," Danny agreed, "But let me ask you something about what you said before. You were telling me the Hashemi have maneuvered themselves into a position where they cannot lose, right?"

"Yes, that's correct."

"What about the Islamic fundamentalists? What happens if the Ayatollah Khomeini actually succeeds in establishing a repressive Islamic theocracy? Sharia law and the Koran would be used to justify harsh measures. Wouldn't the Hashemi and others be destroyed?"

"It won't happen! It's an agrarian dream, like you Americans yearning to restore wilderness in your country. It's a fantasy gone forever, yet thoroughly idealized in your national psyche and culture—and ours. Islamic fundamentalism … is an unachievable dream! We may yearn for it, but we can never have it."

Danny knew in his heart Mohammad Hashemi spoke the truth, but he felt compelled to press his point. "How do you know the Hashemi have covered all the angles?"

Mohammad laughed outright. "Perhaps we lost three years of what you call the 'good times,' but we have outmaneuvered you foreigners on all accounts. Today, we have key individuals in our pocket. For example, we know of a planned assault on Doshan Tappeh Air Force Base two days from now. We know—before it even happens—of the destruction of the Shah's Imperial Guard, the Ten Thousand Immortals. Let no one impugn their name! They were good and true Iranian patriots, but the Bakhtiar government is doomed. Bakhtiar will waste the Imperial Guard at Doshan Tappeh trying to protect his feeble hold on the government. And we know already the airport at Mehrabod will open tomorrow for the triumphant return of the Ayatollah Khomeini from France. He will form a parallel government of his own—an Islamic Republic that will last a thousand years.

"The Hashemi," Mohammad exclaimed, his eyes bright with excitement, "have cultivated interests among the military officers. We have contributed to the dissemination of the fundamentalist viewpoint inside the military, including not only Khomeini's sentiments but those of others, too. We have people obligated to us among the Bakhtiaris, the monarchists, the constitutional monarchists, the Tudeh communists—as well as the *farangi*."

Danny slid a plate of spaghetti over from the edge of the table where the waiter had casually left it. There were no vegetables, but they were probably too much to ask for in the middle of a shooting revolution. "So you've hedged your bets. Is there a place in your planning for any *farangi*?"

"Of course, my friend. I knew you'd understand the reality. Even Iran's greatest archaeological treasure, Persepolis, was built by Egyptians and destroyed by Greeks. That's why I resisted your elimination from the game. In the end, I knew you would be practical. A trusted *farangi* courier like you is, after all, a desirable commodity here. The Hashemi can use you to intervene between the various power centers of the revolution, but first, we must eliminate the *farangi* whore and her influence on you. We will keep her Western-style organization, for it is the most profitable we have ever seen. We have learned a lot from Andrea Wilcox. She was a great manager of people. We would like to keep her too, of course, but that's impossible under the circumstances. She is too independent, too experienced and far beyond the days when she had to rely on protectors. She thinks she can do everything herself, but that's not possible in this political climate. She either needs us, or she doesn't...."

"What about me?"

"You have existed under my personal control and protection for months now. I knew you'd come to accept the practicality of my position one day. I have plans for you. You will be protected and nurtured by the Hashemi under the new regime, whatever it may be. You will make a lot of money and be protected at all times—"

"What do you mean, I've existed under your personal control?" Danny asked suspiciously.

"My sister, Mahvash, is the mother of Lieutenant Khosrow Assadi, captain of the guard at Doshan Tappeh. I have known of your hiding place in his office since the first day you slept on his desk—under three carpets,

I recall. If I had wanted it, I could have had you—how do you say it in English? —'aced?'—at any time."

Mohammad Hashemi's triumph was complete, another victory in a Hashemi strategy of domination. Danny was flabbergasted, but he continued eating the spaghetti until he had cleaned his plate. With food so precious, he couldn't afford to leave it. The meal was only mediocre; he'd eaten much better at Zarech's Restaurant in the "good old days." Finished, he wiped his mouth and quietly refused. "No," he said. "Doing business with you is like sleeping with the last woman left in a bar closing for the night. I don't want to wake up in the morning looking at an ugly truth. I won't work for you."

"What?" Hashemi exclaimed in surprise.

"I have scars I have no memory of, and I have memories that have no scars. I cannot work for you," Danny said. "I want to go home ... to a quiet life in Wyoming. To hell with you and your goddamn revolution. Maybe I'm a rare American, but I believe only those with nothing to lose can win a revolution like this. Maybe something good's going to come from it, but it will happen without me. I've been here too long. I don't care to be a courier between historical forces. To hell with all of you. My loyalties are only to the people who've been good to me."

Mohammad Hashemi was stunned. "Fifty thousand tomans a month and twenty thousand each trick," he offered.

"No."

"A hundred thousand tomans a month and thirty thousand each trick."

"No."

"Two hundred thousand tomans a month, but —with that I can only offer twenty thousand each trick."

"No."

"Three hundred thousand tomans a month, flat rate."

"No."

"I am sorry you feel this way, my friend," Mohammad Hashemi sighed regretfully. "May my God, Allah, go with you. Someday, I hope you understand you just made the biggest mistake of your life." With that, the gangster stood up and walked stiffly away. Instantly, eleven soldiers rose from tables nearby to follow, stopping just long enough to pay the tabs.

Danny finished the last of his tea, oblivious to the fast-emptying restaurant and the growing tension of the night. As he got up, he threw a large tip on the table and smiled at the waiter, but the man just stood in the corner, ignoring him. Yes, Danny thought bitterly, he was sick of these obstinate Iranians and their stupid revolution. Now that he had finally decided to go home, he was glad he would never have to put up with such mulish people again.

———◆———

As an afterthought, Danny paused at the door of the restaurant and then turned aside to visit the men's room, exactly as he had done a hundred times in the past. Pushing open the creaky door, he entered the poorly lit, barren john with its red brick walls, sloping concrete floor, and grimy urinals. Everything in this john was dirty. It was never cleaned, in true Iranian fashion. Stepping up to the crusty urinal on the left, he noisily unzipped his pants.

Seconds later, the door opened again, this time without squeaking at all, and a huge figure stepped silently into the shadows along the wall. Ralf Gruenewald, a man who had long ago chosen his loyalties in this game and who was now firmly in the employ of the Hashemis, stepped silently into the circle of light behind his vulnerable friend's back. Just a few feet away, Danny stood looking down at his fly, neither looking up, nor to the left, nor to the right.

He was pissing his life away, Ralf thought sternly. All those lessons wasted! Those long talks and demonstrations of the soldier's art—how to throw a knife, make a grenade using nails, or alter guns to increase their efficiency—they were wasted time now. His young American friend, a head shorter and a hundred pounds lighter, stood there helpless and exposed, totally unaware of the destiny awaiting him. Doc shouldn't have refused the Hashemi offer, Ralf thought bitterly. Doc had been given a rare second chance by the Hashemi, but he had squandered the opportunity.

Moving as quietly as a mouse, Ralf pulled a simple garrote from the breast pocket of his sport jacket. Stepping lightly across the dirty floor, he threw the loop around Danny's neck. Grinning despite himself, the German twisted the wire tightly and spinning around, jerked the helpless American off the floor onto his shoulder to choke the life out of him. It was all so easy. He had done it dozens of times—

But this time, it didn't go the way he expected. There was a dreadful click—the opening of a big lockback Afghan knife—and a long-armed stab backward into Ralf's kidney. The stab was accompanied by a splattering of blood on the wall and urinal, and then Danny lifted his legs up and swung to the right, freeing himself but falling heavily onto the concrete floor in the process.

Choking, Danny pulled at the collar of his turtleneck, then desperately swiveled the big knife around to cut away the strangling pressure at his throat. The hard blade easily cut through the steel cable of the garrote, and as it fell away, Ralf caught a glimpse of a homemade sheet-metal collar Doc had sewn into the sweater's neck. The garrote, which had cut deep bloody slashes on either side of Doc's jaw, had failed to do any serious damage. The kid had tricked him! Ralf wanted to recover, to do something to finish the job, but he was unable to move, paralyzed with the agony of a burst kidney. There was fire up and down his gutline, and his legs wouldn't work.

Though he was still gagging, Danny shoved Ralf against the wall between the sink and the urinal, then stepped forward into Ralf's outstretched arms and pulled Ralf's shirt out of his pants, bundling it to one side. A look of horror crossed the German's face as he realized what was happening. "N-no," he pleaded.

Looking up into the German's blue eyes, Danny plunged the knife into his friend's chest. Quickly, a little to the left and a little to the right of the sternum, he stabbed twice more, searching for the heart, making sure, just like Ralf had trained him to do, two years before.

Gouts of blood spurted out of the multiple wounds. In a moment, Danny's right arm and sleeve were drenched with hot, red blood, but he stanched the sticky flow with the German's own shirt. Blood soaked through his sleeves, dripped from his elbows, then ran in a rivulet as Ralf's strength bled away. The big man slid weakly down the wall, as Danny applied his shoulder and lowered him to the floor, cradling his head as it drooped to the side. Ralf's fingers twitched convulsively, then the big man lay in a pool of hot, steaming blood, his back against the bare red bricks of the men's room, his head leaning against the slimy urinal. By now, having totally saturated the front of his white shirt, blood began to flow noisily into the dirty drain in the floor.

———◆———

Tears rolling down his face, Danny hung over the sink, wishing he could throw up, but he was not so innocent now. He hated Iran for what it had done to him, but there was no going back. Clinging to the sink for support, he washed his hands, sleeve, and face carefully, then wiped his knife with a handkerchief and dropped it back into his pocket. He would have to oil it soon or it would rust. For five minutes, he knelt beside his friend, wishing things had been different between them. Finally, he pulled Ralf's Beretta from a shoulder holster, then he emptied Ralf's money belt before hurrying out of the restaurant and into the cold night. Not sure where to go—for he could never return to Doshan Tappeh Air Force Base—he walked slowly away, not caring if he were going north or south, towards downtown or the suburbs, towards death or safety.

In the end, what he regretted most was leaving the body of his friend sprawled on the floor of the men's room like that. Did Ralf have family? Would anyone care what had happened to him? Probably not, Danny thought sadly as he walked away, feeling remorseful at the way he had to leave his best friend like that, alone and dead in Iran.

-31-

THE KEY TO A DIFFICULT DOOR

"I knew in my heart all those sons-a-bitches had to die, and I was the only one to do it."

—*Doc*

"Hey, buddy, you speak English?" a man in a freshly pressed bush jacket shouted from an open car window. Danny MacCreary, standing on a sidewalk across the street from the Marmar Hotel, a block north of Ferdowsi Square, had been looking for someone who might remember his friends, the Khodari family, but he had come up empty-handed again. Vainly seeking a safe place to hide until he could get out of the country, he wasn't sure what to try next. He had been walking for three days and two nights without sleep and little food, but as he was hurrying from Ferdowsi, the collar of his dirty field jacket turned up to hide his bearded face, the stranger had called to him.

"Yeah, I speak English," he answered, for it was a bad idea to talk to strangers. Eying the car and its red-faced occupants warily, he added, "I'm an American ... like you."

Curious why the men were riding around so openly just days after the Ayatollah Khomeini had returned to a tumultuous welcome after years in exile, Danny stepped closer to the *djube*, though he still kept a parked car between him and the strangers in case there was gunfire.

"Good. He speaks English. Maybe he can help us deal with this asshole," the man said, jerking his thumb toward the driver in what was, in Iran, an obscene gesture.

He and his friends, obviously new to the country, were newsmen, Danny decided. Figuring the men were unarmed, Danny stepped around the parked car. "Reporters?" he asked, silently clicking on the safety of a

Browning concealed in his pocket. The nine millimeter was just one of a number of recent acquisitions; he carried four pistols now, along with five grenades, three knives, and a length of chain.

"We're journalists. Ted Billingsley, UPI," the man introduced himself, offering his hand. Danny was too cautious to take it, but the man appeared not to notice. He waved at his friends, "Bill Krueger, Reuters, and Bob Norris, *Time* magazine. You live in Iran?"

"You could say that...."

"What do you do for a living?"

"Various nefarious."

"That's funny. Do you speak enough Persian to help us?" Billingsley asked. "Can you explain to this shithead where the fuck we're trying to go?"

"No problem," Danny replied, for he certainly had nothing better to do. Since leaving the relative safety of Doshan Tappeh Air Force Base, he had been aimlessly wandering the streets of Teheran. Hungry and tired, he was thoroughly discouraged. Although he had nowhere to go, he couldn't afford to stop moving.

At that moment, the driver recognized Danny as one of his past fares and certainly one of his best tippers. "Doctor Mary! *Alle shoma khube?*"

"*Bahd nist,*" Danny answered, offering his hand to the Iranian. "*Shoma chetore?*"

He wasn't happy being recognized, but this driver worked for "Freendly Taxicar," a mediocre outfit on Kouroush-e-Kabir Avenue he had used only twice to ferry Marvin's friends out to the airport. The driver probably didn't know Danny was a wanted man.

"*Merci,*" the driver thanked him, before gushing out his story in a torrent. It was a misunderstanding. Picking the three newsmen up at their hotel, the Iranian was told they wanted to cruise near the sites of some of the more recent disturbances. As usual, he had demanded his money up front, two thousand rials an hour, but he was paid for only an hour. Weren't they satisfied? Weren't they near Meidun-e-Ferdowsi, scene of many famous clashes? Couldn't they see it was very dangerous at Ferdowsi? Shouldn't they pay him a tip so he could be on his way?

After listening to the story sympathetically, Danny turned to the three naive *farangis*. "I understand you have a disagreement over the fare."

"The doorman at the hotel told us it would cost five hundred rials an hour," Billingsley explained with a smile. "The driver wanted two thousand up front. He owes us three more hours." Under his crisp bush jacket, the reporter was wearing an orange-and-blue Hawaiian shirt. It was clean and smelled of fabric softener. The man was only sixteen hours away from his home in American normalcy.

"Look, there's definitely been a misunderstanding," Danny explained, not having washed clothes in over a year. "Between three and five hundred rials an hour used to be normal but these are unusual times. The driver thought you understood that to go near some of the hot spots would cost two thousand an hour, and I'm inclined to think you got off lightly. There's military to the west of us near the university because a political rally is scheduled this evening. I think Khomeini himself is going to speak. Lots of troublemakers are to the south and east of us, so this is a dangerous area. I haven't been up near the American Embassy in weeks, but I don't think I'd go there if you paid me in gold...."

"I tell you what—give this man another five hundred rials as a tip and discharge him," Danny offered. "If you buy me a drink over there in the Marmar Hotel, I'll get you an English-speaking driver. What do you say?"

Adamant about not giving their driver a tip, the newsmen began to argue among themselves. "We'll need a receipt for our expense accounts," Billingsley declared.

"You just don't fucking get it, do you asshole?" Danny said, pulling the Iranian aside and shoving a thousand-rial bill of his own into the man's hand. "*Motchakeram*," he thanked the driver, pushing him into his car and hurrying him on his way.

Quickly, Danny herded the newsmen off the street. It was foolhardy making a scene in public, but these newcomers didn't understand they were in the middle of a shooting revolution. Any punk with a gun—and there was an unlimited supply of guns now that the military armories had been "liberated"—would love getting involved in an altercation with foreigners on a public street.

Once settled comfortably in the darkened, smoky bar of the Marmar— smoky because it had been both burned and bombed at least three times in the past two months—the newsmen seemed to relax completely. Danny had encountered their type before. Professional bullshitters, they had honed their newsgathering skills to the point where an afternoon's drinking in a bar resulted in a story that sounded genuine to the audience back home, especially if they played background recordings that sounded like they were really on the streets with people around them. Such men were reluctant to get out in the world to experience the chaos themselves. Ignorant of the roots and causes of the revolution, such men actually promoted the interests of the bearded underdogs as the most worthy. They were the dangerous Fourth Estate, the men who politicized, propagandized, and lied to guide public opinion, revolutions, and murders in their chosen direction. Always the underdog was promoted—even when it was wrong. Thoughtless people followed their reports obsessively.

Danny didn't care for reporters or intelligence agents—and he met plenty—probably because he had a low tolerance for bullshit, dark bars, and alcohol. While the noisy men lounged around the bar on singed vinyl stools, he ordered a liter bottle of mineral water to go, then busied himself wolfing down *lavash* bread and feta cheese from a platter on the bar.

"Double bourbon and ice for each of us," the one named Krueger ordered, waving a twenty-dollar bill at the scruffy man behind the bar.

"No bourbon," the surly bartender replied, scowling at the boisterous strangers. "No ice."

"Whiskey then," the American shouted, trying to sound important.

"No whiskey either," the Iranian answered irritably. "Only vodka."

"Pakdis?" Danny asked.

"Pakdis," the Iranian answered.

"They'll have vodka then," Danny said. "A double shot each," Turning to the Americans, he explained, "Pakdis, a pretty good local brand, is the only thing available—"

"What if I fucking don't like vodka?" one of the newsmen complained.

"Then you can go without you shithead," Danny snapped. "Maybe you don't realize it yet, but these Islamic fundamentalists are pouring all the liquor they find into the *djubes*. Just the other day, they destroyed several million dollars' worth of French wine from the Hilton Hotel's wine cellars. With this newly declared Islamic Republic, you're lucky to get anything alcoholic in Iran."

Disgusted with the reporters, Danny excused himself long enough to use a house phone to call Star Taxi. After ordering a cab, he gulped a triple shot of vodka and stuffed his pockets with pistachios from a bowl on the sooty bar. "Good luck," he waved, heading for the door. "Thanks for the drink. See you around." He laid a thousand-rial bill for the bartender.

"Gotta go so soon?" Billingsley asked, lighting a real American cigarette. "I'm sure you've got some interesting stories to tell. What's it like living in Iran? Had any scary experiences? Seen anything important?"

"It can be dangerous sometimes," Danny replied, pausing at the door. He pulled a Browning Hi-Power out of his pocket to make sure it was loaded. "Thanks for the drink, but I really *must* go. I don't have time to sit around like you newshounds do. Perhaps I could call you...."

"Do that," the reporter answered. "We're staying at the Intercontinental Hotel. Maybe we can get together for dinner, and you can tell us about—"

———◆———

An hour later, the reporters' taxi arrived and so did six heavily armed men: Masud Pooinak, Carl Wolffe, and four of Andrea's new soldiers. Searching the hotel in vain, the gunmen held the three Americans at gunpoint until they were satisfied they didn't know anything. The incident made a deep impression on the journalists.

"God, it's regular cowboys-and-Indians around here! Who the fuck was that American guy in the sunglasses?" Bob Norris asked Masud. "What kind of shit's he involved in?"

"Mind your goddamn business," Masud warned in English, waving a gun in his face. "The man you met is a nightmare ... a nightmare to all of us!"

Later that night, Carl told Andrea, "We're getting closer. It won't be long now before we get him. That was a foolish mistake, calling Star Taxi like that."

"It may have been foolish, but it was daring," Andrea said. Wondering why Danny had called Star—there were, after all, dozens of taxi companies he could have used—she decided it must have been some kind of signal. What could it mean? Before Manucherr Sadeghi's death, the old man had told her he knew Danny's whereabouts. Where had Danny been hiding all this time? And didn't Sadeghi say she had a traitor in her midst? Did that mean Danny was innocent...or were there *two* traitors she had to concern herself with? Why did he call Star Taxi? Was it a message...?

"I'm surprised he is still in Iran," Masud said, taking a seat and picking up a week-old newspaper. "I would like to know where Doc's been all this time."

"I would too," she said, reluctantly opening her accounting books to check the latest figures. The value of her associates' shares in the business had gone up dramatically with each death in the organization. Dieter and Guenther, for instance, had been worth nearly 10% of the value of the Wilcox group, but now, with them and others dead, that amount was distributed among the remaining associates. Newly hired gunmen and drivers were all salaried, the same as Doc had been, but all of the original associates were doing well financially—at least on paper. She needed to spend much of her time working on the accounts just to keep things current.

Masud's shares, for example, were worth somewhere over five million dollars. He'd shit, she smiled wryly to herself, if he knew that.

"Yes, I'm surprised Doc's still in Iran, Masud," she agreed somewhat sadly, looking up with a strange, hurt look in her eyes. "But it makes your job easier. You'll get him. He was pretty obvious this time."

"I hope so," the young Iranian laughed. "I think Doc is a very dangerous man, maybe the most dangerous in Iran."

"Perhaps you're right," she agreed.

———◆———

A day later, Danny called the three newsmen at their hotel to pass on a tip. Intrigued, Bob Norris asked, "Can you give us any more details?"

Danny sounded shaky. Norris could sense he was about to hang up. "Look," Danny said, "I told you everything I know. Act on it or not, I don't care."

"Wait," Norris begged him. "You say there's going to be a fight at a base east of town. What's the name again?"

"Doshan Tappeh Air Force Base. It's in east Teheran, not east of the city," Danny corrected him. "The cadets are mutinying in favor of the Ayatollah Khomeini. Prime Minister Bakhtiar can't allow that if he's to stay in power. There's going to be a showdown. I thought you'd like to know."

"We appreciate the tip," Norris said, "but where did you hear this? We'd like to ask you ... hello? Hello?" he said to a dead line, for Danny had hung up and run away. "Well, this goes along with what we heard earlier today, doesn't it?" he nodded to his two friends.

"Yep, and we're going to be there," Billingsley chortled. "I'm going to get a Pulitzer-prize-winning photograph out of this revolution yet."

———◆———

The assault on Doshan Tappeh the next day was the last major act of the revolution. Danny MacCreary was far across town that day, but he heard rumors that hundreds had died. Blood was said to have flowed in all the *djubes* leading away from the area when Molotov cocktails and automatic-weapons fire from the roofs decimated the Shah's fabled Imperial Guard, the Ten Thousand Immortals, as they drove through narrow streets leading to the base, just as Mohammad Hashemi had predicted in Zarech's

Restaurant. Unfortunately, one of those killed during the fight that day was Bob Norris, the reporter for *Time* magazine, who was shot through the head when he got too close.

In the days following Doshan Tappeh, most Iranian generals were sent to firing squads. The Bakhtiar government collapsed. Traitors abounded, and everyone double-dealt everyone else. Caught in the crossfire of accusations and counter-accusations, Lieutenant Khosrow Assadi, Mohammad Hashemi's nephew, was imprisoned for dubious loyalties and executed. A few months later, his mother, Mahvash Hashemi, was also imprisoned for crimes against Islam; she would never be seen again.

For Danny, however, the fight at Doshan Tappeh was a watershed. More than anyone else, he knew how dangerous the Hashemis' plotting had become. The revolution was playing right into Sadjewi Hashemi's hands, and the old man was grabbing at total power. The remnants of the Sadeghi network had been reduced to smuggling gasoline, so the Hashemis controlled all the drug dealing, extortion, robbery, and murder in the country. Sadjewi, having expanded all of his operations, now employed over four hundred soldiers and several thousand drivers, prostitutes, and hangers-on. Someone had to take care of Sadjewi Hashemi.

The problem was that no one could reach Sadjewi since the few who understood the criminal element in Iran were intimidated by its power. Andrea and her people were holed up in their headquarters off Tavanir Street, catching tricks as best they could. The Sadeghis were impotent without leadership, funds, or soldiers. The Islamic Guard and other revolutionary gangs were being bought off by the Hashemis, while hefty contributions made to the Ayatollahs Beheshti, Shariet-maderi, and Khomeini seemed to be buying time and space, if not full agreement, from them too.

Sadjewi Hashemi lived in splendid isolation at his fortified apartment house in a neighborhood in north-central Teheran called Qulhak. Buildings across the street and to either side were crammed with his people and their families, while *kutches* on all sides were patrolled by his heavily armed men with the grudging agreement of the residents. Amidst the insanity of the revolution, the Hashemi neighborhood was the most peaceful in Teheran.

It was into this nest of vipers Danny MacCreary was determined to travel. Taking a terrible risk to retrieve two of his most secret stashes from brick walls near Marvin's villa—one an incendiary device, timers and detonators, the other a package of twelve kilos of aluminum powder—he then walked the streets for three days looking for a sugar vendor. He finally found an old man hammering an enormous block of coarse brownish sugar tied precariously onto the back of a donkey, a dozen shouting housewives surrounding him. It was the same sugar vendor he had encountered two years before when looking for Parviz Langarudi's house.

Sugar was such a commodity in the revolution that hoarding was common and the price unpredictable; nevertheless, Danny forced his way through the housewives and their angry insults to proposition the old man. "Hello, grandfather," he said, hurrying lest the women summon their menfolk to this intrusion. "I will give you five thousand green-back American dollars for thirty kilos of finely pulverized powdered sugar. Bakery quality." This was nearly seventy dollars a pound for powdered sugar deliverable in a big cardboard box in two days. Handing the man half the money, Danny urged him to grind it finer than confectioner's sugar. Even though it was more work than the old man could comfortably handle, the vendor shouted at the women to get away, then turned his donkey around and headed home to pound his sugar.

Next, Danny visited the last Jewish carpet dealer he knew in Iran, a middling businessman with a small shop in Saltanadabad. The man knew him, or at least knew of him, but he was reluctant to extend a line of credit in these troubled times. Although he expected an unbelievable amount of money for his services, the Iranian gasped when Danny told him what he wanted.

"An old silk Nain, *dozar,* first quality, in blues and tans, deliverable in two days!" the man exclaimed. "Yes, I can find such a carpet, but the cost in these times. Everyone wants such a carpet so they can sell it in another country. You will pay me in greenback dollars, not rials or travelers' checks?"

"No, I can't afford to pay in dollars," Danny admitted, having exhausted his stashes. Having made many carpet deals like this in the last three years, he instinctively knew the man's bargaining had an edge of desperation to it. He figured the dealer was probably ready to go underground to escape the fury of the new Islamic Republic toward the country's many minorities. Chaldeans, Nestorians, Armenians, Zoroastrians, Baha'is, and especially the Jews…they all knew what was coming now. They were going to get killed. Glancing around appraisingly, Danny decided this dealer was secretly stashing cash and carpets elsewhere, for his shop was filled with cheap Pakistani and Turkish rugs that could be left behind in an emergency. Somewhere in a special hiding place, he figured, the dealer had the carpet he needed.

"How about a trade?" he said. "Two similar carpets in return. Both antique silk, first quality, each worth what the Nain will cost. It's a good profit for you."

"What are these carpets? How big are they? Where are they? Why do you wish to trade two carpets for one?" the dealer asked, but in the end his greed got the better of his curiosity. "Okay," he agreed, not able to get any information out of the foreigner.

After making a deposit of thirty thousand tomans cash, appropriated from a stash of Andrea's hidden wealth, Danny signed a document in Farsi pledging to pay the full amount for the Nain carpet in one week or deliver a trade of two antique carpets worth at least twice its value. The carpet dealer seemed to think the American was out of his mind. Smiling craftily, he stashed the document in a floor safe and offered Danny some bread and tea.

"You understand I only do this because you were a friend of the Khodari family. They liked such deals as this."

"Yes, I know," Danny nodded, regarding the man as a snake for mentioning his dead friends' names under these circumstances. Though both Benyamin and Ibrahim Khodari had made decent profits, he was convinced they had never cheated him, unlike other carpet dealers he had known. "Thank you," he replied, putting aside his distaste for the man. "I appreciate your help. I know how difficult it must be for you, a Jew, to do business during this revolution."

"Yes, I trying hard," the Iranian, admitted, shaking his head. "I am not a profiteer, like other carpet dealers in these times, but I must cover my costs too."

The young American nodded, then rose to go. "Thank you for your help," he said, smiling pleasantly though he really felt like laughing in the man's face.

"You are welcome," the man purred, but Danny had hardly gone out the door before the dealer had a helper follow him to be sure the rest of the money would be paid.

Two days later, Danny pulled up in a stolen red *Jyane*, a heavy, sweet-smelling cardboard box filling the passenger seat beside him. Another, heavier box was in the back seat, along with two coils of rope. "I've come to pick up the carpet," he announced, greeting the Iranian like an old friend. As he entered the shop, he noticed three goons seated along a wall drinking tea.

"Here is the Nain," the dealer announced, motioning for his shop boy to spread a carpet on the floor. "Blue and tan, first quality—"

"But not the piece we talked about," Danny smiled, hardly looking at it. "I wanted something special."

"Of course," the dealer replied, feigning embarrassment. Cuffing his shop boy's ears for laying out the wrong carpet, the dealer pulled a tightly rolled bundle from under his desk. "This is it." he said. "Best Nain I see in four years."

It was indeed a prize, tightly woven, worn thin, and aged beautifully, a genuine treasure carpet. "Very nice," Danny sighed, regretting the carpet could not be his. Appreciatively running his hand over the vaginally smooth surface, he thought that in many ways, a carpet like this was better than sex; he smiled the secret smile of an aficionado, satisfied beyond words. When he looked up, his eyes were misty and his fingers tingled. "Very good. You have given me the carpet I need. It is the key to a difficult door. How fitting it's such a precious piece."

"*Khub*," the dealer said, motioning for the shop boy to roll the carpet. "I expect payment within the week."

"Yes." Strangely cold now that the deal was done, Danny shook the man's hand, took a calculating look at the hired help along the wall, then went out and laid the rolled carpet on the big box of sugar in the front seat of the car.

Hardly had he pulled away from the curb, however, than an old Paykan stopped to pick up the dealer's men, who quickly followed after him. Although it had been two years since he had first played with Andrea and her men, this was to be the finest fox-and-hounds game Danny ever ran in Teheran's confusing traffic. Twisting, turning, and even doubling back on his trail, he did not actually lose the men chasing him, but the carpet dealer's goons had a difficult time keeping up.

$-32-$

SUGAR SURPRISE

"Every drug dealer I ever met had long fingernails."

—*Doc*

L ate in the afternoon, Shohreh, the *bargee* of the family Hashemi, answered a knock at the expensive imported Circasian walnut doors
of Sadjewi's personal fifth-floor apartment. Irritated none of the guards
downstairs had bothered to announce a visitor, she promised herself that
even with all the new people the elder Hashemi was hiring lately, such
lapses in etiquette would stop soon. She would see discipline tightened
around this house or—

Her mouth dropped open when she unlatched the carved door to
find the Doctor on the other side. She immediately imagined the young
American was here on some evil errand, but she could hear laughing
among the guards downstairs, and the sound of it echoed reassuringly up
the stairwell.

"Shohreh, hello. It's me, Doctor Mary. *Alle shoma khubay?*" he asked,
a big smile on his face. "I've brought gifts from Andrea Wilcox to make
peace with Sadjewi Hashemi. There's been enough trouble between us. It's
interfering with business."

"D-Doctor," the *bargee* stammered, reluctantly admitting him to the
apartment. "What are you doing here?"

Groaning with effort, MacCreary set a very heavy, sweet-smelling
cardboard box on the floor just inside the door, placed a rolled carpet on
top of it, then stood back and smiled at her without answering.

"It is an unexpected pleasure to see you again," the woman said in
English. "Sadjewi not expect you. He will be surprised. You were passed
by the guards downstairs?" she asked. She could hardly believe the Doctor

had convinced the guards to let him see the old man. Although she knew bounty hunters had been after him for months, aside from two deep, freshly scabbed cuts on either side of his jaw, the bearded young American hardly looked the worse for wear. He needed new clothes, a bath, and a barber, but otherwise, he appeared surprisingly fit.

"Of course I was passed by the guards," he reassured her. "How else could I have come up to the fifth floor of this building? I see Sadjewi brought Reza Malek-Zadeh's brother, Abdul, up from Isfahan. It's been two years since I saw him last."

"Yes, he is here to handle new business for the family," she confided. Personally, she didn't like the reptilian Abdul Malek-zadeh, but she trusted him. If *he* had allowed the Doctor into the Hashemi stronghold, things between the rival gangs must be different now. Poking the sweet-smelling package on the floor with her foot, she questioned Danny's business here.

"Andrea wants peace, "Danny purred, "so she is offering Sadjewi a special gift—well, really *two* gifts. Look at the carpet she's sent!" As he said that, he unrolled the beautiful antique Nain in front of the startled maid.

"Ah!" True to her nature, she gauged its worth at two hundred to three hundred thousand tomans, about thirty-five thousand dollars. Quite a gift for the old man.

"It's from Ali Nassiri's home," Danny said.

Four hundred fifty to five hundred thousand tomans, she adjusted her estimate, knowing of Nassiri's excellent tastes. "Very nice carpet," she laughed nervously. "Sadjewi Hashemi will be pleased."

Again she glanced at the cardboard box, but the Doctor whipped a smaller package from his pocket and handed it to her. "This is for you. I know how you like the *nougat* candy from Isfahan."

She was happy with the thoughtful gift; the doctor had always been good to her in his own way. Although he didn't have the money or the power of those around him, he always remembered to bring her considerate little gifts. Knowing how difficult it must have been to find fresh candy during the revolution, she thanked him, and then said, "I announce you. Sadjewi will listen to your proposition."

"Shohreh," Danny said, reaching out to stop her. "I must see Sadjewi alone. Is he with someone?"

"Yes, two of his men are with him." Struck by inspiration, she smiled slyly. Sadjewi was going to be so pleased with these gifts, there might be benefit for being nice to the American. "I will make sure you are alone."

Danny smiled gratefully, his eyes just slits behind his sunglasses. "Thank you, Shohreh, I will not forget."

"You must wait," she instructed, ushering him into a sitting room. "One of the men is Reza Malek-zadeh. He is not your friend."

Moments later, keeping the surprise to herself, Shohreh interrupted the three men in Sadjewi's sitting room to announce a visitor. The Hashemi gunmen were irritated they were being asked to leave, but at a look from the old man, they nodded obediently and rose to their feet.

In Farsi, Malek-zadeh said, "We will see you soon. We must plan this assault on the Englishwoman very carefully."

"*Balle*," Sadjewi agreed. Thanking the men for coming by on short notice, he promised to arrange a contract on Andrea Wilcox soon. After they had gone, however, he turned to the drapery behind him and patted his thirteen-year-old granddaughter on the shoulder.

In these dangerous times, Shohreh knew, Sadjewi trusted only family so the girl had been watching, secretly ready with a silencer-equipped Uzi in case of trouble. The old man told the girl to stay a little longer to see who the next visitor was.

After smoothing the cushions on the floor in front of the old man and picking up dirty tea glasses, Shohreh smiled and then hurried to bring in the unexpected guest.

At the bottom of the stairs, Reza Malek-zadeh bade the other man goodbye and hurried back to the door of Sadjewi's apartment. He had seen something odd out of the corner of his eye, and, like the good soldier he was, intended to check it out.

Sadjewi's apartment was the highest in a five-story building. A broad marble stair led down to the lower apartments of his most trusted lieutenants, including Reza Malek-zadeh, who lived on the second floor with his wife, in-laws, and three children. Another flight of stairs led up to the roof where the entire household slept during the hottest months of the summer.

There, on the first landing of the stairs above Sadjewi's door, was what he had glimpsed. A light trip wire extended from the steel banister to an eyescrew in the plaster wall a foot above the floor. The wire was connected to an MK3 grenade fastened chest-high on the railing.

Who had authorized this? He knew no one would dare enter the Hashemi stronghold undetected, yet someone worried about this had booby-trapped access to the roof. Reza stepped over the wire and inched up the stairs. Another grenade was wired to the door on the roof, but its trip wire was disconnected. Still another grenade was wired midway across the roof.

The Iranian drew an automatic pistol from a shoulder holster and stepped outside, onto the roof. At first, he saw nothing unusual, but then he spotted a large cardboard box on the building's swamp cooler. On a hunch he examined the parapet around the edge of the roof. When he peeked over the wall on the backside of the house, he spied two ropes dangling from a drainpipe and four strangers threading their way along the back walls of the block toward the building. He rushed downstairs to prepare a proper reception for the unexpected visitors.

Meanwhile, Danny entered Sadjewi Hashemi's sitting room and smiled innocently at the old man, who showed no surprise at seeing him. "It's been a long time, my friend," Danny greeted him. *"Alle shoma khubay?"*

"Merci," the old man thanked him. *"Shoma?"*

"Khub," Danny said, laying the cumbersome package down near the door but keeping the rolled carpet in his hand as he approached the old man. "May I sit down?" he asked politely in Farsi.

"Of course."

Sadjewi motioned for Shohreh, who was waiting at the door to bring tea; he then turned his attention to the young American sitting cross-legged on a cushion in front of him. "I never expected to see you again in my lifetime," Sadjewi remarked truthfully.

"Nor I you." Danny noticed Sadjewi had a gun hidden under a corner of a carpet close to his hand, but otherwise the room hadn't changed from his last visit. The walls and floor were thick with carpets, and one wall, a backdrop behind Sadjewi, was covered with the best Isfahan cloths. Danny detected a slight movement of the drapery behind the old man's shoulder. Someone was breathing there. "I brought you something special," he said.

"I can see that, but why?" The elder Hashemi wasn't giving an inch, his dangerous brown eyes noticing every detail about the American. He could probably see the bulges under Danny's field jacket and obviously wanted to know why his men hadn't disarmed the American downstairs. His wrinkled face twisted with doubt, the old man was probably wondering if there was something about this American that he had overlooked...no, he apparently decided, he had not. Sadjewi relaxed, satisfied that all was as it had been before. His eyes settled on the magnificent carpet Danny had unrolled in front of him, but he allowed not the slightest glimmer of carpet-lust to show on his face.

"I brought you a gift," Danny repeated.

"The question remains: why?"

"For all that I've learned in this country, for all the good times, and all the bad, but mostly for all those who have died because of your scheming."

"You know nothing of my long-term plans, let alone the short-term."

"I know enough. Your son, Mohammad, explained some things to me, like how you've played this out so you can win, no matter what. I could never figure out, though, why you wanted to strike at Andrea and her people—"

"It was my revenge. "

"Yeah, but we didn't do anything to you. I heard your youngest son, Hussain, was murdered, but we didn't—"

"Of course you didn't," the old man snapped. "The big German killed him."

"Ralf couldn't have done it. Andrea had no interest in your son's death!" Danny exclaimed.

"Ralf has worked for me for over a year. My son, Mohammad, lives on the third floor. You want me to summon him to explain this to you a second time? You are so stupid you can't understand? Mohammad tried to educate you in Zarech's Restaurant. I know all about it! Ralf works for me. He killed Hussain on my orders. I also sent him to kill you. I see he did not succeed, but I do not understand why. No one else knew anything about this, not even my sons."

Danny's jaw dropped involuntarily. "On *your* orders! I don't understand. How could you have your own son murdered, then blame it on others and seek revenge?" Appalled at the old man's devious thinking, Danny had no doubt now the Iranian was a dangerous psychopath.

"Hussain was weak," Hashemi commented sadly. "Nobody loved him like his father, but he wasted himself on drugs." Looking up to see Danny's reaction, he admitted, "He was my favorite son—did you know that?"

"You had your favorite son murdered?"

"Not murdered. My son was everything to me, but he wasted his time with women—not Andrea's girls though. I brought only the best women from Europe for him, very expensive but discreet. He loved Swedish and

Norwegian blondes. My son's vices were private. Only his family knew how depraved he was with these women, but he became a problem. The resolution of this gave me a chance to improve the life of his family—"

"So you had him murdered?"

"He was...lost, you know. He was often stoned on cocaine he obtained from your roommate, Marvin. Dirty business! I was able to provide all the opium, heroin, and hashish he could ever use, yet he turns to a drug from the *farangis* instead...."

"How was I to take this? Yes, I had my favorite son killed in order to get my men—how do you say it in English? —juiced?—for a fight. I took advantage of that in order to move on the Sadeghis, who had grown fat and sloppy under the Shah's regime. I claimed it was revenge for my son's murder. It's as good an excuse as any these days. Now the Hashemi are the leaders of the underworld community. We are the leading importers and exporters of illegal goods."

"But look how many have died!" Danny exclaimed. "Your own son was nothing. How many others in your family have died? How many of your soldiers have been killed, how many of your lieutenants? Even Ralf Gruenewald was seduced by you and your money and is now dead."

"He's dead?"

"Yes, and while we're at it, how many thousands of unnecessary deaths in the revolution have been the result of your meddling? What about Doshan Tappeh Air Force Base? Did your family have something to do with that bloodbath?"

"Only a little. We Hashemi are opportunists in some of the actions of history. The revolution is a chance for my family to profit from historical events, since what's happening in the streets creates a perfect climate for our growth. Doshan Tappeh was a minor act to dominate our business. We paid General Rabii to—"

"I don't want to hear it!" Danny shouted, shaking his head in disbelief. "It's an evil fantasy. You plan, you scheme, people die all over the streets, and you win. It doesn't matter that you imagine this bloodshed was according to your plans. Your son, Mohammad, laid this bullshit on me too. This isn't a historic pattern repeating itself for your benefit. In the end, I hope this new guy, this Ayatollah Khomeini, will destroy you and your family. The revolution will burn you up in its hellish fires, and you and your damned family will be forgotten, forever."

"You are wrong, Doctor Mary. The revolution will not destroy the Hashemi. We are too useful for all concerned. You think I do this for *my* benefit? No, I am an old man. I will die someday. My sons, grandchildren, my family will benefit from this period of growth."

"You're an evil old man." Looking at his hands in his lap, Danny sighed, "How many more must die before this ends? This has got to stop—"

"And you think *you* can stop it?" Sadjewi sneered. He seemed unsure of the young American sitting across from him. Danny knew he had once been as transparent as glass, but after nearly three years as a courier, his intentions were now effectively camouflaged from the old man. Not the slightest bit of unease or the least tremble of his hands betrayed him.

He had been around the *farangi* mercenaries too long, Sadjewi apparently decided. He was a true protégé of the great German at last. "It's too bad things have to end this way," the Iranian said regretfully, signaling for his granddaughter to shoot the American. Instead, though, as he turned back around from the backdrop, he faced a .357 Smith and Wesson revolver that Danny had quietly pulled from his jacket.

"No!" the old man exclaimed as his granddaughter moved behind the curtains.

BANG! The muzzle blast from Danny's big gun singed the old man as a slug whizzed past his head into the drapery. BANG! again as the girl lunged forward. There was a muffled thud as she dropped her Uzi and clutched the cloth, leaving a sliding bloodstain as she slowly fell to the floor, dead.

"That was a ... a girl. A mere girl! You shoot a child!" Sadjewi screamed.

"You killed her when you gave her the gun," Danny disagreed.

The old man tore at his shirt, exposing his gray, hairy chest. "Shoot me. Shoot me too! Shoot me now."

"No, I didn't come here to shoot anyone. I came to give you a gift, to deliver a message."

Sadjewi reached down for his own pistol, and then looked up into a smile. "Looking for this?" Danny asked, for he had snatched the gun earlier when Sadjewi waved to the girl, even as he had drawn his own piece from a shoulder holster.

"You cannot escape me and my men," Sadjewi said coldly. "I knew where you were all the time you hid from Andrea's people, but they were as children compared to my hunters. Pray to Allah you die quickly."

Casually unrolling more of the fabulous carpet for the old man to see, Danny said, "A gift. It opened your door for me, and I got to see you this one last time."

Almost lazily, he tossed the carpet closer to the angry Iranian, and despite himself, Sadjewi drew an appraising hand across it, pleased with its quality. He looked up to find the American already collecting the Uzi from under his granddaughter's body.

"It makes no difference," the old man muttered. "I will kill you. You will die soon."

"Nor should my death make a difference," Danny said, opening the door to leave.

———◆———

The unexpected blasts of the magnum pistol hadn't overly alarmed Shohreh, the *bargee*, for the many carpets on the walls and floors had dampened the sound. Thinking the American had probably been shot to death, she was waiting in the foyer for orders from the old man when Danny stepped into the hallway. Stunned, she grabbed at her heart in horror.

"What have you done? Where is the Hashemi?" she screamed.

"He's okay. He's still here—"

As if in answer, Sadjewi began to bellow, "Shohreh, *bia inja, bia inja!*"

Rushing into the room to see what had happened, the loyal maid avoided coming too close to the dangerous American. Tearing two beautiful antique carpets from the wall of the sitting room, Danny ran from the apartment, bundling them hurriedly under his arm.

———◆———

While all of this was happening, Reza and Abdul Malek-zadeh were intercepting the men who were trying to get in the Hashemi home from the garden wall. Although the men swore they were only following some crazy American with an expensive carpet and two very heavy boxes that he had had last evening, none of the Hashemi soldiers believed them for a second.

Who would dare break into a building from the roof? It was too absurd an idea to entertain. And who would think to climb a building to enter from the upper stairwell, the least protected part of a building? Suddenly, two muffled shots rang out. Reza Malek-zadeh looked up to follow the sound of the gunfire and finally realized why the door on the roof had been wired.

He shot and killed the four cowering intruders without a second thought, then shouted for his men to follow him upstairs.

———•———

Reza Malek-zadeh reached the door of the Hashemi apartment just as it opened, but the instant he recognized the Doctor, Danny shot him square in the chest with the Uzi and jumped up the stairs in a hail of bullets. The other Hashemi gunmen ran right over their dying lieutenant in their haste to follow, none of them listening as he croaked a warning about the trip wires. There was a stinging pop, and when the first man rounded the landing, BOOM! Three were killed instantly, and two others were blinded by the grenade's blast. Struggling to his feet and bleeding heavily from shrapnel wounds, Abdul Malek-zadeh shook his head against a terrible ringing in his ears, then ordered the remaining men onto the roof. He glanced regretfully at his dying brother, then rushed up the stairs and burst through the door—right into the second booby trap, and the third.

Meanwhile, Danny had thrown the carpets he was carrying into the garden of a nearby house, and then hurled himself over the edge of the roof to the drainpipe, which he quickly slid down. Retrieving the carpets, he ran along the garden walls in the opposite direction from which he had come, a fortunate decision, he found out later, for having spotted Danny in traffic an hour earlier, Masud Pooinak had not been far behind. The young Iranian was waiting for him with drawn gun at the wrong end of the block.

———•———

Meanwhile, Sadjewi shouted, "Shohreh! Run after my soldiers to see if someone killed the American." The *bargee* hurried out of the apartment and screamed in surprise at the carnage in the stairwell. Reza Malek-zadeh lay dead on his back, staring up at the ceiling, his pooled blood dripping in a stream down the alabaster stairs. Blood and brains were splattered all over the upper landing. Three mutilated bodies were heaped on the stairs beside two wounded soldiers still moaning piteously for help. Another man lay on the roof, blood running out of his ears from burst eardrums. Abdul Malek-zadeh lay dead in a heap nearby.

After hearing her report, Sadjewi Hashemi was completely enraged. Not only had the Doctor invaded his home and shot his granddaughter, he had killed two of the Hashemis' best soldiers. It would take years—and a lot of money—before he could replace the brothers Malek-zadeh. "Go, bring me all my sons," he ordered the maid. "We have urgent business. I must have the doctor's head, and very soon."

Shohreh ran out the door. Phones were ringing everywhere in the building as distant outposts in the neighborhood called to ask about the sound of shots. Sadjewi ignored them. There was plenty of time yet to get the American, but it would be on *his* terms now. After grieving over his dead granddaughter for few seconds, the old man rose stiffly and went to the door of the sitting room to await news. While standing there, numb with the insult given his family and enterprises, he laid eyes on the unwieldy cardboard box on the floor next to the door.

Unconsciously glancing at the fabulous carpet Danny had given him earlier, he allowed greed to sparkle in his eyes. If the carpet were so wonderful, what gift did this mysterious box contain? Dropping down on rickety knees beside the package, the Iranian carefully lifted one end. It was heavy, perhaps forty kilos altogether, and solidly packed, he noticed. Bending over, the old man listened for any ticking, thinking perhaps it was a bomb. Satisfied it was not, he forced a finger into the box, poked a hole through a thick plastic liner and tasted the white powder. Confectionary sugar. A precious gift in these troubled times, but certainly not anything the Hashemis couldn't provide for themselves. Smiling at the American's stupidity, he gently tore at the tape binding the box, feeling carefully under the flaps for some kind of wire or fuse.

The box was filled with finely powdered sugar, which smelled of gasoline and had tiny specs of metal, not an unusual situation with the second-rate goods purchased on the streets these days. Sadjewi smiled. Nothing but impure baker's sugar! Laughing at the credulous American for bringing him such a simple-minded gift, the old man ran his fingers through the sweet, finely-ground dust, until…quite suddenly …the dirty, inch-long nail of his left little finger snagged a trip wire concealed deep in the powdered sugar. He could hear hissing from a fuse.

"Ha, Hah, Ha!" he laughed, appreciating the humor of it. The young man had known him well after all.

—BOOM!—

The first detonation of the sugar bomb, more properly called a dust initiator, knocked out all the walls and windows in the Hashemi apartment, filling every space and living lung with finely powdered, very inflammable sugar and aluminum dust. A moment later, the explosive igniter went off.

—BOOM!—

This was followed by a rushing blast and searing explosion as the sparked dust exploded every conceivable space in the building. The blast roared through the ventilation system to the swamp cooler on the roof—and the concussive bomb waiting there.

—BOOM!—

Like a house of cards, the building collapsed on itself, falling floor by floor into a dusty pile of rubble. The powerful explosion collapsed both apartment houses on either side of the Hashemi building too, while windows as far as six blocks away were shattered by the unexpected blast. Moments later, an illegal cache of cooking gas cylinders exploded in the building to the left, starting a fire that smoldered in the rubble for the next week. Lesser explosions in the next two hours were probably weapons and ammunition.

A towering cloud of dust rose more than five hundred feet in the air, enveloping the entire neighborhood. As the girders screeched and broken windows tinkled and bleeding people ran screaming in every direction, one man raced away, carrying two carpets under his arm. Danny had been blown off a garden wall by the explosion and cut himself on broken glass, but he managed to pick himself up and escape, disappearing into the swirling dust.

At the other end of the block, Masud Pooinak had also been blown off his feet. Covered with shattered glass and broken brick, he struggled to see through the dust. "Doc! Doctor Mary!" he shouted, pursuing his quarry along the tops of the garden walls. He fired twice at a vague figure, but billowing clouds of dust and smoke soon erased Danny from sight.

An hour later, Masud, covering his face with his t-shirt, joined dozens of rescuers pawing through the rubble, looking for survivors. Of Sadjewi Hashemi's apartment building, all that remained were steel columns five stories high sticking obscenely out of a pile of crumbled bricks. A hundred and twenty-six bodies, mostly Hashemi men and their families, were recovered from the ruins, and two hundred-and-ninety injured were taken to hospitals. Seventy Hashemi gunmen were permanently crippled. From blocks around, people had been cut by glass and hit by bricks. Masud shook his head in disbelief. It was the best bombing he'd ever personally seen.

For weeks, neighbors pawed through the rubble looking for guns and ammunition. There was a lot to be found.

———————◆———————

Late that night, Danny limped into the carpet dealer's shop in Saltanadabad and laid two fine, quite dusty antique Persian carpets on the desk. "I think you'll like these," he said, fussing with a rag wrapped around a cut on his wrist. "One's a Nain more than three hundred years old, the other is a Tabriz, about a hundred years old...."

"Oh, yes," the dealer exclaimed, running his hand over each of the antique silk carpets. "Very nice, both of them. It was good doing business with you, Doctor Mary. Perhaps we can do it again someday."

"I don't think so," Danny replied wearily, a sad look on his face. "Business like this comes along only once in a lifetime."

– 3 3 –

THE KURDS

"Do not go there."

—Doc

"**D**o you have a pencil?" asked a gravelly-voiced Iranian woman over the phone.

"*Balle*," Andrea's receptionist, Shamsa, replied in Farsi to let the woman know she didn't have to use English.

"In the name of Allah, the compassionate, the merciful: We, the soldiers of the Islamic People's Committee on eh-Social Reform and Justice announce your location is a target for destruction tonight at eh-seven p.m. Anyone found there will die. Do you under-eh-stand?"

"Yes, but why are you calling with this warning?" Shamsa asked suspiciously.

"Do you under-eh-stand every the word I eh-say to you?"

"Yes, I do."

"Eh-seven o'clock tonight. Are you eh-still copy?" the voice demanded.

Whoever the woman was, the receptionist realized, she wasn't giving any more information than she had been ordered to. "Yes," Shamsa answered cautiously, waving at Andrea to pick up another phone so she could listen.

"There's a eh-second message, very important to you, Shamsa Esfandiari: heads, exclamation point. You must under-eh-stand this second message. It is to you personally … from a friend."

———◆———

For ten days after the destruction of the Hashemi headquarters in Qulhak, Danny MacCreary had wandered the dangerous streets of

Teheran aimlessly. Three times he was attacked, once by a gang of street punks and twice by groups of demonstrators, but there was nowhere to run now. For protection, he still carried the .357 that Andrea had given him so long ago, plus two nine mil's, three grenades, a pipe bomb, and an assortment of other weapons, but the thing he feared more than anything else was sleep. Not once did he encounter a foreigner on the streets, and rarely did he meet a friendly face.

On Valentine's Day, 1979, the American Embassy, in an area of town that Danny avoided, was seized by hundreds of armed "students," most of whom were associated with the Marxist Fedayeen. Police restored order, and Ibrahim Yazdi, one of Khomeini's associates, formally apologized to the American ambassador, but it was apparent Teheran was a city gone wild. Gangs of crazed revolutionaries controlled every street. None of them had a consistent political agenda.

Khomeini, a man so feeble his son had to stand behind him at public appearances to help him wave at his hysterical followers, skillfully pitted his enemies against one another to consolidate his own Machiavellian hold on power. From every lamppost and street sign, from balconies and storefronts, pasted on taxis' windshields and the sides of buses, his stern image glared out upon the bloody revolution he had caused. No Hitler with stamping foot and ranting tirade was this; more often than not, the Ayatollah could only manage a whisper in a noisy room filled with confused followers. For those who did not listen closely enough or could not hear him at all, there was a bedlam of conflicting interpretations. As the weeks passed, his followers became conflicted; even some of his most ardent supporters were sent to firing squads for acting counter to what he had mumbled over tea or breakfast. The Ayatollah's followers claimed everything from the old man's mouth was in the name of God, for God would not allow a man to use His commands in vain.

Kangaroo courts filled the prisons to overflowing; dozens of firing squads were kept busy night and day. Fathers were betrayed by sons; mothers turned in daughters for revolutionary justice, often involving gang-rape and imprisonment. With the sudden, new abundance of guns and explosives, feuds and old scores were settled overnight. There were shootings, murders, kidnappings, robberies, extortions, and rapes in every neighborhood, all in the name of Allah, the compassionate, the merciful.... And Iran became a terrorist state, exporting revolutionary expertise, money, and weapons all over the world, a hate-filled agenda that continues to this day. Iran was ruled by hysteria.

Twice, however, friendly Iranians with ties to America rescued Danny from trouble. "My brother is at the University of Illinois," one man told Doc as he whisked him away from a near miss with a demonstration. "I will never see him again. He will never come home to this. Where do you live?"

"I don't have a place anymore. I've lost everything," Danny replied in a tired, emotionless voice. He looked and felt dirty. A razor hadn't touched his face in more than seven months, and he hadn't changed clothes in nine weeks. He worried his greasy field jacket might stain the BMW's fine leather upholstery.

"You have friends?" the man inquired, speeding through traffic like a banshee on a mission.

"No."

"Where do you go then?" the Iranian asked.

This was a nice man, almost *Christian* in his concern for a stranger, Danny thought, realizing he couldn't ride in the man's car indefinitely. "Oh … thank you. This is fine." He waved at an empty *kutche* and indicated he would get out.

"When last you eat?" the Iranian asked, ignoring his request to stop.

That suddenly struck Danny as a depressing thought, and he was silent. "Four days, I think…maybe five."

Several blocks later, the Iranian pulled to the curb and said, "Wait here. I will come back. Really, you must stay here," he said, touching Danny's hand.

Such was the man's trust that he left his keys in the ignition, and though Danny thought about stealing the car, instead he slid down in the seat so as not to draw attention to himself. Minutes later, the man returned with a paper take-out tray of *chelo kebab*, a warm, dusty bottle of Coca-Cola, a real egg, and a fresh chunk of yellow *sangyak* bread. Sitting quietly while Danny wolfed down the food, the driver kept an eye out for trouble. Danny didn't leave a single grain of rice on the plate.

"I am Baha'i," the man said as his guest finished eating. On the verge of tears and very emotional as he looked out the driver's-side window, he inquired, "Do you have money, my friend?"

"Yes," Danny said. He could not admit to the money easily. He could never explain three Iranian toughs in a dark *kutche* last night, nor the fear of being outnumbered, backed against a wall by their sneers and the glint of knives in the moonlight. Certainly he could never describe to this good Iranian the coldness that gripped him as he looted wallets from the dead men's bodies, still clutching a smoking pistol in one hand. "I have money."

"May God go with you," the man said, looking out at the traffic sadly.

"May the Lord bless you and keep you. May His face shine upon you and be gracious unto you. May His light shine upon you ... and give you peace," Danny responded, making the sign of the cross and getting out of the car to stretch. It was the first time he had felt full in weeks, but the food was making him sleepy, and that was dangerous in the streets of revolutionary Teheran.

The Iranian started his car and pulled into traffic. Although neither of them knew it yet, this kind stranger was the last Baha'i Danny would ever meet in Iran. The Baha'i—like the Jews, Zoroastrians, and Armenians—were being wiped out by the Revolution.

Much later, Danny found himself wandering down Tavanir Street just south of Vanak Circle. Although he would pass within blocks of Andrea's headquarters, the fast traffic here left no time for the insults and thrown debris of slower streets, so he felt the risk worth it. Suddenly, however, his blood ran cold.

"Hello, Doctor," a friendly voice hailed him from across the street.

The only people he could see over there were dusty Kurdish tribesmen squatting around a pile of dirt. Torn by the desire to know who had recognized him and an intuitive dread to stay clear of anything and anyone in Andrea's neighborhood, Danny hesitated only a moment before walking on, but the voice came again, clear and friendly across the traffic. "Hello, Doctor!"

Throwing caution to the wind, he crossed the busy street and approached the Kurdish diggers, both hands holding guns in the pockets of his field jacket. "My friend, the Doctor," a tall Kurd greeted him, abruptly jumping up to embrace him. Danny recognized the digger as one of the bearded tribesmen he had hired to landscape Marvin's villa three years before.

"You are Mohsen," he guessed.

"Mousa," the man laughed, seeming pleased the foreigner nearly remembered him after all this time. "Come sit with us."

Like most Kurdish tribesmen, Mousa was tall, strongly built, and bearded; he was, Danny discovered, the leader of these diggers. Gratefully, he immersed himself among the crowd of Kurds, safe for a few minutes, for the men, very busy with a project, screened him from view of the traffic.

"You want tea?" Mousa offered. A few feet away, a smoking fire of wet cardboard was heating a blackened pot.

"Tea? Yes, I would like some," Danny decided, pausing for a moment to look around guiltily

"You want bread?" the Kurd asked, falling for the look.

"No, I...ah...don't want bread," Danny said, playing the man along. He knew what cheap tea these Kurds drank and that the tealeaves were twice or three times used. "I'm sorry, I prefer black tea," he lied, looking down just long enough for the Kurd to realize such tea was beyond their means, but not long enough to make him feel embarrassed. "I tell you what," Danny offered. "Here's a hundred tomans. Buy a half kilo of tea at the market down the street; I will drink what I want, then all of you can drink the rest...."

The Kurd considered it, fingering his beard and looking at his friends. He had heard recently foreigners were not to be trusted, Americans least of all. Several of the Kurds were so religious they would not drink again from a glass touched by Christian lips. Even now, some of the bearded tribesmen were grumbling because the infidel had been invited to join them, but the offer of black tea was not to be taken lightly. He, himself, hadn't had black tea in years.

"Do you remember when you worked with us digging the dirt in your garden three years ago?" the man asked.

"Yes, it was a very hot day," Danny replied.

"You showed us something. Do you remember it?"

Danny thought back to that day. The Kurds had been breaking the dry, adobe-like dirt of Marvin's back yard. It was 120° degrees in the sunshine, not a cloud in the sky, and he had gone out to labor with the men. Although he didn't know it at the time, the Kurds' estimation of him rose by leaps and bounds as he dug beside them to mulch the dry, dead soil with chopped straw and camel manure; however, when Danny shed his shirt and tied a handkerchief around his head to absorb the sweat, they had, at first, been horrified, then amazed. Not only was he as pale as a dead fish, he had what seemed to them ghastly scars on his left shoulder. Unable to explain to the tribesmen about surgery for a torn cartilage, Danny had told them an imaginative tale about being attacked by a tiger.

"Yes, I remember," he admitted guiltily, for he hadn't meant to actually *lie* to the men.

Shouting for his friends to gather around, the Kurd urged Danny to show the scars once more. Several of the men were amazed the foreigner wore two leather shoulder holsters, one under each arm, but none were surprised that he was carrying weapons, for most of them were also armed during the revolution. As he stripped to the waist, peeling away his sweaters, shirts, long johns and T-shirt to get down to the actual skin, a few leaned forward expectantly. The *sex* was almost too much for them, but sure enough, there were two long scars, one on each side of his shoulder, the mark, Mousa told them proudly, of a tiger in faraway America.

Fascinated, the ragged tribesmen listened attentively as the Kurd recounted, with embellishment, a tale of a tiger attack in the mountains of Wyoming, United States, America. When he finished, the men patted Danny on the back to congratulate him and went back to work, the American welcome in their midst.

"We can have tea now," Mousa told Danny. "The men accept you." After sending a small boy to fetch the tea, Mousa took a break from his labors and leaned against a nearby wall to talk.

"We have had a hard time in this revolution, you know," he told Danny. "This was not our fight. The Shah helped our brothers, the Kurdish people of Iraq, when they fought against Saddam Hussain. In my village in the mountains, we have a teacher to teach little children to read. When I was a boy, the Shah sent workers to pipe fresh water to the village, and we have electricity too. The Shah was good to us, as he was to all village people." Pulling up his left sleeve to show the smallpox scar on his forearm—Iranians were inoculated on their forearms and not their shoulders like Americans—he added, "Doctors visit our village once a month to help us. All of this is from the Shah, so we have no reason to hate him.

"Because of this, the revolutionaries do not trust the Kurdish people. Many have hurt us in the city, and we cannot find work now." Mousa disclosed that some of his fellow Kurds had gone home, fearing trouble from the new Islamic Republic, but still others had come to Teheran looking for something to do since the Revolution had stopped everything but farming.

"Today, though, we get good work," Mousa declared proudly.

"What are you doing? There's no construction in this neighborhood," Danny said, eying the busy tribesmen. Some of the Kurds were cutting lengths of burlap material off a bolt, others were sewing the material into bags. Nearby, a smaller group was shoveling dirt into the bags.

"Ah, it is good work," Mousa laughed mysteriously, evading the question to accept a glass of tea from the errand boy. He did not speak again until the other men had a chance to drink and rest.

An hour later, Danny slapped him on the shoulder and made a move to go. There was no way the ragged men would accept outright charity from him, though they were living more desperately than even he could imagine, but as he thrust his hands in his pockets, wondering how to give them something for the rest and peace they had provided, Mousa looked up and grinned.

"Do you remember Gholamreza Hashemi?" he asked.

"Yes," Danny answered, surprised.

"I saw you, two years ago. You sat in his car. A black BMW car."

Gholamreza was a cousin of Mohammad Hashemi. Danny remembered meeting him only once, on the Vanak Expressway when Andrea had to pay ransom for one of her girls. Ralf had been with Andrea in her car, Bob Fraser walked Danny up to Gholamreza's vehicle, and Masud Pooinak was nearby in a truck filled with gunmen. Those were the good old days, Danny thought bitterly. Gholamreza had been killed just a month later by an irate husband who wrongly suspected his family's honor and his wife's honor had been besmirched.

"I didn't see you, my friend," he admitted, surprised there had been witnesses to what should have been a private exchange. He remembered the prostitute was in bad shape, having been gang-raped by a dozen or more of the Hashemi gunmen assigned to watch her. Sandie, the girl, was badly bruised, but okay; she left afterwards for Greece.

"I saw *you*, Doctor. We were digging a foundation hole for a new apartment building across the street."

"Oh," Danny said, understanding now. No one ever noticed the construction sites. Miserable little men lived among the piles of rubble, but they were never given the slightest attention. They were part of the urban landscape of modern Iran, not participants in its life.

"You came in the car of 'Merican woman, yellow hair and blue eyes—"

"She isn't American. She's English," Danny corrected, a pain stabbing at his heart. Those really were the good old days, when Andrea had been a friend, and not someone trying to kill him.

"Tomorrow night," Mousa confided, glancing at the men behind him, then looking Danny straight in the eye, "We see this woman again. We will kill her."

"Who?"

"The Hashemi. They have come from all over Iran to rebuild their organization."

Stunned, Danny looked with new eyes at the activity around him. The burlap was being sewn into sandbags, tied off with wire. Several of these bags filled with dirt lay off to one side, and just beyond the piles of dirt, three Mercedes dump trucks were parked along the curb.

"What are you going to do?" he asked, his heart hammering in his ears.

"There is a gasline trench blocking access to this woman's building. No car can go in her *kutche*. Tomorrow night, we will fill this hole with bags of dirt and pull the heavy gas pipe down so the trucks," and he indicated the dump trucks nearby, "can drive into the *kutche*."

"Why don't the trucks fill the hole themselves?"

"Kurds no make noise like big trucks! We are making other bags to —" and he ran out of words.

"Cover," Danny prompted, suddenly understanding what the man was trying to tell him.

"Cover the trucks from gunfire," Mousa agreed.

"What time?"

"I don't know," the Kurd shrugged, holding up his arm to show that he had no watch.

"No, I mean what time do you do this tomorrow night?" Danny asked.

"Oh, ha! I misunderstand. I thought you ask the time now. I think seven o'clock, tomorrow the night."

"What will the trucks do?"

"One, parked across the street a few hours earlier, will back up to hook onto the pipe with chains, then pull it down into the trench. My men will fill the trench with these bags of dirt, then the other two trucks will carry Hashemi gunmen into the *kutche*."

Danny wondered whether Mousa had intended telling him all along. Then again, maybe Danny had stumbled on the details of the raid by chance, but either way, it didn't matter. "What about *you*, my friend?" he inquired, a thousand thoughts racing through his head.

"We get five thousand rials for the work."

Cold chills ran up and down Danny's back. Regretfully slipping off his gold watch, a sentimental gift from his father, he gave it to the surprised Iranian. The other Kurds gathered around in amazement, for the watch was expensive. "My friend," Danny began, "I give my watch to help you. Can you read?"

"No."

"Tomorrow night, when this points here and this here," Danny showed him, "it is seven o'clock. Listen to me—DO NOT FOLLOW THE TRUCKS AT THIS TIME. Take your five thousand rials and escape into the night. Also," Danny said, digging in his pockets for money. "I have about 20,000 tomans. It is all the money I have left, but it is for you to divide among my friends, the Kurds. Do as I ask: do not follow the trucks tomorrow night."

"Why you no want us to go kill the whore?" the Kurd wondered.

"Since coming to Iran," Danny said, "I have learned a lot from so many people, but everything I have endured comes down to this moment. The Englishwoman has told me I can never go back to the quiet life I once enjoyed in my own country. I am from Wyoming, and I can never go back home. I can never go back.... She was right. She said I had been changed by what's happened to me here in Iran. Maybe she was right. Maybe she was being honest. She may have been my best friend; I owe her something. I must go to her now. I will be there tomorrow night.

"You Kurds don't have to get involved. You can walk away without being corrupted by the Hashemi," Danny urged. "There may be no glory in it, but survival is a quiet kind of victory. Don't follow the trucks tomorrow, my friend. You must survive. *Khodahafez*." With this, he rose, shook hands all around, and then he walked quickly away into the traffic.

Several hours later, Barbara Towers, an English stewardess who had just finished doing her hair, heard an unusual noise from the back yard. "Marvin, there's someone outside!" she whispered excitedly, grabbing him by the arm and pulling him downstairs. Perhaps twenty people were staying at Marvin's villa that night—a few stewardesses, stray Americans, a Brit or two, a Korean, and several Europeans. Altogether there were eight men behind whom the women banded up for cover, the whole group bristling with baseball bats, chains, and lengths of pipe, though they pushed Marvin out in front since it was *his* house and he was the largest one there.

Hurriedly, he had them snuff their candles to adjust their eyes to the darkness outside. Sure enough, there was someone there, running in a crouch past the dry swimming pool. The man slunk from lounge to lawn chair until he arrived at the edge of the pool only fifty feet from the terrified group, but he obviously couldn't see them standing silently in the shadows of the verandah. Prying up the cover of the pool's pump room, the stranger dropped inside. Moments later, they spotted a shaft of flickering light peeking through a ventilation hole.

"We got him," one of the girls hissed. "Let's put something heavy on the cover so he can't get out."

"I've got an idea," another suggested. "Marvin, you still have gasoline bombs in the gatehouse? Drop one in on him. Nobody needs to know."

"Yeah, that's a good idea!" another exclaimed.

"No," Marvin disagreed. "Let's find out who he is."

"Who gives a fuck," one of the men said. "Let's just fry his goddamn ass. I'm tired of these bounty hunters pushing us around!"

"Sorry," Marvin admitted, "There are no Molotov cocktails. I used the gas in my car a month ago."

"You did what?" a woman asked incredulously. "Do we have anything to kill someone with?"

"Not now," Marvin said, for there wasn't a decent weapon in the house, not even the cheap M-80 firecrackers his former roommate had coated with ball bearings for use as grenades.

The frightened group inched closer, listening fearfully as banging and tearing sounds echoed from the hole. Whoever the intruder was, he was tearing all the pipes loose down there; Marvin hoped he wouldn't damage the pumps so they could get the pool filled next summer in case the Revolution settled down. Just as he was about to jerk the cover off the pump room, however, the light was extinguished and the steel cover slid noisily away.

The stranger looked up, startled to find twenty bandits surrounding him, but then, ignoring them, he smashed another plastic pipe, extracted a tube of grenades hidden inside it, then lifted a heavy pack of ammunition out onto the deck along with a G-3 assault rifle. Seconds later, he retrieved two antitank rockets and their launchers from inside another pipe. Only one person would have thought of such a unique stash for his weapons, Marvin realized, looking closer. The man had a blackened face like a commando, but his long hair and sunglasses were—

"What the shit you doing here?" Marvin bellowed in amazement, jumping forward to hug Danny MacCreary. "Where the fuck have you been? Everybody and his cousin's been hunting your ass."

"I'm sure they have," Danny said. "You saw Ralf, Masud and who else? The Hashemis?"

"Yep. We still see those assholes at least once a week!" Marvin snorted. "It seems you did something recently that really pissed them off." He was relieved to see his roommate still alive, but he was surprised Danny had managed to elude his pursuers. He knew how difficult it must have been to hide out all these months. "How long the fuck you staying? You're hot property right now, you know."

"I'm sure I am." Glancing at the group around him, Danny didn't recognize anyone. "What are all of you doing tonight? Watching TV?"

"Nothing on TV," Marvin replied. "Power's off again, but even when there is TV, it's just fucking Persian music or a propaganda show."

"I know some of you want to tell where I am," Danny said. "There is a reward for information on me, but it's not a good idea."

Marvin felt like a farmer begged by a runaway slave to point the way north and give him time to get out of sight. "No one will say anything," he said. It pained him Danny was not sure of anyone, but in the same situation, Marvin knew he would feel the same way.

"If you don't mind," Danny requested, "I'd appreciate it if you stayed together in a group. Give me an hour to wash clothes, then I'll be gone."

"I've got your gear upstairs," Marvin said. "I packed it up. I was going to send it to your family in Wyoming."

"I'd appreciate it if you would. I've got carpets and stuff."

"Sure." Though neither of them said it, Marvin knew they were still friends, even after all that had happened.

"My family would love the few carpets I have," Danny said sadly. "If you could write a letter too, and tell them you saw me—"

"I will. You want to wash clothes? That's fine," Marvin declared. "Wash your clothes in the damned kitchen and use the oven to dry them. At least that fucking thing still works—it uses bottled gas. No one will tell where the fuck you are," he promised, looking around at his guests. The Hashemis had offered 1,000,000 rials for information about Danny, and he, himself, had been offered a hefty percentage by both Masud and Fraser. The big American, however, was worried his guests were too intimidated to withhold information from the many bounty hunters.

"Okay, everybody," he announced, herding his friends into the house. "We're going to play Monopoly with real money. I've got a million rials with the Shah's picture on them that we can use to play with."

He had been saving the money for Danny's escape, but this was a better use, he decided. A few minutes later, he quietly left the excited group to gather up every telephone he could find in the villa. Remembering the trouble Danny had gone to in marking the phone jacks and electrical outlets in the house so long ago, he sat on the edge of his bed and plugged each of the phones into an electrical outlet to burn their circuits. Danny would have killed him for this three years ago, Marvin grinned wryly, but times had changed.

Ten minutes later, he joined Danny in the kitchen. "You had anything to eat?"

"I ate yesterday afternoon," Danny said. "Do you have any of that stain remover you brought back from America for your shirts?"

"Yeah, I'll get it," Marvin nodded, wondering what was going on.

When he returned, he found Danny unrolling an Iranian Army uniform complete with helmet, combat harness, and a belt he had carried in with his weapons. There was fresh blood along the collar of the field jacket and shirt. Danny unbuttoned and emptied the pockets of the uniform, taking only a moment to glance at a few photos he discovered in a wallet.

"Do you have any razor blades?" Danny inquired, tossing the personal items in the trash. "I need to shave and cut my hair."

"Yes," Marvin answered. "I've got two good blades left, and I have scissors, so I'll cut your hair. I guess you want a military cut—it'll be the first time I've ever seen you without long hair. Where the fuck did you get that uniform? Did you kill somebody for it?"

"You got the stain remover?" Danny asked, ignoring the question.

"Yep. It's supposed to be good on grass, blood ... and other difficult stains," Marvin said. The less he knew the better, he decided, but he was disappointed. His friend had been corrupted; he knew that after tonight he would never see Danny again.

-34-

MAMA GHORBANIFAR

"Moush goush dareh, divar moush dareh—"

—Mama

Like many women of her generation, Mama Ghorbanifar, the mother of the owner and manager of Star Taxi, could not understand the bewildering changes in the new Iran. Born seventy-odd years before in a village south of Isfahan, in a time before the Pahlavis were Shahs and before the superpowers or OPEC oil, she took pride in being a simple woman. Married at fourteen and widowed by twenty-three, she had, in true Iranian fashion, survived on the backs of her children: two daughters, poorly married, and four sons, only two of whom brought any income.

Hamad, her youngest son, insisted on getting an education. Since he showed no inclination to dig or scrape for a living, yet consumed an inordinate amount of food, she shipped him off to a cousin in Teheran. She did not see him again for eighteen years. In all that time, he wrote her only three letters, which she had to have a *mullah* read to her—at twenty rials each. She could only afford to have the religious man write one reply back in all those years.

Hamad finished the schooling he thought he would need—six years—then sat around drinking tea with his friends until he was drafted. While working in the grease pits of an Army motor pool, the young man wondered aloud, "Why do machines operate this way?"

Overhearing him, a trucker put down his clipboard and said, "Hamad, you want to know? Work for me after your national service. I will apprentice you to a mechanic at my trucking company."

Ten years later, Hamad had saved enough money to marry, have a child, and buy a taxi, an orange Paykan with a velvet dash cover and garish tassels framing the windshield. To earn extra money, he took up languages, learned French and English and then began to drive telephone taxis for gullible foreigners. For a while, things went well, and he managed to send his mother a few hundred rials a month, but then he had a run of bad luck. His wife sickened and died, and he sold his only asset, the taxi, to pay bills. Soon after that, he sent his boy to an in-law, and then his mother claimed her right to move in "to take care of him."

Life couldn't have been more miserable. Living in a one-room flat in Narmak, in east Teheran, they shared nearly everything with their noisy neighbors. The Shah's White Revolution had promised change, and there was change: better medical care, better education for the children, better utilities, and even television. Late each night, though, Hamad went home with leaden steps to face his embittered mother and the squalid neighborhood where they lived, his dreams in ruins, his life past the midpoint with no hope of revival.

One hot afternoon in early 1975, after taking a fare out to Mehrabod Airport in a contract taxi, Hamad sat in the car smoking cheap Turkish cigarettes. Waiting for a return fare—preferably some rich *farangi* who didn't know the going rate—he was beginning to wonder if he shouldn't head back into town when a beautiful woman leaned in his open window, took off her sunglasses and asked, "Available?"

"Yes, Miss," he answered, his eyes widening at her cleavage. The woman was attractive, but she knew it, and her eyes were cold as Hell. He had seen this type of *farangi* bitch before. *Farangi* bitches were so tough a look from them could burn the varnish off a table.

"How much to the Hilton Hotel?" she asked.

"Oh, expensive," he remarked, misunderstanding. "Fifty or sixty English pounds a night. I take you?"

"No. How much for a trip downtown?" she inquired, seeming to change her mind.

"Where you go?" he asked suspiciously.

He had learned from experience *farangi* bitches were not to be trusted. This particular one was traveling alone, yet his natural desire to cheat her out of every rial in her purse was suppressed by the strange, knowing look she gave him. It was almost as if she were seeking more than a ride. He noticed she had no luggage on the curb.

"Caravans Hotel," she answered, squinting down the line of cabs and drivers.

"Caravans!" he snorted, and she laughed at his honesty. Apparently satisfied with the answer, she engaged him for a week. Later, she arranged for him to manage a dummy firm of hers called Star Taxi off Tavanir Street, just four blocks south of her business and five blocks from her lavish home. Renting a small apartment over the office, she equipped it with cheap furniture and good carpets, a telephone, and a television, and then had Hamad and his mother move in, rent-free. Although she never knew it—and the two Iranians certainly didn't show gratitude lest it appear they accepted charity—Hamad and Mama Ghorbanifar worshipped the ground on which Andrea Wilcox walked, for they owed everything to her.

It was, however, an odd relationship. After serving tea to the great lady seated on the carpets in her small living room, Mama would never again use a glass that had touched the lips of this infidel. She knew the source of Andrea's wealth, yet Mama basked in the *parti bazee* of the great Ali Nassiri, mixed well with the stylish *farangi* prostitutes, and even came to nag the friendly American courier and the huge German mercenary. Like a typical Iranian, though, Mama Ghorbanifar distrusted good fortune; she believed it would pass in the end. Planning ahead, she made Hamad save his money, buy a Mercedes and hire three more drivers. Within a year, Hamad had financed a BMW and two Fiats through the Bank Markazi Iran. Andrea took care of the maintenance of the taxis at the Beste Body Shop, another of her dummy organizations, and Hamad and Mama kept their private feelings to themselves.

Then, the evening of the day the *farangis* called Christmas, 1978, Andrea walked down to Tavanir Street during a power outage with two of her lieutenants, Bob Fraser and Carl Wolffe. Drinking tea by kerosene lantern light in the small apartment, Andrea and Hamad talked of the past. Although their names were never mentioned now, two of her closest allies, the German and the American, were conspicuous by their absence. Mama knew the Doctor was a traitor and that Andrea had ordered him killed. The German just didn't come around anymore, but these were unusual times, and neither Hamad nor his mother questioned what didn't concern them.

When it was time to go, Andrea had Hamad translate as she explained the customs of Christmas to his mother. "There," she concluded. "Are you sure she understands? These are Christian traditions—not Islamic."

"Yes, I certain of it," Hamad assured her. "Good customs. We have this man you call 'Jesus' in Islam, too, but he is only a prophet."

Andrea laid a small box wrapped in bright and shiny paper in front of Mama, with a bow on it and a card delicately written in Farsi. Hamad instinctively reached for the card to read it to his mother, but Mama snatched it away and put it in an empty drawer, a private treasure between women. She eagerly opened the gift. The written words on the card were not important to her. The gift, several fine gold bracelets, was quickly put to use, for they were a mark of wealth and social standing among Iranian women. Grinning foolishly, Mama walked around the room jangling the expensive ornaments on her skinny arms.

"I am sure my mother thanks you for this great thing," Hamad began uncertainly.

"Merry Christmas to her," Andrea smiled and then she took another package from Bob Fraser. "And to you, too, my friend, for good service."

With that, she and her bodyguards rose. Helping Andrea with her coat, Mama smiled a toothless grin and patted her on the back, but Hamad could only sit there on the floor staring stupidly at the deeds and titles to his own business. He was stunned, for this *farangi* bitch had given Star Taxi away. She had given it to him!

Although events continued to swirl around them, the revolution did not make many changes in the way the office was run. Hamad still sent taxis out with the girls. Occasionally, Fraser or Masud would go along as escorts in place of the lost Doctor. Andrea had Hamad buy and sell a variety of cars and trucks, many of them stolen to order; otherwise, he stuck close to his business and kept his mouth shut.

A loyalist, Hamad had portraits of the Shah and Shahbanou in his office, but as the revolution deepened, his windows were broken, some drivers refused to contract with him, and he lost a Fiat to a torch job. Eventually, Mama urged him to conform before he lost everything, so he reluctantly removed the elegantly framed pictures of the Shah and his queen from the office and hung them upstairs in his apartment.

For her own part, Mama tried her best to continue as before, but the waits at the bakery for fresh bread and at the shops for vegetables and tea grew longer and longer. She considered herself a woman of substance now, for despite being a toothless old hag bent at the waist from years of sweeping rice and dirt off her bare floors, she wrapped herself ever more grandly in her black-and-white-checked *chador*, bundling it just below her dugs and waiting her turn in line with all the grace befitting her new middle-class rank.

One evening, though, as she scurried home after standing in line for three hours for a miserable kilo of hot *barbari* bread, she thought she saw the Doctor again. A man was watching her from across the street, but then he turned away, hiding his face. No, it couldn't have been the Doctor, she decided, for the soldier was dressed in a uniform. That in itself was unusual, for soldiers were almost never seen now, but other troops were undoubtedly nearby. Besides, for nearly as long as she had known him, the Doctor had kept his auburn hair long, and he always wore sunglasses, even at night. This soldier's only real resemblance to the American was his ruddy skin and the fact he was wearing sunglasses.

Mama watched the soldier pace up Tavanir Street before rushing home as fast as her tired legs could carry her. Hamad, who was angry because he was hungry, shouted at her as soon as she came in the door of Star, but she griped back defensively and limped up the narrow metal stairs in the back of the office to their little apartment. Rice, boiling water, some *sabzi* greens, and a bit of meat were her concerns, though she suffered the taunting laughter of the taxi drivers downstairs.

An hour later, at exactly a quarter to seven, she heard a hush fall over the office below. The drivers were leaving, stumbling as one out the door and into the night. Clacking her toothless gums together expectantly— no troublemakers around while she and Hamad ate—she was overcome by the strangest feeling. Waddling over to the narrow steel staircase, she listened intently. Downstairs, a raspy voice she had never heard asked Hamad in Farsi how business was.

"Never better," Hamad answered politely.

"*Khub*," came the harsh voice again, the tone strangely cold. Mama crept closer and peeked down into the office. A large, attractive man in a tailored business suit was walking around, touching things. Two other men, lowborn thugs dressed in cheap suits, stood near the door. Hamad was sweating, but he stood his ground.

"I understand you own this business now," the man declared in Farsi, "yet you still transport the dates of Andrea the Whore."

"It is my business what I do," Hamad answered bravely.

"Yes, it is. But do you have a debt to her that would cause you to do something stupid tonight?" The two guards at the door looked at each other and smirked.

"What do you mean?"

"Would you tell the *farangis* people are coming for them tonight?"

"Hamad!" Mama hissed, suddenly realizing the stranger was a Hashemi. She was afraid. Although Hamad's back was to her, she could sense his fear. "My dear son," she whispered. "*Allah-u-akbar!*"

Hamad stretched his fingers toward the phone on his desk, but he hesitated indecisively. When no one moved, he jerked the earpiece off its cradle.

Crack! The Hashemi shot Hamad with a nine millimeter just below the chin. Hamad staggered off his feet and into the wall. Blood and hair were smeared all over a map of Teheran. Crack! Hamad crashed down, dumping a swivel chair on top of his twitching body. The Hashemi stepped closer to the desk. Crack! Right in the face, and Hamad was dead. The two thugs giggled nervously, then jumped at the Hashemi's orders to turn out the lights. Checking the street outside, the men motioned it was safe.

Meanwhile, Mama limped across the apartment, tears rushing down her cheeks, but she contained her grief long enough to dig a telephone from under a carpet in the corner. "Hallo!" she whined as soon as she recognized Shamsa's voice on the other end. Remembering the code words, she sobbed, *"Moush goush dareh, divar moush dareh—"*

A bullet caught her in the back of the head, and she fell lifeless over the phone, wet with tears and her own blood.

———◆———

"What does it mean?" Andrea asked the anxious faces around her in the girls' lounge. "Did you recognize her voice?" she asked Shamsa.

"No. Her voice was heavy like she was choking on something. There is a big noise, and the phone is dead." Shamsa was in tears, her lower lip trembling. "I am so scared!"

"What did the first message this evening say?" Andrea demanded.

"We will be hit at seven o'clock."

"Same woman?"

"No. Another woman," Shamsa sobbed.

"It's nearly seven o'clock now! What did the second message say tonight? Something about 'heads, exclamation point?' What does that mean?"

Looking around at her girls, all holding pistols except for two toting fire extinguishers, she combed her fingers through her hair. The time for action was upon them, and her men were so relaxed. Bob Fraser carried a Kalashnikov, but Masud Pooinak and most of the others were armed with G-3's; Carl hefted an M-60 machine gun and several belts of ammunition. Grenades, spare magazines, and knives filled the men's combat harnesses. Several of the girls had Molotov cocktails, but they were also ready with buckets of oil and baseball bats in case this was a simple civil disturbance by religious fanatics.

"Heads exclamation point," Carl wondered, scratching his head. It made no sense to him.

"Heads exclamation point," Masud thought out loud. The young Iranian screwed his eyes shut and mouthed the words as if to visualize some meaning to the riddle.

"Heads ... heads! HEADS!" Bob Fraser exclaimed, suddenly understanding the message. "It's kids playing baseball in America—my God, that's it. Heads!" Clapping Masud on the back, he explained, "In America, when kids play baseball, and there's a ball coming straight down, you shout 'heads!' so everyone will look up and not get hit. Heads!"

"I don't understand, Bob," Andrea whispered, though she was beginning to. Her heart began to beat.

"It's a message only an American would send. It's from Doc, it's from Doctor Mary, Andrea! It's a warning—" And at that moment, the lights went out. The neighborhood had gone dark. All electricity had been cut off.

———◆———

Five blocks south, forty Kurdish diggers rose as one in the darkness, most shouldering heavy bags of gravel and dirt, but some carrying shovels or loaded rifles. Two Mercedes dump trucks, their hoods and grills sandbagged to armor them from chance shots, lumbered to life beside them, and twenty-four heavily armed Hashemi gunmen, each with a new G-3 assault rifle, clambered aboard the trucks and squatted down out of sight.

A wolfish face peeked around the corner of the darkened Star Taxi, looking for movement up Shiraz Street. A narrow gasline trench five feet deep, two feet wide, backed up by a four-foot rampart of dirt and topped with a welded, unmovable gas pipe stretched away into the darkness, blocking access to every *kutche* all the way up the hill. Mousa, the Kurd, grinned. Everything looked exactly as he had been told by the Hashemis.

Turning to his men, Mousa motioned for them to follow. Forty gray, turbaned figures moved around the corner, their dusty pantaloons and vests making no sound; eighty black eyes scanned the darkness ahead as they made their way slowly up the uneven, concrete sidewalk toward the second *kutche*. Somewhere off to the right, a third dump truck waited, chains already attached to the pipe across the street, but as yet there was no sound from its engine.

"Baba?" an Iranian tough whispered from the back of the third truck. He could see the long, eerie line of Kurds laboring uphill in the darkness.

It was time to fire up the truck to pull the pipe away from the trench. *"Baba!"* he called more urgently, and then he hurried up alongside the cab to wake his friend. Swinging up on the running board, he was surprised to find the man grinning at him—from ear to ear. There was a soft gurgling of blood, but before the gunman could scream in horror, a man in an army uniform appeared from the shadows behind him and knifed him too.

The armored trucks slowly rounded the corner, followed by eight cars loaded with fifty more Hashemi gunmen. The Kurds were nearing the third *kutche* now, but the soldier seemed in no hurry at all. Walking out into the middle of Shiraz Street, he picked two long bundles off the cracked pavement, and then, before any of the Kurds could react, and long before the drivers of the trucks knew there was any trouble, he expertly stripped and activated two rocket launchers. Seconds later, a wire-guided antitank missile blazed across the street and slammed into the cab of the lead truck, killing it like an elephant stunned in its tracks. A slow-spreading fire of diesel fuel licked out of the truck's engine compartment as it fell to pieces. The second truck swerved and tried gunning around the wreck, but another missile caught it in the front axle, causing it to skid into the gasline trench and crash. Twenty men on fire ran screaming into the darkness.

Immediately, the black night air was filled with tracers. Unsure where the attack was coming from, the Hashemi shot at buildings on every side. They shot out windows, storefronts, and all exposed doors in the neighborhood. Dropping to the ground and crawling for the earthen wall between themselves and the mysterious soldier, the Kurds also opened fire, but they were not sure who their real enemies were. Was the Army here or a unit of the Islamic Guards? Bullets flew in every direction, and it seemed likely there was a double-cross in progress. Some of the Kurds shot at the Hashemi; some of the Hashemi shot back. Neighborhood punks, or self-styled revolutionaries, awakened by the unexpected gunfire in their neighborhood, began to shoot out of apartments lining both sides of the street. Homeowners in possession of looted arms also began to fire back. Within a minute, hundreds of tracers flew in all directions.

In seconds, many of the Hashemi gunmen were sprawled in the street. Ominous red flames licked along the far *djube* and rushed downslope; bottles of gasoline strategically placed beneath parked cars were being methodically shot open, pouring flames downhill to cut off any escape. Wisely, Mohsen Hashemi and a single gunman jumped out of their cars and ran away to fight another day, but rifle fire killed Mohammad Hashemi as he raged at his men in the middle of the street.

———◆———

"LET'S MOVE!" Fraser yelled, sprinting out of Andrea's office and running into the *kutche* to see what was happening. Masud was right on his heels, with Carl and another gunman just behind.

"Dammit, come back here!" Andrea shouted, chasing after them "It's not our fight. Get back here!"

"COVER FIRE!" Bob bellowed, ducking his head out from the wall to check the street. "FUCK ME!" Reaching around the corner, he shot off a quick magazine, then shouted at the others, "Kurds dug in along the storefronts on this side. The street's filled with blown-to-hell trucks, dead men, and junk."

Three quick explosions shattered windows just south of where they stood, followed by three softer thuds. Again, Fraser took a look. "A soldier's running this way. He's laid down grenades and smoke, but there's no covering fire. He's rocking and rolling in full auto all the way."

Carl immediately jumped into the street screaming, "You motherfuckers!" Unloading his machine gun into the scrambling Kurds along the wall, he ordered the other mercenaries to join him. Moments later, he shouted, "Okay, that's it, let's head for home! We did all we could. That soldier helped us by stumbling onto something tonight, but we got more than our butts to protect. Let's go."

"He's down!" Masud gasped, glancing around the building's corner and emptying his G-3 one last time. Shells were ricocheting all around, but Fraser ventured another quick peek. Clutching his side, the soldier was crawling for the gasline trench. Dozens of bullets slapped the asphalt around him, and tracers lit his frightened face. Strangely, he was wearing sunglasses, though it was night.

"Oh, bloody hell!" Wolffe yelled above the din.

Rolling into the trench for cover, the soldier ducked down and ran uphill toward where they were standing at the fourth *kutche*. A foot of slimy mud filled the bottom of the trench, and four feet of slippery dirt kept him from climbing over to where the Kurds lay. Just this one avenue of escape remained, so the man slogged up the trench as fast as he could run, dusting the pipe and dirt to his left with a hot G-3 assault rifle.

The remaining Kurds, sensing the vulnerability of the lone soldier, threw themselves against the rampart and tried to shoot him, oblivious to the heavy fire they had taken from the *kutche* to their left. When Carl came around the corner a second time, with Masud and Bob covering him, the tribesmen were completely exposed. Intent on the kill, six of the Kurds slithered over the pipeline and went into the trench after the soldier, but four more lay dead halfway over. Wolffe's fire caught the rest, splattering brains all over the littered sidewalk. The soldier in the trench killed the other Kurds.

Then, one last Kurd, the wounded leader, hurled himself into the trench, stopping before he reached the panting soldier. He hesitated in surprise. "*Shoma!*" the Kurd exclaimed. He broke into tears.

"Fuck you clean to hell," the soldier answered in English. "You should have listened, you stupid son of a bitch!" And he shot the Kurd in the head.

"*Bia inja!*" Masud shouted, waving at him to come out of the trench. To his surprise, the soldier was looting an expensive gold watch from the tribesman's wrist. Although bullets were raking the dirt nearby, the soldier calmly reached up with his right hand to catch Masud's outstretched arm. As the Iranian pulled him out of the trench, Wolffe gave a final burst of fire downhill, then led the men back up the narrow *kutche* to Andrea's place. Behind them, the gunfire was beginning to die off quickly, and Hashemi gunmen were scattering to the four winds, knowing the firefight would attract attention from Revolutionary Guards. Limping after his rescuers as best he could, the wounded soldier made it to the gate just as Masud was slamming it shut.

"*Moush goush dareh—*" the man panted, begging to be let in. Unable to finish the passwords, he pushed desperately against the heavy steel gate.

"*Khub,*" Masud answered, pulling him inside as soon as he realized the man knew the code.

"Are you okay?" Andrea screamed above the noise. "Anyone hit?" She carried a G-3 in one hand and a pistol in the other, her blonde hair wild in the burning night.

"We're alright, except for this commando," Fraser replied, motioning toward the wounded man collapsed near one of her cars. The soldier was clutching his side, but blood was also gushing from a wounded hand. At the same time, a creeping bloodstain showed just below his right knee.

"But everyone else is unhurt?" she persisted.

"Yeah."

"Thank God! Stash all the weapons. I'm sure the revolutionaries will be doing a house-to-house shortly. Bob, take every girl to the safe house. Masud, get rid of all our papers and phones."

"Right."

"And stop this damn man from bleeding all over my drive," she ordered, pointing at the wounded soldier. "Get rid of him. We don't need any more trouble."

"Gee, thanks," Danny MacCreary wheezed sarcastically, looking up at them for the first time. His long auburn hair had been shorn to the skin in a severe military cut, but his sunglasses and face identified him.

"You've got a lot of fucking nerve coming here again," Fraser swore, halfheartedly unslinging his G-3.

"There's no place left to go," Danny admitted, smiling up at him. He raised the muzzle of a loaded .357 to Bob's face, then swung the heavy pistol around and pointed it at Andrea. "There's nowhere to go except here."

"You realize we've been hunting you all these months?" she asked incredulously.

"Yeah, but I have never known why," he gasped.

"Then it was Ralf, wasn't it?" she decided, the certainty of it hitting her. "*He* was the traitor that almost got us all killed. Do you know I promised lots of money to have you assassinated?"

"Yeah, I know that," he choked after looking at what remained of his left hand. "I heard about it second-hand."

"Yet you came back to me?" Andrea marveled, tears filling her eyes.

Danny's gun hand began to waver, so he thumbed off the hammer and put the revolver in a shoulder holster. For the first time, Andrea noticed the puddle of blood in which he was sitting.

"You're hurt!"

"No kidding," he said weakly. Counting the wounds, he looked up at her and said, "I've been shot five times."

Glancing at the other mercenaries, then at Andrea and a few girls who had already emerged from the house with their suitcases, Masud confessed, "I was wrong to hunt you, my friend. I was in Qulhak the day you killed Sadjewi Hashemi, yet I still shot at you on the wall! I believed all the things I had heard about you. I am sorry I accepted Ralf over you. We will hunt him now and finish the Hashemi."

"No." Danny answered, his head sagging as he panted his strength away. "Somebody got Ralf already—" His eyes half closed with blood loss, he could not admit to killing Ralf. That would have to wait.

———◆———

Much later, Danny became aware of rainbow-colored lights and the deepest blackness. A high whine filled his ears, and his throat could not have been drier if it had been packed with salt. As he lay on someone's desk, an ugly Pakistani nurse labored over his wounds. He found out later twenty-eight stitches had been necessary to close up his right calf, a bullet had been pulled out of his left side, and four broken ribs were taped and bandaged. Although he had other wounds, most of the night he suffered through surgery on his left hand. Occasionally, he puffed on a *hookah* someone held for him, and though the opium helped, the pain was excruciating.

"The hand will require reconstructive surgery," he heard the nurse tell Andrea when she was paid the next morning. "The bullet hit near the wrist and cavitated upward through the palm into his knuckles. I amputated what was left of his middle two fingers, but he will need work on the tendons. A hand is like a piano. Every tendon has tension in harmony with the others. The hand will become deformed unless he gets treatment. It would be best for him to seek a surgeon in the West. For him, the fighting in Iran is over."

Danny felt like his hand was dipped in fire. Towards morning, he awoke with a druggie's headache, but Kabri, one of the girls, knelt beside him and held his head while he sipped tea. She wept; she knew more than he. Later, someone brought breakfast, and there was whispering in Farsi outside his door. As he looked around at sunshine streaming in a window, he realized he had been moved to another residence and was safe. Hardly able to believe his good fortune, he slept well for the first time in ten months.

— 35 —

GOODBYE

"I never paid for it before, and I wasn't even horny—"

—*Doc*

Since the beginning of February, gunmen controlled the streets of Teheran. With civil authority non-existent, bands of bearded young men in field jackets indulged their most violent fantasies. Neighborhoods were squeezed, protected, or looted as the whim of the day dictated; wildcat roadblocks were thrown up across intersections. Pretty women were raped in the name of Allah. Innocent people—even kids—were executed against the walls. Unlucky victims of the revolution were dragged out of their homes and summarily executed for suspected "crimes" while others were marched off to kangaroo courts for "justice."

Demonstrations in front of the American embassy were becoming more hysterical, crowds often chanting *"Margh Bar Amrika!"* while their signs catered to news cameras with the English translation, "Death to America." Sudden arrests were on the increase too, since SAVAK—now risen from the ashes and renamed SAVAMA—was filling the prisons to overflowing. Mangled bodies were found in every empty lot, all shot in the head, many burned by cigarettes.

Even so, the truly dangerous bided their time. The house of Hashemi was rising again, just as distant relatives of the Sadeghi were resurrecting their own organization. Guns were inexpensive, but bombs were cheaper and more accessible. For the first time, lawless expertise was available. During the time of the Shah, terrorists had been inept bumblers as likely to hurt themselves as anyone else, but now, in the time of the Ayatollah, professionals were everywhere. And for every bomb these men made, for every trick and every surprise, at least three eager students learned the trade. Violence was a way of life, for it served as a release of frustrations and a way to express revolutionary zeal. The Iranians would soon carry these skills to distant lands: Palestine, Lebanon, Somalia, Chad, Egypt, Iraq, Syria, and east Africa.

"I sometimes think we should get out of here," Bob Fraser confided one evening in the girls' lounge. Andrea and Masud, playing a game of backgammon nearby, made no response, but Danny MacCreary only sighed and looked away sadly. "I think the revolution is winning," Bob said.

"No," Andrea stopped him, as if she were afraid to let him complete the thought. "There's just too much money here. Do you think Iranians could run this country by themselves? No! There will always be *farangis* here to serve the golden goose. There always have been. Remember: even the ancient Persians had to hire Egyptian stonemasons to build their great monument, Persepolis."

"Maybe," Bob allowed, "But what about this Islamic fervor? It's getting worse every day."

"It may carry them awhile," she conceded, "but it cannot sustain a hollow, worthless revolution for long. They would need a war for that. Only a war could unite these disparate groups."

There may have been something in her eyes or the way she said it that caused Danny to wonder later if she already knew the course events would take. After all she had been through in Lebanon when things fell apart there, perhaps she had learned one of the great principles of political science. It was possible she could already foresee the future: the mangled, young boys hanging in Iraqi barbed wire, whole battalions of fanatical Revolutionary Guards dead and rotting in muddy trenches, a deluded nation betrayed by an old man's vengeful scheming in the name of God, and a faltering revolution buoyed on by the hysteria of *jihad*, or holy war with neighboring Iraq. Perhaps she already knew, though it was hard to say, for Andrea's blue eyes rarely revealed anything.

"I'm worried about the course this revolution is taking," Fraser said

"I am more afraid of the Hashemis," Masud laughed

"Perhaps you're both right," Andrea decreed. "We should find out what the Hashemi are up to. At the same time, with the economy in such a flux, perhaps there's new opportunities for us."

So, in the midst of the horror around them—the shouting, the murders, the demonstrations, and the confusing power struggles as the Ayatollah played off group against group to weaken his opposition—the Wilcox organization began a grueling quest. Fraser collected information on the resurgent Hashemis. Masud tracked the Sadeghis, and Danny followed news from the revolution. Pamela Scardetta, one of Andrea's girls just recently returned from England after a long convalescence, worked to feel out the new regime's attitude toward professional sex. Andrea's new lawyer laid the basis for *parti bazee* influence. Maria Ortega, another of the girls, began the purchase of safe houses, cars, and new friends, in case they were needed later. Lorin Reis, still another of the girls, developed a new business for the organization: smuggling people out of Iran. [Lorin would use this experience in other countries. She wound up working for the UN High Commission on Refugees and was killed in Rwanda in 1994.]

Even with all this new work, however, Danny grew restless, though he didn't know why. He wanted to go home; he wanted to stay. He felt he was in danger; he convinced himself he was safe. The money was good; the money wasn't enough to compensate for the horrors he had endured. His life was filled with conflicts, but the one fact that ruled him was an overweening desire for the peace he had known before coming to Iran. He finally secluded himself and wrote his family in Wyoming, the first letter he'd written in a year and a half, and though it lacked details, he knew his family was sick for news of him, what with all the bullshit on TV. He hadn't had a letter from them in two years.

Days passed into weeks, and still he couldn't make up his mind. Finally, on the last Wednesday of May 1979, there was a hum from downtown, a rushing to work and school that was not quite routine. Rumors were flying about the Shah's return, vague assassinations, or a *coup d'etat* engineered by the Americans. Teheran was a city without sleep. Armed men were everywhere. Every street was closed.

Danny got up soon after dawn and looked out the window of the tiny apartment Andrea had lent him, but there wasn't anything new to see. In the distance, the sky was black with smoke, and on the street below, a half-dozen punks were beating a helpless old man to death. Danny washed dishes and left them in the rack to dry. Everything must look normal, he reminded himself as he prepared to go downtown for the last time. He was on edge and lonely, for he had decided to leave Iran at last.

It took hours to retrieve his money from a secret stash on Shah Abbas Street, let alone do a currency transaction on the black market downtown. Only the most essential businesses were open—bakeries, food stores, and a few gas stations—so, in the afternoon, he caught a taxi up Kouroush-e-Kabir Street to the Beste Body Shop. Masud Pooinak was sitting in the office with the manager, Khani Nassiri. No one else was around. Where formerly there had been a bedlam of hammering and spraying among great piles of engine blocks and rolls of upholstery, now only the vast, haunting quiet that had settled over the city remained.

"*Alle shoma khubay?*" Danny greeted each of the two men.

"*Merci,*" the manager answered, flipping his prayer beads.

"*Shoma chetoray?*" Masud asked.

"*Chai?*"

"No, thanks. It's too hot for tea. Do you happen to have a beer?" Danny asked.

"No." Perhaps the answer was too quick, for Masud quickly reconsidered. "Well ... perhaps there is a beer or two, but don't let anyone see you drinking it—you know how these religious fanatics are."

"I do," Danny laughed, gratefully accepting the dusty bottle Masud dug out of a cluttered desk drawer. "I haven't had anything alcoholic in over a year." Taking a swig of the warm beer, he told them, "I've come to see Ali Nassiri's car."

The two Iranians exchanged a meaningful look, then the manager sadly volunteered, "I show you."

He led Danny to a locked garage at the back of the property, past rusting hulks of cars stolen and cannibalized for parts, past wrecks, scrap, and tools to the darkest corner—the most remote and secret garage of the business. Inside the double-locked doors, he uncovered what was left of the blue Mercedes.

The roof was blown back and sprung like a discarded sardine can. All the doors were gone, the hood was bent over and crammed down into the grill, and the trunk was rippled like an accordion. Of the firewall, engine and interior, nothing recognizable remained. Although it was mostly burned and badly scorched, parts of the rusted limousine still had traces of powder-puff blue paint.

"She wants me to rebuild the car," the Iranian said, waving his hands helplessly.

"You must keep it here, as you've done," Danny told him, glad that he had finally come to see it, for he had always liked Ali Nassiri. "You've done well," he added, patting the man on the shoulder as the Iranian blew his nose on the floor and wiped away a tear. Danny remembered the manager was a distant relative of Nassiri's.

"Of course, I will always keep it," the man promised.

Walking back across the cluttered lot, Danny paused beside another ruined Mercedes and wondered what it was about great events that made people collect souvenirs. Up to now, all of his collectibles had been carpets, jewelry, and gold, but unable to shake the memory of Ali Nassiri, he suddenly walked over to the wrecked car and twisted off its hood ornament. It took a manly effort. Looping it through a gold chain he wore around his neck, he looked up into the eyes of the surprised Iranian. "I wanted to remember...." he said rather lamely.

"Me too," the man confessed sheepishly, a grin sweeping across his face. Pulling a Mercedes logo from a gas cap out of his pocket, he said, "Here, take this. It's from the actual car."

"No," Danny said. "This is good enough for me. You keep that one for yourself. It's very special. He was a relative of yours."

Masud waited patiently while Danny said goodbye to the manager at the gate. Afterwards, Masud walked a short distance along Kouroush-e-Kabir with him. "You will leave soon," he said sadly. "I will miss you."

"Yes, me too," Danny admitted.

"I often think about something you said a year ago. Do you remember you advised me to send my son to his mother in Italia?"

"Yes, I remember."

"I think about this every night before I sleep. Send my son to Italia? Or no? I have decided the boy is Iranian like his father. I will not send him to his mother." Glancing at Danny to see his reaction, the young Iranian asked, "Where do you go from here?"

"Frankfurt, West Germany" Danny lied.

"Will you go to Rome ... for me?"

"Sure." Danny said, taking both of Masud's hands in his own. "What do you want me to do?"

"You are our courier. You are an honorable man. I will pay you fifteen thousand tomans to deliver something to my ex-wife. Give her these," he directed, handing Danny two manila envelopes, the thinner one sealed and addressed to the woman. There was a lot of money in the second envelope, which was not sealed and was very thick.

Danny took the cash out of the envelope and made a show of counting it. Along with some Iranian rials, there were seven foreign currencies, Masud's wedding ring and two gold Pahlavis inside. Putting the money back in the envelope, he sealed it, and then ceremoniously initialed the back. "I'll deliver it," he promised.

"Thanks," Masud said, handing him 150,000 rials cash. "I'm not worried about what's happening, but I promise, if it gets worse, I will send the boy to his mother. The money is for his education."

"Okay."

There was a long silence between them as they stood there. Masud tried to collect his thoughts. A cold breeze came from somewhere, and the traffic noise rose unexpectedly. "Doctor, I loved this Italian woman."

"I know," Danny said. "I'm sure she must've loved you too, Masud. The problem was not in your love for each other; the problem was the differences in your cultures."

"Yes, that's right, of course," Masud agreed. "I see that now. Do you know why Andrea trusted me with her girls? Because I never touched any of them, ever, not one, ever! I have not been with a woman since my wife left me." The young Iranian glanced at the traffic for a moment, then sighed and took Danny by the shoulders. "Goodbye, Doctor Mary, my dearest friend." He was sad and looked down at the sidewalk, tears dripping off his cheeks.

There was this thing about Danny's Irishness, perhaps nothing more than intuition, but he didn't like what he saw in his Iranian friend's face. Saddened, he hugged Masud again, a second time, very tightly, shoulder to shoulder. "Goodbye, Masud, my friend."

As he walked away, the young Iranian called out, "Daniel?" It was the first time Masud had ever used his formal name. "You remember Andrea told us not to get involved with politics?"

"Uh-huh."

"I think I will be political from now on."

A busload of weeping young men bound for Qasr Prison roared by on Kouroush-e-Kabir, momentarily distracting Danny. "Keep your guns loaded," Danny advised, looking with remorse at his friend.

"I will do that," Masud laughed cynically. He waved and walked away.

Marvin's villa was dark, and there was no gate man, but after climbing the wall, Danny found the housekeeper cleaning the house and the gardener feeding chickens beside the dry swimming pool. Danny smiled; he had trained the servants well. The stewardesses were gone, their rooms empty and dirty, but Marvin's bedroom was just as messy as ever. The big American was at his office trying to get some work done, but Danny had no time to go downtown to see him. Sorry he wouldn't be able to say goodbye in person, he sat down for an hour and left a long handwritten letter on his roommate's pillow. It was an honest nine pages long.

Late that evening, Danny caught a taxi over to Andrea's office. Bob Fraser was the only one there, but he was too drunk to talk; Danny left him a note for morning when he would be sober. Because of the good-natured ribbing he had always received from the girls, he had rarely visited their rooms upstairs. Now, though, he took the opportunity to explore. He saw all of the furniture had been sold, and the rooms were empty and growing dusty. On a mirror in one of the bathrooms, one of the girls had written, "Fuck you, Iran."

Wasn't it strange, Danny thought as he read the message, hundreds of thousands of Iranians in the streets were shouting, "Death to this!" and "Death to that!" but in the end, there was more defiance in this simple message from a whore.

Of all the rooms, the lounge and the dressing area on the second floor were the ones he most associated with the girls. He had never been in the dressing area, but he knew the huge chamber—once the living and dining room of an apartment—had been filled with clothes racks, jewelry boxes, and mirrored dressing tables. Now, the room echoed emptily, its expensive marbled floor permanently stained with women's makeup. Tephanie—German, great boobs— how well he remembered her! —Her name was on the bathroom wall, written in …what kind of makeup was it? Mascara? Somehow, it made Danny sad. There had been so much life here where only memories and dust remained. He paused before graffiti scrawled on the wall, "Sophie, '77." Although he couldn't remember which of the girls had called herself "Sophie," his eyes misted over as he recalled that 1977 was the last good year they had enjoyed in Iran.

Emotionally drained, Danny clambered over the high brick wall and walked to Ali Nassiri's luxurious villa to see Andrea, whom he found sitting on a third floor balcony, listening to music and drinking Stolichnaya vodka over ice. Before her on a glass table were the remains of a splendid meal.

"Andrea?" he whispered, quietly coming up behind her and putting his hand on her right arm.

"I thought you might come by this evening," she said, without turning around. Her not being surprised … surprised him. "I haven't anything for you to do tonight, but I need company."

"So do I," he admitted, taking a chair across the table from her. He had never seen her look so disheveled. She hadn't done her hair, and she wasn't wearing makeup; worse than that, she had been crying.

"Fix yourself a drink," she offered, motioning at a portable bar inside the glass door, her voice shaking with emotion. "Let me take a shower. Afterward, we'll have some drinks." She got up before he could answer, and he didn't see her again for an hour.

The housekeeper brought a plate of broiled sturgeon, long-grain rice, and a pot of tea, and he ate with appetite for the first time in weeks.

"There," Andrea said when she returned. Her long hair was carefully styled in a French braid, and she wore a clingy, low-cut silk dress and Egyptian sandals. "Fix me a drink, won't you?"

"Sure," he agreed, suddenly wondering why he was so reluctant to tell her goodbye. Dry-mouthed, he poured her Pakdis vodka in a tall glass, added ice, then mumbled, "I've come to ask you something."

"Yes?"

"I'm going to take thirty days' vacation," he lied, deciding he couldn't trust her at all. "I need to get my hand fixed. It's been hurting, and it's becoming twisted. The tendons are messed up, y'know, and I'm tired of this revolution."

"Why go now? Wait and see how this new government turns out," she suggested. "The school at Doshan Tappeh may reopen, and you can finish your contract. Maybe we could all go on holiday together—I'd love to, perhaps in the autumn! Let's spend time in Cairo. Lovely city! You can get your hand fixed, and we could take a cruise up to Aswan on a riverboat. What do you say? Wait a few months."

"No, I've got to go."

"Wait a few weeks."

"No, I need to go now."

She was silent a long time then, but it was not an uncomfortable gap in the conversation. Andrea tested the sound of it, and supreme actress she was, never showed disappointment. "Perhaps you're right," she said. "Thirty days isn't long. There's not much work for you right now anyway, since no one trusts anyone else. Besides, most of the rich have left for Europe—perhaps I can arrange a few packages for you to deliver there. Yes, that's an idea! Wait a week. Let me see what I can arrange. There's a chance I can get you enough tricks to pay for a handsome holiday in the best hotels in Europe."

"I've got reservations," Danny lied, covering his tracks like he always did with Iranians, for he didn't know whom to trust. Wasn't this the woman who had offered twenty-eight thousand dollars to have him killed just six months ago?

"I leave next Sunday night," he said. That was a terrible lie. He was planning to leave the very next morning, but he figured he couldn't be too careful. Anything could go wrong. The airport at Mehrabod was only open sporadically. Revolutionary Guards were routinely pulling people off planes for last minute questioning. It wouldn't be safe for anyone to know his itinerary.

"Oh?" she said rather distractedly.

"I thought I would take my money with me—"

"Of course," she agreed, getting up to fetch her account books and an attaché case. She placed the case on the table before her and took out a pair of eyeglasses.

"I've never seen you in glasses before," Danny remarked in surprise. She had been so elegant he had a hard time imagining her wearing glasses.

"Yes," she admitted. "I've been doing a lot of reading lately, and my eyes have grown tired."

"You look nice in them."

She melted at the compliment, for in a lifetime of being beautiful, kept, paid, and flattered, few had ever bothered to be genuine with her as Danny MacCreary. "Thank you," she smiled, opening her books to bring his account up to date. "I make it three million, eight hundred thousand rials."

"I'd like it in dollars, if you don't mind."

"You realize the exchanges are charging a premium for green-back dollars. I'll have to charge something too."

"That's fine," he agreed.

"Okay," she decreed. "Do you want your money in dollars?"

"No, some in English pounds. I plan to spend time in London. Wolffe's recommended a private hospital to get my hand fixed."

"Four thousand pounds enough?"

"Yes, fine."

"That's roughly six hundred thousand rials, which I'll do without a premium. That will leave three million, two hundred thousand." Producing a small calculator, she did his account carefully, rial by rial. "You'll want to leave something in your account to keep it open, of course."

"No, I don't think so. I'd like it all—"

"Don't be foolish. You'll have expenses later. You'll need the money. You *are* coming back, aren't you?"

He was caught between a rock and a hard place, for he could not find it in his heart to tell her the truth, yet he was loathe to part with any money. Three times in the past year, Andrea had laughingly taunted he could never go home again. He had changed too much, she had told him. He could never enjoy a simple life in Wyoming; he would never be satisfied without the excitement and money he had enjoyed in Iran. She wanted him to go with her to Brunei or Nigeria or Venezuela to start over again, so how could he tell her he was determined to go home, that all he craved was a quiet life?

"Yes," he lied. "Of course I'll be back-"

"You see? I'll keep thirty-six thousand tomans in reserve for you."

"That's five thousand dollars!"

"Do you think I should keep more?"

Danny fairly choked over loss of the money, but he swallowed hard and nodded, "No, that's fine."

"Good," she said. "That leaves you—" and she did some fast finger-work on the calculator, "with nearly two hundred ninety thousand tomans, about forty thousand dollars."

Strangely depressed by this reduction of more than three years of his life to a sum in dollars, yet surprised that it amounted to so little, he gulped, "Okay."

"Have another drink. I'll get the money from my safe." Andrea had screwed him out of more than eight thousand dollars in ten minutes, but he knew her well enough to realize she wasn't through. Sure enough, when she returned, she had only thirty-two thousand dollars plus an odd assortment of Swiss Francs, German marks, gold coins, and British pounds.

"It's all I had in the safe," she swore, but Danny figured she had just stung him for another thousand dollars. Shaking his head, he accepted it, and she scooped up the money and put it in an expensive eel-skin wallet. "This was Ali's."

Most expensive wallet he had ever purchased, he thought glumly as he finished his drink, but at least he had most of his money. Together with the money he had stashed during the years he had worked for Andrea, he would be going home with about three hundred and fifty thousand dollars in cash. His Persian carpets, gold coins and collection of women's jewelry would fetch another four hundred thousand in London auctions. Not bad for three years work overseas, he decided.

They sat quietly in the darkness for fifteen minutes before he finally picked up the wallet and got to his feet. "Thanks," he said.

"Oh, here," she offered. "This is the address of a good private surgeon in London. See him about your hand. He's the best I know, and he's discreet. Tell him to put it on my account—no bills to you—and I'll see you when you get back," she smiled, though she kept her eyes on her drink.

"Yes, I will," he said." Staring out over the darkness of the garden and the distant lights of the angry city, Danny asked, "You always got a thousand pounds a night, didn't you?"

"Yes," she said, looking up at him sweetly. There was no surprise at all on her face.

Danny bit his lip and laid a wad of money on the glass table in front of her. He had never paid for sex before, not with any of the beautiful women he had slept with in the last three years.

Speculatively, she glanced at the money. She ran a finger through the cash, then up at him. "Dear Danny," she whispered, setting her long-stemmed wine glass on the money to close the deal. Rising immediately, she took his hand and led him into her bedroom. After putting some music on the stereo, she lit a candle on a nightstand, turned off the lights and undid her hair before a mirror. Danny awkwardly put his hands around her waist, marveling at how fragile she really was. Though she was such a *presence* in his life, her head barely reached his shoulders....

"Danny," she sighed seductively, unzipping the back of her dress and letting it fall to her feet. Naked now, she wore no underwear. She was naked in a mere moment.

"Andrea—!" he choked. His head spun; his pulse hammered in his ears. Oh God! Her perfume was intoxicating. "God, I didn't—I really didn't—I mean ... I—Oh please!"

He couldn't breathe.

He couldn't think.

He could only feel.

And then she pressed herself against him. They kissed for the first time, and it was the beginning of a long night of lovemaking. Although it cost him a lot of money, afterwards Danny realized it was a night he could never—and refused to ever—regret. After all he had been through, after all the murders, horror, and bullshit in Iran, he now knew why Andrea Wilcox was, indeed, worth so much treasure, blood, and heartache.

$-36-$

THE COURIER'S LAST TRICK

"Those guys scared the living shit out of me.... Seriously, I was scared to death."

—An American businessman

There was a point at which Danny thought he was going to snap. He couldn't sleep, couldn't sit, couldn't pace, couldn't look out the window, couldn't look inside. He mopped his sweating brow until the skin was chapped. He peed when he didn't have to; he washed his hands when they weren't dirty.

It was five o'clock in the morning, two hours before a taxi was to take him to the airport and six hours before his flight was scheduled—if it flew at all that day. Everything was set. He had a ticket in hand, his reservation was a sure thing—an expensive proposition these days—and he had packed and repacked a hundred times. What could possibly hold him up? The silk carpets in his suitcases? No, the customs bribes had been prepaid. Passport control, visa, residence permit? The officials in charge had all received a fee. Taxi might not show? He had called three different companies to be sure at least one car would come. The owner of the apartment might suspect he was leaving? Danny paid another month's rent to allay suspicion. Was there anything he overlooked?

Only twenty minutes late, a lone telephone taxi finally pulled up before the apartment building, but how Danny had suffered during the delay! Rushing down the marble stairs, he threw his two small suitcases into the back seat and jumped in beside the driver. "Mehrabod," he screamed; the Iranian merely shrugged, apparently having seen this same haste from other *farangis* leaving the country.

They drove through the smoky city past long lines of somber people waiting patiently for morning bread outside the busy bakeries. Danny noticed the gas fires from the ovens were the only lights visible; the streetlights were out again, due to a power emergency or a strike crippling the city. Traffic was frustrating, with wildcat roadblocks to pass, *baksheesh* to pay, and people to lie to. They drove by burned-out banks and theaters, blown-to-hell liquor stores, ruined buildings, wrecked cars, and giant posters of Khomeini's demonic face frowning from every lamppost. On Pahlavi Avenue, a blackened Army truck lay on its side in a wide *djube*, the green, white, and red medallion of Iran visible on an open door. Danny remembered a hundred soldiers had died in a street fight here, and he looked away, sick at heart.

An hour-and-a-half later, they arrived at the international terminal at Mehrabod. Dozens of unkempt Revolutionary Guards stood carelessly playing with their G-3 rifles while an armored car in the parking lot covered the traffic with machine guns. Even so, the taxi driver pulled to the curb fearlessly and nodded for his passenger to get out.

"Five thousand rials," the driver demanded, ten times what the ride once cost, but Danny gave him the money without complaint. There was one more thing to be done: the driver had to be sworn to secrecy, and Danny had the perfect method in mind. Quickly, lest anyone see, he reached under his sport coat and unstrapped the leather harness of his shoulder holster.

"These are dangerous times for you and your family," he said politely in Farsi. "Please accept this gun to protect your loved ones in an emergency."

"Ooh!" the driver sighed, his eyes almost popping out of his head at sight of the revolver.

"It's an American Smith and Wesson," Danny added, saddened at losing the pistol that had saved his life a dozen times. Flipping open the cylinder, he extracted six shiny brass cartridges, closed the gun, and snapped it three times.

"Three five seven?" the driver whispered in awe.

"Three fifty seven, magnum," Danny answered, affectionately wiping the gun's beautiful blue finish one last time.

"Magnum!" the driver exclaimed, obviously not having any idea what "magnum" meant. "Smith and Vesson. Go, go!" he shooed Danny out of the car before the American could change his mind. *"Khodahafez,"* the Iranian called, stuffing the gun under his seat as he sped away.

Feeling strangely naked after more than two years carrying a gun, Danny wished the man goodbye, *"Khodahafez,* motherfucker." He chuckled as he walked inside the terminal and dropped the six cartridges in a trashcan, knowing it was almost impossible to obtain .357 ammunition in Iran now. Someday, the man might learn that .38 Specials would also work, but in the meantime, no one would get killed with *that* gun.

At the ticket counter, Danny confidently bypassed a long line of frantic foreigners trying to get out of the country. "Hey, where the bloody 'ell you think you're going?" a red-faced Englishman shouted, obviously having waited in line for at least twenty-four hours. Danny ignored him, presented himself at the counter, and handed the agent a short note in Farsi.

The clerk immediately broke into a smile of recognition. "Yes, Doctor," he said, although he had never before met the man who had arranged the bribe. "Everything is okay. Your reservation is confirmed through Frankfurt, West Germany, on Pan Am flight 371 from New Delhi. The plane is already here. Take this paper to passport control. They are expect you."

It could have been ominous the way the man said it, but a calm settled over Danny now that he was in the airport. Making his way through the frantically shouting crowd to the customs area, he noticed the baggage carousels weren't working again. They had rarely, if ever, worked the entire time he'd been in Iran. He handed the officials his papers and the note. Uniformed officers and armed rabble alike gathered to look over his gray American passport, work visa, and blue residence permit.

"Your residence permit has expired," one particularly evil-looking punk in a field jacket snarled.

"I couldn't get out of the country before now. Mehrabod was closed a lot before Khomeini came, and I lost my money in a bank fire," Danny lied.

"The Doctor helped the revolution," a customs officer intervened. "He is well known for his medical services to the *mujahadin*." Grabbing Danny's elbow, the man hustled him past the guardsmen toward the last customs checkpoint. "You *are* a medical doctor, aren't you?" the man whispered.

"No, I'm not."

"Allah!" the man swore. "Don't tell anyone. I claimed you are a hero for aiding wounded people in the streets."

A guardsman at another checkpoint accused, "Your work visa shows you are employ by the Imperial Iranian Air Force—"

"The Iranian Air Force is not *imperial* any longer," Danny answered evenly, keeping his true feelings to himself.

"Perhaps that is why you leave now?" the punk sneered.

"No, I'm leaving because my car was burned, my house looted, my wife raped, my children killed in the street, all my Coca-Colas are warm, and rice is a hundred and fifty tomans a kilo," Danny snapped.

Passing him through customs with an insolent wave of his hand, the guardsman warned, "Don't come back to my country."

"Believe me, I won't," Danny said, though he was strangely happy that he had come. As he hurried toward another checkpoint, he reflected on how much he had learned in Iran. Yes, he was glad he had come, but he was happier to be leaving.

The sunny PanAm departure lounge, which was packed with anxious, sweating people, stank of cigarettes and fresh fear. A ticket and a reservation meant nothing at all during the Iranian Revolution, since anyone could be arrested for a trifling offense. Danny found an empty seat as far as possible from other passengers and buried his nose in a book; it was thirty minutes before he realized he was rereading his battered copy of Joseph Heller's *Catch-22*. Twice in two hours, Islamic Guards rushed in to arrest Iranians about to flee the country, and both times, Danny's heart stopped.

Finally, his flight number was called, though he knew the plane had been sitting on the taxiway for over four hours. Typically overbooked by fifty percent, the flight had about a hundred hysterical people jammed against the door of the departure lounge, begging to be let on the plane.

"You are Doctor Mary?" an attendant asked as Danny sauntered up to the back of the mob.

"Yes," he answered.

"You have a reservation. I believe the price was two hundred thousand?"

Danny had the money ready in his hand, but he made a show of extracting every last rial from his pockets, an amount nearly fifty thousand more. "Here, this is for you, if you can help me get through these people."

Without another word, the attendant attacked the crowd from behind. "*Boro, Boro!*" he screamed as he broke his way through the mass, Danny hurrying after him.

"Bloody 'ell," a man complained as he was shoved aside. When Danny pressed past, he realized it was the same Englishman he had seen earlier in the ticket line. "You!" the man snarled when he recognized the young American, but then the door opened, and Danny was pushed outside onto the tarmac with twenty heavily armed militiamen and his two small suitcases. The wall of the concrete building nearby was pockmarked from last-minute executions.

"*Alle shoma?*" one of the scruffy guards asked.

"*Merci,*" Danny answered, producing a pack of Marlboro cigarettes from his sport jacket and giving it to the men. Slinging their rifles over their shoulders and gathering around amiably, the Iranians asked for a light.

"*Befarmae'e,*" Danny offered, giving them a gold Dunhill lighter. Each man took a turn lighting a cigarette with the expensive lighter, the last man pocketing it as an articulated bus pulled up to collect the passengers.

Walking quickly away from the armed men, Danny found a choice seat near the front of the bus and barricaded himself with his suitcases. Moments later, the door to the departure lounge slammed open, and a hundred people rushed the bus. As soon as it was half-filled with screaming passengers, the driver shut the pneumatic doors and pulled away, separating mothers from their children, husbands from wives, and people from carry-on luggage. Almost immediately, three black Mercedes roared up to the terminal, and a dozen shouting gunmen jumped out to surround the Englishman, who had literally missed his bus.

Glancing out the window as the bus pulled onto the taxiway, Danny looked into the man's eyes, a look only fellow prisoners could understand, then lost sight of him as the man was hustled into one of the cars. "I wonder who he was," Danny mused, then put the thought out of his head. There was too much to think about without worrying about strangers. The man's fate was his own....

The bus pulled down the taxiway.

Even at the plane, there were still ten people too many, but Danny retrieved some money from his shoe and slipped it into the hand of a policeman waiting there. Breaking into a grin, the man grabbed his arm and escorted him up the stairs to the waiting *farangi* stewardesses.

"Doc!" one of them laughed, ushering him into the welcome darkness of the plane. As soon as his eyes adjusted to the dim light inside, he recognized her as Brigitte, a French stewardess who had stayed at Marvin's villa, two years ago. Marvin had liked her but didn't like her tiny breasts.

"How are you?" Danny asked, glad to see a friendly face. He remembered Heinz Reibach had a crush on this woman once, but she had refused to go out with him. Too bad. She was a good-looking lady, with fashion-sense, intelligence, and humor. Great legs too, especially in heels.

"I'm happy I don't live in this fucking country," she giggled. "You too?"

"Me too," he said, hugging her warmly.

The interior of the plane was hot and humid; it hadn't had fresh air in four hours. En route from New Delhi to Frankfurt, the jet was packed with two hundred nervous travelers. As he walked down the aisle, he noticed the innocence on their faces. None of the travellers could understand the turmoil outside: the tears, hysteria, bribery, field jackets, beards, and machine guns.

"Was it bad?" a woman inquired, catching at his sleeve.

"Did you witness any of the revolution?" another asked.

"How long have you been in Iran?"

"Did you meet the Ayatollah?"

"Did anybody shoot at you?"

Ignoring the stupid questions, Danny moved like a sleepwalker until he was just behind the wings, an area stewardesses claimed was the safest. Putting his two bags in the overhead compartment, he told an American businessman sitting there, "I'd like to sit near the window, please."

"You would?"

"Yes," Danny said, looking him in the eye. "Please." It didn't take a second request. His sunglasses hid all; the request was firm.

"Of course," the pudgy businessman said, his face torn between surprise and the desire to avoid confrontation in a crazy country. Struggling awkwardly out of his seat, he got up so the two could exchange places in the narrow aisle. The man was sweaty and had a fat gut, a typical businessman on a long hot trip, his dress shirt barely tucked in over his belly.

Danny sat in the warm seat and stared out the window. Now on the opposite side of the plane from the bus and the shouting passengers, he was still able to see their agitated shadows on the tarmac below, bargaining for seats. Again he told himself how glad he was to be leaving this crazy place as he looked out over the dusty runways to Teheran's permanent brown cloud and the distant mountains beyond. Machine-gun-toting militia and armed guards were everywhere in sight, while barbed wire barricades blocked all the gates and sidewalks as far as he could see. There was angry shouting outside, and someone gave permission to board. About thirty sweaty people rushed into the plane to search for seats, but he could still see a large group of shadows below, arguing.

The embarking passengers had barely taken their seats before the doors of the plane slammed shut and the captain's voice purred over the intercom in a British accent, "I _do_ hope you enjoyed a pleasant stay in Teheran."

Faces and memories swirled through Danny's head. The airliner's engines came to life, and on the tarmac below, people scrambled to get out of the way. Technicians, police, a few tearful passengers with no seats, a little boy crying his eyes out all flashed past the window as the 747 jumbo jet turned ponderously towards the taxiway. The pilot was giving the weather in Germany and the stews were going through the safety lecture, but Danny couldn't move, didn't breathe, couldn't think. He could just sit there, his mouth wide open, lost in thought and memories.

"Here," the businessman said helpfully. "Let me help you with the seat belt. They're difficult to click sometimes."

"Oh ... thanks," Danny answered, his ears ringing, his fingers fumbling at the belt. "Thanks."

It took forever for the jet to roll out to the end of the runway. Just beyond the perimeter fences, Danny could see the traffic on the road to Mehrabod Junubi. Through the windows across the aisle, he glimpsed a long row of F-4 Phantoms of the Iranian Air Force, useless beside empty hangars, for the planes were grounded for lack of spare parts. And beyond them, Danny could see two cars rushing out to stop the plane, followed by a tractor dragging a portable stairs onto the runway to block the plane's takeoff. The whine from the engines ceased, and the huge jet lurched to a sudden stop.

Danny felt his heart sinking, for he realized then he could never go home so easily. Andrea had been right all along: no one could leave Iran without paying somehow, either in blood or money. After all the excitement he had been through, he shouldn't have expected such an easy return to the quiet life he had once enjoyed in far-away Wyoming, America. He remembered a passenger in the terminal wearing a T-shirt that said:

> I came
> I saw
> Iran

Stewardesses hurried to answer the intercom. There was a banging on the door outside, and sunlight when the co-pilot opened it to shout at armed men on the ground. More banging followed as the mobile stairs were brought up and five bearded men entered the plane. The leader, who carried a small photo of his quarry, commanded the squad to spread out slowly. Armed with G-3 assault rifles and short-barreled Uzis, the gunmen walked slowly through the plane, each covering the movements of another as they efficiently assumed control of the terrified passengers.

Danny looked out the window. In the distance, even the blue of the mountains and the white of the snow were polluted in this lousy country.

It was no wonder the Farsi word for snow was *barf*. He recalled a business on Saltanadabad Avenue named *Barf* Diaper Service....

"Doctor Mary? Are you Doctor Mary?" a gunman in a new field jacket asked in English, reaching across the businessman to poke Danny in the shoulder with the muzzle of his rifle. The leader held the photo near Danny's face and nodded. Immediately three gunmen clambered over passengers in the rows in front and in back of him to jam the muzzles of their rifles against his head, pinning him to the window.

Keep calm and then go wild when they least expect it, Carl Wolffe had once advised. Remembering his training well, Danny answered, "Yes, I'm Doctor Mary."

"We are surprised with you," the man said, switching to Farsi. He motioned for his men to release the American. "More than anyone, you know there are no secrets in Iran. You try to leave without anyone finding out, and who knows where you will go? What will you do with your life after this? How are we to find you again?"

Find him? He didn't want them to find him again! All he wanted was to return to Wyoming. He would figure out later what to do with his life. Though he was sure the gunmen were toying with him, he had a hard time preventing his lower lip from trembling. More than anything, he wanted to be defiant, but after all he had been through, he was too worn-out. They would do what they were ordered to do....

Producing a key from a jacket pocket, the man handed it to him. Danny accepted it like it was a snake on a cold copper plate headed straight to Hell. "We are disappointed with you, Doctor Mary, leaving Iran like this, but we have an important message for you."

When Danny looked up in surprise, the gunman said, *"Moush goush dareh, divar moush dareh."* And then he smiled with all the teeth he owned— and it wasn't a full set.

Danny felt relief wash over him like a wave of cold surf. He hadn't fooled anyone.

"And I have this for you too," the man grinned, handing him an envelope thick with cash. *"Khodahafez,* Doctor Mary. Your friends wish you well. Do look after your left hand in London as Miss Andrea instructed, then go to Rome for Masud Pooinak."

Clumsily examining the items given him, Danny saw the key was for a safe deposit box in London, England. Later that week, he discovered the box contained a free-and-clear quit-claim deed—in his name—to an expensive, 1,400-acre parcel of irrigated ranch land on the North Platte River south of Saratoga, Wyoming. A check accompanying the deed paid the taxes for ten years. A hand-written note with the deed said, "Thank you for everything you've done for me and for all of us. As the French say, you'll miss me—and you'll miss all of us." It was signed, "Andrea."

In seconds it was over. The gunmen were gone, the banging was done in reverse, the doors shut again, the engines' whine rose, and Danny felt himself pressed into the seat as the plane hurtled down the runway. There was an awful bump as the wheels came up, and a thump and a bump after that, then the plane banked west for Europe—and freedom.

He couldn't help himself—he twisted around in his seat and peered out the window for a last look. Beneath a brown cloud of pollution, Teheran faded into the desert like it had never been there. As he watched the barren land roll away into the distance, the faces of the people he had known filled his head: Ralf, Andrea, Sandy, Sadjewi, the Shah, Shalah Shahlu, Parviz, Puff Omura, Marilyn the Pisser, Leila, Shamsa, Masud, Benyamin, and many, many others. He was overcome with emotion. He couldn't swallow; his heart hammered so loudly he couldn't hear the aircraft's engines. He choked for the least breath, but there didn't seem to be any air to breathe. Tears flowed like rivers down his cheeks, though he wasn't consciously crying.

Then, there was an unexpectedly loud pop next to him. The businessman handed him a small green bottle of chilled French champagne. "Congratulations," the man said.

The stewardess pocketed the man's money and moved down the aisle, handing out other champagne bottles to celebrate similar escapes. Danny accepted the bottle suspiciously; he could only sip it with a skeptical throat.

"Those guys scared the living shit out of me. Really, I was shitting my pants! I was never so scared in my life. Machine guns and such! I thought you were going to get killed right next to me. Blood and brains all over the plane."

"Me too," Danny admitted, a rare smile on his face.

"Good thing they were friendly, huh?"

"Yeah."

"What was it that guy said to you?"

"Huh?"

"He spoke to you in Iranian, and you seemed to understand. And then he said something else in Iranian, and you smiled."

"Yeah. It was Farsi. In Iran, the language is Farsi, or Persian. I understood it. I understand the language pretty well, but I never learned to read and write. He said, *'Moush goush dareh, divar moush dareh.'* It's a Persian proverb."

"What does it mean in English?"

"The walls have mice; the mice have ears."

"No secrets?"

"Not unless you're dead."

"How long were you in Iran?" the man interrupted.

"Three-and-a-half years," Danny answered, feeling worn.

"How'd you hurt your hand?"

Danny had come to Iran to teach English, but he knew he couldn't explain what had happened to him since. How could a stranger on a getaway-flight-to-somewhere-else understand the shooting in the streets, the angry mobs shouting "*Margh Bar Amrika!* (Death to America), the hundreds of bodies hanging from lampposts and signs, the thousands of summary executions and tens of thousands imprisoned without cause, the explosions, the pockmarked garden walls, the stiff and shrouded bodies lying in shallow graves, the generals all dying of "heart attacks," the fiery deaths of his Jewish friends, the hundreds of suicides, rapes, assaults, and deaths that were so normal, let alone months hiding from his friends? Three-quarters of a million people died in the Revolution and the war; three and a half million had to seek refuge in other countries. This—in a country of only forty million. How could any outsider understand drug dealers sitting on a five-hundred-year-old Persian carpet making contracts that might involve the murders of hundreds of innocent people?

What could he say? That he was twenty-nine years old, but felt a hundred and ten? How could he explain anything to a pudgy businessman sitting beside him as they flew away to freedom? And worse: could he ever admit to the smiling man that in the last four months he had killed over two hundred people with guns, a knife, and a couple well placed bombs?

"I caught a bullet in the street," Danny replied sadly.

"I'll bet that hurt like a sonofabitch," the man chuckled nervously.

Holding up his deformed left hand, Danny agreed, "Yes, it did," and then he turned his face to the privacy of the window and wept.

POSTSCRIPT

"An exciting day now is watching a registered bull get off a cow when they're done," Doc joked one cold April morning while we were standing out by his cattle pens in southern Wyoming. We were counting and weighing cattle for shipment to a feedlot in North Platte, Nebraska. Two cowboys on cutting horses awaited instructions in the alley between the six pens. The weigh scale was empty. Nine stock trucks and eighteen people awaited loads from the pens. All were quiet, even the cattle.

"No, it's not. It's when I push you off me on a lazy afternoon here at home," his wife grinned, punching him in the ribs.

Wyoming's spring wind was cold that morning. Our breaths hung in the air around us, but neither Danny nor his wife noticed. They hugged affectionately... and the loading was on.

Four months after Danny MacCreary escaped the horrors of the Iranian Revolution, the ailing Shah was admitted to the United States for cancer treatment. He had some of his chemo at Wilford Hall, on Lackland Air Force Base in San Antonio, Texas—where Danny's story had begun four years before.

On November 4, 1979, a crowd of radicals stormed the American Embassy in Teheran in retaliation and took the diplomats hostage. A tense standoff with the United States would drag on for the next 444 days.

On April 24th, 1980, a military force sent to rescue the hostages landed at a secret airstrip laid out by agents working for the American government. Two Hashemi vehicles smuggling gasoline stumbled into the Americans in the dark, and one of the drivers escaped. Fearing he would alert the Iranian military, the Americans aborted the mission, but then disaster struck as they hurried to leave: a helicopter crashed into a transport plane and eight American servicemen were killed. In a hasty departure after the accident, the rescuers carelessly left behind papers naming friendly Iranians cooperating with the failed mission.

On May 2, 1980, Masud Pooinak and Khani Nassiri were among four hundred people arrested for their involvement in the aborted rescue mission.

On July 27, 1980, the Shah died in Cairo, Egypt, where he was living in exile. Though a few Iranian newspapers claimed, "The bloodsucker of the century is dead," there was surprisingly little reaction in Iran.

Four days later, Masud and Nassiri were executed in Evin Prison.

Andrea's trusted receptionist, Shamsa Esfandiari, was executed in September 1980 for "incorrigibility" after spending months in an Islamic reeducation center. She stood with her back against a brick wall and faced the guns bravely. Her crime was she would not wear a *chador*. Among others who disappeared during this time, Sadeq, Marvin's gatekeeper, and Mr. Davood, his gardener, are rumored to have been executed. Nilufar, Mahsomeh, Kabri, "Star," Behnaz, "Paris," Sahar, "Babe," Nastaran, Fusie, "Babs," and several others of Andrea's girls, plus Hussain, Mehdi, Gholam, Rostom, Mahmad, and Ali, drivers at Star Taxi, were also executed that fall for "crimes against Islam."

Shalah Shahlu, though not an Iranian citizen, was also caught up in the Revolution. As she faced the guns of a firing squad, she opened her clothes and bared her breasts to taunt her killers to their core.

Masud Pooinak's son did not escape the horrors of the Revolution either. In the patriotic fervor that swept the country after the Iraqis invaded western Iran, precipitating the brutal, eight-year Iran-Iraq War, the boy volunteered to fight on the front. During a massed night assault on prepared Iraqi defensive positions, he stepped on a land mine and was killed. He was nine years old. "Martyred," the Islamic government declared after listing eighteen hundred other children who died "defending Islam," though the Iraqis were also Moslems. Iranian children did not merit burials, and their mangled bodies cluttered battlefields until they rotted to bones in the mud.

Amir Abbas Hoveyda, the former Prime Minister of Iran, was executed on direct orders from the Ayatollah Khomeini on April 7, 1979.

Ali Nassiri's palatial home was appropriated by the new government. Today, it houses the Center for the Abolition of Sin. Not a blade of grass grows on the once-beautiful grounds; the swimming pool is filled with trash.

Late one night, Marvin Roberts drove to his company's port facilities in Ahwaz, where he stole a boat and sailed to Kuwait. He now lives in Florida.

Puff Omura invested in restaurants near Washington, D.C. She declined to be interviewed by the author, but she wept when she learned from him that Danny had survived the Revolution.

During the Iran-Iraq War, Second Sergeant Hosseini, the ambitious enlisted man who had bested Danny in a competition to list the fifty-one American states, rose through the ranks. A retired brigadier general, he is a respected member of the *Majlis,* the Iranian parliament. In his spare time, he published a best-selling book about the weaknesses of American culture.

Six weeks after Danny MacCreary left Iran, Andrea Wilcox, Carl Wolffe, and Bob Fraser smuggled themselves over treacherous mountain paths into Turkey. It was very dangerous. Anyone could have cut their throats. They carried over twenty million dollars in cash, jewelry, various currencies, and carpets, which they divvied up in a hotel in Istanbul. Carl retired and lived comfortably in Europe. A heavy smoker, he died of throat cancer in 1989. Last anyone heard, Fraser was working as an "advisor" in South America. Andrea Wilcox collected Ali Nassiri's foreign investments, and then she followed the oil boom and moved to Caracas, Venezuela, where she married a rich businessman in late 1982.

———◆———

Five years after leaving Iran, Danny MacCreary was living in a run-down Airstream trailer at the end of a rutted muddy road in southern Wyoming. Doing his own haying and feeding, he was running over three hundred "cattle units" (cows plus calves) twelve months a year on his ranch, but he didn't have time or inclination to hire help. In fact, he didn't have an appetite for much except working sixteen-hour days, seven days a week, alone. Feeling burned out, he was beyond conversation; he couldn't talk with friends or family about anything that had happened to him overseas. He didn't have a phone, watch television, or subscribe to a newspaper. He avoided get-togethers with neighbors and holiday dinners with family. His only companions were a hundred-pound guard dog, which he named *Sag Bozorg* (the big dog) and a sure-foot Spanish mustang named Bliz.

Danny carried a loaded gun (or two) wherever he went. His favorite was a Browning Hi-Power. "Damned reliable," he said. "It hasn't jammed. Most automatics jam when they're needed. A Hi-Power will bite your hand sometimes, but otherwise it's good. I don't care how many people are shooting at you, a Hi-Power will return fire."

While working on a cattle-loading chute one afternoon in late September

1985, he was surprised when his dog jumped up and growled a warning. There was a shiny, black Mercedes with new Texas plates roaring down the gravel road from the distant highway. It bounced over a cattle guard at the house gate and pulled to a stop in front of his trailer.

"You always did drive like an Iranian truck driver," Danny laughed, tossing his hammer aside. The dog planted itself in front of him and showed its teeth, but it did not growl—and it never did. This visitor was special.

And when she opened the car's door and stepped out, Danny was overcome with emotion. "Thank God," he wept. "You survived."

"Of course, I did," she smiled. Dressed in an elegant wool skirt, fringed Western blouse, a cinnamon-brown Stetson hat, and custom five-thousand-dollar cowboy boots with a colorful Wyoming flag detailed on the fronts, she added in her impeccable English accent, "I've come to check out this 'quiet' life of yours. I was always curious why you pined for it so. What makes this place so special?"

"Now…you," he said, wiping his eyes.

Sag Bozorg reluctantly wagged his tail.

Years later, Andrea Wilcox is still "staying" with Danny MacCreary. Having left her Venezuelan husband for cause—he was a flagrant woman-izer, something she could not accept in marriage—she appears happy in Wyoming. Older and grumpy most of the time now, Sag Bozorg is never more than six feet from her hand. Although Andrea and Danny don't seem to have any agreements between them, they have two adopted children, one a severely disabled Native-American (Arapahoe) child from the Wind River Reservation.

During interviews for this book, conducted at a luxurious six-bedroom log home filled with antique Persian carpets and other Iranian artworks, Andrea claimed she didn't need the legitimacy of marriage. She said she preferred to keep her options open in case something better came along. "You never know what will happen next in life," she laughed gaily. "An intelligent woman has to look out for herself."

Danny ignored her comment. Asked later in the privacy of his cluttered office how he felt about the future of their relationship, he looked out the picture window at the distant ridges of Wyoming's Snowy Range, chuckled skeptically and said, "I'm not worried."

DEDICATION

For my friend, Doctor Mary, shot in the back of the head while on a cattle-buying trip on an otherwise empty highway as he knelt to change a flat tire on his stock trailer, eight miles northwest of Hobbs, New Mexico, April 4, 2016.

—With sorrow—

Butch Denny
Miles City, Montana

Neda—Iran

www.ingramcontent.com/pod-product-compliance
Lightning Source LLC
Chambersburg PA
CBHW070215030726
47505CB00006B/1687